THE WAGES OF SIN

"I hope your stay is profitable, mistress," Hiolanso said mockingly. He turned to go, but a sorcerer was coming up the rain-slick plank, tall and sinister in the darkness.

When he reached the deck, the sorcerer paused, motionless but for the whipping of his gown, his cowled head invisible even in the flare of the lightning. "Return the gold to Mistress Brota, Hiolanso," he commanded, and the little man's hands trembled as he reached into his leather pouch for the money.

Brota shivered, and not only from the wind. How could this stranger know her business, or her name?

"My apologies," the sorcerer was saying in a deep, hard voice. "The wizard will see that this one is punished."

Hiolanso's thin squeal of terror was drowned out by a mind-shattering peal of thunder. He dodged around the sorcerer and bolted for the gangplank.

The sorcerer swung after him and raised an arm. Thunder roared again, and the plank was empty. The fugitive had vanished utterly...

By Dave Duncan
Published by Ballantine Books:

A ROSE-RED CITY

SHADOW

The Seventh Sword
THE RELUCTANT SWORDSMAN
THE COMING OF WISDOM
THE DESTINY OF THE SWORD

THE COMING OF WISDOM

Book Two of *The Seventh Sword*

DAVE DUNCAN

A Del Rey Book

BALLANTINE BOOKS ● NEW YORK

For
MICHAEL
my brother
of course!

CONTENTS

The Fourth Oath

Fortunate is he who saves the life of a colleague, and greatly blessed are two who have saved each other's. To them only is permitted this oath and it shall be paramount, absolute, and irrevocable:

> I am your brother,
> My life is your life,
> Your joy is my joy,
> My honor is your honor,
> Your anger is my anger,
> My friends are your friends,
> Your enemies are my enemies,
> My secrets are your secrets,
> Your oaths are my oaths,
> My goods are your goods,
> You are my brother.

BOOK ONE:

HOW THE SWORDSMAN RAN AWAY

†

"Quili! Wake up! Priestess!"

Whoever was shouting was also banging on the outer door. Quili rolled over and buried her head under the blanket. Surely she had just come to bed?

The outer door squeaked. The banging came again, now on the planks of the inner door, nearer and much louder.

"Apprentice Quili! You must come!" More banging.

The trouble with summer was that there was never enough night for sleeping, yet the little room was still quite black. The roosters had not started yet . . . No, there was one, far away . . . She would have to waken. Someone must be sick or dying.

Then the inner door squealed open, and a man was waving a rush light and shouting. "Priestess! You must come—there are swordsmen, Quili!"

"Swordsmen?" Quili sat up.

Salimono was a roughhewn, lumbering man, a farmer of the Third. Normally imperturbably placid, he was capable on rare occasions of becoming as flustered as a child. Now one of his great hands was waving the sparking rush light all around, threatening to set fire to his own silver hair, or Quili's straw mattress, or the ancient shingles of the roof. It scrolled brilliance in the dark. It flickered on stone walls, and on his haggard face, and in Quili's eyes.

"Swordsmen . . . coming . . . Oh! Beg pardon, priestess!" He

1

turned around quickly, just as Quili fell back and pulled the blanket up to her chin.

"Sal'o, you did say 'swordsmen'?"

"Yes, priestess. In a boat. By the jetty. Piliphanto saw them. You hurry, Quili . . ." He headed for the door.

"Wait!"

Quili wished she could take off her head, shake it, and put it back on again. She had walked away most of the night with Agol's baby, surely the worst case of colic in the history of the People.

Swordsmen? The rush light was filling the tiny room with fumes of goose grease. Piliphanto was not a total idiot. No thinker, but no idiot. He was a keen fisherman, which could explain why he had been down on the jetty before dawn. There would be more light down by the water, and a swordsman's silhouette would be distinctive. It was possible.

"What are you doing about them?"

Standing in the doorway with his back firmly turned, Sali-mono said, "Getting the women out, of course!"

"What! Why?"

"Ach! Swordsmen."

That was wrong. That was all wrong. Quili knew little about swordsmen, but she knew more about them than Sal'o did. Hiding the women would be the absolute worst thing to do.

"You mustn't! It'll be an insult! They'll be furious!"

"But, priestess . . ."

She was not a priestess. She was only a Second, an apprentice. The tenants called her priestess as a courtesy because she was all they had, but she was only seventeen and Sal'o was a farmer of the Third and a grandfather and Motipodi's deputy, so she could not possibly give him orders, but she was also the local expert on swordsmen, and she knew that hiding the women would be a terrible provocation . . . She needed time to think.

"Wait outside! Don't let the women leave. I'll be right there."

"Yes, Quili," Sal'o said, and the room was dark. Plumes of phantom light still floated on blackness in her eyes. The outer door banged, and she heard him shouting.

Quili threw off the blanket and shivered herself a coating of goose bumps. The flags were icy and uneven as she padded across to the window and threw open the shutter. A faint glow entered, accompanied by a hiss of rain and dripping sounds from the roof.

One of her two gowns was muddy, for yesterday she had been thinning the carrots. Her other was almost as shabby, yet somewhere she still had an old one she had brought from the temple. It had been her second best then and was better than her other two now—gardening ruined clothes much faster than being an acolyte did. She found it in the chest, yanked it out, and pulled it over her head in one long, shivery movement. It was surprisingly tight. She must have filled out more than she had thought. What would swordsmen think of a priestess who wore a tight-fitting gown like this? She fumbled for her shoes and a comb at the same time.

Her wooden soles clacked on the paving. She opened the squeaky outer door even as she reached for her cloak, hanging on a peg beside it. The bottom edge of the sky was brightening below a carpet of black cloud. More roosters screamed welcome to the dawn. She was still dragging the comb through her long tangles; her eyes felt puffy and her mouth dry.

On the far side of the pond, four or five of the smoky rush lights hissed amid a crowd of a dozen adults and some frightened children. Two or three more people were heading toward them. Light reflected fuzzily in the rain-pebbled water; other lights danced in a couple of windows. There was no wind, only steady, relentless drizzle; summer rain, not even very cold.

She splashed along the trail, around the pond to the group. Rain soaked her hair and dribbled into her collar. Silence fell at her approach. She was the local expert on swordsmen.

Why would swordsmen be coming here?

Several voices started to speak, but Salimono's drowned them out. "Is it safe, priestess?"

"It isn't safe to hide the women!" Quili said firmly. Kandoru had told stories about deserted villages being burned. "You'd provoke them. No, it's the men!"

"But they didn't do it!" a woman wailed.

"It wasn't us!" said others. "You know that!"

"Hush!" she said, and they hushed. They were all older than she, even Nia, and yet they hushed. They were all bigger than she—husky, raw peasant folk, gentle and bewildered and indistinct in the gloom. "Sal'o, did you send a message to her ladyship?"

"Pil'o went."

"I think maybe all the men should go . . ."

There was another terrified chorus of "We didn't do it!"

"Quiet! I know that. I'll testify to that. But I don't think it was reported."

There was a silence. Then Myi's voice growled, "How could it be reported?"

There had been no swordsmen left to report it to.

Would that matter? Quili did not know.

When an assassination went unreported, was it all the witnesses who were equally guilty, or was there some other, even more horrible formula? Either way, she was sure that the men were in danger. Swordsmen rarely killed women.

"I'll go and greet them. They won't hurt me." Quili spoke with as much confidence as she could manage. The priesthood was sacrosanct, wasn't it? "But I think you men should all go off wood cutting or something until we know why they've come. Women get food ready. They'll want breakfast. They may go straight on to the manor, but we'll try to keep them here as long as we can, if there aren't too many . . . How many of them are there, Sal'o?"

"Don't know."

"Well, go and tell Adept Motipodi. Wood cutting, or land clearing up on the hill until we find out what they want. Arrange signals. Now, off you go!"

All the men ran. Quili huddled her cloak about her. "Myi? Prepare some food. Meat, if you can find any. And beer."

"What if they ask where the men are?"

"Tell lies," Quili said. This was a priestess speaking?

"What if they want us to . . . to go to bed?" That was Nia, and her man Hantula was almost as old as Kandoru had been.

Quili laughed, surprising herself. She was having nightmares of bodies and blood all over the ground, and Nia was dreaming of a tussle with some handsome young swordsman. "Do it, if you want to! Enjoy yourself!"

Incredulously Nona said, "A married woman? It's all right?"

Quili paused to drag up memories of lessons in the temple. But she was sure. "Yes. It's quite all right. Not any swordsman, but with a free sword it's all right. He is on the service of the Goddess and deserves all our hospitality."

Kandoru had always said that it was a great honor for a woman to be chosen by a free, but when Quili had known him he had been no longer a free sword. He had been a resident swordsman, limited to one woman, limited by age; limited also by failing health, although sometimes he had sounded as if that had been her fault.

"Kol'o won't like it," Nona muttered. She had not been married long.

"He should," Quili said. "If you have a baby within a year, it can have a swordsman fathermark." She heard them all hiss with sudden excitement. She was a city girl and expected to know all these things. She was also their priestess; if she said it was all right, then it would be all right. Swordsmen never raped, Kandoru had insisted. They never had to.

"Really? A whole year? How soon?"

Quili did not know, but she glanced up at Nona's face. The flicker from the dying rush lights was too blurred to show expression. If she were pregnant, then that wasn't showing, either. "Hold on to it for a couple of weeks, and I'll testify to the facemarker for you."

Nona blushed, and that did show, and the others laughed. They had little to give their children, these humble folk. A swordsman fathermark would be worth more than much gold. To a girl it would mean a high brideprice. To a boy, if he were nimble, a chance for admission to the craft. Even a young husband would swallow his pride for those and talk of being honored, whatever he truly felt. The laugh broke the tension. Good! Now they would not flee in terror or unwittingly provoke violence.

But Quili had to go and meet the swordsmen. She shivered and clutched her cloak tighter yet. Suddenly she realized that she had met only one swordsman in her whole life—Kandoru, her murdered husband.

The rain might be faltering. Dawn was certainly close, the eastern sky brightening. The roosters were in blatant competition now. Leaving the twittering women, Quili splashed off along the road. One way led to the manor, the other to the River and the jetty. Beyond Salimono's house and the dam, the track dropped swiftly into a little gorge, and into darkness.

She went slowly, hearing the slap of her shoes in puddles, trying not to imagine herself tumbling into the stream and arriving at the jetty all covered in mud. Going to meet swordsmen . . . She should have brought one of the rush lights.

Why would swordsmen be coming here?

They might be coming by chance, but few ships or boats came downstream, because southward lay the Black Lands— rough water and no inhabitants. It was even less likely that swordsmen would have come upstream, from the north, for that way lay Ov.

They might be coming to avenge Kandoru. Swordsmen were utterly merciless against assassins, swordsmen killers. Kandoru had told her so, many times. She would have to convince them that they were looking in the wrong place. A priest or priestess must never tell a lie and was therefore a favored witness, even if she had been his wife and not disinterested. And there were a dozen others. The killers had come from Ov.

But the assassination had not been reported—or at least, she did not think it had been. She did not need to repeat the code of the priesthood to know that *prevent bloodshed* came very high on her list of duties to the Goddess.

A pebble rolled under her foot, and she stumbled. Even in daylight this bend of the gorge was a tunnel, confined between steep walls and overshadowed by trees. The stream bubbled quietly at her side. The rain had stopped, or could not get through the canopy. She picked her way carefully, testing every step, stretching out her hands to feel for branches.

If these swordsmen had come by chance, then they might not

know about Ov. They might not know that they would soon be in terrible danger themselves.

Or they might have been brought by the Hand of the Goddess. In that case, their interest must be more than just one murdered old warrior. Their objective might be Ov itself—*war*! There might be a whole army down by the jetty. That was what Kandoru had said to the first rumors of the massacre in Ov: "Sorcerers are not allowed near the River!"

Then, when the rumors had became more solid, he had said, "The Goddess will not stand for it. She will summon Her swordsmen . . ."

Two days later Kandoru had himself been dead, felled before he even had time to draw his sword, slain by a single trill of music. He had been a good man, in his way. He had lived by the code of the swordsmen, an honorable man, if not a very understanding or exciting husband for a juvenile apprentice priestess. She wished she could have helped him more. She should have pretended a little harder.

The local expert . . . but all she had were vague memories of the stories Kandoru had told her, rambling on for hour upon hour, an old man with nothing but his memories of youth and strength, of wenching and killing; an old man clasping his child bride in clammy embrace in a barren bed through endless winter nights. She should have listened more carefully.

Quili stopped suddenly, heart thumping. Had she heard something ahead of her? A twig snapping?

She listened, hearing only the stream and pattering dripping noises. It must have been her imagination. She went on, more slowly, more cautiously. She had been crazy to come without a light, for she knew that her night vision was poor. The priesthood was sacrosanct. No one, not the worst brigand, would harm a priestess. So they said.

She ought to be rejoicing at the thought of Kandoru being avenged. At fifteen she had been married; at sixteen a widow. At seventeen she found it hard to mourn, however much she reproached herself. She could perhaps have gone back to the temple, when Swordsman Kandoru had no further need for her services, but she had stayed. The tenants had made her welcome and they needed her. So did the slaves, much more so. Her ladyship had let her remain in the cottage and she provided basic fare—sacks of meal and sometimes even meat. She sent small gifts once in a while: sandals not too badly worn, leftover delicacies from the kitchen.

If the swordsmen did know about the sorcerers—if they were planning an attack on Ov—then there must be a whole army of them.

Floundering in the darkness, she almost walked into a vague shape standing square in her path, waiting for her.

She yelped and jumped backward, losing a shoe. "Priestess!" she squealed. Then she managed a slightly lower: "I am a priestess!"

"Good!" said a youth's soft tenor. "And I am a swordsman. In what way may I be of service, holy lady?"

†—†

It was an absurd situation. Standing on one leg in the dark, with her heart still bounding wildly from the surprise, Quili could yet appreciate the absurdity—neither she nor the stranger could see the other's rank. Who saluted and who responded? But of course swordsmen would never send a mere First to scout, nor a Second either. He must outrank her.

So she made the greeting to a superior, managing not to fall over, even in the final bow: "I am Quili, priestess of the second rank, and it is my deepest and most humble wish that the Goddess Herself will see fit to grant you long life and happiness and to induce you to accept my modest and willing service in any way in which I may advance any of your noble purposes."

The swordsman retreated one pace, and she heard, rather than saw, his sword whip from the scabbard on his back. She almost lost her balance again, before remembering that swordsmen had their own rituals, flailing their blades around in salute.

"I am Nnanji, swordsman of the fourth rank, and am honored to accept your gracious service."

The sword shot back into its scabbard again with a hiss and a click. Kandoru had not handled his so slickly.

"Do you always stand on one foot, apprentice?"

She had not thought he would have been able to see. "I've lost a shoe, adept."

He chuckled and moved, and she felt a firm grip on her ankle. "Here it is. Stupid-looking thing!" Then her foot was pushed back where it belonged, and the swordsman straightened up.

"Thank you. You see very well . . ."

"I do most things very well," he remarked cheerfully. He sounded so young, like a boy. Could he really be a Fourth? "Now, where is this, apprentice?"

"The estate of the Honorable Garathondi, adept."

The swordsman grunted softly. "What craft?"

"He is a builder."

"And what does a builder of the Sixth build? Well, never mind. How many swordsmen on this estate?"

"None, adept."

He grunted again, surprised. "What's the nearest village, or town?"

"Pol, adept. A hamlet. About half a day's walk to the north."

"There would be swordsmen there, then . . ."

It was not a question, so she need not say that the resident swordsman of Pol had died on the same day as her husband, or that his assassination could not have been reported, either. *Prevent bloodshed!*

"What city? How far?"

"Ov, adept. About another half day beyond Pol."

"Mm? Do you happen to know the name of the reeve in Ov?"

He was dead, also, and all his men. To answer just "No!" would be a lie. Before she could speak, the swordsman asked another question.

"Is there trouble here, Apprentice Quili? Brigands? Bandits? Work for honest swordsmen? Are we in any immediate danger?"

"No *immediate* danger, adept."

He chuckled. "Pity! Not even a dragon?"

She returned the laugh with relief. "Not one."

"And you haven't seen any sorcerers recently, I suppose?"

So he did know about the sorcerers! "Not recently, adept . . ."

He sighed. "Well, if it's safe, then we must have been brought here to meet someone. Like Ko."

"Ko?"

"Have you never heard the epic *How Aggaranzi of the Seventh Smote the Brigands at Ko*?" He sounded shocked. "It's a great tale! Lots of honor, lots of blood. It's very long, but I'll sing it for you when we have time. Well, if there's no danger, then I'd better go back and report. Come on!"

He took her hand and began to lead her down the road. His hand was very large, his grip powerful; but his palm felt oddly soft, unlike the hands of the farm workers—or even her own hands, these days.

Strangely, she did not feel nervous at being hauled into the unknown by this tall and youthful stranger. She stumbled in the ruts. He muttered, "Careful!" but he slowed down. There were three stream crossings on the trail, and she could barely see the stepping-stones, but he could, and he guided her.

"You were brought by the Most High, adept?"

"We were! The sailor says he's never heard of a ferry being taken before. We've come a long way, too! Very far!" He sounded satisfied, not awed at all. Of course the River was the Goddess, and any ship might arrive at an unexpected destination if it bore a Jonah, someone She wanted elsewhere. Free swords were notorious Jonahs, always being moved by Her Hand. Such manifestations of Her power happened too frequently to be truly miracles, but they were not something that Quili could ever regard as lightly as this brash young swordsman seemed to.

The trees thinned out, the valley widened to admit grayness, and now she could see better. He was even taller than she had thought, lanky and astoundingly young for a Fourth. He seemed no older than herself, but perhaps that was just his carefree manner—he chattered. Kandoru had been a Third. Few in any craft advanced beyond that rank.

"How can you tell how far you were brought?" Quili asked.

"Shonsu could tell. He knows everything! And we didn't come all in one jump. He woke at the first one—I think he must sleep with both eyes open." Whoever Shonsu was, Adept

Nnanji seemed to regard him with more respect than he did the Goddess. "I woke at the third—the cold woke me." The swordsman shivered. "We came from the tropics, you see."

"What are tropics, adept?"

"I'm not sure," he confessed. "Hot lands. Shonsu can explain. But the Dream God is very high and thin there. He got wider as we jumped north. And lower. You can see seven separate bands here, right? When we started, he was fainter and most of the arcs too close together to separate. And we moved east, too, Shonsu says. The rain only came with the last jump."

Shonsu must be a priest, she decided. He certainly did not sound like any swordsman she had ever heard of.

"How could he possibly know about going east?"

"The stars—and the eye of the Dream God! It happened about midnight, and dawn kept coming closer and closer. You'll have to ask Shonsu. He says it's still the middle of the night in Hann."

Hann! "You've been to *Hann*, adept?"

He glanced down at her, surprised at her reaction. She could see well enough now to tell that his face was filthy, smeared with dirt and grease. "Well, not Hann itself. We were trying to cross to Hann, from the holy island."

"The temple!" she exclaimed. "You were visiting the great temple, then?"

Adept Nnanji snorted. "Visiting it? I was born in it."

"No!"

"Yes!" He grinned hugely, big white teeth gleaming. "My mother was near her term. She went to pray for an easy labor, and—*whoosh!* There I was. They only just had time to get her into a back room. The priests thought it might almost rank as a miracle."

He was teasing her. Then the grin grew even wider. "My father had put six coppers in the bowl, and if he'd made it seven, he says, then I'd have been born right there, in front of the Goddess Herself."

That was pure blasphemy, but his grin was irresistible. Quili laughed in spite of herself. "You should not joke about miracles, adept."

"Perhaps." He paused and then spoke more humbly. "I've

seen a lot of miracles in the last two weeks, Apprentice Quili.
Ever since Shonsu arrived."

"He's your mentor?"

"Well, not just at the moment. He released me from my oaths
before the battle . . . but he says I may swear to him again."

Battle?

"Watch this puddle!" Nnanji let go her hand and put his arm
around her, guiding her by a muddy patch. But he kept his arm
there when they were past, and the light was quite good now. She
began to feel alarmed. She was glad of the protection of her cloak.
She had rarely spoken to a Fourth before and certainly never been
hugged by one. He was smiling down at her, being very friendly.
Very.

There were few free men close to her age on the estate, only
two unmarried. They all treated her with awed respect, because
of her craft, and they had nothing to talk about anyway, except
the crops and the herds. She had forgotten what real conversation was like. But she had never had a real conversation with a
man, only with other girls, her friends in the temple, years ago.
He was speaking to her as an equal. That was flattery, and she
was worried by how good it felt.

Why would the Goddess send such a filthy swordsman? It was
not only his face. Now they had reached the bottom of the gully.
Ahead of them lay the River, stretching away to the eastern
horizon, brilliant below the cloud. Color was returning to the
World. The sun god would appear in a few moments. Rain was
still falling, but gently, and she could see water streaking the dirt
on the swordsman's bony shoulders and chest. Even his kilt . . .

Quili gasped. "That's blood! You've been hurt?"

"Not mine!" He grinned again, proudly. "Yesterday we had a
battle—a great feat of arms! Shonsu did six and I drained two!"

She shivered, and his arm tightened around her, so she could
not break loose. She pulled her cloak tight. This intimacy was
appalling behavior for a priestess, but that steely grip gave her
no choice. Kandoru had never held her in public this way. He
had expected her to walk one pace behind him.

"You . . . you killed two men?"

"Three, yesterday. Two in the battle, but earlier I had to
challenge for my promotion, and one of them chose swords

instead of foils. He was trying to scare me, so I killed him. I didn't like him much, anyway."

She began to laugh, and then stared up with growing horror and belief at his satisfied smirk. Two of the swordmarks on his forehead were swollen, obviously new. His hair was black and greasy, but there were patches of red showing through the filth. His eyes were pale, the lashes almost invisible, and the runnels of clean skin washed by the rain were very light-colored. Apparently this murderous, callous youth was normally a redhead. The black in his hair had been applied deliberately, and then it had smeared all over him.

"Please, adept!" She struggled to break loose. They were almost at the jetty. The banks of the River were sheer cliffs of pebbly sand, and the only level land was the patch of shingle in the notch cut by the stream. When the River was high, there was barely room to turn a wagon, but today it was low, the flats were wide, and the landward end of the pier stood completely out of the water.

A small single-masted boat was tied up at the far end. There was no great army of swordsmen waiting, then, but there might still be a couple of dozen of them. Suddenly very frightened, Quili squirmed harder.

But the swordsman held tighter, still smirking down at her as he propelled her toward the jetty. The edge of the sun god's disk rose over the wide waters of the River. "I like you!" he announced. "You're pretty. The Goddess didn't make much of you, but She did very good work on what there is."

Quili wondered if she could slip out of the cloak and run. But he would run much faster than she would.

"I was only a Second in the temple guard," Nnanji remarked, "until the Goddess sent Shonsu. But starting today, I'm a free sword."

"What do you mean?" She knew quite well what he meant.

"Why do you suppose the Goddess sent you to meet me? See, I've always had to pay for women until now—except the slave girls in the barracks, of course. I bought a slave of my own yesterday, but she's no fun. Your Honorable Garathondi will offer us hospitality for a few days . . ."

Quili panicked. "Let me go!"

Nnanji released her at once, looking surprised. "What's wrong?"

"How dare you manhandle a priestess that way?"

She had shouted, trying to bolster her courage. Nnanji looked hurt. "I thought you were enjoying it. Why didn't you ask sooner? Do you mean . . . well, I'll wait until I've got cleaned up. I am a mess, aren't I?"

Quili straightened feathers. "I'll think about it," she said tactfully. Apparently he had meant no violence. He was like a large puppy, fresh from a mudhole somewhere, wanting to romp. She had told Nia that it was her duty. That advice no longer sounded as easy to take as it had been to give, but it would be her duty, also, if he wanted her. Given time to adjust to the idea . . .

"I'd better wait until you've had a look at Shonsu," he said sadly. "Women go glassy when they see him. Well, come on! He's waiting."

What? Did he think she had come down to meet the visitors just so she could get first choice of the swordsmen? Arrogance! Unbelievable arrogance! Speechless, she followed more slowly as Nnanji went striding along the pier. He whistled a four-note signal, although now the sun was shining through the rain, and he was quite visible to whoever was in the boat.

She listened for a reply and was astounded to hear a baby crying. Swordsmen bringing babies?

Nnanji stopped at the end of the jetty, peering down and speaking to whoever was waiting there, doubtless reporting that there was no danger. *Immediate* danger was what he had asked about, so she had not lied. But Quili had not had time to work out how her ladyship might be reacting to these visitors. Uneasily Quili now concluded that Lady Thondi might already be sending word to Ov that swordsmen had arrived. How long did it take a horse to reach Ov? How long for sorcerers to ride back? Perhaps the swordsmen would not interpret *immediate* in quite the same way she had.

Nnanji reached out his arms and caught a baby, as if plucking it out of the sky. He cuddled it to him, and the yells stopped.

As Quili reached him, he turned round and grinned. "This is

my friend Vixini." The baby was about a year old, obviously teething. It was a slave baby— Quili's mind staggered.

Then this so-bewildering swordsman reached down a helping hand, and another man sprang up on to the jetty. Nnanji remarked offhandedly, "My lord, may I have the honor of presenting Apprentice Quili?" Then he went back to tickling the naked baby, as if he were unaware of what he had just produced.

A giant! He was taller even than Nnanji, vastly wider and deeper, thickly muscled. His hair was black, and his black eyes fixed on Quili with a cruel, ruthless intensity that turned her bones to straw. Rape and death and carnage . . .

Nnanji was young to be a Fourth. This huge menace was a few years older, but far too young to be a *Seventh*. Yet there were seven swords marked on his forehead, and although his kilt was dirty, rumpled, and obviously bloodstained, it had undoubtedly started out as the blue of that rank. He must have been sheltering somehow from the rain, for the faint smears of gore on his chest and arms were quite dry.

Momentarily Quili trembled on the verge of turning and fleeing before this terrifying barbarian giant, then she began to stumble through the greeting to a superior, remembering that Nnanji had said women went glassy when they met Shonsu. She did not feel glassy, she felt like an aspen; her hands shook in the gestures. Kandoru had told her that never in his long career had he ever met a swordsman of higher rank than Sixth. She herself had never spoken to a Seventh of any craft—except her ladyship, and everyone knew that her husband had bought that rank for her years ago. But no one would or could buy seven swordmarks.

She bowed, then straightened. The deadly gaze did not waver or shift from her face. The giant's arm rose. The sun god streaked and flashed on a sword blade. "I am Shonsu, swordsman of the seventh rank, and am honored to accept your gracious service." His voice seemed to rise from depths unimaginable. Then the muscles of his arm bunched again as he shot the sword back into its scabbard.

The formalities over, Lord Shonsu put his hands on his hips and smiled.

The transformation was miraculous, as if another man entirely were standing before her. He had a wide, friendly grin, absurdly boyish for his size. Hardness suddenly became male good looks; thoughts of barbarians vanished. This enormous young lord was the most incredibly masculine man she had ever seen.

"My apologies, apprentice!" He had the deepest voice she had ever heard, too, a voice that seemed to echo all through her with shivery promises of confidence and competence, of protection and consideration and good humor. That smile! "We are not in a fit state to come visiting unannounced like this, and at such an unsociable hour."

Glassy now, very glassy.

"You . . . you . . . are welcome, my lord."

The smile grew warmer still, like the rising sun. "You show great hospitality in coming to meet us . . . and no small courage." His eyes twinkled. "I hope that my gory friend did not startle you too much?"

Quili shook her head dumbly.

"There is no swordsman nearby? And what of priests? Have you a mentor?"

"He lives in Pol, my lord."

"Then you are our hostess for now, at least until this Honorable Garathondi appears."

"He lives in Ov, mostly, my lord. His mother, Lady Thondi, is in residence . . ."

"You'll do every bit as well," the giant said with a heart-melting chuckle. "Nnanji tells me that you know of no task that may be awaiting our swords here?"

"Er . . . none, my lord."

Lord Shonsu nodded in satisfaction. "I am glad to hear it. We had our fill of slaughter yesterday, as you can see. Perhaps the Most High has sent us here for some rest and relaxation, then?" He boomed out a laugh and turned back to the boat.

Quili doubted that Adept Nnanji had had his fill of blood-shed. She saw that he was watching her with quiet amusement, rather wistfully. She felt herself blush, and looked away.

Her eyes returned of their own accord to Lord Shonsu, and now she noticed the sword on his so-broad rippling back. The hilt beside his black ponytail was silver, gleaming in the rays of the sun god and the rain. There was a huge blue stone on the top of it, held by a strange but magnificently crafted beast—a griffon. She knew that the griffon was a royal symbol, so that was a king's sword. The great gem could only be a sapphire, and there was another, matching stone, in Lord Shonsu's hairclip.

But . . .

But these men were supposed to be free swords. Free swords were men of poverty. Kandoru had explained often—free swords served only the Goddess, wandering the World to stamp out injustice, to regulate other swordsmen and keep them honest, to guard the helpless. Having no masters, they would accept no reward except their daily needs. A genuine free sword took pride in his penury.

A king's sword? The gem alone was worth a fortune, and the craftsmanship was superb, priceless.

How could any honest swordsman acquire something like that? Bewildered, she looked at Nnanji's sword to compare it. Nnanji was still holding that incongruous baby, which was gurgling and enjoying his attention, but Nnanji's eyes were on Quili.

"It belonged to the Goddess," he said.

"What?"

He nodded solemnly. "It is very old and very famous, probably the finest sword ever made. The man who crafted it was Chioxin, the greatest of all swordmakers, and it was the last and best of his seven masterpieces. He gave it to the Goddess."

Quili turned away to hide the horrible suspicion that flared up in her, which must not show in her face. These men had come from Hann, from the mother of all temples. They had fought a battle. Had someone tried to prevent their leaving— the temple guard that Nnanji had formerly belonged to? Was that sword the reason? Had this Shonsu stolen that royal sword from the treasury of the Goddess' temple?

But if he had, then why had She let the boat leave the dock when he boarded? And why had She moved it here, where there were sorcerers? Swordsmen of the Seventh were very rare and very terrible. Nnanji had said that Shonsu had killed six men in the fight—perhaps the Goddess had few swordsmen capable of bringing such a colossus to justice. But sorcerers certainly could.

Had they been brought here to die?

She felt sick with indecision. Was she supposed to aid these men, or not? What of preventing bloodshed? Whose blood? A mere apprentice should not be faced with such conundrums.

"Apprentice Quili, this is Jja, my love."

The woman smiled shyly, and Quili received another shock. Jja was a slave; her face bore a single stripe from hairline to upper lip, and she wore a slave's black. His *love?* The woman was tall and only that hateful badge of slavery and the close-cropped maltreatment of her dark hair stopped her from being spectacularly beautiful. No, she was beautiful in spite of those. Her figure was magnificently proportioned to her height, yet she moved with a sensual grace: strong and competent and serene. Even a Seventh could not change a slave's rank, but it seemed ironic for a man of such power to love a mere chattel. He was introducing her as if she were a person, though, and watching for Quili's reaction. She smiled carefully and said, "You are welcome, also, Jja."

A faint blush spread over the high cheekbones, the dark eyes were lowered. "Thank you, apprentice." A good voice. Jja turned to take the baby, who was now sitting on Nnanji's shoulders, wedged in place by his sword hilt. Little Vixini resisted, screaming angrily and clutching the swordsman's ponytail.

Then Lord Shonsu's strong arm pulled another woman up from the boat. "This," he said, "is Cowie." There was an odd note in the way he spoke, as if he had said something funny.

Cowie was another slave, and another sort of slave. If Lord Shonsu was the epitome of masculinity, then Cowie was the ultimate sex partner. Quili had never seen a figure so exaggeratedly female, and it was barely concealed at all by the flimsy wisp of garment. Her breasts strained against it, her arms and legs were soft and voluptuously rounded, her face was a lovely and sweet nothing. At the sound of her name, the provocative lips parted in an automatic smile, but her eyes continued to stare blankly at the shore.

Quili remembered her misgivings about her own too-tight gown. In this company she was not going to be noticed.

Nnanji had said something about buying a slave. She glanced at him, and he turned away.

Then another black-clad figure was lifted up by hands below, accepted, and gently set down by Lord Shonsu. He was very tiny and very old, his head totally hairless, his neck a crumple of wrinkles. The gown he wore appeared to be both too large for him and also a woman's garment. A black headband covered his brow. Quili blinked in astonishment at this apparition—babies, slaves, and beggars? What other surprises would Lord Shonsu produce?

"This is Honakura, who prefers to conceal his rank and craft," the swordsman said. "I don't know why, but we humor him."

The little ancient wheeled around angrily, waggling an arthritic finger to scold the giant swordsman towering over him. "You must not speak my name, either! A Nameless One is exactly that—no craft, no rank, no name! Address me as 'old man' if you wish."

Lord Shonsu regarded him with mild amusement. "As you wish . . . old man. Apprentice, meet one old man."

Honakura, if that was really his name, turned back toward Quili. He chuckled and smiled, revealing a mouth devoid of teeth. "Thus I also serve Her," he said.

"You are welcome . . . old man."

Lord Shonsu boomed a laugh. "And this . . ." He dropped on one knee and reached down into the boat. Then he sprang upright, hoisting a youth bodily into the air, a First. He floated there, his shoulders gripped in Shonsu's great hands, and he beamed down at Quili as if there was nothing undignified about such an unorthodox arrival, or as if Sevenths clowned with Firsts all the time.

The big man's voice came from somewhere behind the boy's grubby white kilt. "This is our mascot. Apprentice Quili, may I have the unparalleled honor of presenting the dreaded Novice Katanji, swordsman of the first rank?"

Then he let go. Novice Katanji landed unevenly, stumbled, recovered, and grinned. He fumbled for his sword hilt, which was canted over behind his left shoulder.

"Leave that!" Shonsu said quickly. "You'll decapitate someone—probably yourself."

Katanji shrugged, still grinning, and made the salute to a superior in civilian fashion. Bewildered, Quili responded. It was very rare to make formal presentation of a First; slaves and beggars were always ignored. Lord Shonsu not only had a peculiar sense of humor, he must also dislike formalities and ritual.

The young Katanji was a dark-eyed imp. His single facemark was raw and new, his curly black hair cropped short like a child's. There was a hairclip precariously balanced in it, but no ponytail resulting. He was grubby, but not as filthy as Nnanji, and innocent of bloodstains. Remembering Nnanji's story, Quili could guess that Novice Katanji had sworn to the code of the swordsmen only the previous day. Nnanji must be his mentor, for surely no Seventh would take a First as protégé. Yet perhaps this unconventional Shonsu was capable of even that.

"You are welcome also, novice," Quili said.

His big eyes regarded her solemnly. "Your gracious hospitality is already evident, apprentice." Then those eyes dropped, to linger over her cloak.

Quili glanced down and saw that the right side was stained, the faded yellow cloth marked by streaks of grease, and even perhaps blood, where Nnanji had hugged her against himself. She looked up in mingled shame and anger, as Novice Katanji turned away with a deliberate smirk showing on his face. Impudent little devil!

"No more strays, sailor?" Lord Shonsu was addressing the two men still in the boat. "Then you will come ashore for food and rest before you seek to return?"

"Oh, no, my lord." The captain was a fat and obsequious man. He would probably be very glad to be rid of so strange a cargo. To carry a Jonah reputedly brought good fortune to a vessel and normally the Goddess sent it home again promptly, but Lord Shonsu would be an unnerving passenger.

"We must not keep Her waiting, my lord," the sailor explained.

"May She be with you, then." Shonsu reached in a pouch on his harness and flipped a couple of coins down. They glinted in the sunlight. Free swords paying gold to mere boatmen?

"There we are, apprentice. Seven of us looking for a bite of breakfast." Lord Shonsu had turned to Quili again with high good spirits. He was amused—her astonishment must be showing. Two swordsmen, two slave women, a boy, a baby, and a beggar? What sort of army was that?

Then the menacing frown snapped back, and he stared along the jetty at the road vanishing into the notch of the gorge. He swung around to Nnanji.

"Transportation?"

Horror fell over Nnanji's face, and he jerked to attention. "I forgot, my lord."

"*Forgot?* You?"

Nnanji gulped. "Yes, my lord."

For a moment Shonsu's eyes flicked to Quili, then back to Nnanji. "I suppose there has to be a first time for anything," he said darkly. "Apprentice, we have a problem. I assume that we need to climb at least as high as the top of that cliff?"

"I am afraid so, my lord."

Shonsu turned back to the boatmen, who were fumbling with sails. "Wait! Toss up a couple of those pallets . . . and the awning. Thank you. Good journey!" He stooped to untie a line. Nnanji jumped for the other, watching to see exactly what Shonsu did and copying him.

Kandoru would never have played at being a dockhand, nor a porter, yet now this incredible Seventh gathered up the pallets and tarpaulin and went striding landward along the jetty, the astonished Quili having to trot to keep up with him.

"Apprentice, can you find us a wagon? The old man can probably manage, but Cowie . . ." He smirked again as he said that name. "Dear Cowie has lost one of her sandals. I should hate her beautiful soft feet to be damaged."

"I am sure I can find a cart, my lord," Quili said. A cart for a lord of the seventh rank? And would there be any men left to harness the horse? She had watched it being done often enough . . .

"That would do very well," Shonsu said cheerfully. They had reached the land, where the jetty stood above dry shingle. Quickly he spread the tarpaulin over the planks, then he jumped down and put the pallets below it. As his companions arrived, he reached up and lifted them down effortlessly. "We shall be comfortable enough in here until you return."

"I shall be as quick as I can, my lord."

"There's no hurry. I need to have a private talk with Nnanji, and this seems like a good chance." He flashed that heart-melting smile again.

Confused and unhappy, Quili mumbled something—she was not sure what—and headed for the road. As she entered the gorge, the sun tucked itself up into the clouds, and the World became gloomier and more drab. She had not lied, but she had left these swordsmen in ignorance of their danger. She must try to prevent bloodshed. *Merciful Goddess!* Whom was she supposed to shield—the workers, or the sorcerers, or the swordsmen?

†††

Wallie paced slowly back along the jetty, gathering his thoughts. His boots made hollow drum noises on the weathered planks, and beside him Nnanji's kept time. Nnanji was waiting in excited silence to hear what revelations the great Lord Shonsu was about to impart.

The jetty was stained with cattle dung—probably the estate exported cattle to the nearest city, Ov. The River was very wide, the far shore a faint line of smudge, and no sails marred the empty expanse of gray and lifeless water. At Hann the River had been about the same width, yet Hann lay a quarter of a World away. The River was everywhere, Honakura had said, and in a lifetime of talking with pilgrims in the temple, he had never heard tell of source or mouth. Apparently it was endless and much the same everywhere, a geographical impossibility. The River was the Goddess.

No sails . . . "The ferry's gone!"

"Yes, my lord." Nnanji did not even sound surprised.

Wallie shivered at this evidence of divine surveillance, then forced his mind back to the matter at hand. Twice before he had told his story, but this time would be harder. Honakura had accepted it as an exercise in theology. Believing in many worlds and a ladder of uncountable lives, he had been puzzled only that the dead Wallie Smith should have been reincarnated as the adult Shonsu, instead of as a baby. That was a miracle, and priests could believe in miracles. Honakura had wanted to hear about Earth and Wallie's previous existence, but those would not interest Nnanji.

Jja had not cared about the mechanism or the reason. She was content to know that the man she loved was hidden inside the swordsman, an invisible man with no rank or craft, as alienated from the World as she was. Only thus could a slave dare to love a Seventh. Nnanji's attitude would be very different.

The two men reached the end of the pier and stopped.

"Nnanji, I have a confession to make. I have never lied to you, but I have not told you the whole truth."

Nnanji blinked. "Why should you? It was you the Goddess chose to be Her champion. I am honored to be allowed to help. You need not tell me more, Lord Shonsu."

Wallie sighed. "I did lie to you, then, I suppose. I said my name was Shonsu . . . and it isn't."

Nnanji's eyes grew very wide, strange pale spots in his grimy face. No man of the People could ever look unshaven, but his red hair had been blackened the previous day with a blend of charcoal and grease. Later adventures had added guano and cobwebs, road dust and blood. Now thoroughly smeared, the resulting filth made him look comic and ridiculous. But Nnanji was no joke. Nnanji had become a very deadly killer, much too young to be trusted with either the sword skill his mentor had taught him so rapidly or the power that came with his new rank—a swordsman of the Fourth had the potential to do a mountain of damage. Nnanji would have to be kept under very close control for a few years, until maturity caught up with his abilities. That might be why the gods had ordered that he be irrevocably bound by the arcane oath to which the present conversation must lead.

"I did meet with a god," Wallie said, "and what he told me was this: the Goddess had need of a swordsman. She chose the best in the World, Shonsu of the Seventh. Well, he said that there was none better, which is not quite the same thing, I suppose. Anyway, this swordsman failed, and failed 'disastrously.' "

"What does that mean, my lord?"

"The god wouldn't say. But Shonsu was driven to the temple by a demon. The priests' exorcism failed. The Goddess took his soul—and left the demon. Or what Shonsu thought was a demon. It was me, Wallie Smith. Except I wasn't a demon . . ."

He was not telling this very well, Wallie thought, but he was amused by the puzzled nods he was being given. Others might mock at so absurd a yarn, but Nnanji would want very much to believe. Nnanji had a ruinous case of hero worship. It had suffered an agonizing death the previous day, but then the Goddess had sent a miracle to support Her champion, and Nnanji's adoration had sprung back to life again, stronger than ever. He would grow out of it, and Wallie could only hope that the education would not be too painful, nor too long delayed. No man could live up to Nnanji's standards of heroic behavior.

They turned together and began to wander landward again.

"Another way of looking at it, I suppose, is as a string of beads—that's one of the priests' images. A soul is the string, the beads are the separate lives. In this case, the Goddess broke the rules. She untied the string and moved one of the beads."

Nnanji said, "But . . ." and then fell silent.

"No, I can't explain it. The motives of gods are mysterious. Anyway, I am not Shonsu. I remember nothing of his life before I woke up in the pilgrim cottage with Jja tending me and old Honakura babbling about my doing a fast murder for him. Before that, as far as I recall, I was Wallie Smith."

He did not try to explain language, how he thought in English and spoke in the language of the People. Nnanji would not be able to comprehend the idea of more than one language, and Wallie himself did not know how the translation worked.

"And you were not a swordsman in the other world, my lord?"

Manager of a petrochemical plant? How did one explain that to an iron-age warrior in a preliterate World? Wallie sighed. "No, I wasn't. Our crafts and ranks were different. As near as I can tell you, I was an apothecary of the Fifth."

Nnanji shuddered and bit his lip.

But there had been Detective Inspector Smith, who would have been so horrified by his murdering, idol-worshiping, slave-owning son. "My father was a swordsman."

Nnanji sighed in relief. The Goddess was not as fickle as he had feared.

"And you were a man of honor, my lord?"

Yes, Wallie thought. He had been law-abiding, and a decent sort of guy, honest and conscientious. "I think so. I tried to be, as I try here. Some of our ways were different. I did my best, and I promised the god that I would do my best here also."

Nnanji managed a faint smile.

"But when the reeve of the temple guard claimed that I was

an imposter, he was correct. I did not know the salutes and responses. I did not know one end of a sword from the other."

Nnanji spluttered. "But—but you know the rituals, my lord! You are a great swordsman!"

"That came later," Wallie said, and went on to relate how he had met the demigod three times, how he had managed to find belief in the gods, and how he had then been given Shonsu's skill, the legendary sword, the unknown mission. "The god gave me the ability to use a sword, he gave me the sutras. But he gave me none of Shonsu's private memories at all, Nnanji. I don't know who his parents were, or where he came from, or who taught him. On those things, I am still Wallie Smith."

"And you have no parentmarks!"

"I have one now." He showed Nnanji the sword that had appeared on his right eyelid the previous night, the sign of a swordsman father. "It wasn't there yesterday morning. I think it is a sort of joke by the little god, or perhaps a sign that he approves of what we did yesterday."

Nnanji said he liked the second possibility better. The idea that gods might play jokes did not appeal to him.

They reached the landward end of the jetty and turned to pace Riverward again. It was a strange story, almost as strange in the World as it would have been on Earth, and Wallie took his time, explaining as well as he could how it felt to be two people, how his professional knowledge differed from his personal memories.

"I think I understand, my lord," Nnanji said at last, frowning down ferociously at the rain-slicked, rough-cut planks. "You greatly puzzled me, for you did not behave like other highranks. You spoke to me as a friend when I was only a Second. You did not kill Meliu and Briu when you had the chance—most Sevenths would have welcomed an excuse to cut more notches in their harness. You treat Jja like a lady and you were even friendly to Wild Ani. That was the way of honor in your other world?"

"It was," Wallie said. "Friends are harder to make than enemies, but they are more useful."

Nnanji brightened. "Is that a sutra?"

Wallie laughed. "No, it is just a little saying of my own, but it is based on some of our sutras. It works, though: look how useful Wild Ani turned out to be!"

Nnanji agreed doubtfully—swordsmen should not have to seek help from slaves. "I would swear the second oath to you, my lord, if you will have me as protégé. I still wish to learn swordsmanship from you, and the ways of honor..." He paused and added thoughtfully, "And I think I should like to learn some of this other honor, also."

Wallie was relieved. He had half feared that his young friend would understandably flee from him as a madman. "I shall be proud to be your mentor again, Nnanji, for you are a wonderful pupil and one day you will be a great swordsman."

Nnanji stopped, drew his sword, and dropped to his knees. There were other things that Wallie wanted to tell him, but Nnanji was never plagued by hesitations or deep reflection, and he now proceeded to swear the second oath: "I, Nnanji, swordsman of the Fourth, do take you, Shonsu, swordsman of the Seventh, as my master and mentor and do swear to be faithful, obedient, and humble, to live upon your word, to learn by your example, and to be mindful of your honor, in the name of the Goddess."

Wallie spoke the formal acceptance. Nnanji rose and sheathed his sword with some satisfaction. "You mentioned another oath also, mentor?" The demigod had warned that swordsmen were addicted to fearsome oaths, and Nnanji was no exception.

"I did. But before we get to that, I must tell you about my mission. When I asked what the Goddess required of me, all I was given was a riddle."

"The god gave you a task and didn't tell you what it was? Why?"

"I wish I knew that! He said that it was a matter of free will; that I must do what seemed right to me. If I only followed orders, then I would be less a servant than a tool." Another explanation, of course, might be that the demigod did not trust Wallie—either his courage or his honesty—and that was worrisome.

"This is what I was told:

> "First your brother you must chain.
> And from another wisdom gain.
> When the mighty has been spurned,
> An army earned, a circle turned,
> So the lesson may be learned.

Finally return that sword
And to its destiny accord."

Nnanji pouted in disgust for a moment, his lips moving as he thought over the words. "I'm no good at riddles," he muttered. Then he shrugged. It was Shonsu's problem, not his.

"Nor was I—until Imperkanni said something yesterday, after the battle."

Ah! Nnanji had been waiting to hear this. "Eleven forty-four? The last sutra?"

Wallie nodded. "It concerns the fourth oath, the oath of brotherhood. It is almost as terrible as the blood oath, except that it binds both men equally, not as liege and vassal. In fact it is even more drastic, Nnanji, for it is *paramount, absolute, and irrevocable.*"

"I didn't think the Goddess allowed irrevocable oaths."

"Apparently She does for this one. I think that is why the riddle says *chain*. If we swear this oath, then we're both stuck with it, Nnanji!"

Nnanji nodded, impressed. Again the two men began to walk. Wallie let him think for a moment.

"But . . . you don't know your—Shonsu's—history, mentor. You—he—may have a real brother somewhere?"

"That's what I thought, too, at first: that I had to seek out a brother. But the god did remove Shonsu's parentmarks, and perhaps that was a hint. The oath is restricted, Nnanji. It may only be sworn by two swordsmen who have saved each other's lives. That can never happen in the ways of honor, only in a real battle. I think that is why we were led into that slaughter yesterday. I saved you from Tarru, you saved me from Ghaniri. So you have a part in this mission also, and now we are free to swear the oath."

Given the chance, Nnanji would have sat down cross-legged to hear a sutra, so Wallie began it before he could do so. It was short, as sutras went, and much less paradoxical or obscure than some. He needed only say it through once—Nnanji never forgot anything.

Then they continued to walk in silence, while Nnanji scowled again at the planks and moved his lips. Obviously the fourth oath was causing him trouble, and Wallie began to feel uneasy. He was certain that he had solved the first line of the riddle, and that he was supposed to swear that impossible oath with this gangly young swordsman. But what could he do if Nnanji refused? And why was he not eager to swear? He should be jubilant at the opportunity to be brother to the greatest swordsman in the World.

"It does not seem right, mentor," he said at last. "I am only a Fourth. That oath sounds as if it should be sworn between equals."

"It doesn't say equals."

Nnanji pouted and tugged at his ponytail.

"I need your help, Nnanji," Wallie said.

"Help, mentor?" Nnanji laughed. "Mine?"

"Yes! I am a great swordsman, but I am a stranger in the World. I know less about it than Vixini. There are so many things I do not know. For example: why did you keep your sword on your back all night in the boat? That must have cramped your style a little with Cowie, did it not?"

Nnanji smirked. "Not especially." Then he gave Wallie a startled look. "It is the custom of the frees, mentor."

"It is not in the sutras, not that I can find."

"Then it is just a tradition, I suppose. But a free sword never removes his sword. Except for washing—or to use." He frowned, worried that his mentor did not know something so elementary.

If Shonsu had been a free sword, then the information had not been passed along—Wallie's memory had been cut off in strange places. Even in bed? That would be part of the free swords' mystique, of course, but it must be a very inconvenient habit.

"Well, that shows you how ignorant I am. If you are only my protégé, you will not want to criticize me, or offer advice when you think I am making a mistake. Those are the sorts of things that a brother will do that a mere protégé would not."

"If you would let me swear the blood oath again, mentor," Nnanji suggested hopefully, "then you could *order* me to advise you."

"And I could order you to shut up, too! As my vassal, you were little better than a slave, Nnanji. I may never accept the third oath from any man again and certainly never from you."

Nnanji frowned some more. "But how will I address you? A Fourth can't call a Seventh 'brother'!"

It was not a trivial question. A term of address advertised relationships between swordsmen and could warn a potential challenger that there was an onus of vengeance involved. As soon as they had sworn the second oath, he had begun calling Wallie "mentor" instead of "my lord."

"'Brother' will be fine. Use any term you like. Probably you'll want to call me 'Stupid' half the time."

Nnanji smiled politely. "It is a great honor, mentor . . . if you're sure?"

Wallie hid a sigh of relief. "I am certain—and not all the honor is yours, Adept Nnanji."

Nnanji turned pink under his smears. "What is the ritual?"

"There doesn't seem to be one. Why don't we just say the words and shake hands?"

So, while the waters of the River slapped gently at the base of the jetty beneath them in subtle applause, Shonsu and Nnanji swore the oath of brotherhood and then shook hands. Wallie felt a sense of accomplishment. He had satisfied the first line of the riddle . . . what happened next, though?

Nnanji grinned shyly. "Now I have Shonsu as a mentor and Wallie Smith as a brother?"

Wallie nodded solemnly. "The best of both worlds," he said.

They continued to stroll along the battered little jetty. Rain continued to ooze in summer drizzle from the low, gray-flannel clouds. Gray also was the River, gray were the cliffs that shut off all view of what might lie ahead. This soggy, barren little place ought to be depressing, especially before breakfast and after an extremely short night, yet Wallie's mood remained stubbornly euphoric. He had escaped from the temple, from the dangerous trap that had held him for all of his brief existence in the World. He had proved that he could be a swordsman and could satisfy the Goddess in that role, playing it as he felt it should be played and not necessarily as the native iron-age hop-lites played it. Now he was going to be given a chance to see a whole new planet and an ancient and complex culture, albeit a primitive one. He felt like school was out at last.

Furthermore, the priestess had said that there were no swords-men around. Swordsmen held a monopoly on violence. Without swordsmen, danger was unlikely. Whatever his mission might prove to be, it would surely involve swordsmen, so it had not started yet. There might be more tests or lessons to come, but he might also be due for a vacation. He repeated to himself the instructions of the demigod: *Go and be a swordsman, Shonsu! Be honorable and valorous. And enjoy yourself, for the World is yours to savor.* A male fantasy of that elflike priestess flickered momentarily across his mind, and he hastily reproached himself for being as bad as Nnanji. He had Jja. No man could want more.

"What happens now, my lord brother?" Nnanji inquired im-patiently.

They had reached the tarpaulin that covered the rest of the party. "Let's go and see!" Wallie dropped nimbly to the shingle and peered in under the jetty.

Novice Katanji moved hurriedly away from Cowie. Cud-dling was a good way to keep warm, but his brother would not approve. Nnanji arrived at Wallie's side a second later.

The Goddess had selected a strange assortment of compan-ions to accompany Her champion. Seven was the sacred number, so Wallie's party had to number seven. Nnanji was understandable, and old Honakura was going to be a peerless source of wisdom and information—if he chose to be, for he could be inscrutably obscure at times. But two slave women, a boy, and a baby did not make much sense. On Wallie's back was the seventh sword of Chioxin, which Honakura had defined as the most valuable piece of movable property in the World. The demigod had warned him that alley thieves would prowl after it. Why the mission required such a priceless sword was a mystery in itself; any ordinary blade would suffice when wielded with Shonsu's unsurpassed skill. So why give him a treasure, and then withhold adequate protection?

What he needed, Wallie thought, was a half-dozen hard-eyed, hard-muscled swordsmen, not boys and women; yet he had been balked when he tried to enlist swordsmen from the temple guard. He had hinted to Imperkanni that he needed a few and had almost been challenged on the spot. Now he had been brought to a place with no swordsmen at all. Curiouser and curiousest!

He took a careful look at Honakura. The frail and incredibly ancient priest was accustomed to luxury, not this outdoor adventuring in damp clothes. Nevertheless, he seemed to be in good spirits, beaming his gums at the swordsman. Vixini was fretting, and his mother smiled rather wanly at her owner.

Nnanji directed a bleak gaze toward Katanji, perhaps suspecting what had been going on in his absence. "Lord Shonsu and I have just sworn the oath of brotherhood!" he announced.

Katanji contrived to look impressed, if rather cynically so.

"That makes him your mentor, also!"

Now Katanji looked alarmed.

"It does?" Wallie said. " 'Your oaths are my oaths'? Yes, I suppose it does. And also my brother, perhaps? Well, we shall have to make sure he is a credit to us both, shan't we?" He stepped over and settled on the pallet beside Jja, having to tilt his sword at an angle across his back and keep one leg twisted under him. If this was how free swords had to sit all the time, then he disapproved. Nnanji moved in under cover and squatted on his heels.

"So you have solved the first line of the riddle," Honakura said. "Now what happens?" He smirked mockingly.

"Has your mission begun, then, my lord?" asked Katanji.

Nnanji bristled. In so formal a culture, a mere First must not address a Seventh without invitation, but Katanji had already summed up Lord Shonsu and knew he was in no danger.

Hastily Wallie said, "I don't know, novice. I was explaining to Nnanji that I was not told exactly what my mission is to be. It may have begun, but—"

"My lord brother! He is only a scratcher. He does not know one seventy-five yet!"

Wallie nodded. "Nnanji will instruct you in the sutra 'On Secrecy,' " he told Katanji. "Meanwhile, just remember that this is in confidence, all right?"

The boy nodded, wide-eyed. He had already packed more excitement into his first day as a swordsman than most men would achieve in years. He had even saved Wallie's life the previous evening—and probably Nnanji's, too. Obviously he had a part to play also, but whatever it might be, it would not likely require a sword. Nnanji, in his first flush of excitement at being promoted, had impetuously rushed off, bought that ludicrous slave, and sworn his young brother as his protégé. Cowie might make some old man very happy in a comfortable home somewhere, but she was not a swordsman's woman. Katanji, likewise, was not swordsman material. He completely lacked his brother's natural talents as an athlete, as Wallie had confirmed with his horseplay on the jetty. Katanji had almost fallen over, even in a straight drop of three feet or so. Nnanji would have landed like a cat.

Nnanji was scowling, playing middlerank as he had seen it played in the temple barracks, wearing his topkick-facing-grunt face.

"You say you're not good at riddles," Wallie said. "How is he?"

Reluctantly Nnanji said, "Not bad."

"Then let's try him on this one." Wallie explained the riddle that defined his mission. Katanji frowned. Honakura had heard it before. Jja was certainly trustworthy. Cowie would understand little more than Vixini . . . and yet Cowie had also played an unwitting part in the gods' plans, a reminder that mortals should not jump to conclusions.

"So the question is: what happens now? I do have a couple of clues. No, three, I think. Two of them are things that . . . my predecessor said, just before he died. He said he had come very far. Well, we were moved very far in the night. Secondly, he mentioned sorcerers."

"Rot!" snapped Honakura. "I will never believe in sorcerers. Just legends!"

Wallie knew that he would take a great deal of convincing himself, but he had come to believe in gods and miracles, so he was not going to close his mind on the subject of sorcerers. Shonsu had said they existed.

"There would be no honor fighting sorcerers," Nnanji said grumpily, which was what he had said when Wallie had asked him once before. Then he grinned. "And there aren't any here! I asked Apprentice Quili! No sorcerers and no dragons."

"Dragons? Are there really dragons in the World?"

Nnanji sniggered. "None! What's the third clue, lord brother?"

"You."

"Me?"

Wallie laughed. "I wanted to enlist some good men to guard my back and my sword. I was blocked. I only got one. Of course that one is remarkably good."

Nnanji preened.

"But one is not enough! I'm sure that my mission must involve swordsmen. Now we've been brought to a place where there are no swordsmen, and there can't be many places like that in the World, can there?"

"No."

"So I don't think my mission has begun yet," Wallie said cheerfully. "There must be a few more tests or lessons to come first."

"Dangerous?"

"Probably."

Nnanji smiled contendedly.

"But this sounds like a very safe place. So maybe we've been brought here just to relax for a few days."

"Or to meet someone? Like Ko!"

"Ko?"

"Have you never heard . . . It's a great epic!" Nnanji drew a deep breath, a sign that he was about to start singing. Even if the epic was inordinately long, even if he had only heard it once, or even if that had been years before, he would be capable of rendering the whole thing without a stumble.

Hastily Wallie said, "Just the gist!"

"Oh!" Nnanji deflated and pondered for a moment. "Lord Aggaranzi and his band were moved by Her Hand to Ko but the villagers had no work for their swords, and then Inghollo of the Sixth and his band were brought the next night, and the following day two more . . ."

The Goddess had collected an army at Ko, apparently, and then ambushed a large brigade of brigands, who had been chopped into small fragments. Nnanji approved.

"Sounds reasonable," Wallie said. "So possibly we have been brought to a safe place to meet someone."

Then he heard a distant clanking and jingling that must be the long-awaited transportation arriving.

"So there you are, novice," he said quickly. "Now, why did I tell you all that?"

In the shade, Katanji's eyes gleamed so bright that they almost glowed. "Because 'another' might mean 'another brother,' my lord?"

"Correct!"

"What?" Nnanji shouted. "You think you can gain wisdom from *him?*"

"We just did . . . didn't you?"

Nnanji smiled sheepishly, and then shot another baleful glance at his young brother. "I don't approve of Firsts thinking," he said ominously.

The cart was drawn by one of the strange camel-faced horses of the World, and driven—surprisingly—by the little Apprentice Quili herself. She was clearly having some trouble, but she managed to turn the creaking old vehicle, and then she jumped down and bowed to Wallie.

"Lady Thondi sends her respects, my lord. She will be honored to receive you at the manor at your convenience."

"I don't feel fit to go calling on ladies at the moment."

Quili smiled, seeming almost relieved. "You are most welcome to stop at the tenancy to clean up, my lord. The women have prepared a meal. It will be humble fare, compared to what her ladyship could offer, but they would be greatly honored if you cared to partake of it." She waited hopefully.

"Then let's do that." Wallie began assisting his companions into the cart. There was straw to sit on, and a heap of shabby cloaks and blankets for cover.

He liked this diminutive child priestess. Her long hair was matted by the rain, and her yellow cloak a shabby, disreputable thing, but there was a quickness about her that told of humor and intelligence. Of course she was nervous and jumpy, which was quite understandable, merely emphasizing her youthful charm. Better groomed and garbed, she would be at least pretty and possibly sensational. She probably deserved a better life than the one she was having, if he read correctly the dirt ingrained in her fingers. With her mentor living half a day's walk away, she could have little chance of working toward promotion.

Nnanji was obviously attracted, and she glanced nervously at him as he edged close, beaming down at her . . . no, leering down at her. When she scrambled up to the driver's bench, awkward in her cloak and priestess' long robe, he moved as if to join her. Wallie coughed meaningfully and jerked an imperious thumb at the back. He climbed up and sat beside Quili himself.

She slapped the reins and shouted. After a moment's reflection, the horse decided that there were more interesting places in which to be difficult, and the cart creaked forward.

Tree trunks, valley walls, and streambed crowded in upon their path. The road was no more than a stretch of cleared ground, rough and rutted and spiky with roots. A little work with a dozer and a few truckloads of gravel would work wonders on it, Wallie decided. Twice the horse balked at fords, giving Quili trouble. The stream was rising, encroaching on its banks.

"This rain is unusual, apprentice?"

Quili was concentrating on the horse, but she stopped biting her tongue long enough to say, "Very, my lord. At this time of year. And the first real rain since winter."

Wallie wondered if there could be any relation between the rain and his own arrival. Then he decided that the thought was absurd—he was becoming as bad as Honakura, who was full of weird superstitions. Nevertheless, much more rainfall, and the track to the jetty would become impassable.

The trees were less lush than the tropical varieties at Hann, and he could not identify any of them—hardly surprising, for he was no botanist. Apparently Shonsu had not been much interested in vegetation, for his vocabulary seemed to contain none of the names. Perhaps some had Earthly equivalents, similar but not the same, like the odd-looking horses. Or like the People themselves —a neat, brown-skinned folk, cheerful, fun-loving and lusty, certainly human, but not exactly matching any Earthly race.

He moved his sword to a more comfortable position and stretched out his arm along the backrest. Quili jumped and then blushed furiously.

Damn! Wallie had forgotten that he was no longer the man he

had been on Earth. Women looked at Shonsu in a way women had never looked at the nondescript Wallie Smith. Wallie Smith might have received odd glances had he paraded around bare-chested in a kilt and leather harness, but not those sort of looks.

Which raised the problem of Nnanji's attentions to Quili. Nnanji had never made any secret of his ambition to become a free sword—it had been about the first thing he had imparted to his liege lord Shonsu when he had begun to relax enough in his company to talk at all. Wallie had parried the hidden questions about their joint future until he had gained time to learn from Honakura just what a free sword was. He had been disgusted to learn how much those wandering warriors expected in the way of hospitality. It was not a sutra, it was a universal custom, which meant a law—free swords could have anything they wanted, including access to their hostesses' beds.

That prospect was at least as attractive to Nnanji as the opportunities for bloodshed. Since the onset of adolescence, he had lived within the narrowly male world of the barracks, naïvely absorbing all the macho bragging, believing the tall tales of breathlessly grateful maidens. Now he saw his chance. He had no desire to be a routine policeman in some quiet little town or city. He dreamed of the open road—or, to be precise, open River— and honoring beautiful damsels would be a large part of the romance of it all. Here he was, a free sword at last, and this pretty young priestess had the misfortune to be the first woman he had encountered.

Wallie could admit a certain barbaric logic in the custom. Free swords were the good guys and brigands were the bad guys, but at times the distinction between them must become blurred. So hospitality was given without limits—unstinted generosity could avert pillage, and there was one sure way to avoid rape. Another benefit might be an increase in genetic diversity among the People, for likely few of them ever moved very far from their birthplaces in this primitive culture, and inbreeding would be a problem.

But that was the general case. In the specific instance, young Quili was being molested. Wallie could hardly change the laws of the World, but he could certainly divert Nnanji this time. He glanced back at his companions in the cart, noting his new oath brother's glum expression. Satisfied that the squeaking axles and the roar of the stream would drown out his words, he turned to Quili and remarked, "Adept Nnanji seems very attracted to you, apprentice."

Quili blushed even redder. "I am greatly honored, my lord."

"Are you sure?"

She gasped and somehow managed to go redder still.

"No, no! That wasn't what I meant!" Wallie floundered. "I am very much in love, Quili. I am totally infatuated by Jja. Like a starry-eyed boy! I seek no other woman."

Understandably, she made no reply to such insulting gibberish. She kept her eyes on the plodding horse, although it seemed to be managing without any guidance from her.

"What I meant . . . I mean, if I seem . . . Oh, damn! If Nnanji thinks that I want you, then he will leave you alone. Do I make myself clear?"

"Either . . . Yes, my lord."

"Then I shall pretend. But I'm only pretending!"

"Yes, my lord."

He moved close and put his arm around her. Nnanji would certainly notice. She looked tiny in her yellow cloak, like a half-drowned canary, but there was a surprisingly firm young woman in there. He felt Shonsu's disorderly glands begin to stir and repressed them with thoughts of Jja.

After a moment he said, "I swear I am only playacting, Quili."

"Yes, my lord."

"So there is no reason for you to tremble quite so violently."

†† ††

At first the meal went quite well. The visitors had been squashed in around a group of tables in one of the cottages, while six or seven women flustered around, serving the food by squeezing tactfully past between the guests' backs and the walls. Half a dozen children had managed to slip in, also, and the tiny room was packed and stuffy and dark. The fare was plain, as Quili had

promised, but the fresh bread and lean ham were delicious.
With farm butter and bright vegetables, warm beer in earthen-
ware pitchers, and a mysterious stew, no one was going to complain about the food.

Nor could anyone object to the quality of service. All the
women were brown-clad farmers of the Third, from two white-
haired matrons in long-sleeved gowns, down to the youngest,
whose name was Nia. Nia wore nothing but a short, simple
wrap and looked very good in it.

And there was another young lady named Nona, whose wrap
was so breathtakingly and impractically brief that it must surely
have been shortened for the occasion. At first everyone had
fawned humbly over the swordsmen, but soon Nona found
courage, and then even Nnanji's Trojan appetite could not distract him from her obvious availability. The two of them began
smirking, cracking lewd jokes, and almost striking sparks. Wallie concluded with relief that Quili was out of danger. He intercepted a few eyelash flutters from Nia, which he discouraged
by feigning interest in Quili. Only one swordsman fathermark
would be authorized by this visitation.

That point might have to be stressed to Novice Katanji, who
had made fast progress with a couple of the preadolescent girls,
naked and flat-chested and definitely off-limits in Wallie's view.
There were no girls of his own age around, so perhaps Katanji
was merely being friendly—or perhaps not. As the eating pro-
gressed, though, his socializing slowed down, and he began
directing sharp glances around the whole company and then at
Wallie, who had just made the same discovery himself: there
was too much tension. Something was wrong.

Until that realization struck, Wallie had been fairly content. He
and his companions were clean at last. Their garments had been
rushed away to be laundered and temporary replacements provided. At first an abbreviated brown loincloth had made him feel
as shameless as Nona, but once he was seated at the table he forgot
about it and tucked into the spread with genuine appetite.

Then two minor problems appeared almost simultaneously. As
he ate, he began to feel a strange lethargy. Honakura yawned. Jja
followed suit—and so did Nnanji, in the middle of his animated
flirting. He blinked in surprise and carried on. Wallie smothered a

yawn himself. It had been a short night, but . . . jet lag! They had been moved the equivalent of several time zones by the Hand of the Goddess. Now it was not yawning but laughter that struggled for possession of Wallie's throat. The thought of jet lag in this primitive culture was ludicrous, and the idea of trying to explain it to anyone else even more so. Nevertheless, it was worth remembering, for the resulting mental confusion could seriously warp a man's judgment for a day or two.

His second problem concerned Jja.

The tenancy was a clutter of cottages, all small and mostly shabby, interspersed with barns and sheds, and standing among vegetable patches. Pigs and chickens roamed underfoot, while background noises told of dogs and at least one discordant donkey. The setting was pleasant, centered on a pond that served for washing, stock watering, and irrigation, but in all directions the surrounding countryside was concealed by little bare hillocks and copses of scanty trees.

It was a humble settlement, and the people who inhabited it were humble, also. But they outranked the estate owner's slaves, who lived elsewhere, and they were uncomfortable at having to entertain Jja and Cowie and Vixini. Cowie was quite unaware of the conflict, looking content for the first time since Wallie had met her, stuffing food into herself, apparently impervious to jet lag. Jja had become very quiet. She sat close by Wallie and attended to Vixini and spoke only in reply to questions. He fumed, but there was nothing he could do. The women were trying the best they could. Doubtless Quili had warned them, and the hostility was being suppressed, but it was there. Wallie had not met this prejudice in the temple—Nnanji made no value distinction between free woman and slave—but for these people slaves were a threat to livelihood. The difference was not racial, it was purely an accident of birth, yet the free could not hide their contempt of the unfree. The World of the Goddess was an imperfect place.

So he tried to reassure Jja without at the same time offending the attending women, and he made the best of it. He also made conversation with Quili, on his right. She had discarded her bulky cloak, revealing a threadbare lemon gown that curved satisfactorily in all the right places. Feigning interest called for no effort.

He established that the manor house stood farther up the

hillside, hidden by trees. There were cattle sheds there, and slave barns, and more cottages. The inhabitants of this tenancy seemed to have intermediate status, not quite farmhands and not quite free farmers themselves. They paid their rent in work for the landlord, but they also grew vegetables for sale to the manor. Wallie at once suspected a company store economy and soon confirmed his guess—to obtain imports, like nails and rope, or local products such as lumber, the tenants must deal with Honorable Garathondi's manager, Adept Motipodi. Everything went back to Garathondi in the end.

The ham had vanished. Fresh strawberries appeared, with cream thick as butter. Not for the first time, Wallie mourned the absence of coffee in the World.

Honakura was enthusiastically attacking the dessert, while attempting to discover more about the landowner and his mother, Lady Thondi. Katanji had set out to charm everyone, not merely the young maidens. Jja was being monosyllabic. Cowie was not communicating with anyone. Nnanji was describing the best ways to push a sword into a man and how it felt to do so, making Nona breathe deeply over his courage and the nobility of his motives.

Then Wallie noticed, and Katanji followed a moment later— Quili and the other women were as jumpy as a pondful of frogs.

Somebody had said something. Perhaps it had been only Nnanji's gruesome attempts at shop talk, but something was wrong.

So more than Nnanji's advances had been disturbing the young priestess earlier. Even the older women were nervous, and they were obviously deferring to her, in spite of her youth. Of course in Earthly terms they were peasants entertaining a general or a duke, and some tension was inevitable. Their menfolk were not there to support them, having been called away by Adept Motipodi for a land-clearing project, or so Wallie had been informed. But the guests had not raped or murdered anyone, they had praised the food and hospitality, and the tension was not decreasing. It seemed to be getting worse.

Wallie tried to establish a little local geography. East lay the River, and there were no significant settlements on the far bank. Westward the mountains of RegiVul were normally visible, he was told, but they were hidden today by the rain clouds. To the north lay the hamlet of Pol and then the city of Ov. Perhaps he was expected to head for Ov, but he decided to put off any decisions until he had met with Lady Thondi.

Southward there seemed to be nothing. The Black Lands, Quili said vaguely . . . no people. And even the Black Lands were inaccessible, the older women explained, because there were cliffs. So this place was a curiously isolated dead end? Wallie did not need sutras to warn him that dead ends could be traps. Common prudence would suggest that a move to Ov might be very wise—except that he had no one but Nnanji to guard his back from the alley thieves the demigod had warned about. Stymied!

"You keep no boats here, apprentice?"

Quili shook her head. "Not at the moment, my lord. His honor has one, of course, but he is in Ov." She mentioned a couple of fishing boats that were usually present, and a cattle boat, and one or two others, but for this reason or that reason . . .

Wallie's scalp prickled—too much coincidence. There was a test coming. The Goddess had boxed Shonsu in for some purpose.

And it was then that he remembered the rain and guessed what was happening. He glanced at his companions. Honakura had felt the unease, but seemed more puzzled than worried. Honakura did not know about the climate. He had not heard Quili's comments about it, and his skill was people—he would not have been able to read the appearance of the semiarid landscape as Wallie had done when he arrived at the tenancy, or even to appreciate that irrigation for vegetables meant poor rainfall.

Katanji was suspicious, but a city boy did not have the botanical knowledge, either. He likely did not even know enough about the swordsmen's sutras. Of course old Honakura would not know the actual words of the sutra in question, but he would know what must result from it. Quili obviously did—she was masterminding the deception.

Nnanji naturally suspected nothing and would have to be kept that way . . . and then Wallie remembered the oath he had just sworn. *My secrets are your secrets.* He could keep nothing from Nnanji now.

The gods had tricked him again.

No! He was not going to commit a massacre. It was not fair. He had killed six—no, seven—men the previous day. He had proved that he could be bloody if he had to be. How much slaughter did She want from Her champion?

He was not going to start killing innocent people.

Goddess be damned!

Then he realized that the room had fallen into a horrified silence. He had been glaring at Nnanji, and even Nnanji was wilting under that glare.

"You don't want me to tell about the battle, my lord brother?" he asked nervously. Nona was standing beside him, and he had his arm around her.

Wallie had not heard a word. He pulled his wits together. "I don't care," he said, "although I doubt that these gentle ladies will be interested in such a tale. No, something you said reminded me of another battle. That's all."

Everyone relaxed, including Nnanji. He leered up at Nona. "You don't need me for a little while then, do you, my lord brother? Farmer Nona has offered to show me her house." For him, this sudden interest in domestic architecture was a surprisingly tactful way of describing what the two of them obviously had in mind.

"Yes, I do need you," Wallie said. "I'm putting you in charge for . . . for a little while. I want to see Apprentice Quili's house."

Quili blanched. Then she bared her teeth at Wallie in an attempt at a smile. "I shall be greatly honored, my lord." It came out as a whisper.

"Then let us go right away. Ladies, I thank you for the meal. It was superb."

With varied expressions of surprise and amusement, approval and disapproval, the company moved out of the way as Wallie followed Quili around to the door. The outside air seemed cool and fresh after the stuffy room, flapping his loincloth as if to mock such unswordsmanlike dress. The rain seemed heavier.

Huddled again in her cloak, the priestess pointed to the far side of the pond. "That one, my lord. We should run!"

Hers was the smallest of the cottages, badly in need of a new roof from the look of the sag in the present one.

She would not run very fast in her gown, so Wallie announced that he would carry her. He scooped her up and ran, mud splattering below his boots. She weighed very little, less than Katanji.

The door was not locked. She lifted the latch, and he carried her across the threshold, wondering as he did so if that gesture had the same implications in the World as it did on Earth. He set her down and closed the door and looked around.

It was very small and, obviously, very old. One of the walls leaned inward, and the floor was uneven. Probably the present bowed roof was far from the first that these ancient stones had supported. There were two stools and a chair, a table, and a rough dresser. The floor was made of flagstones, with straw on them by the entrance. Cooking would be done on the fire, of course, and there was an oven built into the fireplace. Faint scents of woodsmoke gave the place a homey air. A bucket and two large baskets stood in a corner; a couple of garments hung on pegs; a small and very rough image of the Goddess sat on a shelf with flowers laid before it . . . There was no great comfort, but the room was clean and friendly.

He looked around to speak to Quili, and she had vanished. Quiet creaking of ropes came from the other room. He ducked through the other doorway in time to see her stretching out on the bed.

"Very pretty," he said harshly, aware of his sudden physical response. Her body was every bit as fine as the tight gown had promised.

She twisted a smile and held out her arms to him, but he could see her hands shaking.

"You're very pretty, apprentice, but you're trying to distract me. Now put your gown on again and come out here. I want to talk to you."

He went and sat on the more solid looking of the two stools. In a moment Quili crept in from the other room, dressed again in her threadbare yellow robe, but barefoot. She lit on the edge of the chair, hands clasped, eyes staring down at the floor, long hair falling to hide her face.

Wallie forced his mind back to business. "Tell me about the murdered swordsmen."

Again, all the color drained from her face. She stared at him.

"Men do not go to clear land on the wettest day since winter, Quili."

She slid to her knees. "My lord, they were not at fault! They are good people!"

"I must be the judge of that."

Quili crouched over and began to weep, covering her face with her hands. That was another approach, and probably the last she had left to try. It might be very effective, though—Wallie was not good at bullying little girls.

He let her sob for a while and then said, "That's enough! Quili, don't you see that I'm trying to help? I want to hear this story before Adept Nnanji does. Now tell me the truth—and quickly!"

Nnanji was sworn to uphold the sutras. His reaction to an assassination would be as automatic as blinking. A cover-up made it much, much worse, and there was no other explanation for the men's absence. Nnanji would snap out a denunciation. He was far too impetuous and idealistic to look for extenuating circumstances first. In fact, to a swordsman, there could be no extenuating circumstances for assassination. Nnanji would be prosecutor and Wallie both judge and executioner. He also was sworn to obey the code of the swordsmen, and if he found against Nnanji, then Nnanji had brought false charges and must pay the penalty. The only penalty in such a case was death.

Once before Wallie had tried to avoid the Draconian responsibilities of a man of honor, and that attempt had merely led to much worse bloodshed. It was another test. He could only hope that the wrong answer the last time would be the right answer now.

"How many swordsmen, Quili?"

"One, my lord." It was a whisper and it came from somewhere near his feet.

"Who?"

"Kandoru of the Third."

"Honorable or not?" He got only silence. "Tell me!"

"He was a man of honor."

"The resident swordsman here, I suppose?"

"Yes. The estate guard, my lord."

It was like pulling teeth with fingers. "Young? Old?"

"He . . . he said he was about fifty, my lord. But I think he was older than that . . . he had bad rheumatism." She fell silent, again staring at the floor. "He was very fond of animals . . . Adept Motipodi called him the finest horse doctor . . ."

"Quili, I am trying to help! I do not want to kill anyone, but I must have the facts."

She straightened up slowly and looked at him with red-rimmed eyes. "He was my husband."

"No!"

He had never guessed that she could have had a husband, alive or dead—she seemed too absurdly young. But why would she protect his killer? To save a lover? Then why were the other women aiding her? Why had the men not reported the assassination to the nearest swordsman?

"How long ago?"

"A little over a year, my lord."

Wallie groaned in horror. "You know what that means? One a week, Quili!" It was utterly barbaric, but that was what the sutras demanded. Of course it would rarely be needed—with that kind of slaughter in the wind, everyone would rush to expose a swordsman killing immediately. That was what the threat was for, to prevent cover-up. But to keep the threat believable, once in a while it must be used.

So Wallie Smith, who had been so reluctant to be a swordsman for the Goddess, was going to be required to prove his bloodthirstiness again? Wholesale, this time.

Slaughter unarmed men? Never! He was not capable.

"Who did it? Someone on the estate, I suppose?"

"No, my lord. They came from Ov."

That was a relief . . . and a surprise. "Then why not . . . For gods' sakes, apprentice, tell me!"

She was weeping again, broken by the strain, unable to betray fifty lives. He rose, lifted her by the shoulders, and sat her roughly on the chair. Then he began to pace, his head barely clearing the rafters.

"Now talk! Start with you. How did you meet him?"

She could talk about herself more easily. She had been an orphan, taken in by the temple at Ov. At puberty she had been accepted as a novice in the priesthood. She had expected to progress to Third, for that was normal, and then a decision would have been made for her—whether she should continue her studies in the temple, or be given a job somewhere, in some hamlet that needed a priest.

When she had gained second rank, Quili had been enrolled in the priestess' choir. One day soon afterward, following a service in which she had taken part, she had been led by her mentor to a meeting with some highrank temple officials. Swordsman Kandoru had been present, and Lady Thondi also.

Swordsman Kandoru had said merely, "Yes, that one."

Thondi, or her son, had recently hired the retired free sword as estate guard. They had supplied a cottage—and now a wife. The owners wanted a swordsman; the workers and slaves would be happier with a priestess in residence; providing one cottage was better economics than providing two. It had been a very convenient arrangement for everyone . . . except Apprentice Quili. By nightfall her oaths had been transferred to a mentor in Pol and she had been legally installed in a stranger's bed.

Wallie wondered what Honakura would think of the tale. It revealed a very sleazy picture of the priesthood. Like swordsmen, priests were corruptible . . . and perhaps even the temple itself had benefited from Thondi's generosity. He wondered briefly if his mission was to clean up a venal local clergy, but that task seemed much too trivial to justify so many miracles. The Goddess had held the Chioxin sword for seven hundred years—surely She would not have returned it to the mortal World for any cause so petty.

"What did your mentor think of this?" he demanded.

Quili sniffed. "I think she disapproved . . . but she didn't say."

"And your present mentor?"

For the first time there was fire. "He is a senile old drunk! He should be replaced."

"Why didn't they put a slavestripe on you?"

"My lord!"

"They bought and sold you, Quili."

She hesitated and then quietly said, "Yes, my lord."

At least he now had her talking.

"All right," he said. "Tell me the rest—who killed Kandoru?"

Wallie's approach had been noted, and the cottage door swung open as he arrived. He stepped inside and wiped the rain from his eyes. Nnanji was on his feet, his face aflame with fury. Nona had been forgotten and only two of the locals remained— the two oldest women, both looking terrified. Cowie was dozing in a corner, Jja and Katanji were being quiet and still and apprehensive, crouched on stools. The room seemed larger and much brighter than it had earlier.

Nnanji exploded into speech. "Lord Shonsu: I, Nnanji—"

"Shut up!"

"But there has been an assassination. And a concealment!"

"I know! But you can't make a denunciation to me, Nnanji. We're oath brothers. I'm not impartial—how could I find against you?"

Nnanji growled angrily. His lips moved as he worked out the complications; then he did not dispute the point. But a priest could act as judge, also. He swung around to Honakura and met a toothless smirk below a black headband—there was no priest present. Had the old man somehow foreseen this? Was that why he was remaining incognito? No, that was ridiculous . . . but very convenient at the moment.

"How did you find out?" Wallie demanded.

It was Honakura who answered. "I could see that there was something wrong, my lord. I asked Adept Nnanji to tell me the exact words that had passed between him and Apprentice Quili when they met."

That would have been no problem for Nnanji. Even Quili had been able to recount enough of it.

Wallie snarled. "He was joking, and she was being too literal."

Nnanji had failed abysmally in his first assignment as a Fourth. Had he questioned Quili properly, then the ferry boat would still be tied to the jetty. He knew that. He came rigidly to attention. "My lord brother—"

"Never mind!" Wallie said. "Do better next time. Meanwhile we have a small problem. Lady Thondi was undoubtedly an accessory to the murder. She is in league with the sorcerers. She has had plenty of time to send word to Ov. Quili knows of no other way out of here than the Ov road."

This might be another test, or it might be the start of Wallie's mission. In either case, the danger was obvious—and extreme.

"We're trapped?"

"Apparently." Wallie looked over his resources: two swords-men, two slave women, a boy, a baby, and a beggar. Not much to fight an approaching army of swordsmen killers. He nodded at the woman he thought was called Myi. "Fetch our clothes, please."

"They're coming," Nnanji said snappily. "These two were witnesses to the assassination."

"In the great hall?" Wallie asked and they nodded dumbly.

"And who killed Swordsman Kandoru?"

"A sorcerer, my lord," Myi whispered.

"With what weapon?"

"With music, my lord . . . three notes from a silver fife."

Which was what Quili had stated.

"Well, old man," Wallie said to the evilly grinning Honakura, "it seems that you and I must both start believing in sorcerers."

†† † ††

Swaddled in a blanket and looking like nothing more than a bundle of trash, Honakura was perched on the driver's bench beside Quili. Wallie had put him there and firmly told him to stop playing stupid games, to bring the girl onto the team. A priest of the Seventh from Hann was the World's equivalent of a Curial cardinal. Once he revealed his identity, he would be able to convince Quili of anything.

Wallie and the rest sat on wet straw in the back under cloaks and blankets. The rain was getting worse, breeding the rivulets of milky mud that ran down the roadway. Patches of silver light in the fields spoke of standing water, while trees in the distance were washed to a pale blue gray. Unfortunately, the road from Ov would still be passable, or so Quili had said.

The cart lurched and squeaked and jingled. It had no springs, but then it was not moving very quickly. Wallie and Nnanji could have reached the manor sooner on foot, had that not meant leaving the rest of the party at the tenancy, potential hostages. A swordsman was both a soldier and a cop, and Wallie was not sure which of his two roles was dominant at the moment. He was likely to be attacked soon by a brigade of sorcerers, but he was also morally certain that Lady Thondi was guilty of murder. Kandoru had been blatantly betrayed, and Nnanji was not the only swordsman hankering for justice. Whether or not Wallie Smith could now bring himself to decapitate a helpless old woman would be an interesting discovery.

He still was seeing very little of the World. Many stretches of the road had been deepened into a trench by long use. It was flanked by hedges—more practical than fences in the absence of barbed wire—and thus he caught few glimpses of the fields. He could tell only that they were small, irregular, and inset in woodland. The country was rising, and surely the manor could not be far off now.

"This must be your mission, my lord brother." Nnanji was in a sulk, furious with his own shortcomings. He was holding the edge of a blanket tight round his neck, leaving his head free, but made him look hunchbacked where it humped over his sword hilt. His wet ponytail was dark red, and even his normally invisible eyelashes were showing more than usual.

"Perhaps." Wallie wore his cover right over himself like a tent, peering out from under it. "But there were only forty or so swordsmen slaughtered in Ov—"

"*Only?*"

"Bad enough, but not much worse than that battle of Ko you were quoting." Miracles and the Chioxin sword suggested something more vast than that. Even if Shonsu had somehow been responsible for the loss of Ov—and the reeve had not been Shonsu, but Zandorphino of the Sixth—that would hardly count as a disaster from a god's viewpoint. "On the other hand, two of the three clues have turned up now—we did come a long way and we are in sorcerer country."

Vixini slapped cheerfully at the edge of the cart; it made interesting splashes. Wagon rides were exciting.

"That's what I meant," Nnanji said. "Sorcerers being found near the River!"

Wallie stared at him. "What do you mean?"

Nnanji tugged his blanket into greater comfort. "Coming down from the hills."

"What . . . what do you know about sorcerers, brother adept?"

"Only the usual stories." Nnanji reached out a hand and patted Cowie's thigh encouragingly.

"But Honakura never heard of sorcerers!"

"He wouldn't, would he? I mean, they worship the Fire God, so no one who had any dealings with a sorcerer would tell a priest. They'd tell a swordsman, though!"

This was a complete revelation to Wallie. Just in time, he restrained a blast of temper: why had Nnanji not told him this sooner?

Then Nnanji's eyes widened. "I thought you would know about them, my lord brother! Did you not have sorcerers in your other—"

"I'm asking you now."

Nnanji rubbed wet eyelids. "Well, the only man in the barracks who had met a sorcerer firsthand was Honorable Tarru. I never heard him tell it, but Briu had." His gaze seemed to go out of focus as he recalled the words . . ."

Tarru? Ironic—Wallie had almost enjoyed killing Tarru. "Just the outline, please, Nnanji."

"Well . . . it was when he was a Second. Long ago. They caught sight of a sorcerer on a donkey and chased him to a village. They surrounded it, but when they searched, he'd vanished. They found the donkey, and his gown, but that was all. They go invisible."

Invisible killers? "You're serious?"

Nnanji nodded glumly. "Seems so. There are other stories. Two frees came on pilgrimage on Leatherworkers' Day last year, and one of them said . . ."

With effortless recall, he rattled off a dozen tales, all retold at least once—yarns spun by members of the guard who had been frees in their youth, or by pilgrim swordsmen granted hospitality in the barracks, or merely tales that had been lying around there for years. The basic theme was always the same. One: Swordsman sees sorcerer. Two: Swordsman kills sorcerer. Three: End of story. A swordsman's invariable reaction to a sorcerer was instant attack—dog versus cat. If there was a contrary story that began with sorcerer seeing swordsman, then the survivor had not reported it to the barracks.

Sorcerers wore gowns with cowls. Sorcerers' facemarks were feathers . . . No, no one knew why. Why were farmers' facemarks triangles? Sorcerers were never found near the River, only in the hills or mountains. There were legends of sorcerer cities—Kra and Pfath and Vul and others—and a few isolated towers. Swordsmen stayed away from those . . . or, again, did not return to report.

Jja caught Wallie's eye, looking very solemn. "There was a place called Kra south of Plo, master. No one ever went there, but I don't remember anyone mentioning sorcerers . . . it was in the mountains." Plo lay far to the south, so that could have nothing to do with these sorcerers.

Nnanji moved on to minstrel ballads. The sorcerers were an evil bunch in those—killing, bewitching, laying on curses—but the minstrels would have selected their material to suit their swordsman audience, so the sampling could be biased. Yet if sorcerers wielded a fraction of the powers attributed to them, then Wallie was facing an impossible situation. The swordsmen's standard murderous reflex would be the only defense—hit him first, before he knew you were there. But almost certainly Lady Thondi had already reported his arrival, so that would not work this time.

Despite Honakura's doubts, there really were sorcerers in the World, only not near Hann.

"Vul?" Wallie said. "That was one of the cities? The mountains here are called RegiVul. Maybe Vul is in these mountains." He thought for a while. "So sorcerers attacked Ov and killed the swordsmen . . . but why? I mean, why now? If they're half as good as your stories say they are, then they could have done this centuries ago." The culture of the World was old beyond imagining.

Nnanji shrugged. "The Goddess does not allow them near the River."

So She had sent Her champion to drive them back into the hills? Nnanji was right—this must be his mission. But Her champion had no idea how to fight invisible killers armed with magic. In fact, Wallie was perhaps the worst swordsman the Goddess could have chosen—his mind retched at the thought of sorcery. All his training was against it. Yet two weeks ago he had not believed in miracles, either.

Then he saw the manor ahead. There were other structures visible in the background—slave quarters, perhaps, and farm buildings—but he ignored those. The big house was doubtless very grand by local standards, but its architecture jarred on him. The proportions were all wrong, and the colors. Most of the stonework was a checker of white and red, its lines cluttered with black or gray pilasters, balconies, and buttresses. The high roofs were tiled in many colors, shining wet, and fussily embellished with green-copper dormers and onion domes. Big windows in the façade looked out over formal gardens, and the rough roadway changed abruptly into a gravel drive leading to a low but imposing staircase. There was his destination, and he could move faster on foot.

He rose, throwing off the cloak. "Nnanji, help the others out when you get there. Katanji, come with me."

He vaulted over the back of the cart. Katanji scrambled and jumped, and Wallie steadied him as he slipped in the mud. Then the two of them ran ahead.

At the foot of the steps, Wallie paused. "Stay here and keep watch," he said.

"For what, my lord?" Katanji looked worried, as he should.

"Archers, mostly. Shout if you see anything suspicious."

Wallie trotted up the staircase, his boots slapping in shallow puddles. The double doors were large enough to take the horse and cart, and very firmly closed and solid. But this was no castle—big mullioned windows reached to the floor on either side.

He kicked the door three times with the sole of his boot, and it boomed like a drum. Then he peered through one of the windows. The panes were small and leaded, glass manufacture still being primitive in the World, and he could see nothing within. The cart had almost reached Katanji, who was rotating slowly, like a lighthouse beacon.

Squat statuettes of dancing nymphs adorned the red granite balustrades. Wallie selected one of the smaller figures and confirmed that he could move it. He could even throw it well enough to collapse a window in a satisfying crash of shattered glass and twisted lead.

He ducked in through the chasm and saw a black-clad woman hesitating irresolutely ahead of him. She was white-haired and matronly, but a slave nevertheless. Send a slave to greet a Seventh, would they? Normally slaves were safe from violence, being property, but this intruder was obviously not respecting property.

"Inform Lady Thondi that I shall see her in the great hall at once."

The woman bowed. "Her ladyship sends . . ."

"At once, or I start smashing things!" Wallie turned his attention to the door, swinging the bar up and pulling. His companions were descending from the cart at the bottom of the steps.

The woman had gone scampering across the wide marble floor toward a grandiose staircase. The entrance hallway was impressive, and evidently intended to be so. Tall black pedestals supported statuary—mostly very ugly, bloated nudes—and the walls were clothed in elaborate tapestries. Wallie had seen true luxury in the temple at Hann; this was rank ostentation. Angrily he compared it with Quili's damp little cottage, but there was probably as much difference again between her humble abode and the estate's slave quarters. He had promised not to tell the Goddess how to run Her World and he knew that many places on Earth had a similar disparity of wealth, but this conspicuous display enraged him. Lands were always the ultimate riches.

Quili was helping Honakura up the steps and the others were following. Katanji came last, walking backward. Surprisingly, he did not trip.

Before Wallie could stop her, Quili dropped to her knees. "My lord . . ."

"No need for apologies, apprentice." He took hold of her elbow and raised her. "You could not have known, and it was not all your fault. Now lead me to this great hall you mentioned."

If the entrance had been vulgarly ostentatious, then the great hall was obscenely so, quite large enough to be the throne room of a palace. Acres of parquet floor were dotted with sumptuous rugs, the fireplace could have garaged a car, and the opposite wall was mainly composed of high windows, their centers emblazoned with medallions and sunbursts of gaudy stained glass. On a clearer day, they would have provided a fine view of the River. Huge chandeliers hung from the high ceiling, and there was even a minstrels' gallery at the far end, above the baronial dining table. Despite several expansive groupings of furniture scattered around, the dominant impression was one of emptiness—a vulgar display of unused space, inhabited only by many more statues. Either someone in the family was a collector, or they were a symbol of wealth in the Ov area.

The visitors paused in the doorway, stunned into silence by such luxury, a truly opulent setting for treachery and murder.

Wallie growled, then said, "I want to see how this crime was committed, Quili. These double doors—were they both open like this?"

"No, my lord. The right one was closed."

Wallie edged his companions out of the way and closed the right flap. "Is that normal?"

"No! I'd never seen it closed before, my lord. I haven't been here very often, but usually both doors are open."

Wallie nodded. That sounded like evidence to him. "Now, put Jja where the Lady Thondi was, and Cowie will be the sorcerers."

Puzzled by this unorthodox procedure, Quili led the women along the hall and placed them near the great fireplace.

"And point out who else was here."

Quili frowned, remembering. Then she indicated where the honored guests from Ov had been grouped, and the senior tenants, including the women who had described the crime to Nnanji. Adept Motipodi had been here, several senior workers there . . . Kandoru had been slaughtered before a distinguished audience.

Jja and Cowie remained by the fireplace, where a cheerful

blaze crackled, although the room was not cold by usual standards. Vixini had dozed off in his sling. Wallie led Quili back to the door. Nnanji was fretting, Katanji twitching nervously.

"Now, where was the other sorcerer?"

Quili pointed and Wallie positioned Katanji in the spot, beside the closed door. Nnanji's face darkened as he recognized an ambush.

Wallie paused, studying the big hall, imagining the crowd of watchers like semitransparent ghosts.

"Tell me again, Quili. Why was the estate guard not invited?"

The little priestess sent him a worried glance; she had told him all this twice already. "Adept Motipodi had sent a message, my lord. His honor was arriving by road, with guests. They might include sorcerers. Kandoru was to remain at the tenancy."

"And you?"

"I had been commanded . . . I stayed with my husband. I was trying to persuade him to leave, my lord."

"And then?"

And then another message had come: Kandoru was to appear and meet the guests after all.

"Was he told to wear his sword?"

"Why would he . . . I mean, he did not wear it when he was digging, or hoeing, but . . ."

"All right. Of course he would. So he knew there was danger."

"Danger?" Nnanji shouted. "From guests?"

Wallie merely nodded. Hospitality should have protected both sides, but so soon after the massacre in Ov there had obviously been danger. Kandoru had known that, but danger would not keep an honorable swordsman from his duty.

With Nnanji playing the victim, Wallie made them act out the crime five or six times, until Quili was sure of her story and Nnanji knew his part. Then he had them run it through without words, while he and the equally intent Honakura watched in silence.

Nnanji-Kandoru marched in through the doorway, Quili a pace behind and slightly to his left. With one side of the door closed, he had no choice in where he walked—good ambush technique. A few steps into the room, he stopped, seeing the audience. Quili almost ran into him.

Then he started to turn and started to draw his sword. When he was facing toward Katanji, the novice whistled three notes to represent the trill of the sorcerer's magic fife. Nnanji paused as he had been directed, arm raised but sword still sheathed, then crumpled realistically to the floor and thrashed a few times. Quili dropped to her knees beside him. Kandoru had tried to speak, she said, but then his eyes had rolled up . . .

"That'll do, I think," Wallie said coldly. Nnanji scrambled to his feet again. "Draw your sword, novice."

Katanji obeyed nervously.

"Put the point on the floor—no, never mind the wood— both hands on the hilt. Right! You stay here . . . Head up! You're a guard. Let people in, but if anyone tries to leave without my permission, hit him with that sword, as hard as you can."

Katanji went pale.

"Use the sharp side." In stern fury Wallie headed for the fireplace, and the others trailed after him.

"What was the playacting for, my lord brother?"

The playacting might not have done any good at all—but it had. Wallie glanced at Honakura. "Well, old man? Did we learn anything?"

"Apparently, my lord." He was grinning toothlessly. Swordsmen behaving unconventionally were a source of great enjoyment to the old priest, and he had just witnessed a World first, a reenactment of a crime.

"How did you know he was there, Nnanji?"

"Who?"

"Katanji—the sorcerer. You started to draw your sword and turn around *before* the music. That's right, Apprentice Quili?"

She bit her lip. "I think so, my lord."

Eyewitnesses in any world were never as reliable as they were in detective stories or the convenient fiction of legal process. Perhaps her memory was at fault—it could only have been a matter of a second or two. But the sequence of events seemed wrong, and the position of the body was significant.

Wallie had thought that his mission would require him to play hero in a barbarian epic, not detective in a whodunnit.

How do you kill a man with music, Holmes?

Elegantly, my dear Watson.

Elegant or not, it had been an ambush, and Lady Thondi had called Kandoru to the meeting.

Everyone except the petrified Katanji had gathered before the blazing fire. Damp clothes steamed, but there was still no sign of Lady Thondi.

"Brother Nnanji? Could you throw that chair through that window?"

Nnanji blinked and said he thought he could manage that.

"Then pray indulge me."

Crash! Vixini awoke with a yelp.

Wallie leaned against a life-size marble statue of a dancer, toppling it down on an exquisitely inlaid table—ebony, ivory, and mother-of-pearl.

Crash!

"Your turn again, brother. Pick another window. Or try a little swordwork on those ropes holding the chandeliers . . . no! Wait—we have company."

Once she might have had beauty, and, if so, it would have been spectacular. Now her body had thickened, and she leaned on a cane, and her height was lost in a dowager hump. She made a slow and impressive progress along the great room, while light flickered on moving jewels. Her gown was ruffled cobalt silk trimmed in silver lace, with thickly massed pearls concealing her neck and wrists. Another fortune sparkled in the high-piled white hair; fingers and ears and bosom were bright with treasure. Behind her came two self-effacing companions, a middle-aged Fourth and an attractive young Second, but no one was looking at either of those, not even Nnanji.

Her hair had always been white. She was an albino, and when she came at last to Wallie and stared up at him with a face of crumpled parchment, its lines etched deep by fury, he realized how accustomed he had already become to the smooth brown faces of the People. This uncanny pallor was shocking to him and must be much more so to anyone else.

"Vandal!"

"Murderess?"

He was younger and a visitor, but he was male and a swordsman. Without turning, she passed her cane to the Fourth behind her, and then made the salute to an equal: "I am Thondi, dancer of the seventh rank, and I give thanks to the Most High . . ."

Wallie drew his sword and spoke the equally hypocritical reply. He then asked if he might have the honor of presenting Adept Nnanji, oath brother and protégé, and Apprentice Quili. Thondi acknowledged them tersely but did not offer to introduce her companions, nor did she deign to notice the rest of Wallie's.

Her eyes were milky pink, filmed by age. There was no other color in the death's-head face that now looked down at Quili—even the lips were the same ivory shade as the cheeks. "Did Adept Motipodi get hold of you, child?"

"No, my lady."

"No? Well, he has been busy. But my son has changed his mind. He has agreed to accept your suggestion about new slave barns. Motipodi will be seeking your help in pacing them out and planning better sanitation."

Wallie watched Quili's reaction with interest. Thondi had bought her once, could she do so again? The priestess flinched and then said quietly, "That is good news, my lady."

Thondi held out a hand without looking, and the cane was placed in it. She headed for a chair.

"When will construction begin, my lady?" Quili asked softly. "As soon as the work in Ov is completed?"

No answer.

"And what work might that be?" Wallie inquired.

"The sorcerers' tower, my lord."

Garathondi was a builder of the Sixth. There was the motive! Good for Quili!

Lady Thondi seated herself stiffly and settled both hands on her cane. She fixed her inhuman pink-pearl eyes on Wallie. The two other woman huddled in behind her chair, as if wanting to be protected from the swordsmen. "You have a strange way of seeking hospitality, Lord Shonsu."

"All I seek from you is justice."

It was an extraordinary face. Momentarily the eyes flickered contempt over Nnanji. "I am to be denounced? When a woman is brought to trial, it is customary for her nearest male relative . . . my son is in Ov at present. But by all means, let us hear the charge."

Two young toughs should have no difficulty in terrorizing one old woman—not when the toughs were armed, and all her menfolk were absent—but this evil old hag was apparently not frightened at all. She was even flaunting a vast fortune in jewelry before the intruders. Wallie's skin crawled in sudden recollection of Nnanji's tales of invisibility. Were there sorcerers present already? Or were the jewels a stupendous bluff?

"For technical reasons my oath brother and I cannot bring a formal denunciation."

"So you will slay me out of hand? Should I kneel?"

"You summoned Swordsman Kandoru here to his death."

"Rubbish."

Time was short, and the evidence clear. Wallie should not let himself be delayed by argument, but he was fascinated by her cold nerve. "Then perhaps you will relate your side of the story?"

A pink worm of a tongue ran along the bone lips. "The facts are indisputable. Rathazaxo of the Sixth came calling with some—"

"A sorcerer?"

"Certainly. A cultivated gentleman, a patron of the arts." She glanced momentarily at the rubble and firewood Wallie had created.

"And he had his man kill your guard."

Lady Thondi wrinkled her nose in disgust. "His honor required assurances that no rebel or fugitive swordsman would be sheltered on our lands. Of course my son and I agreed, and we wished to instruct our retainer accordingly. He was to be allowed to continue his duties here, on condition that he not wear his sword beyond our boundaries. We sent for him. As soon as he walked in that door, he drew and attacked one of our guests. Naturally the man defended himself. It was unfortunate. It was embarrassing."

"It was murder. He did not draw his sword; it was still in his scabbard."

"He was an arthritic old ruin."

"Apprentice, where was his rheumatism, legs or arms?"

"His hips, my lord." Quili was holding her head up defiantly, standing close by Wallie.

"He did not charge across the room. It is a poor swordsman

who cannot draw faster than he can turn, especially one with a sore hip. He was attacked from behind. You had a sorcerer concealed just inside the door."

"Where you presently have that boy."

Exactly! She was a formidable opponent, and Wallie no longer felt guilty about bullying an old woman. "And you send your male employees away to clear land in this downpour? Is that the act of an innocent woman?"

"You are a better butcher than farmer, Lord Shonsu. Try uprooting gorse bushes in dry weather sometime."

Wallie would be enjoying this tussle of wits if he were not himself in urgent danger. "I do not believe you, my lady. I think you are playing for time, until your sorcerer friends arrive."

The albino's eyes narrowed within their enshrouding wrinkles. "I have no need to play for time, Lord Shonsu. If you plan to kill me, then please go ahead and try."

"I would not dirty my sword," Wallie said, and Nnanji growled angrily behind his left shoulder.

At that, a thunderclap of hope hit Wallie. He swung around and smiled at his incensed, quivering young oath brother. "The third clue!"

"What?" said Nnanji blankly.

But Wallie turned back to face Thondi. Now he knew what he needed from this vicious hag. Could he somehow wring cooperation from her?

"I cannot hold a proper trial, so I shall leave you and your son to the justice of the gods, Lady Thondi. But a swordsman was killed in this house. I am going to burn it to the ground."

That was credible.

That hurt.

She snarled at him, opening a pink mouth in the blanched face, showing yellow stumps of teeth. The jewels on her fingers flashed as she gripped her cane more tightly. So she was vulnerable. There were no unseen demons hovering overhead.

"The smoke will bring your servants hurrying back. I shall empower them as a posse—"

"Ambush!" Nnanji whooped with excitement. In theory it would be possible. Although the craft was a closed shop, the sutras allowed a swordsman to arm civilians in an emergency.

An isolated settlement like this would surely have a supply of swords somewhere. But in practice it would not work—not in this case—and Thondi saw that at once.

"My men will hardly be enthusiastic."

Sane men prefer to be on the winning side. Sorcerers apparently slew swordsmen as easily as spitting grape seeds.

"You will be hostage for their cooperation, my lady." Wallie gestured toward Katanji, still guarding the door. "That boy will have a sword at your throat."

"Madness!"

Wallie shrugged and headed for the fireplace, Jja moving out of his way, wide-eyed at his behavior. He lifted a blazing log with the tongs and walked toward the nearest drapes. "When sanity fails, then madness must suffice. It is my only hope—" He glanced back at the old woman. "—for there is no escape route, is there?"

A flicker.

"Yes, there is," said a new voice. "And we had better take it quickly, my lord. The sorcerers will soon be here."

††† †††

Wallie threw the log back in the fireplace and turned to meet the youth who was striding along the room, wiping his hair with a muddy towel. His legs were still wet and very dirty below short leather breeches of a type Wallie had seen muleskinners wear. His feet were bare and dry, so he had removed riding boots before he came in. There were still smears of mud on his face, chest, and arms.

Lady Thondi was rigid with fury, pink blotches like bruises blooming on her cheekbones.

The newcomer stopped before Wallie, dropping the towel. He waited. In vain.

"Present me, Grandmother!"

"I will not own you, idiot!"

The lad shot her an angry glance, his youth making it seem

more petulant than dangerous. He was short and slight, with curly hair and a narrow, pinched face. He was probably no older than Nnanji, but much shorter and even bonier . . . and extraordinarily young for his rank. Being athletes, swordsmen gained promotion much earlier than other crafts, yet this boy's brow already bore three arches. He raised hands in salute. "I am Garadooi, builder of the third rank . . ."

"I am Shonsu . . ." Wallie's suspicious mind was dancing with many dark possibilities. A sorcerer materializing in time to save the house from vandalism? A cleverly prearranged double cross? This newcomer's arrival smacked of miracle, and Wallie had been warned not to expect miracles. Yet he had already seen that flicker in Thondi's eyes—there *was* a way out, and she would probably have shown it to him herself, had he agreed to spare her house.

As he sheathed his sword, the old harridan growled, "There is your hostage, Shonsu!" Surrender confirmed.

"How many grandsons does she have, builder?"

"Only me, my lord. Maybe none tomorrow—my father will disown me or bury me in a foundation somewhere." He grinned somewhat ruefully, but also proudly.

"Then I must question your motives."

A shadow fell. "I had a good friend named Farafini, my lord. My best friend . . ."

"And?"

"He was a swordsman. The demons ripped him to pieces." He turned to regard his grandmother with defiant contempt. "Also, I am ashamed at what was done to Kandoru of the Third in this house. I was not here, but I heard." He looked back at Wallie. "I would make amends, if She will permit it. You are Her servants."

"Young idiot!" Thondi thumped her cane on the floor. "You meddle in affairs that do not concern you. Be silent!"

"What do you suggest, builder?" Wallie asked.

"There are sorcerers coming. She . . ." He gestured at his seething grandmother. "She sent word of you to the tower. The messenger came to the house afterward. I went straight to the stables, but the sorcerers were already on the road. A dozen of them, I was told."

Wallie kept his face as impassive as he could, but a dozen sorcerers sounded like more than enough. Yet, if they were so powerful, why so many? Were they not confident? Then he remembered that the first reports of swordsmen being sighted would not likely have included their numbers. The sorcerers had been prepared to send a dozen against a force of unknown size—plenty confident. By now they must have intercepted a second message, telling them that they need only worry about Nnanji and himself. Would some have turned back?

"How did you overtake them, then?"

"The ferry, my lord."

"There is a bend in the River," Quili said. "A shortcut." It was a shock to hear a new voice break in, but comforting to know that she was vouching for this so-convenient newcomer.

Garadooi nodded. "But it could not carry twelve horsemen and three packhorses."

What baggage did sorcerers need?

"They cannot be more than an hour behind me, my lord, although I ruined a good horse." He was young enough to brag.

"There were no other horsemen on this ferry?" Wallie asked. He would have sent a scout ahead.

The boy shook his head and bent to pick up the towel. "It docked just as I arrived, after they had gone by. Very fortunate! I paid gold to have it leave at once." Again he glared juvenile defiance at his grandmother.

"And this back door?"

Garadooi's eyes went to the windows and the streaming rain.

"I hope the gods have not already closed it, my lord. There is a trail across the mountains. Two days to Aus."

"Aus?"

"A city . . . not as large as Ov, I think. I've never been there. I only know this end of the road. But traders use it."

Land travel was very rare in the World, Wallie knew. A trader road was almost a miracle, and miracles would not be granted. The gods wanted great deeds done by mortals, not their own easy answers. It made sense, but it was suspiciously convenient.

A low growling noise intruded on Wallie's racing thoughts, coming from a red-haired, white-lipped swordsman. "Flight?" Nnanji exclaimed.

"Certainly."

"My lord brother!" He was horrified, outraged. Honor forbade flight and honor could even move Nnanji now to argue with his hero, his mentor and oath brother. "You asked me only this morning to tell you when I thought you were making a mistake . . ."

"It is the third clue, Nnanji. I haven't time to explain, but avoiding battle is no shame in a case like this. Trust me!"

Nnanji fell silent, paler than ever, doubting. He probably still thought that the posse idea would work. He probably would not care very much if it did not—death was preferable to dishonor. Nnanji was certainly no actor, and Wallie was beginning to suspect that he did not perceive fear at all. His was not true courage, the conquest of fear; he seemed to lack the emotion in the first place.

Wallie studied Garadooi. The boy tried to hold his gaze and failed. "You realize that if you betray me to the sorcerers, I shall kill you?"

He nodded. "I shall not betray you, my lord—but time is very short. We must leave soon!"

It could all be a trick to make Wallie spare the family home. Thondi was capable of any deception, but he found it hard to believe that this boy was.

"You are very young to be a Third, builder."

Garadooi flushed under his mud smears. "Money, my lord! I am a flunky for my father; that is all."

Thondi banged her cane on the floor. "And less than that when he hears of this madness!"

Her grandson turned on her. "I don't care!" he shouted in sudden rage. "You know I never wanted to be a builder!"

"What did you want to be?" Wallie asked.

Garadooi was turning very red. "A priest, my lord. And this is one way in which I may serve Her, by helping Her swordsmen against the assassins. And I don't care if they do disown me!"

Poor little rich boy, rebelling against his own guilt . . . if this was acting, it was magnificent. Wallie looked to his companions. "We have no time for discussion, but I want your votes. Can I trust him, yes or no? Old man?"

Honakura had long since settled into a huge, down-filled

chair, being almost swallowed whole by it. "Are there fords on this trail, builder? Or bridges?"

"Both." The boy stared in astonishment at the Nameless One. Perhaps he had not noticed him before.

"Then of course we must trust him," Honakura said. "The rain does seem to be getting heavier, does it not?"

Superstition!

"Nnanji?"

"No! We—"

"Quili?"

The priestess studied Garadooi for a moment and then dropped her eyes. "I think so, my lord."

"But you had never heard of this trail?"

"No, my lord."

"The old mine road?" Garadooi said.

"Oh! Yes, I have heard of that, my lord. I did not know it went anywhere, except up into the mountains."

"Sorcerer country?" Nnanji's scowl faded a little.

Wallie looked back toward the fireplace. "Jja? Should I trust him?"

Jja was horrified that a slave should be asked for an opinion and be required to judge the free. Then she saw that Wallie would insist on an answer. She thought for a moment and then nodded, but it had been Quili she studied, not Garadooi. Wallie wondered why...

"Very well, builder. We shall trust you. But my threat holds."

"Thank you, my lord. How many horses?"

"Six, and a wagon."

The lad said, "Wagon?" as Honakura snapped, "Eight!"

"You are not coming," Wallie said. "We must number seven, remember?"

"Don't be absurd!" Spraying spit, Honakura began to struggle out of the chair. "I am part of the mission. Seven may be increased by temporary guides—or else we do not count babies and Nameless Ones. I am coming! So is Apprentice Quili."

"Lord Shonsu!" Garadooi said. "I would not presume to argue with you, my lord, but horses alone will be much faster than a wagon. The track may not be passable even for them. A wagon . . ."

"If traders use the road, then it must be capable of taking wagons. We need supplies—food, bedding, axes, ropes, chains—and loading a wagon is much faster than loading horses. Anyway, there will be no pursuit. Lady Thondi will advise the sorcerers that we have left by boat. Is that not so, my lady?"

She bared her yellow fangs again. "I wonder why I should lift a hand to save such a fool. He was right—his father will disown him."

"But you will divert the sorcerers, just in case he does not."

Bowing her head over the jewel-encrusted hands on the cane, Thondi whispered, "If you will spare my home." It was a touching note. She must have been a most dramatic performer in her dancing career, even if some of her rank had been acquired by bribery, like her grandson's.

"I shall accompany you also, my lord." That was Quili, sounding quiet but determined.

"That will not be necessary. You have already been more than helpful."

She shook her head stubbornly. "I must not be here."

The sorcerers would question her. If she refused to answer they would know that the story they had been given was false—Honakura had seen that already. And if the wagon could not get through, then she could bring it back with Cowie and the old man, while the others proceeded on horseback.

"Very well. We'll try it with eight. Are there that many horses available?"

"Yes, my lord."

"Then we must go." He looked to the defeated Lady Thondi. "And you will now send a messenger to meet the sorcerers, to say that we have departed the way we came." That would not likely stop them coming to the manor, but it might make them slow down to spare their mounts. "You will divert any pursuit, or I swear that I shall kill your grandson." Wallie could never be ruthless enough to kill a hostage, but formal oaths required drawing his sword and using a ritual formula, so he was not quite committing perjury.

She nodded morosely. "I shall do all I can."

Just for an instant . . . Damn!

Wallie had missed a bet. He had been concentrating on the

old woman, ignoring the two companions who still stood behind her. They were not so skilled at dissimulation, and he had caught a vanishing trace of . . . something . . . on the face of the pretty Second. Now it was gone, leaving him with a nagging certainty that he had overlooked . . . something.

††† † †††

The stable was a long building, barrel-vaulted and gloomy like a tunnel, both musty and acrid with horse smell. For the first time since stepping off the ferry, Wallie found himself in a crowd—forty or fifty male slaves of various ages. Whatever the manor's free servants were doing, wherever they had taken refuge, they were obviously not uprooting gorse bushes—not when the slaves were sitting idle in the warm shelter of the stable, enjoying a holiday. They clustered eagerly around to greet Quili and Garadooi, largely ignoring the swordsmen.

In the interests of haste and mobility, Quili's two-wheel cart would suffice instead of a wagon, and all that was needed was to load it and acquire additional horses. Wallie Smith's equestrian experience had been limited to a few childhood riding lessons, and either Shonsu had avoided horses completely, or his knowledge had not been passed along. Nor had Wallie ever organized a pack trip, although his work with fatherless boys on a certain other planet had given him a fair knowledge of camping.

But young Garadooi seemed to know what was needed and was eager to display his competence. He began shouting orders as soon as the cart rattled in through the big doorway and came to a shuddering halt on the cobbled floor. Wallie stepped back into the shadows and let him take charge, insisting only that axes and chains and ropes be included. He knew what Honakura had in mind; more and more the old man's priestly superstitions seemed to be working out as effective predictions of the ways of gods.

"Hunting, my lord," Garadooi explained proudly at a momentary pause in the confusion. "That's how I know about the trail, too—the men used to take me with them in the fall, when they went hunting."

Those would be free men, of course, yet obviously young Garadooi was friendly with the slaves, also. The younger men, especially, greeted him as a too-long-absent buddy, and he responded in the same fashion—inquiring after this one's health, kidding about that one's love life, promising to investigate complaints. In return they swarmed to help. They ran to fetch the things he wanted and worked with a haste and efficiency quite foreign to slave labor. Wallie's estimation of the poor little rich boy rose by several notches.

Nnanji, also, was now caught up in the excitement of action, yet still not convinced that flight was permissible behavior. "Explain this third clue, my lord brother?"

"I told you—I tried to enlist a half-dozen or so swordsmen. Most Sevenths would have at least that many, wouldn't they?"

"More!"

"And therefore they would stay and fight. I was blocked, Nnanji. I have no army, although my sword needs guarding. It means that I am not supposed to fight. We were brought here to learn, that's all."

"But . . ." Nnanji wrinkled his snub nose. "But when *do* we fight, then?"

"After we get to Aus. Then we enlist an army. Then we come back!" Maybe.

"Ah!"

"And we are going through the mountains, so we may see some sorcerers yet."

Better still. Reassured, Nnanji grinned and unconsciously tested that his sword moved easily in its scabbard.

The previous day the adventurers had escaped from the temple on mules—but the mules had been strung nose to tail. "How are you on a horse?"

The grin melted away. Nnanji confessed that he'd only been on a horse twice. As a First he'd been taken to see the guard post at the jetty, riding there and back. When a mount was produced for him and he clambered aboard, his inexperience was obvious. His long legs hung down like bell ropes, and the horse flattened its ears in contempt. The slaves turned away to hide smirks.

Katanji, displaying his usual ability to astonish, scrambled into the saddle with much greater confidence and ability. The animal was frisky, but he soothed it and brought it under control. Then he smiled down in fake modesty at Wallie and explained that he had helped out muleskinners a time or two.

Wallie wished that he could do as well. The furry, big-nosed steeds were long bodied but low slung. He was assigned the largest available, an ancient and docile cart horse, but he knew he must look as absurd as Nnanji. The saddle was not big enough for him, the stirrup had not yet been invented in the World, and his feet almost touched the ground. Wet kilts were poor riding garb. Moreover, he was still sore from the previous day's mule trip— the coming journey would not be a pleasant experience.

Then they were off, and the rain was certainly growing heavier. Quili drove the cart, loaded with supplies and passengers. Spare horses trailed behind it on tethers, while the swordsmen and Garadooi brought up the rear. At first their way wandered across fields and through orchards, heading inland and uphill. The traders' trail joined the Ov road near Pol, Garadooi explained, but he knew a shortcut to it. Hooves splattered mud and five minutes sufficed to make everyone filthy. Every tiny hollow had become a lake. Then the ascent grew steeper, and the cart slowed the party's progress.

They should be well hidden from any observers—by the hedges, by the many little woods, and by the curtains of mist drifting across the landscape—but they were leaving an obvious trail. Wallie could only hope that the inevitable pursuit would be delayed for a while yet. Even had he trusted Thondi—and he did not—it was inconceivable that the sorcerers would not investigate further. The swordsmen's barbaric ritual of retribution was working against him. Every free man on the estate must be in mortal fear of that, so the sorcerers would have willing allies if they cared to ask. Sooner or later they would give chase.

Again he felt the strange disorientation of jet lag. He was unsure what the time of day was, and the cloud-painted sky provided no clue. He stifled yawns, knowing that he would be much more weary before he could rest.

They had been following the main trail for some distance before he realized that they had reached it, for it was primitive and indistinct, wandering vaguely across open pasture on the hills. In such a downpour he found it hard to remember that this was an arid land, but the prickly trees stood far apart, and scattered pens of piled stones showed that the wild, unfenced moorland was good for little but raising sheep. Lonely shepherd cottages crouched in hollows, seemingly deserted as all sensible men took refuge from the weather.

Axle creaked, hooves plodded, rain fell. Signs of human life dwindled away. Gradually the country grew more hilly, rising and falling on a greater scale. Then the ridges were capped by cindery black rubble, the valleys held running water, and the going had become difficult. The rain increased, moved now by a cold, blustery wind.

If Honakura was reading the gods' program correctly, the door was going to be shut behind the fugitives. By the third ford, Wallie began to fear that it might close before they were through. The water swirled angrily around his horse's knees. Some of the animals balked and had to be soothed by Garadooi.

No one seemed worried about piranha. Honakura had said that they avoided fast water, but this complete lack of concern suggested that they were not found in tributary streams, that only the River itself was instant death. Wallie did not ask.

The fourth crossing was even worse. Here the valley floor was wooded and the trail marked by an obvious cut in the trees. The stream foamed and rumbled, lapping out beyond its banks to conceal its depth.

Garadooi studied it apprehensively. "I think the horses can make it, my lord; but the cart may not."

He rode ahead, being the best horseman, and even he had trouble persuading his mount to enter the stream. He crossed and then returned, shivering and worried.

"Do they continue getting worse?" Wallie asked.

"The next one or two should be better. Then there is a bridge."

"Ah! Could we fell that bridge?"

The lad's eyes widened. "I expect so."

"And that would block the trail?"

Garadooi smiled then. "Probably."

"Then we must trust in the gods!" But Wallie wished he felt as confident as he was trying to appear.

Without little Garadooi's expertise they would never have

managed that fourth ford. He took two horses across, left one, and returned to drive the cart. It skittered sideways in the rush of water, but he controlled the panicking horse and fought through to the far bank. He came back again and formed the more docile animals into a string, then led them across with the other travelers clinging tight on their backs. Finally he persuaded the rest of the horses, one by one. At last the party formed up as before and trailed off wetly through the trees. But they were making poor time. When the sorcerers learned of their flight and followed with fresh mounts, they would rapidly overtake the fugitives.

Another bare ridge . . . another valley . . . After a while they all seemed to blur into a single unending torment of rain, punctuated by the colder ordeals of fords. For long stretches Wallie walked, leading his horse; Shonsu's giant stride had no trouble keeping up with the cart. Once in a while, when downpour yielded briefly to drizzle, he saw a distant gleam off the River, far away beyond the ridges, and far below. The clouds were closer overhead.

Then they came to the bridge. It was built in three spans, logs supported on pilings, but the water was almost level with the deck. This was no mere swollen stream; this was a bloated mountain torrent that had spread far beyond its banks, reaching almost to the trees. The ramps at either end had been bypassed, so that the whole structure stood in the flood, like an anchored raft.

Wallie stopped his horse's feet at the edge of the water. Out as far as the bridge ramps it was smooth and slow-moving, therefore not deep; but in the center it surged and swirled around the pilings. The current would be undermining the supports, for they could not be deep rooted. Even as he watched, floating tree trunks were impacting the bridge.

"I suspect that it will not last long, anyway," he said, having to raise his voice over the noise of the water. "And certainly this can not be forded."

Garadooi nodded, but he was frowning.

"What's wrong?"

"It is not the bridge I remember, my lord. I have not been up here for two or three years. You saw where the trail had been widened?"

Wallie had missed that. "What do you mean?"

"Someone has been improving the road. This bridge is quite new. Do you suppose . . ."

"The sorcerers are using it?"

The lad nodded.

"Where else does it go, apart from Aus?"

"Nowhere. There is supposed to be an old mine along here somewhere, but I thought it was abandoned."

"What did they mine?" Wallie asked automatically.

But Garadooi did not know, and obviously the first task was to cross the bridge. The water was axle-deep on the cart when they reached the gentle ramp leading up to the deck. The bridge quivered and trembled as the travelers crossed, but finally they all stood on the far bank—not exactly on dry ground, but beyond the reach of the flood.

Both upstream and downstream the valley seemed to narrow, and there the River would move more swiftly. "I think this is where we must try to block the road," Wallie said. "And we must stop soon, anyway." Honakura was blue-lipped with cold and exhausted by the jolting of the cart. Even Jja and Cowie looked close to their limits, and Nnanji and his brother were not in much better shape. And the light was failing.

"In about half a league, my lord, there is a cave."

"Good! Then Nnanji and I will deal with the bridge. Leave us the axes and pinch bars. You go on and get a fire going."

Garadooi nodded, teeth chattering. "The chains, also?"

Wallie shook his head. "I could not get a horse back out there again. No—there's no need," he added as the youth was about to offer to try. "I'm sure we can manage with bare hands."

"I'm sure *you* can, my lord!"

Wallie laughed and thumped him on the shoulder. "You have done a great service for the Goddess this day, builder. Tonight I'll tell you just how great. And don't worry if we're some time—I shall keep watch here until dark. Now be gone!"

So Wallie and Nnanji remained and the rest of the party headed off into the trees. Two abandoned horses whinnied anxiously and jerked at their tethers.

Wallie laid ax and bar over his shoulder and studied the bridge for a moment. The piles stood in pairs, each pair topped by a heavy crosspiece. In dry weather, of course, he would simply chop down those piles, but he could not get at them now. Three long and massive wooden beams connected each set, like girders, and the corduroy decking was lashed on with tarred rope. The decking would be easy. After that was removed no horse would be able to cross, but a foolhardy man might walk one of the beams, so those would have to come down, also.

"Let's go, then!" he said, setting out.

"My lord brother" Nnanji sounded wistful as he fell into step, "would this not be good place to set an ambush?"

It would, of course, if an ambush made sense. The trail was a greasy-floored canyon through thick pine woods, already gloomy and about to become very dark. It was little wider than a footpath, and a rope strung at knee height would almost certainly bring down the lead horse, perhaps several.

"For gods' sakes!" Wallie said. "Yes. But why ambush when you can be certain of stopping them? That's stupid!"

"Why?"

"Because—you said it yourself—there's no honor in fighting sorcerers. This is murder, Nnanji! Brigands, swordsmen killers! I wouldn't run from a challenge—"

"I know you—"

"But I'm sure as hell not going to take on impossible odds if I don't have to!" They were back at the water, and Wallie began to wade, testing every step, already feeling the cold through the leather of his boots. "You're a Fourth now. You're supposed to be competent to give orders to Thirds, qualified swordsmen, so think! Don't be so brainless."

His right boot filled with an icy rush, and he winced.

Softly Nnanji said, "Teach me, mentor?"

Wallie shot him a rueful glance. "Sorry!" He was tired and worried and jet-lagged, but he ought not to be taking it out on Nnanji. His left boot filled and tried to fall off as he lifted his foot. "All right. So you're a Fourth. I assume you want to go on and try for Fifth?"

"Seventh!"

"Why not? Well, you'll have to start thinking about responsibility, now—judgment and planning. The sutras will help, of course. You're up to eight hundred and three. You've noticed how they change? The early ones deal with practical things, like looking after your sword. The later ones have begun to teach you tactics, right?" The water was lapping Wallie's kilt and tugging hard at him. He reached out a hand and gripped Nnanji's arm so that they could support each other. The river was certainly still rising.

"From here on, you're into strategy. In fact I'll give you the next sutra right now!"

With icy water halfway up his thighs, Nnanji turned to grin. "Do we have to sit down, my lord brother?"

"I think we'll dispense with—oops!" Wallie recovered his footing, and they pushed on through the sadistic cold torrent. "I shall *try* to dispense with sitting down. I didn't mean the whole sutra, anyway, just the epigram: 'Only cats fight in the dark.'"

"Explain, mentor."

"You tell me." Wallie stumbled again. The bridge stood higher than the banks, ending in low ramps of dirt and corduroy, but now the current was sucking away the fill, and most of the logs had gone, also. He scrambled blindly up the remains to get out of the water. Then he helped Nnanji up. He bent his legs to tip water from his boots, wondering if his toes had died.

"What's it called?" Nnanji was doing similar gymnastics.

Wallie chuckled. "'On Evaluation of Opponents.'"

"Oh!" Nnanji was silent as they squelched along the shivering bridge to the third support. "It means 'Don't fight without knowing who you're fighting'?"

"More or less. You take that side, I'll do this." They began chopping the bindings that held the wooden deck. "Who, or what, or how . . . appropriate, is it not?"

They soon established a pattern. The pinch bars were not needed, for only lashings held the logs to the beams. Wallie cut one side and Nnanji the other. Then Nnanji hit the center tie and Wallie pushed the freed log sideways, away into the stream. The water was halfway up the beams now.

"We need to know more about sorcerers?"

"Much more."

Of course! Now he saw. That was why Wallie Smith had been chosen to succeed Shonsu. True, he had a deeply ingrained prejudice against believing in sorcery, but he had already accepted that it could exist in this World. The evidence of Kandoru's murder was convincing, and Garadooi had been telling of demons loose in Ov. So Wallie would believe in sorcerers. But he also had scientific training. He could analyze a problem in a way that no other swordsman ever could.

Half the center span had been stripped, exposing the three long beams. A circus horse might cross on one of those in dry weather, but the bravest of riders would never risk such a feat in rain, above a roaring torrent. Yet an agile man on foot might try it.

"We need to know what they can do?" Nnanji asked, pausing to catch his breath. Bridge smashing was warm work, even in heavy rain.

"Yes. But we need even more to know what they can't do."

The bridge uttered a loud warning. Wallie stopped and regarded it warily. He did not intend to go down with the ship, and the gods might be about to complete his work for him. There was a definite sideways sag now, the structure starting to fail under the combined efforts of men and river. Flotsam had collected thickly on the upstream side, creating drag. Piles were tilting as their supporting rubble was washed away.

"Let's go!" The two of them began to run. They had barely reached the ramp when an even louder creaking announced the end. Weakened by their work, the center span succumbed. Beams split, lashings snapped, spars splintered and sprang skyward. An instant's foam, and the middle of the bridge had vanished. Floating debris showed momentarily, rushing away downstream.

"That ought to hold them," Wallie said with some satisfaction. Quite likely the rest of the structure would follow of its own accord now. Perhaps the whole thing would have gone anyway, but gods were well known for helping those who helped themselves.

That left the problem of returning to shore, and it proved to be harder than the journey out. Twice Nnanji's feet were swept from under him, and only Wallie's stout grip saved him from following the center of the bridge away into the unknown. Once Wallie stepped in a hollow, sat down, and submerged completely. But eventually they staggered out of the water, shivering and coughing.

They emptied their boots again and began jumping up and

down and thumping arms to get warm. The sky was darkening, and they had a cave to find, but some hunch told Wallie that he ought to wait around a little while yet.

"What did you mean, 'Need even more to know what they can't do'?" The question came out in puffs as he jogged in place, but Nnanji was notable for his tenacity.

"One of your minstrel ballads told how a sorcerer changed himself into an eagle, didn't it?"

"Yes, my lord brother."

"Well, they didn't fly from Ov; they rode horses. And that's why I'm waiting here. Maybe they can fly across the river."

"Oh!" said Nnanji.

"There must be a way to fight sorcerers. The Goddess wouldn't have given me an impossible task, would She?"

"No."

"So they must have a weakness, and I have to find it. Forty men died in Ov."

Garadooi had told them. He had not been present, but he had been awakened by the noise—half the city had. A line of sorcerers had appeared in the main square before dawn and sent a challenge to the reeve. The Honorable Zandorphino had marched out with his entire force. The sorcerers had begun a chant. The swordsmen had charged. Fire demons had appeared and slaughtered them to the last man. No one had survived. Even trees and statues had been demolished by the demons' fury, walls and storefronts smashed in, blood splattered over upper-story windows. In minutes the whole garrison had been shredded. Garadooi had found the body of his friend Farafini, charred and chewed and mangled, with one leg ripped off and his sword broken.

But there had to be a way to fight sorcerers.

"Look!"

Wallie's hunch had paid off. Against a dark sky, across a darker skyline, figures moved—three or more. He might have missed some, but riders had just come over the top of the opposite ridge and vanished down into the gloom, heading his way.

"They're coming!" Nnanji said, unnecessarily.

"They are! Let's move the horses—quick!"

Wallie ran for the mounts, with Nnanji close behind, inevitably asking, "Why?"

"Because they'll whinny!"

That might not be true. Rain might stifle the scent, but it would be a wise precaution. So they rode the wet and unhappy horses farther away from the river and tethered them again. Then the two men hurried back along a trail that was rapidly becoming a stream in its own right.

Wallie removed his sword and laid it by his feet, then made Nnanji do the same—another precaution, against reflections. They stood shivering in the shadows and waited to see if sorcerers could fly across rivers. Could they sense watching swordsmen and send demons against them?

Nothing seemed to happen. Another span of the bridge had gone, and the third was awash. The light was so poor now that the forest on the opposite bank was a black wall, and the roar of the bright silver river drowned out everything except the thumping of Wallie's heart and a faint chattering of teeth from Nnanji.

A whisper: "My lord brother?"

"Yes?"

"I don't think I would mind a *small* fire demon, right now."

Wallie chuckled softly. "Get two."

Then light blazed on the far side of the river, among the trees. Nnanji hissed.

Sorcery!

In a world of flint and steel, there was no way to make fire appear like that—no matches or cigarette lighters. It flickered between the trunks, and Wallie thought he caught a glimpse of cowled figures, a flash of orange that might mean a sorcerer of the Fourth. Then the glow faded away, and darkness returned.

"A demon?"

"I don't think so," Wallie said. "I'm only guessing, but I think they were checking our tracks. They've seen the bridge. Now they know they've lost us. Unless they can fly."

Another sorcerer ability—they could magic up fire at will. But why so brief? In a dark, wet forest, light would be useful. Why let it go out so soon? Was that a limit to their ability, even if not a very useful one to know?

There was no more fire. There were no more signs of the sorcerers among the trees. Time crawled like glaciers. Frozen to his soul, Wallie was about to give up when Nnanji muttered and pointed. Vague figures crossed the skyline again. This time they counted four of them and a pack horse, retreating. The sorcerers had departed, balked of their quarry, heading home on a long ride over the hills.

Whereas the two chilled swordsmen could now go in search of warmth and shelter only half a league away. They were coming off best this time.

"Let's go," Wallie said. "It's been an instructive day, but don't overlook that last lesson, my young friend!"

"What's that, my lord brother?"

Wallie laughed. "Never trust a dancing girl."

BOOK TWO:

HOW THE SWORDSMAN BLUNDERED

†

"So that's what a mountain looks like!" said Nnanji, emerging from the ground at Wallie's side.

Morning was dawning, clear and fresh and virginal, with not a cloud in sight. Light flashed on distant whorls of the River to the east. To the north the view was blocked by a great humped peak, snowcapped and majestic, while its brothers and sisters stretched out beyond the limits of sight to the south. The travelers stood on the flank of a long range of volcanoes, a saddle to the west showing where the crossing must lie.

Wallie had guessed about volcanoes from the black rock he had seen the night before. Garadooi's cave was a lava tube, a portion of whose roof had fallen in, providing a rubbly access slope. Obviously it had been used by generations of hunters and traders, for a fair path had been cut in the debris, smooth enough for the horses to descend, and the interior was roughly fitted out as a stable in one direction and human quarters in the other. When the two swordsmen had arrived the previous night —guided by Katanji, who had been shivering to death on the trail, waiting for them—there had been a blazing fire and hot food and crumbly old boughs to sleep on.

"That's a mountain," Wallie agreed. "And a good big one to start with! The Goddess be with you, builder!"

Not formal enough—this was a new day. "I am Garadooi, builder of the third rank . . ."

79

Salute and response completed, the lad stretched and looked around, then pushed fingers through tousled curls. "You will ask Apprentice Quili to lead us in prayer, my lord?"

He had called for prayers the previous night, also. Wallie could believe in gods now, but he was still not a great praying man, being mildly embarrassed by even the swordsmen's dedication that he performed every morning with Nnanji. Garadooi was the first religious zealot he had met in the World. Honakura and Jja and Nnanji were all pious servants of the Goddess, but they did not flaunt their beliefs as the young builder did. After being told about Wallie's mission and the sword, he had prayed loudly and publicly.

Still, Wallie had much to be grateful for. "I have no objection to prayers, provided they are brief. We must hurry, I fear. How long until that river is fordable?"

"About a day, I suppose?"

Perhaps not even that, Wallie thought. These rubbly volcanic rocks would absorb water quickly. He turned to study the slope ahead and the trail faintly visible on it. It would be a long climb to the pass, and there was no cover. Any watcher with good eyes would be able to keep them in sight, without using sorcery.

"The western side is more wooded, my lord," Garadooi remarked, clearly thinking on the same lines.

"Then I shall be happy to reach it."

They crested the pass around noon, hot and already tired by the climb. Ahead the sun beat down upon a flat, barren upland that showed more rock than grass, with a few pustular cinder cones here and there, and some widely separated cairns to mark the trail. Wallie turned in the saddle for a last glimpse of the distant River, then waited anxiously for the western slopes to come into view. Every bone ached, and he felt sure that he had blistered the blisters on his blisters.

He had passed time during the ascent by questioning Garadooi about sorcerers. Rather reluctantly, the lad had admitted that the citizens of Ov did not seem to be greatly oppressed by them, nor even very resentful of the new regime. Even more reluctantly, and in reply to direct queries, he had confessed that the late Reeve Zandorphino had been disliked. He had not kept his men under firm control. Swordsmen, as Wallie well knew, could be arrogant bullies.

The elderly king of Ov had been left in charge, the only change being that now sorcerers kept order for him, instead of swordsmen. He had imposed a tax to finance the building of a tower for the sorcerers and had demolished buildings to make room for it. That had been an unpopular measure and was believed to be the result of a spell cast upon the old man by the chief sorcerer, a Seventh. But Garathondi was the contractor and was waxing even richer than before. Then the discussion had naturally come around to slavery. The family fortune was fertilized by the sweat and blood of slaves, and young Garadooi's conscience tortured him over that. There was the source of his rebellion, and of Wallie's present salvation.

"So a slave is a slave, my lord! He is still a child of the Most High. It is no reason to treat a man as an animal, is it?"

Wallie had not previously met antislavery sentiment in the World to match his own and he agreed wholeheartedly.

Nnanji had listened with open disgust to the tales of sorcerers. Probably he had never concerned himself with the ethics of slavery before, but his hero disapproved of it, so he had been adjusting his views to match. Now he intervened to tell how Lord Shonsu had befriended a slave in the temple and had thereby been assisted to escape. Wallie would just as soon not have had the incident mentioned, but Garadooi heard it with great approval.

On another point he set Wallie's mind at rest and enraged Nnanji. Soon after the massacre—or so he claimed—Garadooi himself had slipped away by ship to Gi, the next city downriver. He had personally informed the reeve about the destruction of the Ov swordsmen. He had not been the first to do so, and no action had followed, for Gi was a much smaller place, and the garrison was neither able nor willing to attack the sorcerers now entrenched at Ov. Wallie was relieved to hear that there had been no cover-up. If he ever returned to the Garathondi estate, he would not have to judge a concealment. Nnanji muttered angrily about cowardice in Gi.

Yet Nnanji and Garadooi, two highly dissimilar young men, were forging a very unlikely friendship, based upon their respective obsessions with honor and religion. And perhaps, Wallie decided, he was a charter member, also, if a somewhat more cynical one.

He had ridden forward and was chatting with Jja and Honakura, riding at ease in the cart, when the upland began to tilt westward and the trail descend. Southwest and northwest stood more snowy peaks, and straight ahead, far off and glinting . . .

"I told you it was everywhere!" Honakura remarked smugly. Of course Aus would lie on the River—all cities did.

"It flows northward at Ov," Wallie said, "so here it must run south?"

That was geometry, not theology, and Honakura had to ponder the problem for some time before he agreed that such was probably the case. Even then he would not admit that it must necessarily be so—the Goddess could do anything She wanted.

The descent became steep, the trail a stony gash through thick brush that soon prospered into hot, still forest. As Garadooi had said, the western slope was more lush than the eastern. The cover and the shade were welcome; the resident insects were not. Wallie saw trees very much like oaks and chestnuts and ash, with brambles and nettles and dogwood filling the spaces between. The trail wound to and fro and up and down, following old lava flows, scree slopes, riverbeds—any feature whose original vegetation had been sparse. As the land fell, small streams appeared in the hollows.

Now he organized his expedition on better military lines, with Katanji and Garadooi riding ahead as scouts. The procedure was primitive—the first man chose a point with as long a view as he could find, then waited for the second man to catch up to him before proceeding farther. The second waited for the cart and the rest of the party, then went ahead to find the first again. Their rear was unprotected, except for Wallie's own presence behind the cart, but he lacked the manpower to cover that direction and he thought he should be safe from pursuit, for the rest of this day at least. Katanji was excited at being chosen, and also amused, flashing smug glances at his brother. Nnanji pretended not to notice, but in truth he was unable to control his horse well enough for such work—it would have refused to leave the others for him.

As afternoon wore on, Wallie noted more signs that the trail had recently been improved. He also saw traces of horses and wheels that had passed by not long since.

Then the cart caught up with Garadooi, who had sent Katanji ahead as first scout. "The mine road, my lord!"

Two identical trails ran off into the woods. Wallie studied the fork. "Again I am glad you are here to guide us, builder. One looks much like the other."

"And they are both being used, my lord."

No need for a Mohican on that problem—there happened to be horse dung visible on both trails. So the mine had been reopened; more sorcerer activity, or just coincidence?

"I should dearly love to know what is going on here," Wallie said. "Is this the work of these cowled characters? If so, what do they mine? What gets transported to and fro on this road—and does the garrison in Aus know about it?"

He pondered for a moment. "How far to the mine?"

The youth shrugged. "I think it is a long way, my lord, but I don't know."

Wallie hesitated and then decided to risk it. "Take over, adept. Proceed with all deliberate speed. I'm going to explore up this other road a little way."

Responsibility! Beaming, Nnanji thumped fist on heart in salute. Wallie turned his mount along the mine road and met rebellion at the first bend. Eventually he convinced the brute that a swordsman of the Seventh outranked a mere horse, no matter how stubborn, and then he managed to kick it into an excruciating trot. The road was just as narrow and winding as the one he had left, and he thought he had brought much more than his fair share of the flies.

Leaving Nnanji in charge was a risk. If he blundered into a caravan of sorcerers he might react in ways that Wallie would find irrational. Moreover, it was unlikely that this digression of Wallie's would yield any useful information at all. At best he could only hope to find some evidence of what was being mined—a spillage from a tipped wagon, perhaps. But the change of pace and the solitude were a welcome break. He resolved to limit himself to a quarter of an hour and then turn back.

He found much more than he had bargained for. At first all he saw was more trees; road bending to the right followed by road bending to the left; a hill up and a slope down; bushes and outcrops and ruts. Just as he was beginning to feel that his time must be up, he reached the edge of a recent lava flow. The forest ended abruptly, giving a wide view across bare, black rock flooring a valley. The hill on the far side was bare also, probably burned off by an even later flow, and the road descending it was clearly visible . . . and in use.

Hastily Wallie applied brakes and then reverse, moving back under cover. He counted three wagons. He estimated that the work gang marching behind numbered about thirty—those would be slaves, of course—and the mounted band in front about a dozen. They were too far off to see if they wore cowls, but they were certainly dressed in robes and therefore could only be priests or old men . . . or sorcerers. Browns, mostly, but the one in front was either a Fourth or a Fifth, an orange or a red.

He turned his horse and kicked it savagely until it achieved a canter. Had he come along the road half an hour later, he would have blundered right into that procession. He cursed himself for a reckless idiot.

That was not the worst of it, though. If Garadooi's geography was correct, the men were coming from the mine, so obviously it was being operated by the sorcerers. Two of the wagons had been drays carrying lumber, dressed tree trunks. The sorcerers were heading for the downed bridge, to replace it.

How did they know about *that*?

His companions looked up in alarm as he cantered his foam-flecked horse alongside. They had stopped in the center of a wide, almost dry, riverbed to water the livestock, and also to exchange mounts and spares. It was an exposed position, but one where they were not likely to leave conspicuous traces on the ground. That might be Garadooi thinking like a woodsman, or mere chance. Wallie did not care which it was, for he knew that the expedition had been leaving an obvious trail. The sorcerers would need no magic to follow it.

Unsaddling his own horse, he quickly explained the new problem. If the sorcerers were aware of the bridge, then surely they must also know of the fugitives.

"Twelve?" Nnanji said thoughtfully. "Six each way?"

"Perhaps. Except that they will soon see that we have gone by the junction, so maybe ten in this direction." And in less than half an hour, likely.

"You think they can send messages?" Honakura remarked, leaning over the tailgate and leering. "Or can they see at a distance?" He was enjoying watching Wallie struggle with the concept of sorcery.

"Messages, I hope." But the sorcerers would have needed time to load the drays after learning of the downed bridge . . . why had they not sent men off after the fugitives immediately? Either they knew exactly what the swordsmen were doing and where they were, or they expected to catch them easily on the trail. Or there might be another force ahead somewhere.

"Eagles?" Nnanji tilted his head to study the high blue sky. Faint dots floated there—kites or vultures . . . or sorcerers?

"I'm going to ignore that possibility," Wallie said firmly, "because if they're that powerful, then nothing we do will be of any use at all. But we've got to get off the road."

"The horses need a rest, my lord!" Quili's chin was raised in respectful but determined revolt. "We have been pushing them much too hard and too long." Wallie resisted a temptation to consign the horses to perdition. The people needed more than rest.

"If we leave the road," Garadooi said, "we'll lay a trail as obvious as that mountain."

Wallie stared along the river valley. "That mountain" showed fainter and bluer than it had been, higher and surprisingly far off. He turned and looked the other way. The river was typical of rivers he had seen near mountains before—more gravel than water, a very wide bed of shingle with scattered little streams and puddles in it, and a few grassy or scrubby islands. It would be easier terrain than the road.

"We can't be very far from the River itself!" he said. "Let's head that way. And stay in the water."

"It's safe enough," Quili nodded to where some of the horses were wading.

Could animals sense piranha? Not wanting to show his ignorance, he did not ask. "Let's move!"

"Her powers are always most manifest near the River," Honakura said sagely.

"Indeed, in affliction we should seek Her aid," Garadooi agreed.

"Katanji?" Nnanji asked, but as he did so, a sound of hooves announced that the scout was coming back to see what the delay was. Better and better.

So move they did, splashing along the stream. When one branch gave out, they crossed shingle to another. Soon the winding of the valley and the tufty islands had hidden them from the road, and then they left the water and walked dry-shod on the pebbles. A good tracker would find them soon enough, but, with any luck, pursuing sorcerers would go farther on toward Aus before realizing they had missed their prey.

After a while Wallie drew alongside Garadooi. "What are the chances that we shall find a hamlet or village on the River?"

The boy shook his head, looking worried and lost now. "We can only trust in the Most High, my lord. If there is a village, of course, they will have boats."

Which was what Wallie had been thinking. He could acquire safer transportation on the River with gold, or with steel.

An hour or so went by with no signs of pursuit. Late-afternoon sun glared fiercely down and reflected back as savagely from the dark shingle. There was no wind. The horses were visibly flagging, footsore from the hard going, and making very slow time. The passengers in the cart were bone-weary from the endless lurching and bumping, the riders sore and raw. They were all eaten away by mosquitoes. Twisting and winding, the valley yet continued unchanged between thickly wooded walls.

Wallie chewed at his problems without tasting any answers. Boats and an escape by water had the greatest appeal, but the River might be far off—he had no way of knowing. Alternatively, common sense suggested that he find a campsite somewhere and leave the civilians. Hopefully only the swordsmen were in great danger, so they could retrace their steps and try to reach Aus, traveling by night. Then they could return with help. He did not like that program at all. He did not want to leave Jja undefended.

Suddenly the river changed and became a small lake, almost

filling the valley. Its far bank was a rocky dam—an obvious lava flow to Wallie's eye—and beyond that was open sky and a remote horizon of blue water, framed by the valley walls. Cheering broke out.

"Master!" Jja exclaimed. "Look—smoke!"

The cheering grew louder as the others also saw the filmy white cloud rising from somewhere ahead. Smoke meant people.

It had long been obvious that the previous day's rain had not touched this side of the mountains. The lake was low, and the cart was able to skirt it on a shingle beach with only two or three dips into water. A low rumble ahead warned of falls. Even the horses seemed to feel the excitement as the expedition reached the end of the lake and began to cross over the hummocky black barrier. The river foamed along a narrow trench, then fell away into a rising cloud of spray.

Katanji had pushed his horse to the fore and was standing silhouetted against the sky. He yelled something into the noise.

Wallie dismounted, dropped his reins, and walked forward stiffly to see. When he reached the cliff edge, he was looking down into a small and boxy canyon, floored by grass and scrub. The waterfall cascaded down in giant steps into a pool, from which a stream wandered along through the trees to enter the River beside a rough pier of black stonework. There were no boats tied there, and it seemed deserted. A couple of roofless cottages guarded the landward end, overgrown and obviously ancient.

Jja came and stood at his side. He put his mouth close to her ear and shouted. "We're a century or so too late!"

"But the smoke . . ."

"Steam!"

He had forgotten that volcanic country could nurture hot springs. One side of the canyon was wooded, but the other was mostly bare and knobby rock, glistening and steaming like a motionless cascade of porridge.

The others had come to see, also. After a while they all retreated back to the cart, away from the tumult.

"It's a quarry," Wallie said, "or it was, once. The hot water makes . . . that brownish marble stuff." Evidently Shonsu had never heard of travertine, for he could not put a name to it.

"Looks like no one's been here in a lifetime. Well, it's a sheltered spot, and we can have hot baths."

"There are boats out there, my lord," Katanji said, squinting into the westering sun.

The boats were much too far off to be of use, but a leader must keep his followers' spirits up. Wallie looked meaningfully at Nnanji's red ponytail. "We'll take your brother down to the dock and wave him," he suggested.

As a campsite, the quarry canyon could not have been bettered. There were indeed warm pools at the base of the cliff. Nettles had taken possession of the ruined cottages, but there was grass on which to pitch the two small tents the adventurers had brought, and they could build a fire without being seen by watchers inland. There was fresh water to drink and there would be shelter from wind, if wind came.

Getting there was the problem. It took another hour to move all the people, the supplies, and the horses safely to the valley floor, and by that time the sun was nearing the horizon. The cart was pushed a little way down the slope and wedged against a tree, less visible from the lake above.

Wallie had never felt more weary in two lifetimes, and everyone else looked equally bedraggled by the long, hard day. He sent the women off to try the hot pools while the men pitched camp. He himself went down and inspected the jetty. Built of discarded stone from the quarry, it was obviously very old, but probably still usable.

Then he joined the other men in a luxurious hot soak that unknotted muscles and soothed blisters, taming aching fatigue into sleepy weariness. When that was over, food was waiting.

The sun set in a celebration of gold and crimson, sky and River in duet. Water birds flew homeward.

There was little talk around the campfire as the valley gradually filled with darkness. Cowie fell over, asleep, and Nnanji ordered her to go to bed. She smiled vaguely and wandered away to the tents. Silence returned. Even the normally bubbly Katanji had lost his air of excitement, while Honakura looked dangerously spent. Wallie had arrived the previous day at a deserted jetty by a little canyon, and now he had reached the same sort of place on the same River on the other side of the mountains. Somehow it did not feel like much progress.

"Well, novice?" he said. "Three days you've been a swordsman now. You're not getting bored yet, are you?"

Katanji managed a grin. "No, my lord."

Nnanji snorted in mock disapproval. "When I was a scratcher, I spent my first three days doing sword drill. I thought my arm was going to fall off."

His brother shifted position. "My arm is not the problem, mentor."

"I know how you feel, and where. He's done well, has he not, my lord brother?"

"Very well. We all have."

Nnanji nodded proudly and asked, "What do we do now?"

"Suggestions will be welcome."

"We should pray," Garadooi said primly, "throwing ourselves on the mercy—"

"Rot!" Honakura deepened his wrinkles into a pout.

"Blasphemy, old man!"

"Rot, I say! I assure you that the Goddess knows exactly what She's doing. You've been on hunting trips, builder? Did you ever find a campsite with hot and cold water, with sweet hay, with a view like this . . . safer, better sheltered, or more obviously a special provision of the gods?"

"But—"

"Lord Shonsu is Her champion, and we are being well cared for."

"—You're a priest?" Garadooi reddened.

"I was," the old man admitted testily. "And I say that we were led to this place for a purpose, so any requests from you would be mere presumption. The only person here with brains is Cowie." At that he clambered stiffly to his feet and headed for the tents. Evidently he did not enjoy being sermonized by a mere layman, although that was part of the price of anonymity.

Sparks flew up into the darkness, and the yellow light flickered over the circle of weary faces. The fire's tenor crackling sang over the waterfall's baritone. Katanji yawned mightily, rolled himself up in a blanket, and was still.

The problem remained. Garadooi and Quili began conversing quietly. Wallie put his arm around Jja. Nnanji poked idly at the fire with a long stick.

There was driftwood. On any other River, Wallie might have contemplated building a raft, but these waters were deadly. The sails in the distance would have been fishing boats or trading ships, but he could think of no way to signal them. Even smoke would not work in this case, for the plume of steam must be a well-known local landmark.

"We have a couple of days' food, I suppose," he mused. "At least on short rations. You and I could try to make Aus, Nnanji. Then we could bring a boat for the others."

Nnanji grunted quietly in agreement and yawned.

"We haven't had much sleep in recent memory," Wallie said. "A good long rest may brighten our wits a little."

"You wish me to take first watch, my lord brother?"

"Not much point. Nowhere to run and no way to fight."

Nnanji frowned doubtfully. If Wallie asked, he would willingly stand guard until he fell over.

"I know what the sutras say," Wallie admited, "but I just think this case is unusual. We both need sleep more than anything."

Nnanji nodded obediently and wished him good rest. He pushed off his boots and began wrapping his long legs in a blanket. Soon he was stretched out like a mummy and in two more minutes was snoring.

Jja cuddled closer to Wallie and sniggered playfully. "Cowie has been given the evening off again, master. She's not having to work very hard, is she, for a night slave?"

He tightened his arm around her. "No, she's having a real easy time." Pause. "At least he isn't attempting to honor any priestesses."

Jja smiled up at him. "I think the apprentice seeks honor elsewhere."

Wallie looked across the fire. Quili and Garadooi were sitting very close together, still talking . . . discussing slave barns?

"Uh! I hadn't noticed."

"I was very bold, master—I mentioned it to Adept Nnanji, also. He hadn't noticed, either."

"He wouldn't."

"But he approves of Builder Garadooi. And Builder Garadooi is very impressed by Apprentice Quili. Never really appreciated her before, he says. He hasn't spent much time on the estate since he swore to his craft."

Wallie kissed her ear. "I forgive your presumption, slave. Well done!"

Jja yawned and fell silent. Then she said, "Lord Honakura is actually enjoying this, isn't he?"

"He . . ." Wallie was about to say "He is having a ball," but he stopped in time. It might come out literally. "Yes. He's weary, of course. But, yes. He's happy."

"Have you noticed something else, master? You changed my life, and Nnanji's. Lord Honakura is happy. And Wild Ani . . ."

"I gave her gold?"

"Gold is little use to a slave, master. She could buy wine or sweetmeats with it, not much else. But you let her make fools of the whole temple guard. She would have loved that, more than anything."

"What are you implying, my darling?"

"I think that all those who help your mission are rewarded. Novice Katanji was going to have to apprentice to his father, and he didn't want that."

No, Katanji would not have been content to knot rugs all his life. Wallie recalled also Briu's twin sons, and Imperkanni being appointed reeve of the temple guard. And Coningu would be reunited with his long lost son by now.

"Maybe you're right," he said sleepily. "I hope for Quili's sake that you are, and that we can all get out of this alive to enjoy our rewards."

Then Jja kissed him. It was a vigorous, inventive sort of kiss, and they ended lying prone together. "You'll think of something to do, master."

"Tonight I can't think of anything," he said. "Rewards must wait. Go to sleep."

He remembered shivering briefly in the night, and Jja tucking a blanket around him. The sun god in summer needed much less rest than mortals, especially mortals so travel-weary that they could sleep on the hard ground as soundly as they would have done in feather beds. Birds made encouraging noises at dawn and were ignored.

Morning was half gone . . .

"Mentor?"

Nnanji? No—that was Katanji's voice. Shonsu's warrior reflexes could leap from sleep to full awareness instantly. Wallie sat up and said, "Yes?"

Katanji's impish grin hung against the sky. "May I have the honor, my lord, of presenting Novice Matarro, swordsman of the first rank?"

††

"The honor shall be entirely mine," Wallie said, "if you will allow me a moment to find my hairclip."

The boy at Katanji's side had cowered back in shock as he registered Wallie's rank. He was taller than Katanji and farther along in his adolescent metamorphosis, but probably little older. He looked healthy and well fed, his skin burned dark by sunlight. He wore a harness and sword, and the single craftmark on his forehead was certainly a sword and long since healed, unlike Katanji's, which was now infected into a festering red sore.

Yet Matarro did not look like a swordsman. He had no ponytail, or kilt, or fancy swordsman boots. His hair was cropped short and his only garment was a breechclout, a long strip of white cloth that he had tied around his hips, with one end hanging down as a tail behind and the other passed between his legs and looped over to form another tail in front.

Having clipped his hair back and disentangled himself from his blanket, Wallie took hold of his harness and scabbard and scrambled to his feet. He fastened buckles, putting on his most friendly smile for the nervous newcomer.

Somewhat reassured, the boy drew and began the salute to a superior. "I am Matarro . . ." He moved his sword with confidence, but he made two of the postures in the wrong order and did not seem to realize his error.

"I am Shonsu . . ." Even as he replied, Wallie was staring over the lad's head at the jetty. The campsite lay at the rear of the valley, hidden by scrub. When the ship had arrived, the crew had seen only a deserted quarry and a few grazing horses. Novice Matarro had come ashore to scout, or had perhaps been ordered to do so as a joke.

One question that would need to be resolved was how Katanji had met him. If he had seen the ship first, then he should have wakened Wallie or Nnanji—who was now sitting up in bleary surprise, hearing the voices. Katanji, of course, had turned on his charm and invited Matarro to come and meet his mentor. He had then chosen Wallie because he had been told that Wallie was now his mentor, also, and he was grinning broadly at Matarro's stunned reaction.

Nnanji bounced to his feet. "Allow me to present you, novice," Wallie said, "to Adept . . ."

The little ship had a blue hull and white masts—three masts, which seemed excessive for her size. She had a definite list to starboard. Two gangplanks had been set out, and men were carrying lumber down one, piling it on shore, and trotting up the other. Any sound of voices had been drowned out by the noise of the waterfall.

"What vessel?" Wallie inquired when the formalities were over.

Matarro's alarmed eyes were flickering around the campsite, counting and inspecting as the rest of the party began to stir.

"Her name is *Sapphire*!" Katanji said quickly, smirking. Wallie wilted him into silence with a Seventh's killer glare.

"*Sapphire*, my lord."

"And what brings you to this deserted place?"

Matarro hesitated, uncertain how much he should reveal. Likely he had never met a Seventh of any craft before and he was right to be nervous. Highrank swordsmen were dangerous, especially to other swordsmen. Wallie could challenge the boy if he did not like his looks or the way he spoke. It would not be honorable to maim or kill a novice, but no one would argue the point with Shonsu, and it would be quite legal.

"We were brought by the Hand of the Goddess, my lord. We

dragged our anchor last night . . . That has never happened to us before, my lord."

"And the cargo has shifted?"

Matarro nodded, seeming surprised that a landlubber could make such a guess.

"And who is the master?"

"Tomiyano of the Third, my lord."

Wallie smiled. "Then pray present my compliments to Sailor Tomiyano and inform him that I shall call upon him in a few minutes. We are on the service of the Most High and are in need of some transportation."

The lad nodded once more. He began to turn, before remembering that he should speak a formal farewell. He made an even worse mess of that ritual than he had of the salute; but he knew how to handle a sword. Then he shot off through the scrub like a startled hare, heading for the jetty.

Nnanji snorted and said, "Water rat!" with bottomless scorn. "*Sapphire*, huh?" he added, grinning at Wallie. Then he turned to Katanji with a face like a Demon of Retribution—time to impart a few truths about proper military procedure.

Wallie headed for the tents. Honakura had already emerged and was beaming toothlessly.

"The Goddess be with you, old man."

"And with you, my lord."

"You were right again!"

"Aren't I always?"

"So far," Wallie admitted. "So tell me what has happened to the sorcerers? And I thought I was not supposed to benefit from miracles?"

Honakura's tiny shoulders shrugged within his black gown. "As far as sorcerers are concerned, perhaps you have been overestimating them? Men may have great powers and yet make mistakes, you know. They are only human. They may still be on their way here, but too late. And I wouldn't call this a miracle; it is the Hand of the Goddess. Besides, I never said you would not be granted miracles, only that you must not count on them. Heroes are allowed to be lucky, my lord. That is quite different."

He smirked. Honakura could have knotted a college of Jesuits into a lace counterpane.

Chuckling, admiring the fine weather, savoring this dramatic solution the gods had provided to his problem, Wallie continued over to the pool at the base of the waterfall to spruce himself up. In a few moments Nnanji joined him, muttering under his breath about scratchers and figuratively wiping Katanji's blood from his hands. He could not see that three days was not long enough to turn his brother into a textbook swordsman, or that he would never rise to Nnanji's own impossible standards.

"Let me guess," Wallie said. "He asked you to describe the proper procedure, and then you had to admit that we were not following it, because I had not posted pickets . . ."

Nnanji growled wordlessly. He could pull rank on his brother, but too often he allowed him to talk back and then he invariably lost the argument. Grinning to himself, Wallie dropped the subject.

When the morning's usual routine was completed, he said, "Now let's go and call on *Sapphire*. What are the formalities for boarding a ship, Nnanji? Does one ask permission?"

"Permission?" Nnanji looked shocked. Deep in thought, he followed after Wallie for a moment and then said, "Yes! Adept Hagarando mentioned that once. And a captain expects the salute to a superior from anyone, regardless of rank. No swords drawn on board . . ."

These were the sort of things that Wallie did not know about the World. This was the reason that the gods had assigned Nnanji as his assistant, with his flawless memory packed full of lifetimes of experience from the whole temple guard. But Nnanji's pride was in his swordsmanship, and Wallie must be careful not to let him suspect that his main purpose was to be a human reference library. He would be crushed if he suspected.

So Wallie thanked him offhandedly, as if the matter were trivial, pushing his way through the bushes. "A water rat is a swordsman who lives on a ship?" Shonsu's knowledge of swordsman slang had been passed along. "How many types of swordsmen are there?"

Nnanji blinked in surprise. "Three, I suppose: garrisons, frees, and water rats."

"No ponytail, no kilt? Water rats are really sailors with sword craftmarks?"

"That may be, my lord brother—I never met one before. The frees always spoke of them with contempt. I'd have to think—"

"Don't worry about it now," Wallie said hastily, not wanting to call up another retrieval from the mental databank. "With a name like *Sapphire*, this ship has obviously been brought by the Goddess for—"

Nnanji shouted, *"Devilspit!"*

Blue and green sails spread, *Sapphire* was a hundred paces out in the River, still listing, but making good time downstream. A pile of lumber lay abandoned on the jetty.

Wallie had erred. He should have gone straight to the ship with Matarro.

How long until the sorcerers arrived?

"My lord brother! What do we do now?"

Wallie stood for a moment in angry silence, watching the ship dwindle, aware for the first time that there was a fair breeze blowing this fine morning out there on the River.

"I think we leave the problem to a friend of mine," he said weakly.

"What friend?"

"I call him Shorty."

Nnanji frowned. "Shorty?"

"You haven't met him. He's a god."

Very funny, Mr. Smith! He had been told that he must not call for miracles. He had also been warned that he might fail, as Shonsu had failed. He could die on this mission. Now he had been given good fortune ranking close to a miracle, and he had let it slip through his fingers.

How long until the sorcerers arrived?

Jja and Quili had prepared breakfast. Wallie was too mad at his own folly to have much appetite. He brusquely ordered Katanji down to the jetty to watch the disappearing *Sapphire*. He assured the others that she would soon be returned. His fake confidence certainly did not fool Honakura, who smirked, or Jja, who looked worried. The others seemed to believe his prophecy, especially Garadooi.

Accepting a pile of roasted pork ribs and pancakes heaped on a wad of dock leaves, Wallie signaled Nnanji to accompany him. Once they were out of earshot of the others, he sat on the grass. Nnanji copied him, carefully balancing a triple helping of his own. Katanji appeared, puffing, to report that the ship had vanished. Wallie told him to go back and wait until it unvanished.

"Talk and eat at the same time," he said; Nnanji usually did so, anyway. "I want to hear all the stories you can remember about sailors and free swords. The exact words this time, if you can."

"Of course!" Nnanji looked surprised that there should be any question. He thought for a moment, chewing on a bone, then he chuckled. "At lunch on Potters' Day, two years ago . . ."

That was a humorous story of a Fifth who claimed to have killed, in the course of his career, four men and eight ship captains. The other tales were more specific, all told in Nnanji's unconscious mimicry of the voices he had originally heard recount them. Free swords expected free transportation—they were on Her service. Sailors who declined to supply it, or who got cheeky with swordsmen, might lose an ear, or worse. Sometimes, of course, the swordsmen had to put up with the impertinence until the ship reached port. Then they were free to impose penalties, and did so. A couple of incidents sounded perilously close to rape. Not surprisingly, there were also rumors of swordsmen mysteriously disappearing in transit.

Of course these were the tales that had been worth repeating; for each of those there might have been a hundred uneventful, or even friendly, encounters. But the overall trend was clear.

"That'll do! Thank you, Nnanji."

"I've lots more!"

"That's enough. They're a revolting bunch, aren't they?"

Nnanji nodded vigorously, chewing a lump of gristle. Then his eyes widened, and he swallowed it, half choking. "You mean the sailors, my lord?"

"No." Wallie rose and stalked away, leaving his protégé openmouthed with horror.

* * *

"My lord, you do not need us now." Garadooi had no doubts. "Apprentice Quili and I would take our leave, if you will permit it."

"But the sorcerers . . ."

"They will not harm her, my lord. Nor, I think, myself."

"You can't know that." Wallie had expected to take these two with him when the ship returned, if it did. If it did not, of course, they might be safer away from his company, but the young builder was not thinking of that.

"My father is one of their main supporters among the guild-masters." He did not like to admit that. Then he grinned innocently. "And how have I offended? Three swordsmen arrived, lost. I escorted them out of the sorcerers' domain by the quickest route."

"I am very grateful to you both." Wallie put on his sternest face. "Go, if you wish, with my blessings. But I shall require an oath from you, builder."

"I shall tell them nothing, my lord!"

"You will tell them everything! Answer all their questions. You must swear to that—I will not have you tortured on my account. Otherwise you stay here."

The lad's thin features took on their familiar fanatic sheen. "I am aiding Her cause. She will protect me!"

That might be so, but Wallie extracted a solemn oath from him regardless. Being preliterate, and having no other form of contract, the People put great weight on oaths.

"You will take the cart?"

Garadooi looked surprised. "And the horses."

"Two would be enough? I will buy the rest from you."

"But . . ."

Wallie put a finger to his lips.

Surprise became a smile. "We never discussed it! But I will not take your gold, Lord Shonsu. My family can afford to contribute a few hacks—'I lost them, Grandmother.'"

Wallie let him win the argument that time. The secluded jetty might be more than an escape route. It could also be his access to the sorcerers' mine and the back door to Ov, an ideal place to land and muster a small army. The unwanted horses would not likely stray from such an equine heaven. They would be useful again.

Down at the jetty, Katanji was still sitting in lonely boredom on the lumber. Garadooi caught the two horses he wanted, and they were quickly loaded with supplies and a tent. Then Wallie accompanied him and Quili to the top of the cliff and helped drag the cart back to the flat. The River valley stretched off beyond the lake, with no signs of sorcerers yet.

The second horse, he noted, was tethered behind the cart as a spare; Garadooi was going to ride beside Quili. As he once more thanked them both, shouting over the noise of the falls, Wallie did not need Jja to point out a change in the little priestess—in both of them. They stood close. They had the undefinable air of two people wanting to be alone together. He wished them good luck and Goddess-speed . . . and very nearly offered congratulations, also. But perhaps that would be premature.

Then he saw that a tiny, distant figure on the jetty was jumping up and down and waving both arms.

"I must go," Wallie said. Again he thanked them both, smothering the priestess' renewed apologies for the initial misunderstanding. He shook Garadooi's hand. Quili he kissed—her honor maybe, his pleasure certainly. She blushed crimson, but cooperated, seeming to enjoy the encounter as much as he did. Then he went scrambling and sliding down the hill again. The expedition was back to seven.

By the time he joined Nnanji and his brother on the jetty, *Sapphire* was close enough for sounds of angry voices to be floating in across the water. The wind had dropped completely, and her sails hung limp in the noon heat as she drifted toward the dock. She was not listing so badly as before.

Katanji was impressed, Nnanji triumphant—

"I just looked away for an instant, my lord—then there she was!"

"This time they'll do as She requires of them, my lord brother!"

Wallie was not convinced. Obviously some of *Sapphire*'s crew were not, either. Now he knew how swordsmen regarded sailors and, therefore, why Matarro's news had caused them to depart so hurriedly. The Goddess had brought them back to the same place, but he wished he could make out the words of the arguments going on aboard. The largest and loudest discussion was taking place on the raised deck aft . . . poop? The high bit at the front would be the fo'c'sle in English, but he seemed to lack maritime terms in his vocabulary. That was odd, because Shonsu must have traveled by ship. Then two men ran up on the fo'c'sle and the anchor ran out with a roar of chain. It stopped with a clang and sudden silence as it reached the water, apparently jammed. Oaths and screams of rage were followed by hammering noises. *Sapphire* continued to drift closer.

Wallie turned to see how the rest of his party was proceeding, coming at Honakura's slow pace. "Nnanji! Look!"

A solitary figure was dancing up and down on the cliff top —Garadooi. He had a horse beside him. Wallie waved to show that he had noticed, and the lad acknowledged. He remounted and rode away.

Nnanji's eyes had narrowed to slits. "They're coming?"

"That's how I take it."

How long for mounted men unencumbered by a cart to travel the length of the lake? How long to scramble down the hill? And that might not even be necessary, if a spell cast from up there could summon demons to down here.

Wallie wiped sweat from his brow, but some of that was from the heat, for the sun was glaring off the water and the dark stonework. The still air was dead and enervating. *Sapphire* was very close, obviously about to reach the jetty at the exact place she had been tied up earlier. The arguments were over, and so were attempts to free the anchor. Two men were adjusting fenders, but most of the rest seemed to have disappeared. Jja, Vixini, Cowie, and Honakura had reached the jetty.

Gentle as falling feathers, *Sapphire* nestled against the pier. Wallie stepped to a bollard, waiting for a line. Nothing happened. No gangplank?

He jumped up on the pile of lumber, which put him almost level with the men standing on deck, and some distance back from the ship.

"You forgot this?" he asked politely.

For a while there was no reply, only a staring match. Five men were visible, and no one else. They were standing along the near side, well spaced to repel boarders and holding their hands down, out of sight below the gunwale, so he could not tell if they were armed. All he could see were bare brown chests and angry faces. He thought briefly of a line-up of wrestlers.

The one in the center was closest, and therefore likely the spokesman. He must be the captain, Tomiyano. He was visibly furious, eyes slitted, powerful white teeth bared in a grimace. Three shipmarks just below a Caesar haircut told of his rank and craft. He was young and well built, bone upholstered with muscle, and he was barely keeping control of himself. His hair was reddish—not as red as Nnanji's—but his skin was burned to the same dark rosewood shade. In spite of his youth, he looked like a man accustomed to having his own way. He looked dangerous.

Wallie was not on board yet. He made the sign of acknowledgement of an inferior.

The sailor snarled. "What do you want, swordsman?"

"Permission to come aboard, Captain?"

"Why?"

"I seek passage for myself and these companions."

"This is a family ship—we have no room for passengers."

"I am willing to pay any reasonable fare."

"That will not make the ship larger."

"Then put your Jonahs ashore."

The sailor's weathered face flamed even brighter, although there was no shame in being a Jonah. "What the hell do you mean by that, swordsman?"

Wallie waited a moment to cool his own rising temper. To address a highrank by his craft was deliberate insult. He was also fighting a searing desire to turn and look at the cliff, to see if sorcerers had appeared there yet, but that would be a tactical error in this nasty negotiation. He could only hope that Nnanji was watching and would tell him when it happened.

"If you have no Jonahs aboard, then perhaps you were brought here to get some?"

Tomiyano, if that was who he was, drummed fists on the rail in frustration and looked up longingly at the limp sails.

"Sailor, this is benefiting no one. Let me come aboard and I shall salute you. Or you salute me here. Then we can resume our discussion in civilized fashion."

The captain was silent. A whole minute seemed to drag by in wordless glaring. Then he snapped: "I am Tomiyano, sailor of the third rank, master of *Sapphire* . . ." He gabbled off the rest with a few careless gestures. It was the cultural equivalent of spitting on a man's foot.

Wallie let the rudeness sit in the air for a moment, then drew his sword. "I am Shonsu, swordsman of the seventh rank, chosen champion of the Goddess, and am . . ."

"Chosen *what?*"

"Champion. This is Her own sword, Captain. It was given to me by a god. Note the sapphire? My hairclip is another sapphire, and also came from him. I am on a mission for the Most High. I am presently in need of transportation, and your ship was brought here, I understand, by Her Hand."

Tomiyano spat. "Firsts talk too much."

"He was lying?"

"No," admitted the captain.

Katanji coughed loudly. Wallie's head turned before he could stop it. Five men in cowled gowns were standing on the cliff top.

Tomiyano had noticed. He smiled with joy. "Running from someone, swordsman?"

"Yes, sailor. Sorcerers."

"Sorcerers? This close to the River? Hah!"

Wallie glanced at the other four men. They were frowning, perhaps wavering, but he must convince their captain first. He turned to the cliff again. The sorcerers were hurrying toward the easiest descent. Nnanji was paler than Wallie had ever seen him. It was not fear of the sorcerers that was eating at Nnanji— he wanted to get at this insolent sailor. The rest of Wallie's party were huddled behind the lumber, unhappily waiting. This might be another of the gods' tests—Wallie had very little time left to negotiate his way onto the ship.

Tomiyano jeered. "You've been gulled, swordsman! You're running from bogeymen."

Keeping his voice calm with an immense effort, Wallie said, "Not so. A year ago, in Ov, forty swordsmen were slain by sorcerers."

"They can have three more as far as I'm concerned."

"And Matarro of the First? Save him, then! Sail away quick, Captain."

The fury blazed up again in the sailor's face. That reminder of his own impotence seemed to rob him of speech. His ship had been hijacked, and he could do nothing about it.

"The sorcerers summon fire demons, Captain. You wouldn't want those near *Sapphire*, now, would you?"

Tomiyano seemed ready to start grinding his teeth. He turned to look at the River. For some distance out from the jetty, the water was as clear and smooth as plate glass. Beyond that it was rippled by wind.

"If I let you and your riffraff on board, then these sorcerers will come after you."

"Let us on board and you can depart. It is Her will you are flouting, not mine. I did not summon you here."

"*No!*" Tomiyano had thought of another solution—dead men do not need to go anywhere. His hand appeared, holding a knife. Wallie had no need to call on Shonsu's encyclopedic knowledge of blades to tell him that it was a throwing knife; the way the sailor was holding it showed that. Suddenly he felt very mortal. He was utterly vulnerable at that range, but too far away to use his sword.

"No damned landlubber swordsman will ever set foot on my deck again! I swore at Yok that—"

"Quiet!" shouted a new voice. The captain's arm dropped, and he turned to glare as a newcomer emerging from a door in the fo'c'sle. Wallie relaxed with a gasp. He stole another glance landward; the sorcerers were invisible, hidden in the trees, but they must be close to the valley floor by now. He looked at the River. The edge of that mysterious calm was racing landward— the wind was coming. He could only have minutes left before *Sapphire* began to move. If he could not board, then he and Nnanji should be heading for the trees, to meet the enemy under cover . . .

"I'll handle this, Tom'o," said the new voice, and Wallie turned to stare in bewilderment at the figure now standing beside the captain—a Fifth, in red. A swordsman, for there was a sword hilt beside the gray-streaked ponytail, but old enough to wear a sleeveless gown; short and enormously fat, and the harness was a strange type, with the chest straps crossing in an X instead of being vertical . . . Too fat. Fat in the wrong places . . .

Then she began her salute: "I am Brota, swordsman of the fifth rank, owner of *Sapphire* . . ."

A fat, middle-aged, *female* swordsman? As he drew his sword to respond, Wallie's mind was reeling from this latest shock, and he could hear Nnanji growling. Tomiyano began to argue; the woman told him to be quiet, and he obeyed. Owner? She was obviously the true master of the ship, almost certainly Tomiyano's mother. When the seventh sword clicked back into its scabbard, she turned her head briefly to study the River, then the apparently empty valley on the other side. Her ponytail was bound by an incongruous pink bow.

"What talk is this of sorcerers, my lord?"

"They slaughtered the garrison in Ov a year ago, mistress. The Goddess has sent me to deal with them—but at the moment I do not have the forces to do so. Five of them will be here in a few moments. I am not the only one in danger. You and Novice Matarro . . ."

She was not as tall as Wild Ani, but probably fatter. Yet that pillowed brown face held none of the sullen air of defeat that haunted always the face of a slave. There was an ominous hardness there, and Wallie tracked it down to her eyes. The rest of her features were soft and rounded, but the eyes sat in dark caves like lurking dragons. Her eyebrows were bushy, white more than brown. They were an old man's eyes peering out from a woman's face.

"Thirty years we have traded on the River, Lord Shonsu, and never have we been taken by Her Hand. Never has She troubled us, nor we Her. Never have I heard of a ship being taken while at anchor, either. Perhaps you and I are indeed intended to do business together." Again she glanced at the River, studying the telltale ripple of wind approaching. Above them the sails stirred very slightly. She was playing for time.

"Then we had better do it quickly, Mistress Brota."

She shrugged bulky shoulders beneath crimson cotton. "What exactly do you seek from us?"

Wallie hesitated a second to line up his thoughts. With this woman he would prefer a signed, sealed, and witnessed contract backed up by affidavits and secured by a performance bond, but he would have to settle for a handshake. He glanced again at the innocent-seeming valley.

"Immediate embarkation. Safe passage for my companions and myself to . . ."

Careful! The geography of the World was variable—Aus might not be the next city by River. "Safe passage to the nearest city where I can enlist some swordsmen. Food and shelter, of course."

Again Tomiyano tried to speak, and again she slapped him down with a word. "Very well. The fare will be two hundred golds."

Nnanji's blasphemous shriek was lost in a bellow of relieved laughter from the captain. The other sailors grinned. The sails rippled.

Shrubbery rippled also, close to the two ruined cottages at the landward end of the jetty.

Two hundred golds was blatant extortion, far beyond the means of anyone but the rich. It would buy a farm.

"Done!" Wallie said.

Her eyes narrowed in anger, those dangerous male eyes behind a rubber female mask. "I would see your money, my lord."

Wallie was already fumbling in his money pouch, two fingers feeling among the coins for the jewels that the demigod had given him. He found one and held it up between thumb and forefinger. "I sold one just like this for three hundred, mistress. So I have the fare. We have a deal."

She scowled, staring at the tiny blue star. Greed won. "Get them aboard!"

The crew members jumped to obey. Two gates flew open in the ship's side, and hands reached down. Wind caressed the sails and they billowed joyfully. As Wallie jumped off the lumber, figures emerged from the trees. Tomiyano ran for the poop deck to take the tiller. Jja and Vixini went in one gate, Honakura was almost thrown through the other by Nnanji. More crew members began to spill out from doors in fo'c'sle and poop. Wallie dragged a bewildered Cowie behind him and hurled her up, also. *Sapphire* began to drift away, a gap opening between her fenders and the edge of the dock. Katanji scrambled aboard, pushed by his brother and pulled clear by a sailor. Sorcerers were running for the jetty, anonymous monks in their brown robes and cowls. Nnanji and Wallie grabbed at the sides of their respective gates and their feet were dragged free of the dock. They fell against the ship's side and for a moment dangled there, boots only inches above the piranha-infested waters. Then they scrambled up and were hauled aboard.

As Wallie rose to his feet, the gate banged shut behind him. Whew!

†††

The sorcerers had halted halfway along the jetty, beaten. Their leader was a Fourth, and he shook his fist. Wallie waited for spell-casting to begin, but the sinister figures just stood there. Already *Sapphire* was a surprising distance out, turning her bow to open River. Either she was now out of range of magic, or the sorcerers were too winded by their run to chant.

Brota was standing in front of Wallie, feet firmly planted, hand outstretched. Male sailors had clustered around. Their faces were unfriendly, and their hands were behind their backs.

If it had been a test of Wallie's ability to win his way on board, then he had succeeded. If the right answer had been to stay and fight, then he had failed utterly, delivering the sword of the Goddess to a gang of pirates. He would be feeding fish in minutes.

Nnanji's boots drummed on the deck, and he appeared from around a dinghy that hung in davits amidships, next to the rail. He stopped, started to raise his hand, and then froze, nonplussed.

Wallie fumbled again in his pouch, deliberately taking much longer than necessary so the watchers would not know that there were more jewels there. "Ah!" He brought out a sapphire and dropped it onto Brota's fat palm.

She studied it carefully, then slid it into a pocket without offering to give him any change. She held out both hands. Awkwardly he did the same, and they made a four-handed shake, a new custom to Wallie. He thought the tension decreased then.

"Come with me, my lord." Brota turned on her heel, and sailors made way for her as she headed aft. Nnanji stepped back and almost fell into the hold.

Brota had a rolling, ponderous gait. Wallie followed with his head up, waiting for the knife in his back. It did not come, and a moment later Nnanji fell into step behind him.

Sapphire's main deck was small and very cluttered. Wallie had boarded alongside a large open hatch. Immediately aft of that, dinghies restricted the deck on either side. Then he had to detour again for the main mast, and a second hatch behind that, avoiding the stays slanting up from the rail, the bollards and racks of pins and fire buckets that seemed to obtrude everywhere, and also piles of lumber, including planks that he decided must be the hatch covers. It was an obstacle course, and dangerous with the two big hatches open. Women and children had emerged from somewhere to study the intruders with sullen resentment.

Brota was heading to a door below the poop deck—that at least was an empty area, with Tomiyano sitting on a helmsman's bench, holding the tiller and scowling. Two flights of steps led up there, one in each corner of the main deck, further crowding it. Wallie followed her through the doorway, ducking his head. Nnanji was at his heels.

The room was bright and airy, as big as the poop deck above it, although Wallie's sword hilt almost touched the beams. The only furniture was a pair of big wooden chests at the back, and the only obstruction the mizzenmast, close to the door—that was why the door was off center, then. There were two large windows in each wall, their louvered shutters open to admit a fine view in all directions.

"This we call the deckhouse, my lord. If you are to be aboard overnight, then it must suffice, for we have no spare cabins."

"It will serve very well," Wallie said. "But what do you use this for normally? I wish to inconvenience you as little as possible, mistress."

The bristly white eyebrows rose slightly. "We eat here when the weather is bad. The children play in it. The watch uses it at night. We can dispense with it for a day or so and not suffer unduly."

He smiled. He got no answering smile, but her manner was not so hostile as her son's had been; business was business. Wallie realized that he was not going to be tossed overboard . . . not just yet, at least.

"And what rules would you have us obey, as passengers? I want no trouble, mistress. I come in peace."

Again mild surprise. "Heads and showers are through the forward door, my lord. I ask that you not go below."

"Agreed."

She studied him for a moment and glanced at Nnanji.

"Permit me," Wallie said, and presented him. Both he and Brota used the civilian gestures—it would be difficult to draw a sword under so low a ceiling. Nnanji was curt, obviously still furious.

"There is one matter that often causes trouble, my lord. I am sure that you are honorable swordsmen—"

"Adept Nnanji and I brought our own slaves. The old man is harmless, and we shall warn the novice. If there is any friction at all, Mistress Brota, please inform me at once."

She nodded, chins bulging. "You are gracious, Lord Shonsu."

"And you on your side . . ."

She frowned. "I apologize for my son's brusque manner. He . . . You are welcome aboard. We shall serve as the Goddess wills."

If Tomiyano had been brusque, then Wallie had no need to meet hostile. "I understand that the closest city is Aus, about a half-day's ride to the north."

She glanced out at the scenery. *Sapphire* was already in mid-River, heading upstream. "That will be our destination, then. One port will do as well as any other for us. When we have restored trim, we shall make better time."

Wallie turned to look at the main deck outside. Voices and thumps revealed that work was going on in the holds. From time to time one end of a plank would appear and then disappear again. Some children were kneeling on the deck, watching what was going on below. The cargo had shifted and was being rearranged.

"If a couple of strong backs can be of assistance, mistress . . ."

He had moved too far out of character; surprise turned to suspicion. "We have more hands available than room to use them, my lord. You will excuse me?"

Wallie watched her waddle out to the deck, that incongruous sword hanging on the plump red back, gray ponytail wagging, fleshy arms swinging. He turned to Nnanji and cut off the protests bursting to emerge. "Tell me about female swordsmen, brother?"

Nnanji scowled horribly. "It is one of the things about the water rats that annoy other swordsmen. I have heard it argued several times." Then he quoted three separate conversations between people whom Wallie had never met. More familiar with legal arguments than Nnanji could ever be, he concluded in his own mind that the sutras did not prohibit female swordsmen. They were ambiguous on the subject, and so the water rats were entitled to their interpretation, but it would be unnerving to find oneself fighting a woman. Strictly speaking *swordsman* had no gender. Swordsperson? How could he think of Nnanji, say, as a *swordsperson*?

"She must have been good in her youth," he said, "to have won her red. She could probably put up a good defense even now. Too slow for much of an attack . . ."

Nnanji smirked. "We're safe enough, then. I saw no others, except Novice Matarro."

"Did you get a good look at the sailors?"

"Yes. Why?"

Wallie grinned and headed for the door. He was not quick enough. "My lord brother! Two hundred golds is robbery!"

"I agree."

"Then you will take it back when we reach Aus?" Nnanji's eyes burned. He was still under the influence of the barracks propaganda, planning to cut off ears, perhaps.

"No, I will not! When I shake hands I stay bound. I certainly hope Mistress Brota does, also."

Nnanji stared back blankly.

"You didn't look at the sailors. You're not thinking. Come on!"

Honakura had perched himself on a fire bucket just outside the door.

"Did you miss any of that?" Wallie inquired waspishly.

The shriveled old face looked up at him. "I don't think so, my lord. An interesting lady!"

"And a bloodthirsty son!"

"True. Tell me, do you feel spurned now?" The shrewd old eyes were mocking.

Wallie had never considered that he himself might be the mighty one of the riddle. And he had criticized Nnanji for not thinking? There could be none mightier than a swordsman of the Seventh.

"I hope so," he said thoughtfully. "I should not like to be spurned much more than that. *An army earned?*" He had done nothing so far to earn an army. He tried to guess what Honakura was hinting at. The sly old rogue had seen something. "You think that maybe recruiting in Aus will not be as easy as I am hoping?"

"Perhaps. Have you found any circles to turn, yet?"

"Dammit! What have you worked out?"

"Me, my lord? I am but a poor beggar, an old and humble servant . . ."

Wallie muttered something vulgar and walked away. The little priest was intolerable when he was in that mood.

The clamor in the holds continued, but *Sapphire* was not listing so badly. Jja was sitting on the deck near the fo'c'sle door, patiently restraining Vixini's desire to explore the hatch. Cowie was slumped beside them. Katanji was in conversation with two adolescent girls and also Matarro, who was now swordless. He had no ponytail and wore nothing but his breechclout. At this distance, there was no way to tell that he was not a novice sailor. How many more of the crew were swordsmen?

But the sun was shining, the wind cheerful, and the ship was sliding serenely through the water at a fair rate. Snowcapped peaks of RegiVul loomed along the northeastern skyline, majestic and beautiful.

Wallie walked over to the rail and leaned back against it, studying the deck, the coming and going of people. Nnanji stood beside him, frowning and trying to do the same. Jja rose and came over with Vixini in her arms and Cowie trailing behind.

"You've been on ships before, my love," Wallie said. "How does this one compare?"

She smiled and glanced around the deck. "Only once, master. This one is cleaner."

"Yes, she's been well cared for." *Sapphire* was old—the knots in the deck planks were raised lumps, evidence of many years of wear—but brass shone, paint and varnish glistened, the cables looked strong and new. The people were well groomed and healthy. Except for a couple of old women in gowns and a few bare children, everyone wore a breechclout. The women supplemented it with a bra sash, tied at the back. On some of them the bikini effect could catch male eyes like flypaper.

"You can take that rascal into the deckhouse," Wallie said as Vixini began struggling furiously. A preadolescent girl had just shepherded two toddlers in there. Cowie followed behind Jja like a tame sheep.

Nnanji growled throatily. A lanky, dark-haired girl of about his own age was scrambling up the ratlines on the far side. Her twin sashes were yellow and even skimpier than most. The action was very interesting.

"Drop it!" Wallie said.

"I can look, can't I?" Nnanji protested, with mock hurt.

"Not like that, you can't! There's steam coming out of your ears, and your ponytail is standing straight up."

Nnanji chuckled, but he continued to watch intently, craning his head farther and farther back as the girl went higher.

Brota was seated at the tiller, swordless now—a harness would be uncomfortable over a gown. Tomiyano and another sailor had gone up to the fo'c'sle and were working on the capstan, probably trying to free the jammed anchor chain. Both wore brown breechclouts, but the captain also had a leather belt to support the dagger that was his symbol of office. Everyone else was unarmed; there were no weapons in sight.

"When I came aboard and was paying Brota, the men crowded around. Were they holding weapons behind their backs?"

"Yes, my lord brother. Long knives."

"Where did they put them afterward, did you notice?"

"No," Nnanji said grumpily. "They're not very respectful, are they?"

The passengers were mostly being ignored, but Wallie caught

hints of resentful glances that he was not supposed to have seen. Apparently the work in the hold was completed, and two men replaced the planks over the hatches. They walked by the two swordsmen several times without even seeming to notice them.

"None too friendly," Wallie agreed. "What was it the captain said when he was about to knife me?" Then he quickly added, "Quietly!" as Nnanji drew a deep breath. Tomiyano had shouted, so Nnanji had been about to shout.

"Oh. Right. 'No damned landlubber swordsman will ever set foot on my deck again! I swore at Yok that—' That was all I heard."

Wallie nodded. "It's what I heard, too." Back at the tenancy the women had been nervous and jumpy and too friendly. These riverfolk were being not friendly enough, yet somehow he felt a similarity. Again, there was too much tension.

There was one exception. The girl in the yellow sashes came sliding down a rope and then pranced along the deck toward the fo'c'sle. She was too slim to bounce very much, but that did not seem to matter—Nnanji growled once more. If she was trying to attract his attention, she was winning all the medals. She was younger than Wallie had thought at first, about Quili's age, and tall, dark, and toothsome.

Nnanji sighed, a stupid leer still on his face as he watched her go. "First-rate equipment."

"Try looking at some of the other sailors, protégé."

"The others are a bit young for me. I ought to warn the nipper, I suppose . . ."

"The men."

Nnanji frowned. "What am I supposed to see, my lord brother?"

"Scars." Tiny marks on shoulders and ribs, usually on the right side—old scrapes and recent bruises.

Nnanji had been leaning back dreamily against the gunwale. Now he sprang erect, glaring, as his eyes confirmed what Wallie had said. He began spitting sutras. Fifteen: a civilian must not be allowed to touch a sword, except in emergency. Ninety-five: never could he be given a foil. Ninety-nine: never, never, never might a civilian practice fencing with foil or stick . . . He fell silent, staring at Wallie in shock.

"The women have them also," Wallie said softly. "I suspect that every person on this ship can use a sword."

"But Brota is a swordsman! This is abomination, my lord brother!"

"Common sense, though. Ships are prey to pirates, are they not? No garrisons to shout for in the middle of the River."

Nnanji's reaction had been a surprise. Probably he had not noticed the scars himself because he was so accustomed to seeing them on his friends, but Wallie had been expecting an explanation. If they were truly evidence of an abomination, that could be why Tomiyano was averse to allowing swordsmen aboard. Yet the marks were obvious on every adult Wallie had been able to see, and every port must contain swordsmen to notice them, also. In some respects Nnanji was as innocent of the World as Wallie, and there must be many things he had not heard mentioned in the barracks. Foil scars on sailors might be an example.

"You don't want me to denounce them?"

"Oh, Nnanji, Nnanji! Think! Brota and I shook hands. We're guests, of a sort. That's all that's standing between us and the fish. I've got a fortune on my back and another in my hair. Now—be nice to sailors, please?"

Nnanji could not appreciate danger except from other swordsmen, but he looked uneasily at the sun-bright waters on either side of the ship, at the far-off smudges of shore. A few fishing boats to starboard were the only signs of human life.

"How many in the crew?"

Nnanji shook his head.

"So far I've seen five men, six women, five adolescents, and half a dozen children. That must be about all. I *think* they're all sailors—apart from Brota and Matarro, of course—but I haven't had a good look at all the faces."

"Yes, my lord brother."

"Now, where did they hide the knives?"

"Hide?" Nnanji looked even more wary.

He peered carefully around the deck. Wallie had never seen him so uneasy; perhaps the landlubber was beginning to appreciate how much of a trap a ship could be. In a few minutes he began to mutter, laying out his logic like playing cards. "Those buckets of sand . . . they don't grow vegetables . . . fire fighting? Big enough to sit on, but I couldn't lift one. You could. Why not stack smaller buckets to sit on?" He looked hopefully at Wallie.

"Well done! See, thinking isn't so hard, is it?"

"It makes my head ache." But he was pleased by the praise. "Mentor?"

Wallie turned around to meet Katanji's earnest gaze. Novice Matarro stood nervously behind him.

"Katanji, we'd better straighten this out—I'm not your mentor, except because of that strange oath Nnanji and I swore, and that's not standard procedure. So let's say that I am only your mentor if Nnanji's not around, all right?"

"Yes, my lord." Katanji turned glumly to his brother.

Wallie caught Matarro's eye and winked. The boy twitched in astonishment and then grinned.

"Mentor, may I take my sword off? Mat'o, here, says he'll take me up the ratlines to the crow's nest. But swords aren't allowed aloft."

Nnanji frowned at the sailor jargon Katanji was flaunting. Wallie could guess at the meanings, but his need to guess showed that Shonsu had never bothered to learn the terms. To a swordsman, evidently, a ship was merely a convenience. "I expect he thinks a landlubber wouldn't have the nerve to go out on those—what do you call the crosspieces, novice?"

Katanji shot Wallie an alarmed glance to say that he did not need help of that caliber.

"Yards, my lord," said Matarro.

"Show him, then!" Nnanji said heartily. "Turn cartwheels! I'll hold your sword. Perhaps he can find you a breechclout, too? A kilt isn't very suitable for sailoring."

Astonished by this unexpected indulgence, Katanji hastily stripped off his harness and handed it over, kicked off his boots, then ran off with Matarro. Nnanji's eyes slid round to Wallie's again.

Wallie nodded approvingly. "They are more useful."

Nnanji was a quick learner.

For some time Wallie leaned back against the rail and watched ship life. Two youngsters were playing a board game on one of the hatches, three women peeling vegetables on the other. A very skinny young sailor had begun holystoning the deck. Tomiyano and a couple of other men sat cross-legged in a corner, pretending to splice cable, but mostly keeping a careful eye on the visitors. Laughter drifted out from the deckhouse and down from the rigging, where Katanji and a group of adolescents were apparently clowning, invisible among clouds of sails. The sun was high and warm. Honakura had disappeared. Brota sat like a red mountain at the tiller, chatting to an elderly woman in brown. Traffic on the River was increasing, and that might be a sign that *Sapphire* was approaching Aus. Or somewhere.

Then Nnanji hissed in astonishment. The girl in the yellow bikini had emerged from the fo'c'sle door. Smiling, she sauntered toward the swordsmen, taking her time so that they could enjoy the hip movement. She was wearing a sword.

Not merely female swordsmen, but young, beautiful, and *sexy* female swordsmen? Nnanji muttered, "How could a man ever fight *that?*" Wallie was wondering the same thing.

Tomiyano roared, "Thana!" and leaped to his feet. She turned and frowned as he bounded across to bar her path. He whispered something angrily and tried to stop her, but she dodged past him.

She walked quickly over to Wallie and saluted, while he stared in disbelief at the two swordmarks on her flawless brow. She had shiny black curls and a smooth, coffee-colored skin— an all-over perfect complexion, very little of it not visible. Her face was lovely, with a classic chiseled beauty. She was too young and too slim for his taste, which preferred Jja's more ample curves; but he thought of fashion models and he could readily admit that few men would spurn this lithesome warrior maiden. Nnanji was almost panting.

Wallie responded and presented Apprentice Thana to his oath brother. Tomiyano hovered in the background, fingering his dagger.

Thana stood demurely with hands folded and eyes downcast below long lashes, waiting for the highrank to speak first. It had not been Nnanji she had been trying to impress. For a moment Wallie was at a loss for words. The crossed straps of her harness pulled the light cotton of her bra sash very tight, with outstanding results, worthy of much study.

He tore his eyes away and took a deep breath. "I was already enjoying my voyage on your fine ship, apprentice. Your company increases the pleasure greatly."

She contrived a maidenly blush and fanned him with those eyelashes. "You honor us with your presence, my lord."

"I am not sure that the captain altogether agrees."

Thana pouted slightly and glanced around to see what Tomiyano was doing—he was leaning against the mainmast and still fingering the dagger.

"Forgive my brother's rough tongue, my lord. He means no harm."

The devil he didn't! Brother? Then this svelte Thana was great, fat Brota's daughter—incredible! There was no resemblance at all.

Before Wallie could think of a rejoinder, Thana said, "I can see that you bear a remarkable sword, Lord Shonsu. Would you be so gracious as to let me examine it?"

The obvious undertones were not accidental. Wallie drew the seventh sword for her to see. She had probably not been genuinely interested, but that weapon would impress anyone, and she was startled when she saw the Chioxin craftsmanship. He nodded to Nnanji, who eagerly recounted the legend as she studied the great sapphire, the griffon guard, and the chasing on the blade itself.

Tomiyano was not alone among the crew in disapproving of Thana's fraternization. The women were frowning and the men openly furious. Wallie decided that Thana was a self-willed young minx. Perhaps her mother could handle her, but her brother clearly could not.

"It is wonderful, my lord," she said at last, gazing earnestly up at Wallie and ignoring Nnanji. "We are fortunate to have this opportunity to aid the chosen champion of the Goddess."

Wallie sheathed the sword. "I was fortunate to have *Sapphire* arrive when she did—although I hardly think that it was by chance. She is a fine vessel, and I can see that she is well looked after."

More fluttering of lashes. "You are kind, Lord Shonsu."

"Thirty years old, I think your mother said?"

"Oh, she is older than that! My grandfather . . . bought her. He was captain until about two years ago. He died of a fever. He was a great sailor. Then Tom'o took over." She shrugged. "He's crude, but not a bad sailor, I suppose."

"Why not your father?"

Thana sighed conspicuously. "Daddy died a long time ago. Besides, he was a trader. We riverfolk have a saying, my lord, 'A trader for the head, a swordsman for the hands, and a sailor for the feet.' We lack a trader at the moment. My older brother, Tomiyarro—now there was a trader! He could buy the shell off a turtle and sell it feathers, Mother always said."

"Then how do you trade?" asked Wallie, who could guess. He was being vamped. She was too young to have much skill at it, but that very youth made even her clumsy efforts effective.

"Oh, Mother handles it," Thana said offhandedly.

"Mistress Brota is a very shrewd negotiator."

Thana sniggered. "You outsmarted her, my lord."

"I did?"

"She got a nice sapphire out of you, but she was really after your hairclip."

Not knowing what to say to that, Wallie looked at Nnanji, but Nnanji was glassy-eyed. Time to change the subject. "Your brother said this was a family ship. Who are the others, apart from your mother and brother?"

"Cousins," Thana said. "Uncles and aunts. Dull! I so rarely get to meet any—" She sighed deeply. "—*real* men."

"So obviously you have no Jonahs, yet you were brought here by Her Hand last night?"

"It is exciting!" Thana said, with a nervous glance at the landscape. "That has never happened to us before."

"So your mother said. I expect you will be returned to your home waters as soon as we disembark."

"Well, I hope not!" She tossed her curls. "We've been trading between Hool and Ki for years and years and years. It's very dull. I keep telling Mother to try somewhere new."

"And why does she not, then?"

"Profit!" Thana spoke with contempt. "She knows the markets. Sandalwood from Hool to Ki, pots and baskets from Ki to Hool. Back and forth, back and forth. Dull! This is an adventure! We're not even in the tropics any more, are we?"

"No, we're not. But excitement can be dangerous."

Thana smiled winningly. "What should we fear when we have a swordsman of the Seventh on board? I'm sure you could handle a whole shipful of pirates all by yourself, Lord Shonsu."

"I certainly hope I don't have to!"

Pirates could be a tricky subject, bringing in the matter of sailors using swords. No sooner had that thought occurred to Wallie than Nnanji blundered into the conversation. "It must be very difficult for you to get fencing practice, Apprentice Thana?"

The topic did not seem to bother her. She turned to look at him rather calculatingly. "Indeed it is, adept. Would you be so kind as to give me a lesson after lunch?"

Nnanji beamed. "I should be delighted!"

Thana smiled and turned back to her main business, Wallie. Wallie had not liked that smile.

"We must be getting close to Aus," he said. "So there may not be any 'after lunch.' But surely we are your Jonahs, and it is said that Jonahs bring a ship good luck."

"We need it!" Thana dropped her voice conspiratorially. "I have wondered sometimes, Lord Shonsu, if we were cursed."

"How so?" Wallie sensed the approach of some creative storytelling.

"Well, first my grandfather . . . then Uncle Matyrri died of a cut on his hand . . . and then pirates! A year ago. They killed my brother, and another uncle, and one of my cousins died of wounds later."

"That's terrible!"

"Yes. It was tragic. I've gotten over the worst of it, you know, but of course I still miss them terribly."

"This was at Yok?" Wallie inquired.

She reeled backward as if he had struck her, turning so pale that he thought she might be going to faint.

Out of the corner of his eye, he saw that Tomiyano had half drawn his dagger. He was too far off to have heard the words, but he had seen his sister's reaction.

What had Wallie provoked? "Your brother mentioned Yok."

She nodded dumbly, staring at him, trembling.

"I assume that these pirates were renegade swordsmen?"

Thana licked white lips and then merely nodded again, seemingly incapable of speech. Wallie felt that he was walking a sheet of glass over an abyss. Tomiyano was not the only one to have noticed.

Wallie lowered his voice. "Of course I would not say this to anyone outside our craft, apprentice, but a bent swordsman is a terrible abomination . . . deserving of no mercy." He glanced swiftly at the perplexed Nnanji. Even he had noticed Thana's terror, but he had not yet worked out the only possible explanation. "My oath brother and I ran into a band of renegades two days ago. We dealt with them severely. The World is a better place without such scum."

Thana seemed to relax slightly, and a trace of color crept back into her cheeks. "That . . . that sentiment does you great honor, my lord."

"Such things are better not discussed," Wallie said pompously, and looked to Nnanji for agreement.

Nnanji said, "Er? What?"

Then adults and children began emerging from the fo'c'sle carrying baskets of fruit and loaves. Wallie felt relief like a cool breeze. "Ah! Here comes lunch! You watch what happens now, apprentice. This is where Adept Nnanji gets back all the profit your mother hopes to make on my sapphire."

†† ††

By the People's standards, the riverfolk were an informal lot. Lunch was laid out on the forward hatch cover, and the people sat around wherever they liked, on hatches or buckets or the deck. The food was plain but satisfying: fruit and cheese and sausage. Brota yielded the tiller to Tomiyano after a heated discussion that included covert glances toward the swordsmen. Then she parked her massive form on the rear hatch and proceeded to demonstrate how she had acquired her bulk, almost rivaling Nnanji's Gargantuan efforts.

Crew and passengers separated into clumps. Wallie was given

a wide berth, but Katanji had won acceptance by the younger sailors. Nnanji attached himself to Thana and was gobbling without pause, while animatedly relating how Lord Shonsu had been given the seventh sword. He was using the version Wallie had given Garadooi, almost word for word, and that was safe.

Wallie sat crooked-leg on the deck, leaning against the starboard bulwark with Jja at his side, trying not to seem as worried as he felt. Clearly his mission was going to be more complex than he had thought. Granted that *Sapphire* had been sent to rescue him from the sorcerers, her purpose must be more than merely transporting him to Aus. What exactly had happened at Yok a year ago? Thana had mentioned pirates, but that was not what Tomiyano had said. Thana's panic had been horribly reminiscent of Quili's apprehension when Wallie had brought up the subject of assassinations. These sailors were not humble peasants who would flee into the hills; any hint that Lord Shonsu was prying into a murky past would bring the knives out of the fire buckets very quickly. Hostility hung over the sunny deck like invisible fog.

There had been no concealment at Ov—Garadooi had proved that—but *Sapphire* could have reported a crime to swordsmen in any city on the River, so the first answer did not work for the second problem. The next city up ahead might not be Aus. It might be Yok.

Wallie had chosen the wrong side to sit for a good view of the mountains, but *Sapphire*'s tacking let him catch a glimpse of them now and again. They were faint and blue in the noon heat, not visibly changing.

He needed a talk with Honakura, but private conversation was impossible on this crowded deck. The old man was sitting happily on a hatch cover, chatting to a woman as ancient as himself.

The meal drew to a close. Children began clearing up the food. Without a glance at Lord Shonsu, Brota stumped off to relieve her son at the tiller. Tomiyano trotted down from the poop and began assembling a meal for himself before the baskets were removed.

People were staring out to starboard. Wallie rose. *Sapphire* was arriving at a city.

At first glance he could see nothing remarkable about it. The mountains of RegiVul stood unchanged to the northeast, so it could only be Aus, and it looked much as Wallie would have expected a city of the World to look. Lying on flat ground, it was already largely obscured by the high warehouses of the dockyards—two- and three-story wooden buildings, weathered silver and topped by red tile roofs. Beyond those roofs a few gold spires and taller buildings of gray stone with the same red tiles stood stark against the cobalt noontime sky. The frontage of warehouses was broken by narrow alleylike streets winding back into the town. The bustling crowds were too far off to distinguish the colors of their ranks, but seemed to be composed of quite unexceptional people going about unexceptional business. *Sapphire* was picking her way among anchored ships of many types and sizes, and others were moored along the quay. Horse-drawn wagons rumbled along the streets, their sound wafted over the water by the wind.

Wallie studied the roadway for a while, looking for swordsmen, but it was still too distant. Then he took another look at the buildings.

Then he took three long strides over to the hatch cover where Tomiyano was eating.

"Captain? What is that tower?"

The sailor flashed him a hostile glance and then stared at the city. He chewed for a while, swallowed, and said, "No idea."

"You've never seen one like it?"

"No." He laughed contemptuously. "You thinking it might be full of sorcerers, swordsman?"

Yes. Garadooi had talked of sorcerers building a tower in Ov. Several of Nnanji's stories had mentioned towers, although none of them had described what sorcerer towers should look like. The structure that concerned Wallie was quite unlike anything else visible in Aus—assuming that this was Aus. It was square and dark and much taller than anything else. It stood close behind the row of warehouses, a block from the riverfront. Its windows were blacker gaps in the black stonework. It was sinister.

"I have never seen anything like that, either," Wallie said, without mentioning that he had never seen a city of the World before. "If my suspicions are correct, then it is not only me who will be at risk, Captain. Your mother and sister are swordsmen also."

Tomiyano snorted. "I am sure they will defend you. You paid your fare to here, Lord Shonsu. Here you are. Here you stay."

Then he added, "Good riddance."

Nnanji caught Wallie's eye. Nnanji was thinking the same thing he was.

Wallie marched to the nearer steps, trotted up to the poop, and strode over to where Brota sat by the tiller.

"That tower, mistress? Have you ever seen anything like that before?"

"Down, please, my lord. I need to see."

Restraining his warming temper, Wallie knelt. *Please do not speak to the driver.* Now he saw that Brota was performing some tricky maneuvers, bringing her ship in through a crowded anchorage in a fitful breeze. The wind seemed to be failing.

"No," she said. She frowned. "No, I haven't."

Neither Quili nor Garadooi had ever been to Aus, and suddenly Wallie remembered the inexplicable *something* he had seen on the face of one of Lady Thondi's companions. Thondi associated with highrank sorcerers. If they had taken over Aus as well as Ov, then both she and her friends would know about it. Hilarious—Wallie had been heading from frying pan to fire. That would also explain why the pursuit in the mountains had not been more strenuous.

He did not need to explain for Brota. She glowered at the mysterious building, her strangely masculine eyebrows lowered in thought. "You bought passage to this city, my lord."

"No, I did not. I bought passage to the nearest city where I could enlist swordsmen."

She grunted. "So you did. Well, I have never heard of sorcerers near the River. Yes, I've heard tell of them in mountain lands, but they worship the Fire God. The Goddess would not . . ." She glanced at Wallie's sword and stopped.

Tomiyano wandered up the steps, munching a peach. He leaned against the gunwale and regarded the kneeling swordsman with disdain. The city was coming closer. Wallie twisted around to study the crowded dock road again, wishing heartily that he had a good pair of binoculars. "If I am correct, mistress, then you are in danger also."

"Not as many as I would have expected for a place this

size." Brota was counting the ships tied along the dock and those anchored out in the River. "But every ship carries water rats, my lord."

"Maybe not here."

She reached up and untied the bow that held her ponytail. The graying hair fell loose about her shoulders. "One city is much like another to a trader. I have cargo to sell. You take your swordsmen into the deckhouse, my lord, and we shall see."

Wallie could not argue further, not with the contemptuous sailor listening. He rose and stalked away.

As he stood by the deckhouse door, ushering his charges ahead of him, he stared again at the approaching dock. It was still just too far off to distinguish either swordsmen or cowled sorcerers, but getting close enough that he, in turn, would soon be visible to them. He ducked inside quickly.

Nnanji was pouting at this concealment, but had the sense to say nothing. Wallie walked around, closing the shutters and opening their louvers so that he could see out without being seen. Honakura had parked his tiny form on one of the big chests and was smirking.

"Don't tell me I should have expected this!" Wallie growled.

"I would never be so crass, my lord."

Wallie sat down beside him. They were directly below the helmsman, but enough shouting and wagon noises were drifting across the water to drown quiet voices. Quickly he recounted the mysteries he had uncovered on *Sapphire*: the interview with Thana, and the problem of sailors with foil scars.

The old man reacted with some glee. He was enjoying himself immensely. "As far as the scars are concerned, my lord, I think I have observed them on sailors."

"But never on other civilians?"

Honakura shook his head. "And I have known sailors to seek absolution for killing men in sword fights."

"There must be a sutra, then. Certainly it would make sense to let sailors defend themselves against pirates." Not that the World always made sense. Wallie pondered and caught himself rubbing his chin, a mannerism Nnanji had begun to copy. But eleven hundred and forty-four sutras took too long to search and must wait until another time.

"Also," Honakura remarked innocently, "I was talking to Swordsman Lina . . ."

"Who? I didn't know there was another—you mean that antique crone you were sitting beside at lunch?"

"Well, if you think her age discredits her testimony . . ."

"Beg pardon, old man! Forgive me."

Honakura snorted. "She said one thing I ought to pass along. 'Warn that fine lord of yours not to try his swordwork on the captain.'"

"She's color-blind!"

Honakura bridled. "Senile, I expect." He went into a sulk and refused to say more.

Sapphire nudged gently against fenders.

Wallie stood by a window, next to Nnanji, who was cuddling Vixini in sullen silence. Lines had been thrown, and men were making them fast . . . perhaps sailors from other ships, for they waved cheerily as crewmen called down thanks. One of the gates was thrown open, and a gangplank laid ready, but it was not run out.

Nothing more seemed to be happening. Jja and Katanji and Honakura had gathered around the other dockside window. Even Cowie was peering out at another, although she probably did not know what she was looking for.

The dock road was much too narrow for its traffic, squeezed between the water and the warehouses. A much larger ship directly aft was unloading bales of cloth and gray sacks, with many slaves milling around and wagons lined up to be loaded. Carts full of firewood rumbled slowly past at intervals in one direction, wagons loaded with building lumber in the other, the iron-shod wheels deafening on the cobbles. Solitary horsemen and sedan chairs and handcarts provided more hazards for the dodging pedestrians. It all looked like a port should. It smelled of dust and horses and fish and river.

Then Nnanji hissed and pointed. Two sorcerers were progressing through the crowd, a brown Third and an orange Fourth. Cowls hid their faces and long hems their feet; their arms were folded inside voluminous sleeves. The effect was sinister and impersonal. They strolled as if patrolling, heads moving slightly from side to side, pace slow and regular. The other pedestrians made way for them. After a few heart-stopping moments they had passed the ship and were continuing on their way. Wallie released a long breath that he had not known he was holding.

The door flew open and Brota rolled in. She scowled at Wallie and then stood aside as Thana followed. Then came young Matarro, struggling with a long leather bag, and finally the very old woman who had to be Swordsman Lina. Brota banged the door closed. She had seen the sorcerers, obviously, and was going into hiding, along with the *Sapphire*'s other swordsmen. None of them bore swords, and only Brota had long hair.

Matarro dropped the bag and it clinked. Nnanji stiffened. He thrust Vixini back at Jja and went prowling over to inspect that bag.

"It is not my doing," Wallie said. "You would have come here anyway—there are only Black Lands downstream."

Brota pulled a face and lifted flabby arms to tie up her ponytail.

"What are we waiting for, mistress?"

"Port officer."

"Is that a craft?"

She rolled her eyes at such ignorance. "No. It is a sinecure. The king's nephew or an elder's son or such trash—swindlers, bloodsuckers, and bastards . . .

"They're usually faster after our money than this," she added sourly.

Having to bend forward under the low ceiling, Wallie drew his sword . . . just in case. Nnanji had been rummaging in the bag of swords that Matarro had brought; he drew his own and rose. The gangplank ran out with a screech and a thud. The watchers moved to the windows on the deck side.

Thana stood very close by Wallie, peering through the louvers. "Oo!" she whispered. "That's very nice!"

Her enthusiasm was understandable. The young man striding up the plank was almost as tall as Wallie, moving with a smooth grace. He could have been carved from oiled walnut—very dark and notably handsome, wearing orange sandals and breechclout, with a gaudily embossed leather pouch slung over his shoulder. Wallie thought of beachwear advertisements.

The newcomer flashed white teeth at Tomiyano and made his salute. "I am Ixiphino, sailor of the fourth rank, port officer of Aus, and it is my deepest and most humble wish that the Goddess Herself will see fit to grant you long life and happiness and to induce you to accept my modest and willing service in any way in which I may advance any of your noble purposes."

Tomiyano made his reply with surprising grace, while the visitor's eyes slid back and forth, studying the assembled sailors. The men were all near to fire buckets, Wallie noticed. Dislike of swordsmen did not automatically make them sorcerer supporters.

"I welcome you and your ship to Aus, Captain," said the beachwear model with another shimmering smile, "on behalf of the elders and the wizard."

"Wizard?"

"Ah! Your first visit to these parts? Yes, the wizard is the ominous Lord Yzarazzo, sorcerer of the Seventh. Aus has long been free of swordsman barbarism."

"What about water rats?"

Again the teeth shone. "They will not be molested if they stay on board. We have two local laws I must explain, Captain. The first is simply that any swordsman setting foot ashore will be delisted. Permanently."

Tomiyano reddened. "My mother is a swordsman. She normally handles our trading."

"That is unfortunate. She may trade from the deck. If she steps off the plank, she will violate the law." Ixiphino shrugged and then chuckled. "But she will find that Aus is a good place to trade. Trading on deck is not uncommon, and the profits will probably be higher than you are used to."

"Why?"

"Because some ships have a prejudice against sorcerer towns, so fewer call than before. But the traders are honest—relatively speaking, of course—and the people are peaceable."

"Then the sorcerers keep order?"

The port officer laughed. "They do, and very well, too."

The man had not once looked at the deckhouse, although the crew members were carefully leaving that side of him clear, for the benefit of the watchers. Curious!

"What does a sorcerer do if, say, the apprentices riot?" To-miyano asked.

Another laugh. "We keep our apprentices under better control than that, Captain. But we have had violent persons—visiting swordsmen have attempted violence on occasion. I can tell you that the sorcerers' methods are just as effective as the swordsmen's. More so, I should say. A spell can be cast from a distance."

Tomiyano was a skeptic. "Turning them into frogs?"

"Turning them into corpses, Captain. Sometimes charred corpses." Pause. Within the dim deckhouse, glances were exchanged.

The officer was still being amiable. "But apart from that one restriction, Captain, Aus is like any other city and more pleasant than most. The trading fee is two golds."

The captain raised his eyebrows into the fringe of his hair. "That seems very reasonable."

"In most cities that is the fee. The difference is graft, and my masters do not permit that."

Tomiyano silently handed over two coins and shook hands. The young man bowed his handsome head slightly and turned as if to go.

"You said two laws?"

"Oh, yes. Stupid of me." The port officer flashed his smile again. "There is an absolute restriction against swordsmen of high rank—Sixths or Sevenths. They are not even allowed in port. But such are rare. You have no free swords aboard, do you?"

"Of course not," said Tomiyano.

The officer turned to look at the deckhouse, then back to Tomiyano with quiet amusement. "And you swear that by your ship, sailor?"

Sweat broke out on Wallie's brow. His hand tightened on the hilt of the seventh sword.

"I do."

Nnanji drew breath with a hiss.

The port officer gave the captain a long cynical smile, shaking his head as one might disapprove of a naughty child. Then he spun on his heel and departed, his sandals slapping on the gangplank. Tomiyano absentmindedly wiped his forehead with the back of his hand and began shouting orders.

"My lord brother!"

Here it came. Ever since the first time they had met, Wallie had known of Nnanji's impossible idealism. He had known that some day it must lead to trouble. And here Nnanji had an open-and-shut case.

"I have told you that you cannot make a denunciation to me, Nnanji. Will you denounce the captain to his mother?"

Nnanji flushed scarlet and glared around the group. Even in the gloom of the shuttered deckhouse, Thana, Lina, and Matarro were visibly hostile. Brota's eyes were chips of steel.

"I think my son's remark was made for your benefit, adept!"

"I do not hide behind perjury, mistress! Then my own honor would be sullied."

This was insanity! Suicide! Wallie had two cities full of sorcerers to worry about now, and Nnanji was provoking the sailors as if he actually wanted to be thrown ashore. He would certainly not live to the next port, nor would Wallie. Then Wallie saw a way out.

"It was not perjury, Nnanji. It was simple, honest-to-Goddess truth. We are not free swords."

Nnanji turned to stare at him blankly.

"You told me there were three types of swordsmen. You missed one—mercenaries."

"Well, that's not really a type, lord brother. I mean the chance doesn't come up very often." Nnanji was ambivalent about mercenaries. Taking money to wage war was barely honorable. On the other hand, mercenaries could wallow in blood and feats of honor.

"Nevertheless, we are on a specific mission for the Goddess. Therefore we are mercenaries, not free swords! So the captain spoke the truth. Now shut up!"

"Yes, mentor."

Brota gave Wallie a long, hard look and then almost smiled. "You swear that, my lord?"

"By my sword."

She nodded, apparently satisfied.

Tomiyano marched in and pulled the door closed behind. He

leaned against it and glared at Wallie. Old Lina threw open a shutter on the River side, admitting gratifying light and fresh air.

"Thank you, Captain," Wallie said.

"He knew you were here!"

"Apparently."

"I think we should leave," Brota muttered. "I don't like this."

"Can't!" her son snapped. "No wind now. Calm as milk."

Wallie was not surprised. "I should prefer that you stay awhile, anyway."

Brota scowled. "You mean that? Why?"

"Because," Wallie said, "I have to learn more about sorcerers. The Goddess would not have given me an impossible task, so there must be some way to fight them. They must have a weakness. I can't guess what it is, and the only way to find out is to ask questions in places like this. How many more cities have been captured? When? How? Where is the nearest swordsman city? Those sorts of questions. You can find out for me, mistress; you and your crew. It will be a service to the Most High."

It might be a penance, also, but Wallie was not about to inquire about *Sapphire*'s cryptic past.

Tomiyano looked at his mother and she nodded. "I'll lay out some samples, then," he said grudgingly.

"Two questions," Wallie said. "You shook the port officer's hand. Was it smooth or calloused?"

"Smooth. Why?"

"Not a sailor's hand?"

The captain's eyes narrowed. "I expect his father is an elder, or something. He's just a playboy sailor. Never mind that—"

"Second question: have you ever in your life queried a tax for being too low?"

Tomiyano's face reddened. "What the demons does that matter? You saw and heard, didn't you? He knew about you. The sorcerers have told him."

"He *was* a sorcerer," Wallie said.

Facemarks were so basic to their culture that the idea took a while to sink in. Brota seemed to accept it first, and her shrewd eyes shrank to slits within their wrinkles. "Why do you say that?"

"Because he refused the extra money," Wallie said. "If that really is the custom, as he said?" She nodded. "So? He did that to persuade us that his masters were all-seeing, all-powerful. But he didn't act like a flunky being watched by his masters— he was amused, relaxed. And you can't buy that sort of higher loyalty, because he could take the extra salary and demand the graft, too. His hand is smooth. He is a sorcerer."

The others exchanged frightened glances.

"Well, we're here," Wallie said. "Go and do your trading. But remember that anyone may be a sorcerer, regardless of facemarks. I suggest you don't allow more than one stranger on board at a time."

"My lord brother?"

"Yes?"

"Sorcerers can make themselves invisible. The ship may be full of them already."

Wallie groaned. "Thanks, Nnanji. Good thinking."

†† † ††

A display of lumber and a few brass pots had been set up on the quay. Brota settled into a chair on deck and waited for customers. Sailors slipped down into the crowd and wandered off in search of information, river lore as well as military intelligence. Honakura went also, at his tortoise pace, and he was sure to be a shrewd investigator. Hawkers came by with carts, calling wares. Old Lina tottered down to haggle over pink plucked fowls and baskets of strawberries. From time to time sorcerers went by in pairs, paying no especial attention to *Sapphire*. The afternoon wore on, hot and airless.

Nnanji had gone back to sit by Matarro's bag of swords. He had scowled over each one in turn, finding them much shorter than he expected, and had finally pulled out his whetstone and started to sharpen them.

Vixini had gone to sleep. Jja and Cowie sat like sculptures, with slaves' unlimited patience. Wallie watched through the shutters.

"Mentor," Katanji said. "May I go out on deck?"

"No. Why aren't you wearing your sword?"

"My kilt is downst—below decks, in Mat'o's cabin."

Nnanji grunted and went back to whetting. Wallie did not interfere, although he saw no reason why Katanji should be imprisoned as he and Nnanji were. Katanji had no ponytail and his facemark was a festering red sore, almost unreadable even at close quarters.

Time passed. Nothing much happened. A trader sniffed disparagingly at Brota's lumber and walked on. The first two sorcerers went by again. Nnanji's whetstone scraped nastily and untiringly. Honakura wandered back past the ship to explore in the other direction. Katanji fretted, mooning from window to window. Wallie grew tired of standing, rolling his problems around in his mind until he was giddy. Always the answer was the same—he must have more information.

It was not fair! How could he wage a war unless he knew his enemies' powers? Military intelligence was what he needed. Mata Hari . . . George Smiley . . . In Thondi's house he had been a whodunnit detective. Now he found himself in a spy thriller, and the damnable facemarks of the People made it impossible. He needed to become, for a while, James Bond, or even Travis McGee. A few days as a longshoreman or a porter in Aus would let him uncover the data he needed, but he had seven swords indelibly engraved on his forehead.

Nnanji's whetstone made a tooth-jarring screech.

That did it.

Several times, Wallie had been forced to remember that emotions were not a mental process. In acquiring Shonsu's body, he had also acquired his glands. He had learned to look out for danger signals when he had his sword in his hand and adrenaline could be expected, but sometimes those glands could sneak up on him.

As now.

Frustration, impotence, the ignominy of hiding, even perhaps some residual jet lag, all suddenly boiled over. Wallie Smith lost Shonsu's temper.

"Hell!" he snapped. "I'm going ashore!"

Nnanji looked up approvingly. "Right!" he said, and put away his whetstone.

"You're staying here," Wallie told him. "You'll guard my sword and my hairclip. Katanji, go to Brota and ask her for some black cloth. Shut up, Nnanji."

Ten minutes later, he had stripped down to a piece of black burlap around his loins and a rag around his brow. He had never felt more naked, and his conscience was whimpering cautions at him, but it was too late to back down. He started for the door.

"My lord brother!" Clutching Wallie's harness and sword, Nnanji was glaring mutinously. "This is wrong! A swordsman without his sword is without his honor. You asked me to tell you—"

"Your objection is noted." Wallie stepped around him and marched out on deck.

Brota stood with fists on hips and looked him over without expression. "You're all beef and no brains. What are you trying to prove? It's stupid!"

Insolence! But he was not a lord of the Seventh when his head was bound. He walked by her without a word.

Jja stood at the top of the plank, pale and troubled. He smiled cheerfully and tried to get by her, also, but she stepped in his path and put her arms around him.

"Master, please? I know a slave should not say such things, but please do not do this! It is very dangerous."

"Danger is my business, Jja."

He kissed her forehead and eased her out of his way.

She clung to him. "Please . . . Wallie?"

She never called him that except when they were making love. He shook his head. "We must trust in the Goddess, darling."

He looked both ways for sorcerers. Not seeing any, he trotted down the plank and mingled into the pedestrians, settling to their pace. He had a good view over people's heads, and no one seemed to pay much attention to him, although he intercepted a few scowls that he found more puzzling than threatening. He strolled past display tables loaded with wares and guarded by traders; past hawkers' carts bearing piles of bright fruits, golden loaves, and heaps of bloody meat encrusted with flies; past stationary wagons with horses tossing their nose bags in a jingle of harness. He stepped out of the way of other wagons rumbling along; he jostled in and out of the crowd and was careful not to get his bare toes stepped on, or stub them on the cobbles. He scanned the litter of trade goods being loaded and unloaded. He began to enjoy himself.

The air was still; hot and sticky. The docks of Aus stank, but he was having fun.

Then he saw a couple of cowls approaching. Turning his back on them, he squeezed into a group around a hawker's cart where lumps of something were being roasted on a brazier and offered on sticks. The old man tending it gave him one of the scowls he had noticed and then muttered, "Here, then," and handed him a stick.

Now Wallie recalled that beggars also wore black and bound their heads. So the mighty Shonsu was a beggar, a big, husky beggar who should go and find an honest job? He suppressed a grin, thinking of his pocketful of jewels back at the ship. He bit into the offering and found it rubbery but delicious, hot and spicy. On a second mouthful he decided that it was octopus, or squid. Fresh-water octopus?

In return he mumbled a benediction: "May She strengthen your arm and sharpen your eye."

The scruffy old hawker recoiled in shock, and at once Wallie wished he could bite back his words, for that was a swordsman's blessing. The hawker was frowning—an athletic young man with long hair...

Wallie grinned. "As they say."

The hawker's eye flickered over Wallie's shoulder, to about the spot where the sorcerers might have reached. "Not any more," he whispered. "Not here." Then he shouted, "Be off with you!"

Wallie glanced round and the sorcerers had passed. He set off again through the crowd, chewing on his snack. He passed a ship unloading baskets of vegetables, another loading tiles. Then he stopped in surprise, causing a man behind to bump into him and curse. Just ahead was a large, two-horse wagon, parked by a small ship. Sacks from the wagon were being carried up the plank by a gang of youths, and the plank squeaked loudly with every step. Beyond it the dock was heaped with goods, mostly long rolls of cloth, with a few anonymous bales and bundles. In front of the plank, closer to Wallie, the rest of the ship's cargo had been spread out all over the ground, from ship to wagon: boxes and jars, but mainly copper and brass pots, shining bright in the sunshine.

What had caught Wallie's eye among this clutter were two large, snakelike copper coils. Studying the collection of pots, he identified a couple that were as big as garbage cans and had lids and narrow spouts at the top. Hypothesis: the coils fitted on top of the pots. That meant distillation.

Wine, yes; beer, yes; but he knew of no words for brandy or moonshine or spirits or alcohol. Was this sorcery? Excited by his discovery, he headed toward the ship.

And there was Tomiyano, talking to a sailor. He saw Wallie at the same moment as Wallie saw him, and his face blazed with rage. He broke off his conversation and strode over.

"What in hell are you doing, Shonsu?" he demanded in a low and furious voice.

"Snooping," Wallie said. "I am a Nameless One, though. Only swordsmen may search me."

The captain was not amused. "There's enough under that headband to kill you seven times over. You're endangering my ship!"

Perhaps he was, but Wallie smiled innocently. "No I'm not. Your ship is safer with me ashore. Now tell me, see those copper snakes? What are they, and what are they for?"

Tomiyano looked around reluctantly. "I've no idea," he said. "Come over here, out of sight."

He returned to the bottom of the plank, and Wallie followed, safely hidden from general view by the high-piled wagon. The gang of grubby adolescents and young men continued bearing sacks on board, many of them trailing a trickle of yellow dust behind them, while a blowsy woman leaned over the rail and counted on an abacus. The older sailor wore a captain's dagger and he was pulling sacks down from the wagon for his workers.

The ship's hull was shabby and badly in need of paint. It was a mean and dirty parody of the family ship that Wallie had left.

The captain was overweight, gray-haired, and looked both stupid and lazy, compared to the sinewy Tomiyano as their respective ships compared. He eyed Wallie suspiciously, but greeted Tomiyano's return as an opportunity to break off work once more and continue their chat. When the next adolescent came for a sack, Wallie hauled one down and loaded it on his back. Then he did the same for the others; that would keep the captain talking.

Wallie eavesdropped. Down from Aus were shoals, said the sailor, and beyond those the Black Lands—no cities and no people for two weeks' sailing. Captain Tomiyano should head up. Next city was Ki San, big and rich. No sorcerers there. Things had been slack in Aus ever since the sorcerers came. Ki San would pay more for luxury stuff like sandalwood. A big copper and brass city, Ki San. That was a natural opening for Tomiyano to ask about the coils—and the sailor closed like a constipated clam, an obstinate oyster. Coils he would not discuss.

Now Tomiyano's curiosity was aroused, also, and he went over to examine the mysteries. Wallie joined him. The tubing was made from soldered copper sheeting, but it was skillfully wrought, and when Wallie picked one up he had no trouble in attaching it to one of the two big pots. The lids were tight-fitting, and both pots were empty, but they could only be intended for distillation. The old sailor was nervous and trying to change the subject, although in answer to a direct question he admitted that the goods were headed for the tower. Tomiyano, obviously intrigued now and being helpful to his silent companion, offered to buy one and was emphatically turned down.

"What would a sailor want with those?" asked a high-pitched voice behind them.

Wallie spun around and found himself facing two sorcerers.

One of them was holding a silver fife.

Both were strangely bulky in their cumbersome garments. The taller was a man of about forty, wearing a Fourth's orange.

A thin, suspicious face showed from under his hood, and his arms were folded inside his sleeves.

The other was in brown and had three feather marks. He was plumper and younger. His lips were curled in an arrogant sneer, close to the mouthpiece of that slim silver tube. Three notes on one of those had been enough to kill Kandoru.

The remark had been addressed to Tomiyano, but both sorcerers were looking at Wallie.

Trickles of sweat ran cold on his ribs; he was trapped. On one side was the wagon and on the other the ship, with the sorcerers blocking the exit toward *Sapphire*. Behind him the way was obstructed by the litter of trade goods and the gangplank and the mountain of rolled cloth. He could think of at least three sutras that should have warned him, quite apart from common sense. Nnanji's honor, Brota's practicality, Jja's love —he had spurned them all and now must pay for his folly.

Worst of all, he did not know what dangers he faced. Could a man outrun a spell? Even if he were facing only knives or swords, he would have little hope of escaping by dodging and taking to his heels, although the sorcerers' gowns would impede them if it came to a chase. If all they had to do was blow into that fife, or they could chant some words to turn him into a charred corpse...

"Just curious, adept," Tomiyano said in a voice unusually humble. "We hadn't seen anything like them before."

"Curiosity is dangerous, sailor," the Fourth replied, without looking at him, "especially for swordsmen of the seventh rank. Would you not agree now... Wallie?"

††† †††

Impossible! Jja knew that name, and Honakura, and Nnanji. No one else in the World. Even had one of them been captured, there had been no time to extract information, by torture or... or by any means that Wallie could imagine.

Jja had spoken his name at the top of the gangplank. There

had been no one within earshot. Not even Brota could possibly have heard that. It had to be invisibility. Or telepathy.

But if the sorcerers had either of those abilities, then they were unbeatable.

"Oh, you do look worried!" The sorcerer smirked. "And you told Jja that you would trust in the Goddess?"

No one could have overheard that.

Wallie knew he had gone pale and he was struggling desperately to keep himself from trembling. Fear, yes. Fear of the unknown, more so. But mostly fury at his own utter brainlessness. Idiot!

"Move!" the Fourth snapped. "Move over there!" He nodded toward the plank.

The ship's captain was perhaps not as stupid as he seemed—he had fled up to the safety of his deck. Work had stopped.

Wallie hesitated, then shrugged and turned. He picked his way through the pots, halting when he reached the plank to look back at the sorcerer.

"The other side—against the ship!" the Fourth commanded in his squeaky voice.

Obediently Wallie moved to the edge of the dock and ducked under the plank.

The sorcerer nodded in satisfaction. "I don't like the smell of swordsmen." His laugh was as shrill as his voice.

The junior sorcerer grinned. "Take off that headband!" he ordered. He had folded his arms like his superior, and the flute had disappeared. Was that perhaps a short-range magic?

Wallie shook his head and spoke for the first time. "I am a Nameless One, serving the Goddess." His voice sounded steadier than he had expected.

"You are a swordsman of the seventh rank! And here we honor the Fire God. Take off that rag and tie your hair back."

Wallie obeyed in silence.

Why did both sorcerers now have their hands hidden inside their voluminous sleeves? They seemed to be holding something in there, either a weapon or some sort of magical charm, Wallie assumed. A knife would be bad enough, and he had no idea how to fight magic. Their eyes were cold in the shadow of their cowls, but they seemed more relaxed, now that their captive was farther away. Could that mean that their spells would take time to operate, and they needed distance between them and their victims? If so, then Wallie had already been outsmarted, for now he was even more hemmed in than before, by the drop to the water on one side, the rolls of cloth behind him, and the chest-high plank in front.

He glanced down. The fenders and the curve of the bow left a gap between the dock and the peeling wood of the ship. There was room enough to jump there, into the deceptively innocent water. On Earth he would not have hesitated, but here even in harbor the water was free of floating litter except for a few fragments of wood. He could no longer trust to the gods to recognize his ignorance and save him from the piranha. He had been warned—miracles were never performed upon demand. That way of escape was closed.

"Jump if you wish," mocked the senior sorcerer. "It will save me a spell and save the trouble of pushing you over afterward."

"I'll wait," Wallie replied, as calmly as he could manage.

The sorcerer sneered at him triumphantly. Then he spoke to his companion without taking his eyes off the swordsman. "We should deal with the sailor accomplice first."

"Leave him out of this!" Wallie shouted. "He never met me before today. I took his ship at sword point."

"He tells fibs, swordsman. The usual penalty for perjury is a mouthful of hot coals."

"He had no choice, adept! I was listening, in the deckhouse, with my sword at his sister's throat."

The Fourth hesitated. "I think you are lying, swordsman. But we shall be merciful. Show him what we use the kettles for, since he is so curious."

The Third moved toward Tomiyano, gliding through the copperware pots like a ghost, seeming not to touch the ground. He went very close, peering into the captain's eyes, causing him to step back warily, hard against the copper stills.

"So you want to know our business, do you?" The sorcerer sounded amused. He seemed the more confident of the two, and therefore by comparison the older sorcerer was not confident. That must mean there was hope—but where, and how?

Wallie could not see Tomiyano's face, only his back, but he could hear the anger in his voice: "I apologize. I did not know they belonged to you."

There was devilry brewing; the sorcerer's voice was mocking. "Well, pick one up, and I will show you."

"No," Tomiyano snapped.

The sorcerer snapped also: "Pick it up!"

The sailor put his hands on his hips. "No!"

The sorcerer muttered something and waved a hand before the captain's face. Tomiyano recoiled angrily; then he screamed and clutched at his cheek. He doubled over, cursing and stamping his feet.

Wallie clenched his fists and glanced at the Fourth. He was still watching the swordsman, apparently enjoying his impotent rage and fear.

Furiously Tomiyano straightened and grabbed for his knife.

It had vanished. The shock seemed to sober him; he turned a fear-filled face toward Wallie. He was pale with pain and there was a hideous burn at the side of his mouth. He was shaking his left hand as if the fingers hurt, also.

"Swordsmen cut off ears when people annoy them," the Third said. "We are not so barbarous, but we like to remember those who transgress. That will warn any of my brethren who meet you in future that you are not to be trusted. Now, Captain Tomiyano, pick up that kettle!"

A crowd was gathering at a respectful distance behind the sorcerers, and the sailors were watching from above. Tomiyano shot Wallie a glance of fury. He knelt and wrapped his arms around the big pot. It was not heavy, and he straightened up, turning again to face his tormentor.

"We use them, Captain, to breed birds in," said the Third. "You don't believe me? Look!"

He reached out and pulled off the lid. With a loud flutter, a white bird flew up into Tomiyano's face. Startled, he stepped back, tripped over a cauldron, and crashed to the ground in a clamorous rattle of metal and bouncing pots. The two sorcerers laughed heartily, and after a moment there was laughter from the sailor audience on the ship and also from the steadily growing crowd at the end of the wagon. Tomiyano rose shakily, while the bird circled away into the sky.

The junior sorcerer turned and floated back to the side of his superior, and they both looked across at Wallie.

"Now it is your turn, swordsman," the Fourth said in his high voice. Wallie's heart was racing, and he was wondering how long a spell took and how fast he could jump. He should have done it while the other was busy tormenting the sailor.

There was a pause, an agonizingly long pause, while sorcerers stared at swordsman, and swordsman stared back. Wallie kept his breathing slow and tried not to tense his muscles, but he was soon wishing that they would get on with whatever they planned.

"You were astonishingly stupid, Wallie," said the Fourth. "Even for a swordsman, you were very stupid."

"I don't dispute that," Wallie said. What was going on here?

The Fourth nodded faintly inside his cowl. "This is a very humble swordsman, Sorcerer Resalipi."

Studying the shadowed face, Wallie thought he saw beads of sweat on it—the man did not want to kill. Perhaps if Wallie were to attack them, he could do it; but killing in cold blood is not to everyone's taste. Wallie knew.

The brown hood turned toward the orange and whispered something inaudible. Was the Third offering to perform the execution?

"No, Resalipi," the Fourth said, "I think a humble swordsman could be instructive. I give you a choice, Lord Wallie. You can die now, or you can crawl back to your ship on your belly, as a demonstration of your humility."

Hope! Hope like a small flame rising in dead embers. Wallie Smith would rather crawl than die any day. "And then I and the ship may leave safely? You will give me your oath?"

Even that tiny show of resistance was almost enough to change the sorcerer's mind. "You are in no position to bargain!" he squeaked. Then the junior prompted him again. "Good idea! Know, swordsman, that we of the sorcerers' craft swear by fire. Take off that sack and throw it over."

Wallie hesitated for a fraction of a second as realization of what was coming began to dawn. Then he reached down to rip off his loincloth. He wadded it and threw it over the plank toward the sorcerers. As long as they played with him, he was still alive. He glanced ruefully at Tomiyano, watching in angry and surprised silence. He did not look at the crowd.

The Third glided forward and picked up the burlap, carried it back and dropped it in front of his superior, who held out a hand and mumbled something over it. It began to smoke, then burst into flames. Both men looked at Wallie to see if he was impressed, so he looked impressed.

"I so swear," the Fourth said. "Now—over there and lie down." He pointed at the bottom of the plank.

Again Wallie was momentarily tempted to refuse. The Shonsu part of him was rebelling violently at the thought of a swordsman humiliated. Naked except for the tie around his ponytail, feeling mortally ashamed and vulnerable, he walked to the place indicated, knelt, and then lay down, head raised to watch them.

The sorcerer stared at him for a minute, apparently surprised. "Well! Start crawling! If you stop, then you will die."

Wallie looked to his companion and even he was astonished. "I have a hot-blooded junior on board," he said. "Captain, please go back to the ship and warn them. Nail Nnanji to the mast if you have to. I want no more trouble."

"But tell him to watch," the junior sorcerer said. He laughed, and the captain jumped over some pots and ran.

"Crawl, swordsman!"

Wallie rose to his hands and knees.

"On your belly, I said!"

Wallie lowered himself flat and began to drag himself along the cold, lumpy, and incredibly foul road. They used a lot of horses on that road. He passed the litter of copperware and the end of the wagon, and the crowd parted for him.

He had only five ship-lengths to go.

It took about ten years.

"Keep your head up, swordsman!"

The sorcerers followed behind him, shouting to the crowd to make way for a swordsman. A corridor opened in front of him, a corridor lined with surprised, mocking faces and loud with ribald comment. He detoured around the piles of goods on the dock. He passed by the wheels of the hawkers' carts and the legs of the display tables. He told himself to be pragmatic—humiliation was greatly preferable to death.

The laughter started before he reached the end of the first ship. Then the throwing: filth and rotted fish and a few harder things.

"Keep your head up, swordsman!"

He saw bare feet and boots and sandals and then gowns that reached to the ground, so he knew that more sorcerers had arrived. The crowd told him to move faster and to be careful not to scrape anything off. The children started building an obstacle course with bales and boxes, so that he had to drag himself around them.

"Keep your head up, swordsman," said that high-pitched voice behind him. He had been mocked by a crowd before, when he was on his way to the Judgment of the Goddess, but then he had been Wallie Smith, a confused Wallie Smith and in pain. Now he was a swordsman of the Seventh and already accustomed to thinking of himself as such. Now the scorn cut deeper.

"Make way for a swordsman!"

The corridor of people and boxes twisted around until it led to a wagon, and he obediently crawled through underneath and was cheered when he emerged. He wondered what he was crawling away from—music? A white bird or a burning cloth? Perhaps the sorcerers had been bluffing all the time. Yet Kandoru had died. The garrison in Ov had died, and probably the garrison of Aus. The fat sailor had run up his gangplank.

He might not have made it at all had he not suddenly thought of Nnanji. Nnanji had denounced him to Imperkanni for using a disguise. Disguise was not honorable, but this—Nnanji could never forgive this. And Wallie had made the kid swear the fourth oath, *Your honor is my honor*. So he had destroyed Nnanji's honor as well as his own. Nnanji would kill him, strike him down unarmed as a reprobate, without as much as a warning . . . except that Nnanji in his own eyes would be a reprobate also and hence not have the right. Perhaps Nnanji was more likely to kill himself, proper behavior in a shame culture. Frantically Wallie scanned sutras. What was the World's equivalent of the Roman falling on his sword, or the Prussian officer cleaning his pistol? He could find nothing in the sutras to show that the Goddess expected *seppuku*. Swordsman slang, then: "He washed his sword." Of course.

Now he saw the full extent of his stupidity. Shonsu or Nnanji would never have gone ashore unarmed, but had either somehow been trapped as Wallie had been trapped, then he would have jumped from the dock. That had been what the sorcerers expected; probably what the gods expected, too. He should have had more faith. He had failed not once, but twice.

Nnanji valued his honor above all else in the World, and Wallie was literally dragging it in the dirt. There could be no forgiveness, no forgetting, no understanding. The fourth oath was irrevocable. He could not have been more cruel had he planned it, and it was entirely possible that he would arrive back at *Sapphire* to find Nnanji already dead. He was still frantically hunting for a solution when he realized that he had reached almost to the end of his torment and in worrying about his protégé he had been crawling automatically and had forgotten to listen to the jeering around him.

Sapphire's gangplank was in view: an oasis, the Holy Grail. He finished the distance and dragged himself onto the plank. He rose to his knees and then to his feet, waiting for some final treachery, but all he got was a derisive cheer from the onlookers.

He was filthy beyond words, scraped and shaking. He turned and looked at the sorcerers. He thought they were watching him with satisfied amusement, but it was hard to tell under the cowls. He nodded his head in a hint of a bow, then he spun round and walked up the plank.

One: Sorcerer sees swordsman. Two: Swordsman crawls.

But not end of story.

At the top of the plank a very pale Jja handed him a cloth, and he wrapped it around himself. They stared at each other in silence for a moment, and then he glanced around the deck. There were sailors there, and Brota and Thana, but there were no faces. No one was looking at him. He was invisible.

Except to Jja. Slaves were supposed to keep their eyes lowered. Jja never looked him in the face unless they were alone together.

"Only you!" he whispered. "Only you do not care about honor?"

"Honor? Honor to a slave?" She grabbed his arm and pulled him toward the fo'c'sle. Astounded, he let himself be led through the door and into a cramped shower cubicle, dark and smelling of mold. She pulled the wrap away from him and worked the pump handle, getting almost as wet as he did as he rubbed away the filth.

"Jja . . . I'm sorry," he said.

"Sorry? I told you!"

She was furious with him, terror turned to rage, and the transformation in a meek and obedient slave was more unexpected than all the sorceries he had witnessed.

"Where is Nnanji?" he asked.

"I have no idea!"

Clean at last, he clutched her and kissed her, and she tried to struggle against his vastly greater strength—and that was another sorcery—but he forced his kiss on her until she acquiesced and returned it. When they parted she stared at him again for a moment in the gloom and then burst into tears. He held her tightly, both of them soaking wet.

"You did tell me, my love, and I should have listened. I am very sorry."

She leaned her head against his chest and whispered, "No, it is I who must be sorry, master, for speaking to you so."

"You will never call me 'master' again! Never!"

"But . . ." She looked up in dismay. "What can I call you?"

"Call me 'lover' when I deserve it," he said, "and 'idiot' the rest of the time—and that is positively the last order I shall ever give you. Oh, Jja, you are the only sane person in the World, and I love you madly. Come. Let's go and see what we can rescue from this mess I've made."

She handed him his kilt and his boots. He ran a comb hastily through his hair and then braced himself to go out on deck once more in the stark, pitiless sunshine. Brota, Thana, Tomiyano, other sailors . . . still none of them was acknowledging his presence, the invisible swordsman. His appearance provoked a cheer from the dock. He did not look that way.

His hairclip and sword were in the deckhouse. He marched across. As he rounded the aft hatch cover, the door opened, and Honakura came out, very wearily, reminding Wallie of the stereotype of the kindly old country doctor leaving the sickroom. *You may go in now.* The old priest walked forward and tried to go by Wallie, who moved to block him.

"Well, old man?"

He looked up, his face giving nothing away. "That young man has a head like a coconut. I have never met a harder. But he understands now."

"I am very grateful, holy one."

The bleary old eyes seemed suddenly to flash. "I did not do it for you. You are a contemptible lunatic." The old man walked away.

Wallie went in and pulled the door closed.

Cowie was sitting on one of the chests at the far side, staring blankly into space. Nnanji stood in the middle of the floor, very pale . . . young and hurt and vulnerable. He was still holding the seventh sword in its scabbard, the straps and buckles of the harness dangling. Wallie walked over to him. He should have prepared something to say, but for a moment he could only stare at the strangely bruised look in Nnanji's colorless eyes.

"The gods are cruel, my lord brother."

"Nnanji . . ."

"I could not have done it."

That was absurd. *I could not have displayed such cowardice, and therefore you have more courage than I have?* Some of Honakura's contorted logic, no doubt.

"Nnanji, I am sorry."

Nnanji shook his head sadly. "The gods are cruel. 'When the mighty has been spurned'? The old man explained that you had to suffer that, brother . . . but I could not have done it. Not even for the Goddess Herself." He looked as if he wanted to comfort Wallie with a hug.

"Oh . . . Oh, hell!" That cute little solecism might excuse Wallie's behavior to Nnanji, but it was a lie. He could not hide behind such deception, no matter how hateful the truth. "I did not think of the riddle. It never entered my mind. I crawled because I did not want to die."

Nnanji closed his eyes and shivered.

"It was the way of honor in my other world." There was no way Wallie could ever reconcile a shame culture and a guilt culture. The ways of thinking were too unlike. But he had to try—try to show Nnanji that what he had done was not such an atrocity to him. "I had broken a law. I paid the penalty. It hurt no one but me, you see. It was better than dying, I thought. I told you I was doing my best in this world . . . but I warned you. I said that I was not really a swordsman."

"Uh!" Nnanji shook his head as if to clear it and turned away to hide his face. "But the gods must have known that you would do that thing."

"I suppose so. Perhaps I should have jumped. Perhaps She would have let me . . . return safely." There was no easy word for swimming.

Moments crawled by. Crowd noises drifted in from the dock.

"I did warn you, Nnanji. That first day, when we sat on the wall in the temple gardens . . ."

"'I am not one of those heroes you find in epics.' I remember."

"I can't release you from the fourth oath. It is irrevocable. But the second has lapsed, if that is what you want. We remain oath brothers, but we need never meet again. At the next port you can leave."

After another moment, Nnanji turned around and straightened his bony shoulders. "No. I also have a part to play. The old man still thinks so. I will stay." He held out Wallie's hairclip.

Surprised and gratified, Wallie took it and scooped his hair back to fasten. "It may not be for very long. The little god warned me—punishment for failure is death, or worse. Honakura may be mistaken about the riddle. I may have screwed everything up. So it may not be for very long."

Nnanji swallowed hard. "Worse? You have been punished already, then. Maybe not . . . And it was my fault, too, brother!"

"Never! What do you mean?"

"You told me to warn you when you were making a mistake. Taking off your sword—"

"You did warn me. I ignored you."

Nnanji drew the seventh sword.

Wallie's heart skipped a beat and then began working a little harder than usual. He was unarmed. Nnanji with a naked sword in his hand was a matter to consider very carefully.

"I could have stopped you, brother," he said softly.

Wallie said nothing. In the dimness of the deckhouse, light flashed from the deadly blade as Nnanji twisted it to and fro, looking down at it pensively. "I should have stopped you. But you were Her champion."

Were? One thing certainly had died this day—Nnanji had been brutally cured of his hero worship.

Then he looked up at Wallie and forced a thin smile—as insubstantial as dust, a smile that registered much more wry than joyous.

"Are," he said. "Her champion, I mean." He held out the scabbard and harness. He retained the sword.

Very uneasy now, Wallie took the harness and began buckling it on, wondering what was happening under that red hair.

"I hope I still am. But I don't feel like a champion today."

Again Nnanji looked down at the sword in his hand, watching the play of light on the sapphire, the silver, and the razor steel. "Do you remember the last thing Briu said, my lord brother?"

"No."

"The last-but-one thing. He said, 'I suppose we must keep trying to do better.'"

Perhaps Nnanji was regretting his change of mentors.

No; he stared calculatingly at Wallie for a moment, and then went down on one knee. He held out the seventh sword in both hands, proffering it. He said solemnly: "Live by this. Wield it in Her service. Die holding it."

It was the ceremony of dedication. The sutras required it for a recruit's first sword, but the swordsmen applied it to any new blade. Nnanji was using it for a rededication—a renewal, Shonsu reborn. But it also meant *friendship*, for when a swordsman acquired a new sword he would ask his best friend to give it to him. So it meant forgiveness and reconciliation, affirmation and a fresh start. It meant: "Be a swordsman now." It was full of squishy swordsman romanticism that was typical of Nnanji and now felt absurdly reassuring and right.

Angry at the childish lump in his throat, Wallie spoke the reply: "It shall be my honor and my pride."

He took the sword and smiled at Nnanji as he rose. "Thank you, brother. I shall try to do better."

Nnanji did not return the smile. He said softly, "So shall I."

They both swung around as the door opened.

"Master!" Jja said urgently. "The ship is about to leave. Novice Katanji is not on board."

††† † †††

Nnanji was almost at the door when Wallie's hand closed like a lion's jaw on his shoulder. "Bad tactics, brother!"

"Oh, right!" Nnanji said.

So he remained to fret unseen, and it was Wallie who marched out to investigate. Ironic cheers from the dock greeted him. Lumber and pots had been retrieved and untidily piled on the deck. The wind had returned. Hands stood at lines, Brota was at the tiller, and two men were already stooping to take hold of the gangplank. They straightened up angrily as Wallie's boot came down on it.

One of them was Tomiyano, and his eyes spat fire at Wallie. The burn on his left cheek was black and cracked like charred alligator hide. Even under a thick wad of grease, it had to be hurting like hell. His voice was slurred as he tried not to move that side of his mouth. "What the demons are you doing now, swordsman?"

"Our First is still ashore."

"The bag-heads told us to leave," the captain mumbled. "You going to go argue with them?"

"I suppose I must." Wallie stepped out on the plank, and the crowd hushed at once.

There were eight or nine sorcerers down on the dock now. They had closed off the roadway from the water across to the warehouses, and spectators massed behind the cordon on both sides. There were people leaning from the warehouse windows and people precarious on wagons and people in the rigging of the nearby ships, apparently assembled to view this unobtrusive scouting mission by the Shonsu expedition, sneaking unnoticed around Aus.

The Fourth with the squeaky voice was still there, but a Fifth now stood beside him, an impersonal red monk with a blotch of shadow instead of a face—so the *Sapphire* affair was bringing out the big fish. Katanji might be miles away, but hopefully he was somewhere close, trapped in one crowd or the other with empty roadway between him and the gangplank. His facemark had been a suppurating mess, but it would not stand a close scrutiny.

Wallie paraded down the plank with all eyes on him, his skin tingling in expectation of some unpredictable supernatural attack. He stopped a foot from the end, folded his arms, and stared across at the Fourth and Fifth.

"I would speak with you, Adept Sorcerer," he called. The two cowled heads, one red and one orange, turned toward each other, conferring for a few moments. Then the Fourth came slowly forward and stopped a few feet away, out of sword range from the plank. The cold eyes stared out of the cowl.

"What more do you want, swordsman?" asked the squeaky voice.

Wallie tried to read the thin features. There was something new there—less triumph? Resentment? A reprimand, perhaps?

"I wished to thank you for sparing my life, adept. Indeed, I would shake your hand if you would allow it." *Of course, if you can read my mind, you'll see what I am doing is distracting you and your friends.*

"Shake hands with a sorcerer? Have you asked any swordsmen to shake your hand yet, Shonsu?"

Hurry, Katanji!

Shonsu!

"You did not know me by that name earlier, sorcerer."

A flush swept over the shadowed face. "That is not true!"

Wallie had not planned to do more than create a diversion. To rouse the sorcerers' ire further might be dangerous folly—but instructive. He smiled. "You are lying, adept!"

The sorcerer bared his teeth. "No! It would have been fun to have carried out the original sentence, but this way is better. We shall have no further trouble from you now. You might have displayed heroism, which could have been dangerous. Your friends will be impressed by this."

Original sentence? Tell me more!

"No, adept. You were being merciful, and I appreciate that. Again I offer you my hand."

"Again I spurn it. My masters' patience is not unlimited. Only my oath has protected you this far. Get back on that ship, Shonsu! You will have more crawling to do when you return to your nest."

Out of the corner of his eye, Wallie saw someone break out of the crowd and come running along the edge of the dock. He dared not turn. The sorcerers' cowls must restrict their peripheral vision hopelessly.

Where is my nest? You know more about Shonsu than I do.

"Well, I hope that your leniency has not caused you trouble." It had—the sorcerer colored again.

Someone jumped up on the plank behind Wallie and ran up to the deck. Wallie turned, as if surprised, and caught a glimpse of Katanji's skinny form, breechclout tail flapping.

"Who was that?" the sorcerer squeaked.

Wallie shrugged. "Some sailor brat. Well, I bid you farewell, adept. The Goddess be with you. The next sorcerer I meet, I shall spare for your sake."

"It is the next swordsman you need worry about, Shonsu!" The sorcerer turned and swept away.

Wallie started back up the plank, beginning to shiver with the release of tension. But the sorcerer had been correct. Now that he was known by name, Shonsu's reputation had gone to much less than zero. How could he ever earn an army now?

"Invisibility," Wallie said. "It has to be."

He stood beside the starboard poop steps with an arm around Jja. Honakura sat halfway up, at eye level for once, a tatty black monkey with his elbows resting on his knees. Nnanji leaned against the rail with one boot on the bottom step, looking bleak as tundra. His eyes were dull, as if somehow turned inward. At his side Novice Katanji, restored now to proper swordsman dress, was being small and humble and inconspicuous, waiting for the skies to fall when his brother got him alone—or sooner, if Lord Shonsu chose to pull them down personally. The other two were in the deckhouse, Cowie caring for Vixini or possibly vice versa.

Aus was sliding away into the distance, *Sapphire* starting to roll as the wind blustered in mid-River. The sun rode high yet, and the evening was far from over. Being champion for the Goddess was exacting work—in the first three days of his mission, Wallie had managed to antagonize two cities' worth of sorcerers, the entire swordsmen's craft, and a shipful of sailors. And perhaps the gods themselves.

The sailors were the most important at the moment.

And in return he had learned . . . what?

He had described what he had seen—a burning rag, a bird appearing, a dagger disappearing, an inexplicably scorched sailor. Add in the stories from Ov, stories of magic fifes and rampaging fire demons. Add in the tales Nnanji had recounted from the temple barracks. Yet worse than what he had seen was what he had heard.

"I thought perhaps they could tell people's thoughts," he said—Shonsu had known no word for telepathy. "Listen to our minds? But we can rule that out, because I fooled them when I was covering for Katanji; they didn't know what I was thinking then. So it has to be invisibility. When Jja spoke to me, there was a sorcerer standing beside us."

Honakura sighed. "And how many on board now?"

"Who can say? Keep talking and we may hear them start to laugh."

Nnanji lifted his head and began looking around, as if counting invisible sorcerers. Or perhaps he was watching the sailors. They had almost finished tidying up the deck, and the glances they directed at the passengers from time to time bore a nasty flavor of menace. Tomiyano had run up the other steps to the poop, going to talk to his mother at the tiller. He had replaced his stolen dagger.

"My mind chokes when I ask it to swallow invisibility," the old man complained. He had not previously heard Nnanji tell Tarru's story of the sorcerer on the donkey, the first mention of the subject, so Nnanji had repeated it for him. Honakura bared his gums in a hideous scowl.

Wallie agreed. "Mine, also. But I can see no other explanation. Perhaps . . . if my folly in going ashore had any value at all, it was in giving me a chance to talk with sorcerers. And I learned that much. So my stupidity was not a total loss."

"Why not invisible swordsmen?" Nnanji remarked glumly. "Make me invisible, my lord brother, and I'll clean up Ov and Aus for you."

He would, too—and enjoy doing it.

Tomiyano came down the steps and hurried to the far end of the deck. Sailors, men and women, clustered around him like a huddle of children plotting mischief.

"Honorable Tarru's story could have another explanation," Honakura mused. "The sorcerers may be able to alter face-marks. Then the man on the donkey just became a tanner or a serf, or something."

"I had seen that," Wallie said patiently. The old man could not adjust to the idea of a swordsman using brains.

"And that would explain the fake port officer, too, if you were correct in believing that he was a sorcerer."

"That also! But facemarks cannot explain how they over-heard Jja and me. There must have been a sorcerer on deck."

Honakura sighed. "Yes. And if I could change my shape, I suppose I should choose to look much like that port officer—young and beautiful. Would you love me then, Jja?"

"He was very handsome," Jja said tactfully. She smiled and reached up to kiss Wallie's cheek. "But I love only swordsmen."

"One swordsman," Wallie said.

"One big, strong swordsman."

He kissed her for that. It was a long time since they had shared the feather bed in the royal suite of the temple barracks, a long time when a man had a body as lusty as Shonsu's. Already the temple was beginning to feel like the good old days.

There was trouble brewing among the crew. The surreptitious glances were now revealing amusement. Something had been decided, and the word was being passed. Wallie's disgrace had changed their fear into contempt. The captain had been disfigured for life, the ship itself put in danger. Whatever the cause of the sailors' original hostility, they had valid reasons now to resent these swordsman intruders—and less cause to fear the Goddess. Champions do not crawl in the mire.

"Next topic," Wallie said. "How did they know I was on board? The port officer did. I went into the deckhouse before I was visible from the shore—I'm sure of that. My eyes are as good as any, and I couldn't make out the people on the quay."

Honakura's wrinkles writhed as he screwed up his monkey face in thought. "We thought they could send messages, my lord. The sorcerers at the quarry saw you board a blue ship. I didn't see many blue ships in Aus." In an illiterate World, of course, ships did not bear their names emblazoned on their stems.

"Possible," Wallie said. "Although I am convinced that the sorcerers did not know me as Shonsu. Not at first. Thondi would have told them my name, but that message did not get transmitted all the way to Aus. Someone in the crowd recognized me." He was distinctive. Big swordsmen were rare.

"Then they can see at a distance," the priest said. "They saw that the bridge was down, but perhaps not that swordsmen had crossed it. Then sorcerers from both sides met at the ruined bridge . . . That would fit! That was why they were so long in following us to the quarry!"

"Possibly," Wallie conceded. "And they saw me on board as *Sapphire* came into port? Possible, possible!"

The sailors were spreading unobtrusively around the aft end of the deck. The children had been taken below. Nnanji straightened and reached up as if to feel that his sword moved freely. Just in time he changed the gesture into one of gripping the nearest mainstay and leaning against it. He could recognize danger from civilians now—he was growing more tense by the minute.

"You are amassing an impressive list of your opponents' powers, my lord," Honakura remarked. There was enough cynicism in his tone that Nnanji flashed him an irritated glance.

"So what did you learn, old man?" Wallie asked.

"Very little, I admit. I could see nobody watching the ship. I saw you come down the plank and then I saw two sorcerers go after you, but I did not see where they came from. They had not passed me."

Wallie grunted. Had those two been invisible until then? Invisible men on that tumultuous dock road would have been trampled to death in minutes. So had they been invisible on board *Sapphire* and then followed him ashore?

"The locals were reluctant to discuss sorcerers with a stranger," Honakura said crossly. "Naturally. But I did learn that they have been there a long time—ten years or more."

"Ten years?" Wallie had not expected that. "How many more cities have they seized, then?"

"I don't know."

A small voice said, "My lord?"

"Yes, novice?"

"With respect, my lord, it was eleven years ago, Swordsmen's Day, 27,344."

"Indeed?" Wallie said. "Who told you that?"

The boy colored slightly. "A wench, my lord. She was selling perry in mugs. She had a swordsman fathermark."

Wallie felt a smile escape him. He glanced at Nnanji, who frowned warily.

"Was the perry good?"

Katanji grimaced. "Horrible, my lord. It was the fathermark; I don't like perry."

This time Wallie laughed, in spite of the tension building around the deck. "What else did she tell you, then, after you had complimented her on her excellent perry?"

Gathering confidence, Katanji said: "Her father was killed by the sorcerers, my lord, so I didn't think she would betray me, although she noticed my facemark. They didn't use fire demons here. The garrison was hosting their annual banquet and the sorcerers came. They sent in a challenge."

"And the swordsmen would all be two-thirds drunk—or four-thirds. What happened?"

"They all ran out the front door, waving their swords and . . . and shouting, my lord. She said the sorcerers slew them by calling down thunderbolts."

"Thunderbolts?" That was new.

"A flash of lightning," Katanji said solemnly, "and a clap of thunder. As each one came out, he was struck down. It wasn't like Ov. They weren't torn to pieces or chewed, my lord. Almost no marks on the bodies at all, she said. A few burns, but almost no blood."

And from another wisdom gain . . . "Go on!" Wallie said.

"Then the sorcerers ordered everyone out, checking for survivors hiding among the guests, she said. They found a couple trying to climb out a back window and they killed them, too. Then the sorcerers burned down the hall to make sure. Eighteen died, the whole garrison. And she thought about another dozen had come to town since and been killed, at various times, my lord."

"*Very* well done!" Wallie said. "Nnanji, I think you should overlook the matter of going ashore without permission."

Nnanji nodded, grinning proudly.

Katanji looked relieved. "The sorcerers have driven out the dyers."

"They've done *what*?"

"All the dyers have left town. The woman did not know why, but it has raised the price of textiles, and clothes." He glanced over at the crew. "And leather . . . I thought the sailors might be interested."

Nnanji growled. "Never mind that! What else that matters?"

"That's about all . . . Oh, my lord? The next city up is Ki San, and there are no sorcerers there. But the next one on this side is Wal, and there are. Are sorcerers, I mean. She didn't know about any other towns, not even Ov."

The People did not travel much, except for traders and sailors and minstrels. There were no newspapers or TV stations.

"You have done very well, novice! That is excellent information. And you uncovered all that in very little time."

Katanji flushed, obviously very pleased with himself and enjoying the praise. "I didn't have time to talk with anyone else, my lord."

"Nnanji, you will instruct your protégé in sutras seven seventy-two, seven eighty-three, and seven ninety."

Nnanji nodded—those dealt with military intelligence and espionage. "And eight hundred and four, my lord brother!" He grinned briefly—cats.

"However," Wallie said, "that facemark of yours will heal properly in a few days, novice. I don't suppose that we shall be sailing back into Aus again, but if we do, you will not try that same trick again, is that clear?"

"Of course, my lord," Katanji said, not quite humbly enough to stop Nnanji scowling at him suspiciously. Then he was distracted. The shapely Thana had come out of the fo'c'sle door and been greeted by broad grins. Was this what the sailors had been waiting for? She was not wearing her sword. There were no weapons in sight except for the captain's dagger.

"So?" Honakura remarked. "You think that now the mighty has been spurned and you have gathered wisdom from another? What about earning armies and turning circles?"

Wallie glared at him. "You tell me!"

"It is your riddle, my lord."

"Yes, but you've seen something, haven't you?"

"I think so." The old man leered. "It was something you said yourself, my lord, but it seems so obvious that I hesitate to—"

"Trouble!" Nnanji said.

Thana was holding two foils and two fencing masks and she was heading aft, toward the swordsmen.

"Adept Nnanji?" She stopped alongside the mainmast, slim and ravishing and still clad in only the two skimpy strips of yellow cotton. She smiled endearingly. "You promised me a fencing lesson?"

Nnanji gulped audibly. "How can I fight facing that?" he whispered.

Wallie had other worries. "It's some sort of trap. For gods' sakes, check her foil before you start." That notion did not come from the sutras or from Shonsu's swordsman instincts—Shonsu would never have thought of that sort of treachery. Shonsu had never seen *Hamlet*, Act V.

Nnanji shot him a look of incredulity. "And anyway there isn't room to draw, let alone fence!" He glanced up at the more open area of the poop deck. That would still be small.

Wallie shook his head. "See how short those foils are? And this is where the fight would be if pirates boarded, so it makes sense to practice here."

The largest clear space on *Sapphire*'s main deck was before the mainmast, where Thana was standing, but it was minuscule by a landlubber's standards, cramped between the dinghies and the forward hatch. The crew were spread all around it, waiting with unconcealed glee.

"Delighted, Apprentice Thana." Nnanji did not sound convincing.

"Let me hold your sword," Wallie said, thinking of all those overhead ropes. "And don't underestimate her!"

Again Nnanji registered disbelief—he might be suspicious of trouble, but he obviously did not doubt his ability to outfence a female Second. Wallie was not so sure. The swordsmen sported very long swords, as long as a man could possibly manage with one hand, and they were fond of flamboyant leapings and swashbuckling strokes that would certainly not work on shipboard.

Nnanji glanced overhead, drew his sword carefully, and handed it to Wallie. He paced over to inspect the foils Thana was offering. Frowning, almost as if she had guessed Wallie's warning, she held out both and let him choose. He obviously liked neither, but he took one and tried a few swings with it. Then he stepped to the center of the cramped space and turned to face her. They donned their masks.

"Best of seven, adept?"

Nnanji lowered his foil. "I thought this was a lesson, apprentice?"

"Of course, adept. Foolish of me." She guarded at quarte.

"Try that a little higher," Nnanji's mask said. "Better. Now?"

Thana lunged, Nnanji recovered and fell flat on his back on the hatch cover. Thana shouted, "One!" The crew howled.

He lasted a fraction longer on the next passage, standing his ground as well as he could while the blades whirled. But then he started to recover again and either he was uncertain what was behind him, or the effort of remembering spoiled his concentration. A cut to the head connected. "Two!"

He had overlooked the possibility of jumping up on the hatch cover, which would have given him more room, but then Nnanji had never seen pirate movies. On the third pass he attacked furiously and managed to gain ground. Thana recovered easily, backing away between the mast and the stays. It was fast and devilish close-in work, quite unlike the style Nnanji was used to. He caught his foil in the shrouds, and Thana jabbed him in the ribs. "Three!"

The crew was screaming like an aviary of parrots. Wallie was clenching his teeth and cursing through them at the same time. If Thana was a Second then the water rats judged rank much harder than landlubbers, but he was impressed with the swordsmanship being displayed and thinking that he wouldn't mind some of that close-in practice for himself.

The ship rolled . . .

"Four!" Thana yelled triumphantly. She pulled off her mask and capered about, taking bows and being loudly cheered.

Scarlet-faced, Nnanji slunk back to his friends like a whipped dog, still holding his foil and his kilt, and mask. He had been gone about three minutes. Avoiding his mentor's eye, he leaned forward against the rail as if he were about to double over and throw up.

The unwelcome guests had been shamed at their own game. After the fun would come the business.

Tomiyano sauntered across, jumped up on the aft hatch cover, and put fists on hips. Three sailors slipped by behind him to stand opposite the visitors—close to fire buckets.

"We're going to put you off at the first jetty, Shonsu. You can walk from there."

Nnanji straightened and turned around.

The ship had crossed the River and was skirting the bank at a safe distance. Wallie saw farms. There would be jetties. "I remind you, Captain," he said with faked calm, "that I paid our fare to the first port at which I can enlist a band of swordsmen."

The sailor sneered lopsidedly. "Who would serve under you, Shonsu? The first swordsmen you meet will put you on trial for cowardice. The contract can never be fulfilled. You're going ashore, and good riddance!"

To call a swordsman a coward must lead to blood as surely as lightning led to thunder. Tomiyano might be seeking to provoke a fight so he could kill the passengers, gaining the seventh sword and whatever else of value they possessed. The absence of the children was ominous. However, the adolescents like Matarro were present, so probably bloodshed was not the main intention. But it was certainly being offered as an option.

It was not an option Wallie could accept. Nnanji had just

been shown up as useless under shipboard conditions, and even Shonsu could not prevail against a blizzard of flying knives.

Nor, even if his pride would allow it, could he appeal to Brota, for she had been informed in advance and so must have agreed. He could acquiesce and go ashore, relying on the Goddess to prevent the ship from leaving, but obviously the sailors were no longer worried about divine intervention, and Wallie thought they were probably right. He must not demand more help from that quarter. He had been given *Sapphire* as a man might be given a cantankerous steed, and it was up to him to ride her. In epics, heroes never fell off.

To go ashore meekly now would be to resign his commission—he felt certain of that. It might be another test, or the start of punishment. But there was absolutely no satisfactory way out.

And Nnanji was waiting to see what he would do. *Be a swordsman now!*

Wallie still held Nnanji's sword. "Catch!" he shouted and threw it, hilt first. Tomiyano caught it like a circus juggler. The other sailors reached hands down to the buckets and then froze.

"What the hell?" the captain demanded furiously.

Wallie took the foil and mask from Nnanji's nerveless hands, ignoring his startled stare.

Again he shouted, "Catch!" He threw the mask.

Tomiyano dodged. It struck the shrouds, fell, and clattered away across the deck.

"What the demons are you doing?" he roared.

"As you please." Wallie walked forward to the edge of the hatch. "Sailor Tomiyano, I, Shonsu, swordsman of the seventh rank, do hereby empower you as a posse for the purpose of resisting a passenger, armed with a foil."

"What? You're crazy!"

"We'll see."

"What are you playing at?"

Wallie sprang up on the hatch cover. "Sailor, you are an insolent dog. You are about to be whipped. Guard!"

He leaped forward and struck with the foil. Tomiyano parried and instinctively riposted. Wallie parried that and lunged. In the background, Nnanji's voice said, *"Devilspit!"*

Clang-clang-clang . . . For a few moments Wallie summed him up. He was fast and he had some very good routines. Much better than Thana. About a Sixth, maybe? Then Wallie got down to business. He smashed the foil across the sailor's chest, raising a red welt. The captain swore, lunged, was parried. On Wallie's riposte, the foil button ripped a strip across the sailor's ribs. Then Wallie deliberately bloodied his nose; it was dangerous to strike so close to his eyes, but it would hurt. The torrent of blood was very satisfying.

Recovering before the onslaught, Tomiyano jumped down backward from the hatch cover. Wallie followed and drove him in fast reverse around his own deck, thrashing and cudgeling without mercy.

And why had he embarked on this insanity? Not just to impress Nnanji. Nor the sailors. He was signaling to the gods: *Here is my flesh, and there is a sword. If my life is forfeit, take it. If sentence has been passed, then carry it out.*

Foil against sword was an impossible handicap. Tomiyano could take risks that Wallie could not, for all he would suffer was another welt, while Wallie's first miscalculation would be his last. He must also hit hard, while Tomiyano was wielding Nnanji's sword, and none could ever be better sharpened—it would cut flesh as easily as air; a touch could be fatal.

Yet Wallie had two advantages. It was astonishing how much Shonsu's muscles could accelerate that foil within a few inches of movement, how hard he could hit with it. And, although the captain was astonishingly good, Shonsu was the best in the World.

There was no contest. It was a massacre.

And the crew could do nothing. Their captain was in no real danger. They could hardly intervene unless he called for help. And Tomiyano would not call for help when the odds were so much in his favor—Wallie had judged his man correctly.

There was no sound but the rasping of breath, the strident clamor of metal, and the steady pounding of Wallie's boots as he stamped, left foot following right. Horrified sailors scrambled clear as the butchery came their way. He had done this before—Shonsu knew how to fight on a ship's deck. His style of fighting had changed completely. Neither the clutter nor the moving deck impeded him at all.

Foil and sword whirled in noisy silver fog. Tomiyano backstepped almost as fast as he could go, parrying as well as he could, never connecting. Wallie followed relentlessly, knocking the man's offense aside as if he were a paralytic, shredding his defense like paper. Soon both men were gasping and sweating, but the captain was also pouring blood. His back and chest and ribs were battered and skinned, as if he had been flogged.

"That'll do!" Wallie panted. "Throw down the sword."

But the fight went on.

Tomiyano was a proud man. He would not quit. He would not call for help. He had tried everything he knew and been thrashed in spite of it, and still he would not quit.

Wallie stopped striking and continued to parry.

"I said to drop that sword!"

Still Tomiyano was trying to kill his opponent. Their mad progression around the deck had ended, and his strokes were slower and shaky, but he was not going to quit.

Wallie would have to break his collarbone. "Last chance, sailor!"

Suddenly the captain switched to a two-handed grip and made a hard, long, slow downward cut like a scythe stroke or a golf swing. Wallie made an easy parry and the sword cut through his foil and his kilt, and severed his femoral artery. *Impact!*

He lay on his back, staring up at two triumphant, pain-maddened eyes behind a blade drawn back for the *coup de grâce*, stark against a whirling brightness of sails and sky, and he heard only the thunder of his own heart as it sprayed his life out in a scarlet fountain. Time was frozen into eternity. No one breathed. Then the sailor cursed and turned away, removing the sword.

Wallie tried to sit up, and someone turned out all the lights.

BOOK THREE:

HOW ANOTHER BORE THE SWORD

†

Nnanji was reviewing the sutra "On Staunching Blood" as he jumped forward, but a sailor was there before him, with his thumbs already pressed in Shonsu's groin. Thana arrived with a bucket of water—obviously the riverfolk knew what to do when there were no healers around. And one did not package fish food.

So he let them tend the wounded swordsman and contented himself with pulling Jja out of the way. She was accomplishing nothing except getting herself covered with blood. Brota's shadow fell over Shonsu as she knelt down to take charge, and she seemed to be capable.

"He'll need a warm bed," he told Jja as he led her back toward the deckhouse. "There are blankets in those chests."

They reached the doorway and were met by a strange wailing noise. It was coming from Cowie, who must have emerged to watch the fight. She had done this howling before, he remembered angrily—what an error she had turned out to be! He slapped her face. She reverted at once to her normal silent blankness. Jja pushed past her.

The priest was still sitting on the steps, looking a thousand years old, totally shocked.

"You all right, old man?" Nnanji demanded. Honakura nodded and then took hold of himself and smiled.

Katanji . . .

"Catching flies, novice?"

162

"Er, no!"

"No, *what*?"

"No, mentor."

"Then close your mouth and stand up straight."

Responsibility, Shonsu had said.

Brota's voice came from inside the huddle: "He's coming round. Put that hilt between his teeth . . . needlecase . . ." Yes, she knew what she was doing.

Nnanji took a deep breath and glanced around. The mood had changed. Even river riffraff must appreciate the show of swordsmanship they had just seen—incredible! They couldn't feed a champion like that to the fish, and now it seemed like they didn't want to. So he could relax a little, wait for Shonsu to come round. But he needed his sword; he headed forward again in search of the captain.

Tomiyano was leaning against the rail, barely able to stand from the look of him. An elderly woman was fussing beside him, trying to dab at him with a towel. He was resisting her attentions, holding a rag to his bleeding nose with one hand and clutching Nnanji's sword in the other. His eyes were bleary with pain and he was still choking for breath, one big mess of bruises and welts and scrapes, from sweat-matted hair to feet soaked in Shonsu's blood.

For a civilian, he'd put up quite a fight, perhaps the best fight Nnanji had ever seen. Even if Shonsu had pulped him, the sailor had managed to parry many of the strokes, and even one would have been a feat against Shonsu. He'd stayed upright, which spoke in trumpets for his toughness. Considering the punishment he had taken, it was amazing he was still on his feet now. He forced his eyes back into focus when he saw Nnanji, and the woman retreated apprehensively.

Nnanji held out a hand. "May I have my sword back please, captain?"

Tomiyano took the rag away from his face and raised the sword so that the point was almost touching Nnanji's navel. The sailor's arm was shaking, which was hardly surprising, and the needle point wavered before its target. "What will you do with it, sonny?"

"Sheath it, sailor."

They continued to glare at each other for several minutes.

Blood trickled from the captain's battered nose and oozed from his scrapes. If the sailors were pirates and planning to feed Shonsu to the piranha, then now was the moment, and Nnanji would be getting his sword back point first. But it was not the first time he had been threatened with a sword, and there was nothing else to do but wait and see, so he waited. His hand was steady—it was the captain who was shaking. Other sailors were watching. This was important.

The two of them seemed to stand there for a long time, while the sailor's breathing gradually slowed, but eventually Nnanji felt the challenge reverse itself—instead of the sailor inquiring whether he was afraid of the sword at his belly, he himself was inquiring whether the sailor was afraid to return it. Finally Tomiyano lowered it, wiped the blade with the cloth, and held it out hilt first.

Nnanji took it, sheathed it, and said, "Thank you."

He walked away.

That had gone rather well.

The huddle around the wounded man was still there, so he headed for the deckhouse to see if the slave had got the bed ready . . . and by the door he came face to face with Honakura again. The old relic had apparently recovered from his shock—he was smiling in an irritating manner.

"Well, old man? Have you an explanation for this also?"

"Explanation is like wine, adept," the priest said. "Too much of it in one day can be harmful."

Damned slippery priest-talk! "It can also be like my mother's homemade bread: very good when new, but harder to swallow as it gets older."

The old man just shook his head, and Nnanji blurted, "Why didn't She save him?"

"She did."

He glanced at the watchers grouped around Brota and the stricken swordsman. "That's saving? I saw no miracle."

Honakura chuckled drily. "I saw two! Could you take that sort of a beating and then not finish the job?"

Nnanji thought about that. "Perhaps not. And he'd been totally humiliated in front of his crew."

"That made it easier, though."

"Why? Never mind. What was the second miracle, then?"

The old man cackled in his infuriating way. "I'll let you work that out for yourself, adept."

"I haven't got time to play games," Nnanji snapped. "I've got responsibilities."

He marched into the deckhouse, feeling strangely annoyed by the old man's stupid grin.

Shonsu had been bandaged and now was carried into the deckhouse and laid on a blue cotton pallet. Brota looked him over, glanced at Nnanji without speaking, then waddled out. The rest of the crew followed her.

Jja began washing blood off her master. He was unconscious and pale as . . . very pale. Nnanji took his hairclip, his harness and sword. He went over to sit on one of the chests and checked the pockets. Shonsu had told him of the sapphires, but he whistled at the sight of them and hurriedly put them in his own pouch before anyone else saw. Then he counted all his mentor's money. *My goods are your goods*, but he was going to keep them separate. He laid his own coins on the chest for now. There was a cool breeze blowing in from the window beside him, waving his ponytail.

He removed his scabbard and replaced it with Shonsu's and then he sat and studied the seventh sword for a while before sheathing it on his back. He wished he had a mirror—certainly no Fourth had ever worn a sword like that. Reluctantly he put the hairclip in his pouch, also.

Katanji peered in, still pale. Nnanji beckoned him over.

"How much money have you got, protégé?"

Katanji looked surprised. "Five gold, two silver, three tin, and fourteen copper, mentor."

Where had the little scoundrel gotten that much?

"Okay. Count mine for me, will you?"

Katanji blinked, but he knelt down by the chest and counted without having to use his fingers. "Forty-three gold, nineteen silver, one tin, and six copper."

Right. "Then take it and look after it for me," Nnanji said.

His brother obeyed, stuffing the coins into his pouch.

"They're not going to put us ashore," he said. "The others wanted to and Brota refused—for now. The captain's been taken below. Is . . . is he going to live?"

"Shonsu? Of course."

Katanji looked over doubtfully at the wounded man, then he put on what their mother called his soft-boiled look. "Nanj? They won't speak to me when I'm wearing this sword."

Nnanji opened his mouth to impart some truths about proper swordsman behavior . . . and remembered. "Take it off, then."

The expression on the nipper's face was almost laughable. So was the speed with which he wrapped himself in that stupid breechclout—as if Nnanji would change his mind. Then he tied on his money pouch and ran. But there would be time enough to turn him into a swordsman when they all got off this rotten floating barnyard.

There were two or three hours of daylight left; Nnanji decided to stay where he was. It was the best defensive position he could have found, and he could keep an eye on Shonsu. The wounded man was neither conscious nor unconscious. When spoken to he would open his eyes and seem to understand, but mostly he just lay and thrashed around restlessly, often asking for drinks, which Jja gave him through a reed. Then he would lay his head back again and close his eyes. He shivered sometimes and sweated. She did not leave him. She had laid a rolled pallet across the door to keep Vixini from straying, but the baby was behaving himself for once.

Nnanji played with Vixini a little and talked to the slave woman a little, but mostly he thought swordsmanship. This shipboard technique was very interesting: very little footwork, and then only short steps. Tremendous armwork; point, not edge. He wouldn't give Tomiyano a fair match, even on land, but he would certainly beat Thana there—she'd never get near him. Yet obviously on the ship he was a scratcher again. A good swordsman ought to know both ways, and clearly Shonsu did.

How good was Tomiyano? Two or three ranks below Shonsu. But he had been fighting with a longer sword than he was used to. Give him a half rank for that and take one off for being on his own deck, and at least two for wielding sword against foil. The trouble was knowing how to grade Shonsu.

There was no measuring Sevenths. "To be a Seventh," Briu had liked to say, "is simply to be unbeatable." Shonsu was the best in the World, maybe a ten?

He finally judged that Tomiyano was a high Fifth or low Sixth. And a sailor! Where had he got his practice? Perhaps from that dead brother that Thana had mentioned. If not him, then there must be others around almost as good, for it was very hard to be greatly better than one's fencing partners.

Yes, he would learn this new way of fighting. As a start, he reviewed his match with Thana, and then Shonsu's, carefully going over every step and every stroke.

The morning sun climbed very slowly; it seemed uncannily slow to a woman who had lived all her life in the tropics. Fair wind, and the River wide and bright. It was a fine day, she could admit; this was a better climate for one of her size. The word in Aus had been that there were no dangers in this direction, no shallows or unexpected bars. Traffic was light. Wisely, the crew were staying away from her while she ground away at her decision, so she sat alone at the tiller with no distractions.

She had slept badly and awakened no closer to a solution, although she usually found that sleeping on problems was the best way to straighten them out. The only progress her dreaming mind had made was that it had seen what was missing. It would come, she was sure, so she was just going to wait for it—for him. A good trader knew when to be patient, so she would let him make the first move.

The swordsman was still alive, and somehow she had known he would be. He seemed to understand when he was spoken to, but he would answer in grunts and nods. She had never seen so much blood come out of one body before. Even at Yok, her deck had not looked so like a slaughterhouse.

Tom'o was still sedated, and she was going to keep him that way for a while. If he had offended the gods, then he had most surely paid for it. No bones broken, thanks to the Most High, but a terrible beating. It might make him a little easier to handle for a while. He had been getting fractious, even before this torment began, and so had Thana. In fact, Thana had been growing into quite a problem. After Yok they had seemed to settle back into much the same steady, routine life as before, except that they stayed down from Hool and never gone near Yok or Joof; those had been once-a-year destinations, anyway, for the spring crops. But no, it had not been the same. Change had been in the wind, although she had been refusing to admit it. Now they all had much more change than they could ever have wanted.

Something was going on . . . people beginning to crowd out on the main deck. She watched warily, out of the corner of her eye, not showing that she was paying attention. Then she saw the tiny figure come into view, painfully climbing the starboard steps. Here he was. This was what had been missing.

He advanced slowly, puffing a little, and smiled at her. He made no greeting and he sat himself beside her on the bench without waiting for an invitation. Only his toes touched the deck.

She glared down at the shiny skin on the top of his head. "You'll have to move off there when I tack," she growled—he had trapped her into speaking first.

"I shan't be long. Have you made a decision, mistress?"

"I've decided I like beggars on my ship as little as swordsmen."

His eyes were surprisingly bright for his obvious great age. "I outrank you."

Lina had been right—he was a priest. She could tell by the way he spoke. A Sixth? For a moment she thought of telling him to prove it, then changed her mind quickly. The mood the crew was in, they'd all fall flat on their faces before him if he really was a priest of the Sixth. He would be giving the orders, instead of her.

She grunted, trying to make him say more, but he stayed silent, hands clasped in his lap, looking straight ahead, scuffing his feet like a child. Waiting for her, of course. Impudence! Then her attention was drawn back to the main deck again.

"What's going on down there?" She hoped her guess was wrong.

"Another fencing lesson."

Oh, no! She reached for her whistle.

"His idea."

"I don't believe it! A male Fourth asking lessons from a female Second?"

The old man nodded, grinning. He was not looking at Brota. Probably it hurt to turn his neck up at that angle. "Adept Nnanji is an ambitious young man. He says your fencing is different. Is it?"

"Yes. But I never met a landlubber who would admit it was better."

"I'm not sure he went quite that far. But he is always eager to learn."

The fencers were in position, most of the ship's company standing around to watch the sport again. The old man was silent once more, still letting her lead the conversation.

"I could put you all ashore," she said. She had seen many local jetties, most of which would likely handle *Sapphire*'s modest draft. No settlements of any size, though—none that would have a healer able to tell a sword cut from a snakebite.

"You're not going to."

"Don't be so sure."

"I'm sure you won't, mistress. I didn't say you might not try."

"So you came to warn me?"

This time he twisted his head around far enough to flash his gums at her in a smile. Then he went back to watching the fencing. The sound of clashing foils drifted up in the wind, but the crowd was oddly silent.

"You're a priest!"

"Yes."

"What's a priest doing running after swordsmen?"

"Collecting miracles."

"Such as?"

"Such as your son not finishing off Shonsu when he had him on the floor. On the deck."

"You think he's still the Goddess' champion after that fool trick he pulled in Aus?"

The little man adjusted himself on the bench. "Don't try to outguess the gods, Mistress Brota. If She wanted a swordsman to do that, Shonsu was the only one she could have chosen. Right?"

"But why—"

"I don't know. But I shall find out if I live long enough . . .

or not, as the case may be. I learned patience a couple of lifetimes ago."

She studied the pennant and adjusted course. The sails filled
more fully, and the ship leaned over happily, like a sleepy dog
relaxing. "Tell me another miracle, then."

"Have you ever seen a slave so loved? Or a Fourth so
young? Anyone who has helped Shonsu has been rewarded."

"And my son was punished for being difficult?"

He nodded.

"Even if I agree to let you all stay, the rest of the family may
not go along."

He chuckled without looking up.

"One!" That was the swordsman's voice. The crowd muttered.

"He's *beating* her!" Brota exclaimed.

"He is a very fast learner. Don't underestimate Adept
Nnanji. He is not nearly as stupid as he would like to be. Youth!
He will grow out of it."

"Shonsu lost a lot of blood," she said. "If that's all, then
he'll be up and about in a few days—before we even reach Ki
San, likely. Then what? He'll need revenge on Tom'o for
wounding him."

The old man chuckled again. "Not Shonsu. He'll shake his
hand and offer him some lessons."

"Then he's like no swordsman in the whole World!"

"That's very true." He did not explain.

"Besides, I never heard of a landlubber giving a sailor fencing lessons. Some of them won't even admit it's legal."

"Is it?"

"There's some sutra or other," she muttered. Water rats did
not bother much with sutras. "And what if he dies? I've seen
wounds become cursed, old man. My brother-in-law had a nick
on his hand, and it killed him. My nephew—"

"A sword cut?"

Was that a threat? How had this nasty little busybody learned
about that? But he was still apparently intent on the fencing, as
though he had not spoken.

"Two!" Nnanji shouted.

"Shonsu is not going to die. He may be very sick . . ." The
old man paused as if considering a sudden idea. "Yes, he may

be quite sick. But he won't die. And you'll have no trouble with the rest of us. Your daughter can handle Adept Nnanji for you. His brother is—"

"His brother is a little imp! He was getting a lesson on knots from Oligarro this morning. Why would a landlubber need to know knots?"

He laughed aloud, spraying spit. "That's what Nnanji asked him. But you can guess. And the slave won't leave her master's side, so she's no problem."

"It's that other one. I don't like ship's whores. That Katanji was dropping hints to the boys. Does he?"

"I wouldn't put it past him." He looked up at her in surprise. "I don't think Cowie's important any more. You can get rid of Cowie if you want to, mistress."

"How?"

His eye twinkled, and they suddenly laughed together.

"And young Thana has her heart firmly on Lord Shonsu's tray," the priest said. "Isn't youth wonderful? Do you remember what that was like, mistress? The burning? The agony of being apart? How one person became the sun and all the rest of the World only stars?" He sighed.

How could she forget? Tomiy, young and slender, handsome as a string of diamonds. What could landlubbers ever know of the whirlwind courtships of the riverfolk, the few scattered hours together when the two ships met in port? The awesome commitment, a leap of faith, knowing that one might never see one's family again? And what was left now of Tomiy but a son who'd been manic enough to sauce a swordsman of the Seventh and a wayward, shrewd little minx of a daughter . . .

Another yell of triumph from Nnanji. Thana had not scored at all yet. She would not now; not if the red-haired youth had mastered water rat footwork already.

"Thana has always insisted she would marry a Seventh," Brota admitted. "Tom'o says a nightsoil carrier of the Seventh . . ." She had allowed the confrontation to be turned into a conversation, almost a conspiracy, as if the two of them were arranging everything between them. This shriveled antiquity was as sharp as any trader she could think of.

"Not this Seventh, though," he said. "No matter how long she has to try."

"Expect to be on board for some time, do you?"

He nodded and rose stiffly. "It will be quite a long voyage, I think."

"Where to? There are swordsmen in Ki San."

"But Shonsu is not able to recruit them, because of the wound your son gave him. So the contract will still be in force." He beamed at her. Even standing, his eyes were no more than level with hers.

She glared angrily. "I could give back his jewel."

He shook his head. "You shook hands. I have given you your warning, Mistress Brota. Don't antagonize the Goddess any further. Serve Her well and you will be rewarded."

"And what if he dies?"

"He won't."

"You can't know that." Yet his eerie confidence impressed her, and she could usually smell lies at a hundred paces.

"I do know that," the old man said simply. "I am certain."

"Certain is a strong word!"

"There is a prophecy, mistress. I know that Shonsu is not going to die this time, because I know who is going to kill him. And it is not your son."

He walked away, unsteady on the sloping deck.

Nnanji shouted, "Four!" He had won the *lesson*.

††

"It's too late to drop them overboard," Tomiyano said angrily. *Sapphire* had just overtaken a wallowing ore barge and was about to pass on the leeward side of a cattle boat. It would not steal their wind, but the neighborhood would be low-class for a few minutes.

Yes, it was much too late—there were witnesses. The River was busy as a marketplace. Morning sunlight danced on the bustling waters. River gulls screamed and swooped overhead. Brota said nothing.

"We could buy a ship apiece with that damned sword. Not to mention his hairclip. And however many more gems he may have in his pouch." In four days he had made a remarkable recovery. The swellings were going down, although his shoulders were striped in more shades than a seamstress' silk box, and he moved his arms as if they were old as the sutras. He was leaning on the rail at her side, grumbling. She did not think he was serious, but if she showed interest he might be. Trying her out, tempting. His ordeal had not made him easier to handle. Whatever the cost, he had felled a swordsman of the Seventh, and very few sailors had ever been able to claim that.

"Company astern," he added.

She turned to eye the galley overtaking, its gilded oars moving like wings, its prow embellished with shiny enameled arabesques. It was heading to cut her off before she passed the cattle boat. The stench caught *Sapphire* briefly. Ugh!

"He's going to die," Tomiyano said. He turned around and cautiously leaned elbows on the rail. His chest was almost as gaudy as his back, and his burned face was flaking. "His leg looks like a melon. Have you listened to him? Not a word makes any sense. Gibberish!"

"I told you to stay out of the deckhouse."

"I did. I looked in the window. And you can smell his wound from the hold. Damned landlubbers all over the ship! That Nnanji is dangerous. Every time I look at him, I expect him to start denouncing someone. Self-righteous young whelp!"

Brota did not speak. Nnanji had promised no denunciation in Ki San. Nnanji was under control. Thana had needed very little coaching. He revolved around her like a trained moth.

"And that Katanji!" Tomiyano spat over the rail.

Obviously his liver had been tainted by the bruised blood. A rhubarb purgative was what he needed. She wondered if beer would disguise the taste, for he would never take it voluntarily. "You're the only one to complain about him. He seems to get along with everyone else."

"That's what I mean! Have you seen how Diwa looks at

him? And Mei? But we *are* going to throw them off in Ki San, aren't we?"

Brota nudged the tiller judiciously. Perhaps it had been a mistake never to accept passengers before—Tomiyano was reacting as if he'd been raped, and some of the others were almost as bad. He had been born on *Sapphire* and had never slept anywhere else in his life. He worshiped the old hulk.

Roars of fury came floating across from the galley. It veered, and then feathered oars and lost way, in danger of stripping its sweeps against the cattle boat. Brota began planning her next tack. A couple of huge cargo ships, three times *Sapphire*'s size, were lumbering along ahead, while tiny luxury yachts flitted in and out like dragonflies—the owners coming to escort their cargoes, perhaps. She had never seen so much traffic so far from a dock. The great manor houses stood ranked along the shore; suburbs coming into sight. Ki San must be huge, and she felt excitement mounting, even in herself. The crew were expectantly lining the rail on the main deck.

"You *are* going to kick them out in Ki San?"

"Wait and see what the boy says."

"Him? He told Thana he'd never seen a city before Aus. This Ki San is . . ." Tomiyano considered the shore and the river traffic. "It's going to be worth seeing. It'll snuff 'em all up and not even sneeze. He'll stay aboard!"

Of course Nnanji would decide to stay, but likely he had not worked that out yet. He was down on the main deck with the rest, his ponytail shining copper in the morning sun, the silver griffon and its sapphire shining more brightly beside it. Everyone was down there, except Shonsu and his slave. Real devotion, there. She never seemed to sleep.

Evidently Tomiyano had also been looking at the sword and suddenly he realized its significance. "But he can't go ashore, can he? Swordsmen would be a bigger threat than sorcerers!" He laughed, then muttered something scornful about swordsmen, but under his breath so Brota could pretend not to have heard.

A challenger needed no reason. That sword would be Nnanji's death warrant if any highrank caught him wearing it. Of course in theory he could carry it in a sheath and wear his own, but Adept Nnanji would surely regard that as beneath his honor. And it would not save him from civilians, or swordsmen low on scruples.

A lumber boat and two fishing smacks ahead . . . "My head's aching," she said. "Eyestrain. Pity you're not fit enough to handle this for me."

"Move over!"

"But your shoulders . . ."

"Move over, I said!"

She left him to it and headed for the steps. She was tired of his griping, and the rest of the family was as bad, although they were more subtle about it. She was going to let the swordsmen stay—until she had sold her sandalwood. She would pitch them off just before *Sapphire* sailed. Safer that way. Unless, of course, the gods were feeling generous, as the old man had predicted. She was a trader and words were cheap. Let them show it.

Brota was down with the rest of the family, sitting on a hatch cover, when Ki San itself came into view, glorious in the sunlight. She had seen more of the World than any of them, but even she was impressed. A million green copper roofs spread out over many hills in a forest of spires, cupolas, and domes. On the highest summit a palace shone in white and gold. The bustling dock front stretched out of sight, outlining a bend of the River, a giant hedge of masts, and rigging dwindling away in an arc into the far distance. Lighters and barges flitted about like gnats. Windlasses and wagon wheels sent a continuous rumble of noise floating out over the water.

Watching the hubbub of the docks drift by, Brota began to wonder if they would ever find a berth. Then a little ferryboat pulled out ahead, and Tomiyano shot *Sapphire* into the gap as easily as he could have hit a spittoon. He grinned in lopsided triumph. The crew cheered and jumped to furl the sails and throw lines.

Brota heaved herself up and walked over to Adept Nnanji.

"Well, adept? You wish to remain on board?"

He gulped and nodded, still staring in horror at the city. "I do. You will send for a healer, mistress?"

"Very well."

"Ah, mistress?" He turned his attention from the view and squirmed slightly. "I want to sell Cowie. A slave who has hysterics at the sight of blood is not a suitable companion for a swordsman."

"That's true." Brota nodded solemnly. Well done, Thana!

Nnanji stammered. "Er, I wondered if you would sell her for me? You would get a higher price than I would."

"Probably. A man selling a slave like that means she's no good. A woman selling her can claim she's too good. Of course I'll want a commission. A sixth?"

His face fell. "Thana said you'd only want a fifth."

"All right. For you, a fifth."

He beamed. "That's very kind of you, mistress."

"My pleasure, adept."

The port officer departed, Matarro was sent for a healer.

The chance of a Seventh as patient brought a Sixth with no less than three juniors to carry his bags. He was a butterball of a man with a low, oily voice and a smooth manner; green linen gown freshly pressed, black hair slick on his scalp. He frowned when he saw the invalid. The healers clustered around, muttering and prodding, while the laymen retreated into an anxious group in the far corner of the deckhouse. Brota carefully placed herself on Nnanji's right.

Finally the Sixth rose and regarded the group in some doubt. "To whom do I have the honor to report?" he asked.

"To me," said Nnanji, stepping forward. Brota moved with him.

"The wound is cursed," the healer said cautiously.

Obviously.

"In the case of a civilian, I would recommend that a chirurgeon be summoned to remove the limb."

Brota braced herself, but Nnanji's sword arm barely twitched.

"No."

The healer nodded. "I thought not. Then I regret to announce that I cannot take this case."

Brota was ready to intervene, but the lad knew the correct response. "We respect your learning, your honor. While you are here, however, perhaps you would advise us on . . . on these foil bruises on my ribs. What would you recommend?" He had a tear glistening in one eye, but he did not seem to have noticed.

The healer nodded gravely and recommended that Nnanji be kept cool, given plenty to drink but take care not to choke on it, put hot compresses on the bruises every two hours and in between apply a balm, which one of the juniors produced from a bag. Nnanji solemnly thanked him and paid gold for the balm and the advice.

"And you will return tomorrow, your honor?" Brota asked. Nnanji looked surprised, but the Sixth beamed and said of course he would come back to check on the adept's bruises. She had no intention of remaining overnight, but she did not want the man tattling to the garrison about a Seventh in port. Not yet.

She accompanied the healers as they went out on deck.

"How long, your honor?" she asked.

"Five days?" said the oily Sixth. "At the outside. But he was a strong man. You could, of course, call in the priests."

Five days, Brota thought.

The healer was almost a sword victim himself as he left, for Matarro and Katanji had appointed themselves a ceremonial guard at the top of the gangplank, like those the big ships had, and their salutes were erratic. Brota concealed a smile and shouted for Nnanji to come and give them a lesson. He came boiling out of the deckhouse and did so in flames.

"Gods' armbones!" Matarro said when the monster had gone. "Does he really expect us to stand like this all day?"

"No." Katanji melted back into a comfortable position. "He's just upset about Shonsu. Nanj is okay mostly."

Then Brota was going ashore, and they flashed their swords again, but less dangerously.

They watched as samples of wares were set out on the dock, sandalwood and a few brass pots. Brota settled herself in a chair, and the busy dock life of Ki San thronged by in the hot sunshine. Wagons, rumbling along with loads of barrels and bales, raised clouds of acrid, horsey-smelling dust while highrank traders strolled by with their followers to sneer at the displays. Hawkers pushed loaded barrows, calling their wares to the ships; porters trundled carts. Sedan chairs and pedestrians and mules and pedlars wound their way in and out through the traffic. Robes and loincloths and wraps, in white and black, yellow, brown, and orange flashed by in the bustle and noise. There were many swordsmen patrolling the area.

"What happens now?" Katanji asked, fascinated.

"Puke all," Matarro said. "If some trader fancies what we've got out, he'll come and inspect it and say it's all crap, and Brota'll tell him he's an armpit and it's great stuff. Then they'll both try to make the other name a price so they can say that it's unthinkable. After that they get down to business. If he's serious, he'll come on board and look over the stock itself. Finally they shake hands."

Not much happened for a while. A few traders sniffed like dogs and wandered away. Then Thana led out Cowie, cleaned, coiffed, and appropriately clad, and took her down to the dock. The Firsts saluted and ogled as they went by.

"You never did," Matarro said.

"Did, too!" Katanji rolled his eyes. "Last night again! Nanj was snoring like a grindstone. I crawled over and helped myself. Three times."

"She looks like a lump!" the ship boy said doubtfully.

"Never!" Katanji assured him. "As soon as I start, she just goes wild. Loves it! Heaving and panting! Great stuff!" He went into slavering detail.

Matarro was impressed, but not quite convinced. "Swear on your sword?"

Certainly he swore on his sword, Katanji said, with the confidence of one who could not be discredited. Then their attention was called to the dock.

Cowie's appearance had proved more interesting than a whole mountain of sandalwood. A trader of the Sixth broke off negotiations at the next ship and hurried over, which was enough to get Brota off her chair right away. A Fifth crossed the roadway at the same time, then another Sixth. Their followers streamed in behind them, forming a crowd, which began to grow and jostle. Matarro swore a few oaths of disbelief, and Nnanji emerged from the deckhouse to watch. It looked as if Brota might be holding an auction, for hands were waving and voices bellowing.

"Haven't they ever seen boobs before?" Katanji demanded.

"Not like those!" Matarro said longingly.

Then there was a disturbance at the back of the crowd and it hastily opened for the latest newcomers, swordsmen.

"Holy ships!" said Matarro. "A *Sixth?*"

Nnanji bolted back into the deckhouse. He peered out through the windows, muttering under his breath, trembling with rage and frustration.

Jja was applying balm. She looked up, white-faced and red-eyed, brushing her hair aside with the back of one hand. She smiled slightly. "Adept? If you put the sword under the edge of the bedding and stayed close to the door, then it would come to no harm."

But Nnanji could not dispose of a trust so easily. He remained in the deckhouse, fretting angrily by the shutters.

The crowd rapidly dispersed, leaving only the troop of swordsmen and a few curious onlookers. Then Nnanji suddenly exclaimed, "Jja! Look at this!"

Together they watched Cowie being assisted into a sedan chair. Incredulous, they saw her borne away with an armed escort. "I have seen many miracles around Shonsu," Nnanji whispered, "but never one like that. A slave in a sedan chair?"

Brota stopped a moment to talk to one of the traders, then came stumping up the gangplank. When she reached the safety of her own deck she threw her head back and roared a carillon of river oaths, waving her fists in the air. Her crew melted away, knowing better than to speak to her in that mood. She wheeled round and stormed the deckhouse. Katanji trotted after her. Matarro followed more circumspectly.

She almost took the door off its hinges. "There's your money!" she snarled, smiting a small leather bag into Nnanji's hand with considerable force. "Twenty golds!"

"The Sixth bought her?"

"Yes! The Honorable Farandako, swordsman of the Sixth, reeve of Ki San!" She spat the words. "I had them up to fifty and they would have gone higher—eighty or ninety. Then your *noble* swordsman comes up and says that twenty is more than enough for a slave and takes her. Swordsmen!"

Armed robbery! Nnanji looked at the little bag that still lay in his oversize hand, looked at Brota . . . looked down at the restless, flushed face of Shonsu. "Brother," he said sadly, "we have need of an honorable swordsman."

There was no reply.

"He was generous, his honor!" Brota was still quivering with rage. "He needn't have paid more than one. Or none at all!"

"Why, mistress?" Nnanji asked. "What is so special about Cowie? Why a sedan chair?"

"The king," Brota said, lowering her voice almost to conversation level. "He collects slaves like her. He need only deliver her to the palace steward and he can be sure of at least a hundred." And if she had thought to research her market properly, she could have done that.

"I'm happy for poor Cowie," said Jja. "She goes to live in a palace. The Goddess rewards those who help my master."

Nnanji and Brota looked at each other, startled and rather shamefaced at not having thought of that.

"Well, you got them up to fifty golds," Nnanji said, spilling the coins into his other palm. "A fifth of that is . . . ten, right? So ten for you and ten for me, which is what I paid for her."

Brota snorted, but took the money before he came to his senses.

"Here, Katanji, keep those for me," Nnanji said. Then he remembered that the two Firsts had been left on guard duty. He exploded at them, driving them from the deckhouse with prophecies of cataclysms and doom.

"Five score gold pieces!" Katanji growled when they were back at their posts, safely out of range. "For a mattress?" He pulled a face in disgust. "Boy, someone's going to get a king-size disappointment!"

Matarro grinned, knowing that now he was getting closer to the truth. Then they started to laugh. They laughed so hard that they almost dropped their swords.

"Three hundred!" Tomiyano glanced hurriedly over his shoulder to see if the traders had overheard his astonishment. But they were watching their slaves carry the sandalwood down from the ship and load it onto the wagon.

Brota merely nodded and continued weighing coins from the table into a leather sack. Never had *Sapphire* carried a more profitable cargo, and at those rates they had left thirty golds' worth sitting on the jetty where Shonsu had boarded.

It was not yet quite noon, and good sailing weather was going to waste.

"Next port?" she asked.

"Three days to Wal. After that three, maybe four, to Dri."

Five days! "Cargo?"

"Brass," her son said, and she nodded. Ki San was proud of its brass and copperwork. Her own collection of pots had been greeted with derision, but fortunately there were only a few score in the hold, leftovers. Load up with this good stuff, and they would all sell together. Moreover there was a brass warehouse directly opposite their berth—that might be a clue from the Goddess or it might not, but it could save the rent of a wagon. Indeed, the trader was already standing at the front, hoping. She handed the bag to Tomiyano and led the way across the road. Had they had to go far, she would have donned her sword. Had it then been needed, he would have wielded it.

The trader was a Third—young, nervous, probably just started on his own. His establishment was small by local standards, yet he had an open-fronted shed large enough to have taken *Sapphire*. New businesses had debts. She made the conventional opening remarks and he replied. There were the customary objections about traders only trading with traders, but she had already found the local way around that, and few traders ever put a sutra ahead of a profit. The quality impressed her, and Tomiyano signaled that it was as good as any he had found. Cauldrons, tankards, pans, knives, and plates—above all, plates. Plates were heavy. She wandered around between the piles, eyes busy. Metal gleamed everywhere, even hanging from the ceiling. She found the dark corner with the junk and allowed for that. Volume, weight, packing, damage . . .

Then she gratefully accepted a chair and put on her helpless widow act. Tomiyano played skillfully along, reading her signals as she seemed to fidget. How much brass could they carry? Depends how many plates, how many pots. She appealed to the trader for help, knowing that *Sapphire* was much roomier than she looked—the cabins were small. They discussed hold size. She said big and Tomiyano patiently said small. The trader believed the sailor.

"Here," she said suddenly, dumping the bag down. "Three hundred that we just got for our lumber. You take that and we take as much as we can carry. That's easiest, isn't it?" She smiled innocently.

Tomiyano roared at her: three hundred golds—they could never carry that much. Yet the trader was suspicious. "You are serious, mistress?"

"Certainly." Keep him off balance. "Three hundred for all we can carry, our choice. Delivered on deck."

He laughed. "Mistress! A thousand, perhaps."

Hooked!

"Three hundred in that bag, that we just got for our lumber. If you have it brought at once, we can get in half a day's sailing. If I go elsewhere I haggle and we stay the night."

He nodded, staring across at the ship, calculating. "For a shipload . . . eight hundred."

She waddled out of the shed and looked at Tomiyano. "Two more this way, three that," he said, pointing. The trader called to her, and she kept walking. Seven hundred. She kept on, Tomiyano blustering at one elbow and the trader at the other.

"All the best craftsmen in the city—"

"There just isn't room for three hundred golds' worth! It'll get scratched and dented. And weight! It'll sink us."

She snorted. "With Shonsu on board? Ha!"

The cobbles were hard on her ankles and slowed her pace.

"Five hundred, my last offer." The trader was still with them, and the next brass dealer coming up ahead.

"What if he dies?" Tomiyano snarled. No talk of throwing overboard now.

"The healer said we had five days. We've used half of one."

"Four hundred," the trader said.

They had reached the next warehouse, a much larger place. The proprietor had been warned by his spies and was waiting. He made the sign of greeting. "Done!" said the young man behind her in a sob, and she turned round and held out both hands.

There were pots everywhere: in the cabins, along the passages, in the dinghies, on the decks. The plates had gone in the hold, and Tomiyano fretted about draft and shifting cargo and incomplete repairs and ballast and trim. The trader had wept hysterically, screaming that he was ruined. The crew were astounded and wondered if she had taken leave of her senses. With pots all over the deck, what do you do if it rains? How do you get to the ratlines in an emergency? Brota ignored all of the comments. She knew an opportunity when it barked loud enough and she did not think Shonsu was going to be drowned. She could get three fifty for this lot, perhaps more. Five days. A slow death, that, and his leg had not started to turn black yet.

The only place without metal was the deckhouse. One load had been placed in there. Nnanji had moved it all outside and stood glaring in the doorway, his arms folded and the seventh sword on his back. He might be a simple swordsman, but he seemed to have made a good guess as to what was happening and why. The deckhouse stayed clear.

Sapphire moved drunkenly away from the dock, responding to her tiller with a reluctance that felt like resentment.

The deckhouse was the only place left to eat, so when the anchor fell, it was there that the food came—roast dodo and rich-smelling manatee pie; fresh brown loaves and steaming dishes of fresh vegetables from Ki San. Brota sat on one of the chests, and everyone else crowded in on the floor.

She sensed strange moods in the company. The crew were worried about the trim and the cargo, anxious about tomorrow's weather; but they were also jubilant over the windfall from the sandalwood, believing now that the Goddess was smiling on them. Hool was a discarded memory. Their only sadness was a certainty that the wounded man in the corner was going to die of his wound as Matyrri and Brokaro had died. The passengers were morose, but were equally certain that he would live. As dishes passed around, little conversations would start up and then fade away again uneasily.

Then Tomiyano came in, carrying a large copper pot with a strange coil on the top of it. Brota held her breath. He glanced around until he located Nnanji, then picked his way cautiously over legs and around people to reach him, and laid the pot gently on the deck.

"Adept Nnanji," he said in a gruff voice. "Do you know what this is for?"

Nnanji frowned at it, looked up, and shook his head.

"Your mentor saw some like these in Aus," Tomiyano said, "but larger than this. He was very interested in them for some reason. I had hoped you would know. We got it with the others."

Nnanji closed his eyes. "All he told us was: 'I saw some copper coils that I thought might have something to do with sorcerers and I went over to look at them.'" His voice had taken on some of Shonsu's low rumble. He opened his eyes again. "I can't help you, captain. But perhaps you would let me buy that, so he can look at it when he recovers."

"I'll give it to you," Tomiyano said gruffly.

Brota thought a prayer to the Holiest: a peace offering! Incredible! But would the swordsman take it?

"I cannot accept a gift from you, Captain," Nnanji said. "How much to buy the pot?"

Tom'o flushed furiously. "Five golds!"

Nnanji calmly reached into his money pouch and counted out four golds and twenty-one silvers, laying them on the deck at the sailor's feet. *Madness!*

As soon as he had finished, the sailor kicked the coins away across the floor. He stamped over to the other side of the deckhouse, his face dark with rage, leaving the pot where it was.

Brota sighed and decided not to interfere. When men behave like children, women should stay out.

"What's the next port, my lady, and how long?" Honakura asked from a corner.

"Wal, in about three days," she said with her mouth full.

"There are sorcerers in Wal!" Nnanji said sharply.

Brota looked quickly at Tomiyano. "Is that right?"

"I didn't think to ask," he confessed, frowning, angry with himself. "Times and current and landmarks and shallows and trading, but I didn't ask about sorcerers! I didn't ask about Dri, either; the one after."

"Dri's all right," Katanji said.

He had a great gift for throwing rocks into still pools, that lad, thought Brota.

"I didn't give you permission to go ashore," Nnanji growled in the silence.

Katanji didn't say anything, kept eating.

Nnanji admitted defeat. "All right. What did you discover?"

"The left bank is sorcerer country," said his brother, waving a crust in the general direction of the mountains.

"Don't you know your right hand from your left?"

"He's right, adept," Brota said. "We're going upstream, so that side is the left bank."

Nnanji glared, seeing that he had been trapped. Katanji's eyes were twinkling, but he was careful not to smile. "There are Black Lands to the south, mentor," he said. "The sorcerers have taken over at least three cities on the left bank: Aus, Wal, and Sen, maybe more. And Ov, of course, on the other side of RegiVul, the mountains. Even the sailors don't seem to know much farther than two or three cities. But there are no sorcerers on the right bank, at least near here. Ki San and Dri and then Casr—they're all right."

His brother nodded and growled, "Well done, novice." Again he sounded like Shonsu—Katanji noticed and hid a grin in a mouthful of pie.

"Well done," Nnanji muttered again, scrunching up his forehead in thought. He looked at Brota. "We'll bypass Wal, then?"

"No more sorcerers for me," she said. "We can go on to Dri." But they couldn't reach it in five days.

The food was eaten and the dishes removed. Oligarro brought out his mandolin and played awhile. Then Holiyi shrilled a few tunes on his pan pipes. Then a sleepy silence . . . It was almost dark. The Dream God was starting to shine, this strangely low Dream God, wider and brighter.

"Nanj?" said his brother. "Sing us a song."

"No," Nnanji said.

"Yes!" said everyone else. The passengers were in favor now. Jonahs brought profit.

So Nnanji let himself be persuaded. His voice was reedy and not strong enough for a minstrel's, but his unconscious gift of mimicry led him through the tune, and the words were apparently no problem. He chose one of the great sagas, about the tryst of Illi and the ten-year siege, about the great hero Akiliso of the Seventh and how he had sulked in his tent because his liege had taken away one of his slave girls. It was a familiar tale, but he sounded like a minstrel and he had the cadences and the pauses and the triumphs and griefs in all the right places.

But when he got to the place where Akiliso's oath brother went to fight in his stead, he suddenly stopped. "I think that's enough for one night," Nnanji said. "Finish it another day."

The deckhouse applauded and praised and wiped a few eyes. Brota flexed her shoulders stiffly. She had been as much caught up in the song as any of them. The old man might be right. Shonsu might recover before they reached Dri, where there were swordsmen. Then the Goddess would release *Sapphire*. Three hundred golds for a load of sandalwood!

But she thought that Shonsu was going to die.

Matarro's young voice came out of the shadows, for it was quite dark now. Only the windows glowed. Reflected ripples of light played over the ceiling. "Adept Nnanji? What will you do if Lord Shonsu dies?"

"That's none of your business, my lad," his mother snapped.

"It's all right," said Nnanji's soft voice out of the blackness on the other side. "It's a swordsman problem, so he's right to be interested. I die also, novice."

A terrible coldness ran through Brota. "Bedtime!" she called loudly, surging to her feet. One or two of the children copied her, but everyone else stayed still, waiting.

"Nanj!" squealed his brother. "What do you mean?"

"There was no abomination!" Brota shouted. "Tom'o had been empowered as a posse!"

"That's correct," Nnanji said. "No denunciation. You see, novice, if I were only bound to Lord Shonsu by the first oath, as a follower, or the second oath, as his protégé, then there would be no difficulty. But we two swore a greater oath, so I would have to try to avenge him."

Tomiyano snarled wordlessly from somewhere to Brota's right.

"It isn't going to happen, though." Nnanji might have been discussing the price of fish, so quiet and level was his voice. "But it would be an interesting problem. The captain isn't a swordsman, so I couldn't challenge him, and there was no abomination, so I couldn't just pronounce sentence and kill him. Probably I would have to give him a sword and empower him as a posse again, to kill me. But it doesn't matter, because Shonsu isn't going to die."

"Filthy landlubber sword-jockey!" Tomiyano snarled. "You think you can get away with that?"

"Not a chance. You would knife me or run me through with the sword. And even if I did do you, the others would get me."

The men growled in angry agreement.

"So don't worry about it," Nnanji said. "I wouldn't do it without warning you. Shonsu isn't going to die, and even if he does, you'll easily get me first."

"That means all of you!" Brota screamed. "Witnesses, your brother for certain. Yes, all of you!"

"I expect so," Nnanji said coldly. "But an oath is an oath."

She swore loudly, silencing the rising noise. "That settles it!" she snapped. "You go ashore tomorrow at the first jetty we see. All of you. I've never broken a deal in my life, but this one is finished!"

The crew shouted agreement.

In the darkness to her left the little old priest coughed. "You did well on your lumber, mistress?"

The coldness increased, filling her with ice. She had not only accepted Shonsu's gem—now she had also taken gold from the Goddess. And she had so overloaded the ship that any sudden squall would lay her on her beam ends.

"Well . . . we'll see tomorrow," she said faintly.

The deckhouse filled with shouts of disbelief. They thought she was crazy. So did she.

†† ††

Four days out of Ki San, in late afternoon, Brota sent Tomiyano to fetch Nnanji. The lanky young swordsman, pale-skinned and bony, was leaning morosely on the rail, staring out over the River. Flashes of sunlight streaked on the silver handle of his great sword; the sapphire gleamed against his red ponytail. Very few people on the ship would even answer him now, let alone venture to address him.

She watched from the tiller as Tomiyano approached and saw him deliberately jostle a few of the copper vessels so that Nnanji would hear him coming. Oligarro and Holiyi were on deck, also, keeping a wary eye on things.

The captain spoke; Nnanji glanced up toward her and then shrugged and led the way aft. If he was uneasy at turning his back on the knife-bearing sailor, he did not show it. The poop was even more closely packed with pots than the deck and the two men edged their way through.

"Mistress?" Nnanji was curious but cautious.

Brota pointed to starboard. Far off over the bright waters, the eastern shore was a thin line, on which sharp eyes could just discern the tops of buildings and a good imagination could see a tower. Beyond lay the remote mountains of RegiVul, crumpled blue like crystallized sky.

"Wal?" said Nnanji.

"Wal," she agreed, then pointed over the port bow.

He turned and studied the swampy, desolate bush flowing past only a few cable-lengths away. There had been no hamlets or even shacks on that bank for hours. Then he looked up at the rigging and back to her, puzzled. "What am I supposed to see?"

Landlubber! "The sky," she said.

"Oh!"

It could not have been more obvious—a gigantic, boiling thunderhead, dazzling white on its foaming top, lightning flickering in the dark below its flat base.

"You overloaded the ship, didn't you?" he said, turning to her with amusement.

"Even if I hadn't, I'd want a port for that thing," she said. "I've never seen one grow so fast."

Suddenly he grinned, broadly. "She wants us to visit Wal."

Brota could see nothing to grin about. She leaned on the tiller, and grudgingly *Sapphire* began to respond. "We have no choice," she said grimly.

"Fine," Nnanji said. "I'll stay in the deckhouse."

Tomiyano's face held hatred and resentment. He fingered the sorcerer brand on his cheek. "So will I," he said.

An hour later she sent for Nnanji again, and this time he came alone. The ship was carrying every stitch that Brota and Tomiyano dared hoist, rolling uneasily in a fitful breeze, and Wal was dismally far away. He was wearing his own sword again, instead of Shonsu's—evidently ready for trouble.

"We may not be going to make this," she told him. Perhaps she had been wrong; perhaps Shonsu was destined to drown, and she was to be punished for greed.

The swordsman looked puzzled. The fingers of the storm were reaching out above them and about to seize the sun, but Nnanji ignored that. He pointed at Wal. "I thought you were going there, mistress?"

"We're tacking," she snapped. "Can't sail straight upwind, Nnanji!"

"Oh!" he said, not interested in technicalities.

"We have to clear the decks," she told him, clenching her teeth at his smile.

"The pots will fill with rain?" he asked.

"They'll roll. We're going to put as many as we can in the deckhouse."

His smile vanished and for a moment she thought he would

argue, but then he nodded. "If we put Shonsu behind those two chests he will be safe?"

"We had thought of that. He will be safe from rolling pots, at least."

Nnanji nodded. "Anything I can do to help?" he asked.

She gestured at the cluttered poop. "You can throw these overboard, if you like."

He blinked. "You are serious, mistress?"

"Yes!"

He did a fair job of not laughing at her, but it was an effort. "Fine!" he said, and started tossing the pots and urns and ewers over the rail. Lae and Mata were already doing the same on the main deck, while others were starting to pack the deckhouse. Tomiyano was emptying the dinghies. Then an army of shadow came racing over the water after them, and the sunshine died.

Sapphire staggered along, leaving a trail of bobbing brass and copper behind her. Brota avoided Nnanji's eye.

Suddenly there was no wind. The sails flapped listlessly, the ship lost way and then wallowed in waves outrunning the storm. Pots dropped alongside now stayed there, no longer falling astern.

"What's happened?" Nnanji demanded suspiciously.

"It is the calm before the storm. We expected it. When the wind comes, it will be from behind us—and strong. That's why I said that we may not be going to make it. All we can do now is wait."

They could also shorten sail. Tomiyano's whistle shrilled, and the hands started for the ratlines. Nnanji shrugged and went back to heaving cargo overboard.

". . . nothing of which I may be ashamed . . . avoid no honor . . ." declaimed a voice below them, a deep voice, but faint; audible now only because the wind had dropped.

"What's *that*?" Brota exclaimed, taken by surprise.

Nnanji looked uncomfortable. "It is Lord Shonsu. He is repeating the code of the swordsmen. Usually what he says makes no sense, but today he keeps quoting bits of the code."

Brota and Nnanji looked at each other uneasily. "Like a prayer?" she muttered.

A prayer for forgiveness?

Above them the sky grew steadily blacker, and to the west was the father of all blacknesses.

Brota yielded the tiller to Tomiyano and Oligarro. It might take both of them to hold it when the time came. The air was calm, humid, and menacing. *Sapphire* drifted aimlessly on the great River.

Little deck cargo remained, all securely tethered. The dim deckhouse was packed tightly, and when Brota and Nnanji went to inspect it they could not see the patient. Jja was sitting in a far corner on a chest. Shonsu lay at her feet, safely barricaded behind it. She smiled bravely across the forest of pots at them. "The sorcerers will find it difficult to reach my master here," she said.

Brota made a cheerful reply, but if they had to abandon ship there would be no quick way to get Shonsu and his slave out of that corner. Nnanji did not seem to have thought of that. She wondered if Jja had.

". . . sutras of the swordsmen . . . the will of the Goddess . . ." the sick man said.

Then the wind came.

Tossing and rolling, creaking angrily in every timber and rope, *Sapphire* ran before the storm. Brota huddled in a leather cape in the shelter of the deckhouse wall and wept for the old ship. It had been an unkindness to load her so, a breach of trust. At every roll or pitch, there was a muffled clashing of metal from the cabins below, but Tom'o was magnificent. His grandfather could have done no better, reading the air by the look of the water, angling the old vessel along the edge of the wind, arrowing toward Wal, staying out of the calm before them and out of the fury behind.

Still there was no rain, only cold blasts of wind and darkness, pitchings and creakings. Wal gleamed in sunshine ahead of them for a while, growing closer now, but oh! so slowly. The tower became obvious, an ironic beacon of hope. Then the shadow fell on Wal, also, and only the distant mountains knew sunlight. The children were already stowed in a dinghy. The adults stood by the rails and tried to seem unconcerned as the storm pursued them, marching on pillars of lightning across the waters, grumbling thunder like a cursing of giants.

Wal looked much like Aus, wooden walls and red tile roofs. There were no ships at anchor here; all lay safely moored at the dock, stirring nervously as the waves grew. Tomiyano took *Sapphire* in and found a berth.

Then he marched angrily down to the deckhouse to hide his face from the sorcerers. Brota, watching him go, suddenly realized that he was going to be shut up in there with Nnanji. There was room for two people inside the door, but not much room. She shouted, and the captain paused, nodded, and passed his belt and dagger to Oligarro. Then he stamped inside and shut the door. She went over and stood close by, just in case there would be trouble; but the sailor was unarmed, the swordsman could not easily draw his sword under that roof—and if he tried, Tom'o would snap him like a twig before he succeeded.

Through the shutters she heard only silence and a distant, hoarse rumble: ". . . sutras of the swordsmen . . ."

Brota stayed by the deckhouse door to watch over Oligarro, a heavyset, white-haired man, quiet spoken; usually reliable, but cursed with an unpredictable temper. The docks were deserted before the coming storm, strangely empty, dust blowing over the stones, the litter, and the horse droppings. The only visible life was a slave gang carrying timber from the next ship and loading it on a wagon. The horses had been removed to safety, but slaves were waterproof and did not shy at thunder. Thunder! It rolled almost unceasingly from the coal-dark sky that hung like a black tent overhead.

Brota and Oligarro . . . everyone else, adults and children, had fled below to tidy up down there and rejoice at reaching safe haven. She supposed it was safe, glanced up unhappily at that all-seeing tower, so like the tower at Aus, but here doubly ominous in the gloom, black on black. She hoped that the sorcerers' rules would be the same here, that a swordswoman was safe on board. Then she saw that one other person had stayed —Katanji was sitting cross-legged in the sheltered spot below a dinghy, watching and grinning like an imp, disappearing as the lightning threw shadow over him, reappearing in the subsequent gloom. He was not wearing his sword, so he should be all right. Sharp kid; he liked to see, liked to know.

Then a port officer arrived, and the plank was run out for him. He came hobbling up slowly, an emaciated old sailor of the Third, and she disliked him on sight. He paused to make the salute to a superior to Oligarro, his brown robe writhing around his thin shape, his eyes watering in the wind. His name was Hiolanso. Shonsu had said that the port officer in Aus was a sorcerer. If this was also one, he had chosen a much less attractive shape—meager white hair, scraggy neck, many wrinkles, and liver spots.

Oligarro responded as captain of *Sapphire*.

Hiolanso bid him welcome to Wal on behalf of the elders and the wizard, then headed for the deckhouse, seeking shelter. She stepped in front of it to block him. Frowning, he eyed her face-marks and saw who made the decisions. He saluted wryly and she responded.

"You are aware that swordsmen are not allowed ashore, mistress?"

"I guessed as much."

Hiolanso looked suspiciously at the deckhouse, turned to study the deck cargo and then to face Oligarro. "You seemed heavy laden when you came in, Captain. Low in the water?"

"We made it," Oligarro said without expression.

The old man made a twisted smile and shouted over the wind, "Then let us do our business quickly. I have no wish to hang around in this weather. The fee is twenty golds."

"Twenty!" shouted Brota and Oligarro together. Thunder bellowed above them in celestial outrage.

"I have never heard of such a fee for a ship this size!" Brota roared.

The officer smiled again, suddenly illuminated by lightning. He winced at the ensuing noise and then said, "Nevertheless, that is the fee—today."

Oligarro was turning red. "It is absurd! We cannot pay!"

"Then you must leave."

Brota wondered how Tomiyano's temper was holding up, for

he must be listening behind the door. Was this old man a sorcerer?

"I have five golds here," Oligarro said, blustering and uncertain. "Take it and be gone."

"Twenty."

They had no choice and he knew it. Brota glanced down at the dock, and there were four or five youths standing there, accomplices undoubtedly. The old crook would order their lines cast off if they did not pay him. She had met corruption before in port officers, but never this blatant, never with a monster hanging over the River and waiting to smash her ship.

"I must go and get the money, then," she said, flashing a warning glance at Oligarro. Veins bulged in his ruddy, stolid face.

"Be quick! Or I shall make it thirty." Hiolanso was shivering in the cold.

Angrily Brota gave Oligarro another meaningful look, then stamped away, heading for the companionway door. She hoped he was using his head—*don't lose your temper, keep that man out of the deckhouse*. If that scoundrel discovered a highrank swordsman on board, his fee would become fifty at once. But the money was in her cabin, aft, and the passages were cluttered with copperware. Katanji scampered ahead of her and held the door open against the gale.

She muttered thanks. She had gone only two steps when he said, "I have fifteen golds here, mistress."

She swung round, unable to see him properly in the dark.

"That would be a kindness," she replied.

"Two silvers?"

"You're as bad as he is! All right, two silvers."

He chuckled and counted fifteen coins into her hand. She wondered how a mere First could have so much. These swordsmen tossed money around in a way she found disgusting. Sharp kid—not many people would have seen the opportunity for fast usury.

Lightning and thunder greeted her again as she staggered back across the deck, noting Oligarro's surprise at her speedy return. She handed over the money.

"I hope your stay at Wal is profitable, mistress," Hiolanso said mockingly. "I bid you good day, Captain."

He bowed and turned.

He walked three steps and stopped.

A man was coming up the plank.

When he reached the deck, he paused, standing tall and sinister in the darkness, motionless except for the whipping of his gown, arms folded inside his sleeves, face invisible inside his sorcerer's cowl. Then a flare of lightning showed his red robe and a momentary glimpse within the hood: heavy black eyebrows, a square, strong face, confident and severe.

The darkness returned, and he glided forward through the thunder as if he moved on wheels.

"Return the twenty golds to Mistress Brota, Hiolanso," he said.

Brota shivered and not from the wind. He knew her name? The port officer's teeth were chattering, and his hands trembled visibly as he reached in his leather pouch and counted out the money.

"My apologies, mistress, Captain," the sorcerer said in a deep, hard voice. "The elders and the wizard have been much concerned at the corruption among their officials. Now we have caught one and he will be punished. We offer the shelter of our port for your ship, and there will be no fee."

"Punished how?" Brota asked, thinking of the many times she had cursed officers.

"That's up to the court." The sorcerer turned his hood slightly to study the criminal. "At least one hand in the fire, and for so large a theft, probably both."

Hiolanso's squeal of terror was drowned out by a mind-shattering peal of thunder. He dodged around the sorcerer and bolted for the gangplank.

The sorcerer swung round to face after him and raised an arm. Thunder roared again, deafening. A cloud of smoke swirled for an instant and was wiped away by the wind.

The plank was empty. The fugitive had totally vanished.

Brota heard a whimper of terror and realized that it was

coming from herself. Now it was Oligarro's teeth that were chattering.

Tap . . . tap . . . Rain was starting.

The sorcerer turned to the sailor and made the salute to a superior. "I am Zarakano, sorcerer of the Fifth rank . . ."

Oligarro's voice quavered as he responded. The sorcerer looked to Brota and made the salute to an equal, and her voice was no steadier. The port officer had disappeared before her eyes. It was true, then. She had not believed in sorcerers before she met Shonsu. Now there was one on her deck and he had destroyed a man on her gangplank. One instant there had been a man running down the plank; next instant, only smoke. Never in her life had she worried that she might faint, but the thought now crossed her mind.

Tap . . . tap . . . tap tap tap . . .

"Let us take cover for a moment," Zarakano said. He reached for the deckhouse door handle, and Brota was too paralyzed to do anything. The wind grabbed the door and hurled it open with a crash.

Nnanji stood in the entrance, his arms folded, his face a pale blur in the gloom—for an instant. Then lightning flared again, highlighting him in a brilliance of red hair and orange kilt against a million flames of copper. A murderous explosion of thunder rattled the whole ship. The sorcerer recoiled in surprise, started to raise an arm, and then lowered it. This was no water rat swordsman he was seeing—harness, kilt, even the proper boots. Sword. For a moment nobody moved or spoke, and the wind suddenly dropped—the calm before the storm again; silence, no thunder.

". . . no less than justice . . ." That was Shonsu, still raving in the far corner.

Nnanji could not draw under that roof.

Swordsman and sorcerer faced each other for a long, blood-freezing minute, then the sorcerer made the acknowledgment of an inferior. Nnanji's face was unreadable in the gloom. He paused, then made the salute: "I am Nnanji, swordsman of the fourth rank . . ."

There had been much talk about sorcerers on *Sapphire* lately

—Katanji had passed on the stories. Had swordsman and sorcerer ever saluted each other like this? Water rats did not count. This was a meeting of snake and mongoose, and the mongoose had saluted.

"I am Zarakano, sorcerer of the fifth rank . . ." The snake responded.

"I will be evermore true to . . ." growled Shonsu in the background. Lightning sizzled and thunder bellowed simultaneously, drowning him out.

Tomiyano was keeping to one side, still invisible, but what if the sorcerer went into the deckhouse and saw his branded face? What if he heard Shonsu and recognized the code of the swordsmen?

Plop! Plop! Huge drops began to hit the deck.

Without taking his eyes from Nnanji, Zarakano asked, "How many free swords are you carrying, mistress?"

"Only Adept Nnanji and a First," she muttered, wondering if Katanji was back on deck, wondering if the sorcerer's powers could detect her lie. The rain noise was beating louder, and the wind rising again, muffling Shonsu's mumblings.

"Adept Nnanji is a man of discretion," the sorcerer said, in what seemed meant to be a jovial tone. "But so am I. I think I shall bid you good day, mistress." Lightning flared blue white again, blazing off the swordsman in his orange kilt, flaming red and yellow from copper and bronze behind him. "I see you carry much cargo. I will cast a spell of good fortune on it for you."

Brota stepped in front of him and reached for the door. With Oligarro's help she pushed it shut, hiding Nnanji, whose feet had never moved. Then she leaned on it, feeling weak and horribly shaken. "I thank you, Master Zarakano," she said. "And wish you good day, also." Meaning that she would keep his back safe from the swordsman.

Rain exploded from the sky, torrents of rain, a universe of rain, furring the deck with white fog.

The sorcerer nodded at her, pulling his cowl farther over his face, then hurried for the plank. She saw him reach the dock and the two yellow-robed sorcerers of the Second waiting for him. Then all three sped across the street and were hidden by the rain.

Even the greatest of storms must pass eventually. Brota had retired to pamper a headache, but she must have dozed, for a tap on the door awoke her.

"Who is it?"

"Novice Katanji, mistress."

"Just a minute."

The storm had almost gone. The ship was rocking less, creaking less, and sunlight was streaming in the window.

Her cabin was a wooden box, but a larger box than the others, with space for a dresser as well as a chest, and a raised bed that was her sole concession to age. The lantern on the dresser was the only one aboard, a greater badge of authority than her son's dagger. She had a rug, drapes, and three small wool tapestries to brighten the box.

She eased herself up and took a moment to gather her wits. The wind was dying. Two hours until sunset, perhaps, with the light coming in low under the fringe of the storm. They would be able to sail soon. She grunted to her feet and padded across to admit Katanji. He was grinning, his face grimy and his hair smelling wet.

"Come for your money, have you?" She chuckled. She counted out his fifteen golds onto the dresser. "These two silvers? What happens if I tell your brother?"

He studied her a moment and shrugged. "Then I don't help you the next time," he said.

What next time? "Where does a First get fifteen golds?"

"Oh, most of it's Nanj's," he said. "I'm holding the ten he got for Cowie, remember?"

She passed over two silvers. "Thank you, *swordsman*."

"You're welcome, *swordsman*," he replied impudently, but the charm of his grin let Katanji get away with such insolence. All the coins went in the same pocket, she noted. "Are you going to sail or stay the night, mistress?"

"Sail. The cowls know your brother's on board."

"You don't believe in the spell of good fortune, then?" His eyes glinted.

She was not in the habit of debating her decisions—not with Tomiyano, certainly not with landlubber Firsts, yet . . .

"No. Do you?"

He chuckled. "Of course! Besides, Holiyi was complaining only today how long it was since he had a night in port."

"You let Sailor Holiyi worry about his own sex life, novice, or I'll start Nnanji worrying about yours."

He blushed scarlet and looked uneasy. He was, after all, only a kid, and yet she was matching wits with him as if he were a trader of the Fifth. "Anything else?" she asked, thinking that she had time for a shower before they cast off.

He nodded. "I have some information for you. I think it's worth a gold. Maybe two."

She sat down on the bed, making the ropes creak loudly, and she stared at him suspiciously. "Two golds! What is it, the elixir of life?"

He shook his head.

"Where did you get information?"

He shook his head again. "Can't say. Do you want to hear?"

"Who decides if it's worth one gold, or two, or nothing?"

He hesitated and shrugged. "I suppose you do."

"If I don't want it, then I don't pay?"

He nodded doubtfully. Then he grinned again. "You'll want it. There are two brass merchants in town, Jasiulko and Fenner-olomini."

He had her attention. "How did you find that out? You been ashore in a sorcerer town? You're crazy!"

He shook his damp curls. "Swordsmen don't go ashore here, mistress."

She glanced at his feet. "I'd better tell Tom'o to clean up the deck, then."

He looked down and then bit his lip, vexed at having missed that. "Don't ask questions, mistress, please."

How had the kid got his face so dirty? It looked greasy, smeared. This lad had promise. In fact he was one of those Shonsu miracles, she decided. "It's worth knowing about the merchants, Katanji, but it's not worth two golds."

"There's more," he said, grinning wildly.

"Let's have it then."

The words spilled out excitedly. "Two nights ago there was a fire. Jasiulko's warehouse burned down. He lost his whole stock."

Brota stared at him for a long minute without a word. She had no doubt at all that he was speaking the truth. She reached in her money bag and silently handed him two more golds.

†† † ††

It might have been the sorcerer's spell, but she preferred to think it was the handiwork of the Goddess. Whichever it was, Brota kept her ship in port overnight and next morning sent word to both the brass merchants. She made them bid against each other, for Fennerolomini dearly wanted to keep Jasiulko out of business. In the end Jasiulko took the whole cargo for five hundred and twenty-three golds. Brota shook hands on it, then went down to her cabin and danced a jig.

Lae had been scouting and came back exulting about furniture, carved from a type of oak that grew nowhere else but near Wal. When the dealers brought samples, Brota agreed with her judgment and loaded shiny tables, ornate chairs, and intricately inlaid chests. *Sapphire* spent a second night in port, and the sorcerers did not trouble her. Nnanji skulked in the deckhouse. Shonsu's ravings grew quieter, and his wound more obviously cursed. His death seemed closer than ever.

No one asked where Novice Katanji was, but next morning he was aboard when *Sapphire* set sail in the sunshine for Dri, three days upriver, still carrying the dying swordsman.

The days passed, but Dri came no closer. With all her canvas spread, *Sapphire* wallowed on a river of glass, barely holding her way against the current in a sickly, fitful wind.

Honakura was becoming concerned. Even he, with a professional faith in miracles and Shonsu's mission, was finding increasing difficulty in believing that the swordsman was going to survive his wound. Each morning the great frame was more wasted and its continuing survival seemed more like a direct intervention by the gods. Jja was eroded to a wraith by effort and worry, Nnanji morose and sullen.

The sailors had prepared their plans. They had consulted Honakura about them, for at first they had been unable to believe that Nnanji was serious. The old man had assured them that he was, that no danger to himself or his friends would ever distract the young swordsman for a moment from whatever he saw as his duty and the call of honor. If Shonsu died, then Nnanji would head for Tomiyano with a sword.

If that happened—or so the plan went—he would be caught in a net, trussed like a pig for market, and put ashore, together with the rest of the passengers.

Tomiyano himself had other ideas. His vitriolic hatred of swordsmen allowed no room for nets in his view of the future. Any nonsense from Nnanji's direction was going to be countered with a fast knife, the consequences be damned. Some of the men agreed with him.

Sapphire was not a tranquil ship.

Yet now she was becalmed and so was the quest. The old priest knew that the matter was urgent—a process that should have taken years was being squashed into a few short days. The gods were in a hurry, but things had come to a halt. Obviously someone ought to be doing something and had failed to pick up his cue. Honakura was quite willing to help, but he was a minor character in the drama and would not be permitted to meddle greatly. And he did not know what was supposed to happen next, or who was supposed to make it happen.

The Ikondorina prophecies were some guide for him, of course, and the demigod's riddle was beginning to make sense. He knew more than anyone else about Shonsu's mission—certainly more than Shonsu did—but at the moment he was baffled.

It was a hot and still afternoon. The banks were far off on either side, the mountains faint in the eastern haze, the water an azure mirror. High above him—and looking straight up was a tricky procedure for Honakura—the youngsters hung in the rigging like sloths, Katanji among them. A group of women sat on the poop deck, chattering quietly and knitting, preparing warmer clothes for winter in this nontropical climate. Holiyi, Maloli, and Oligarro were splicing ropes, which was a peaceful and sedentary task. Linihyo and Sinboro dangled lines in silence from the fo'c'sle. Young Matarro held the tiller with obvious pride, although the ship was virtually stationary, her wake a faint ripple on the silken sheen.

The only person being energetic was Tomiyano. Down on his knees beside the aft hatch cover, he was scraping one side of it with a sandstone block. It seemed an unpleasant task. He was probably demonstrating that he had recovered his health, and the spare sanders he had laid out in clear view were a strong hint that he would appreciate some help. The hint was being ignored. After some thought, Honakura decided that the purpose was to remove the old paint before applying new—he had not had to worry about such practical matters since he was a child, but that seemed logical. At any rate, Tomiyano was the only really active person in sight, and the screech of his block was the only loud noise.

And there was Nnanji, leaning on the rail, staring out at distant fishing boats. No one in the crew spoke to him now. He was being treated like a dangerous animal.

Honakura sauntered over and laid black sleeves beside sinewy young arms. Nnanji turned to regard him for a moment in silence.

"Any change?" he asked.

Honakura shook his head.

The swordsman nodded and looked out at the water again for a while. The strain was telling on him, inevitably. The smooth juvenile planes of his face had become more angular. Even this silent contemplation was new.

"I was not always popular in the barracks, either, you know," he said softly.

"What do you mean?"

"I mean that you don't need to follow me around with that

worried expression. You look like my mother, wondering if I'm constipated."

Honakura was taken aback—an unfamiliar sensation, he admitted to himself.

Then Nnanji asked, "Did I make an error?"

That also was unexpected. "When?"

"When I sold Cowie. She was one of the seven."

"There was no miracle to stop you, so I don't suppose so."

Nnanji groaned. "It feels like an error. I've never been so horny in my life."

He had, of course, sported quite a reputation in the barracks. "Why did you sell her, then?"

Nnanji's pale eyes stayed fixed on the far-off fishing boats, but a slight smile tugged one corner of his mouth. "I interpreted a hint as a promise."

Interesting! The lad was poking fun at himself, and that was another new development. Of course he had not been able to go ashore with the other bachelors in Ki San and Wal. He could not romp in the rigging with his sword, either, and the crew did not invite him to join in their chores.

"What you need is some exercise, adept."

Nnanji nodded, still facing the water. "That's what I meant. But even other exercise would help, I suppose. Would you care for a fencing lesson, old man?"

"A fencing lesson is just what I need," Honakura said wryly, "but it would not be legal, would it? Try Thana—she might agree to that sort of exercise."

Nnanji shook his head. "I think I must have lost weight. She doesn't see me now, even when I speak. I work the nipper to distraction; he hates it, and I don't want to sicken him of it too much." He sighed.

Honakura had heard Brota's opinion of Katanji as a swordsman and seen him head off to hide in the chain locker when his mentor appeared with foils.

Then Nnanji half turned, leaned on one elbow, and grinned at the priest. "I shall have to ask the captain."

Yet again Honakura was startled. "You're joking!"

"No." The grin grew wider. "The sutras say I can't give a civilian a foil—but they don't say I can't accept one from a civilian. I left mine back in Hann. And I can't give a civilian a lesson..."

"But he's better than you are? You are thinking like a priest, adept."

"Where could I have picked up such a bad habit, I wonder? Still, he can't do more than throw me overboard for asking, can he? And in return for a fencing lesson, I can get a sailoring lesson, also—I'll offer to help him with whatever that noisy job is."

This was all very much out of character! A swordsman doing manual labor? Asking fencing lessons from a sailor? Honakura prided himself on being able to predict people. He did not welcome such anomalous behavior. A twinge of intuition whispered that this might be what the gods were waiting for, but...

But there was also something new in Nnanji's eyes, hidden behind the grin. Most people, in Honakura's experience, used their eyes only to *look*, few used them to *see*. Nnanji had just changed categories, for he had noticed Honakura's reaction, and the old man very seldom gave himself away like that.

The grin grew wider. "Well?"

"He might do much worse. He may flog you as Shonsu flogged him."

Nnanji shook his head. "No. He's not that much better than I am. It would slow him. I'd butcher him, too, if he started that."

"But why should he agree to give a fencing lesson to a man who may try to kill him? That's crazy!"

"Panache?" Nnanji said. "He likes to impress the others. He gave me my sword back, remember?"

Where had this swordsman found such an insight? From Katanji? Yet Honakura did not think Katanji had been consulted. That would be even more out of character...

"Want to make a bet, old man?"

"No, I don't! I think you should stay away from Tomiyano. He's dangerous." But that, Honakura realized as soon as he said it, was not likely to be an effective argument in this case. "He'll try to cripple you!"

Nnanji registered astonishment. "No! Yes, he will, won't he? Well, then! There's a real incentive for him!" He flashed a truly wicked smirk and went striding off toward the deckhouse door, emerging a few moments later without his sword and harness.

Tomiyano looked up warily as he heard boots approach. He sat back on his heels, scowling, reached for his knife, and then showed surprise at seeing a swordsman unarmed.

Honakura had spent a long lifetime analyzing people and knew he could read expressions better than most. He saw the dark flush of fury on the sailor's face when Nnanji made his request. He saw it change to disbelief. He saw the attraction of the idea dawn. Nnanji pointed to the sanding job, looking hopeful and earnest and totally lacking in guile. Then he grinned broadly across at Honakura as the captain rose, heading for the fo'c'sle, obviously going to fetch the foils.

Still apprehensive, the old man perched himself on a nearby sand bucket and prepared to watch. The tension among the crew was far too high to risk such nonsense; the memories of the fight between Shonsu and the captain much too vivid. There would be too many opportunities for things to go wrong. It was a blatant challenge to the gods. He should have more faith, but he wished he knew what to expect, or how this could possibly help.

Tomiyano was gone some time. Quite likely his mother had hidden the equipment. Few people noticed the foils and masks in his hand when he returned, but the first clash of steel rang through the silent ship like an alarm bell, and the reaction was frenzied. Youngsters came swarming down the ropes, the knitting party on the poop disintegrated, people erupted from the companionway to stare in disbelief and then gaze at one another. Brota came out screaming, her nerves ragged from the days of uncertainty.

"What in hell are you doing!" she yelled, even as she burst through the crowd around the doorway like a surfacing whale.

The fencing stopped, and the captain pulled off his mask and looked around at the watchers, then at his mother.

"I'm teaching a swordsman to fence," he said. "If all of you would get out of the way and give us some room." Then he put the mask on again and went to guard.

Brota ground out an incredulous oath. For a moment she seemed about to argue, then she fell back with the others and watched as the lesson proceeded, quietly wringing her fat hands.

Honakura knew nothing about fencing and cared less, but he could study the spectators. At the beginning, the women looked worried and the men mostly pleased, eager to see the captain return some of the medicine he had taken from Shonsu.

It seemed to be a very static match. The two men were standing their ground, left foot planted, left arm high. Nnanji's right boot would stamp forward, *Clump*, and then retreat, *Tap*. The captain's bare foot moved in silent counterpoint. Foils rang. *Clump . . . Tap . . . Clump . . . Tap . . .* Back and forth they disputed for that one spot on the deck. Evidently this was not orthodox—eyebrows began to rise. Glances were being exchanged. The smiles became frowns. But Thana, watching intently, was beginning to smirk. *Clump . . . Tap . . .*

Neither man was claiming any hits. The noise increased, the pace grew more ferocious. Then the captain stepped back instead of forward, and Nnanji followed. *Clump . . . Clump . . .* Spectators muttered in astonishment. Again the captain had to retreat, and this time he kept going, being driven by Nnanji as he had been driven by Shonsu. The watchers scrambled clear . . . faster yet . . . along one side of the aft hatch . . . past the fo'c'sle door. *Clump . . . Clump . . . Clump . . .* Forward again toward the main mast.

"One!" Nnanji yelled.

The match stopped. Tomiyano whipped off his mask and hurled it to the deck. He was red-faced, gasping for breath, and obviously furious; glaring murder at the swordsman.

Nnanji unmasked, also. He was equally breathless, but his grin said more than all the other faces put together. "Sorry!" He panted. "That was a little harder than I meant."

Tomiyano was holding one hand to his incompletely healed, still-variegated ribs. He brought it away, and there was blood on his fingers. Thana stifled a noise like a giggle. The captain transferred his glare from the swordsman to his sister, then pushed past Nnanji and marched toward the fo'c'sle door, the crowd parting for him in silence. Nnanji looked around at the circle of scowling faces. "I didn't mean to," he said.

The sailors turned away.

He shrugged, laid the mask and foil tidily on the hatch cover, and walked toward the deckhouse. The spectators began to disperse in angry silence.

Honakura slid off the bucket and followed the swordsman.

Even with all the shutters open, the deckhouse was airless and hot. Shonsu lay in his usual corner, wasted and soaked in sweat, his breathing labored. Pus oozed from his tumescent thigh. Jja was asleep on the bare floor at his side, exhausted from her vigil.

Nnanji stood at the far end, by a window, wiping himself with a towel. He had removed his hairclip, and his hair was a red mop. He was panting still, and grinning still. Without ponytail and harness he looked astonishingly young and innocent.

Honakura eyed him with concern. "You can beat him, then?"

He nodded and wiped his face. "He fooled me."

"*He* fooled *you?*"

"Yes." Puff. "He's very fast . . . has some good routines . . . but now I know them . . ." He wiped some more and panted some more. "He's not a swordsman. A swordsman would have others . . . he doesn't. I didn't realize!"

"And he tried to hurt you?"

Nnanji laughed, unable to suppress his joy. "At first. But I truly didn't mean . . . to hit like that. We were going very fast. It does happen."

Shonsu had said that Nnanji's memory worked in fencing, also. He never forgot anything. So now he had the captain's measure. He knew his tricks.

"You have hardly calmed the crew's worries, adept."

Nnanji had draped the towel over one shoulder and was combing back his hair with his fingers, about to replace his hairclip. His juvenile grin faded. "No." He frowned, lowering his arms. "And this does change things, doesn't it? I could hardly give him a sword if he might lose, could I?"

He gazed at the speechless Honakura with that strange new stare of his. It was Shonsu's stare. Then he waved at the oak chests.

"Pray sit, my lord." That was Shonsu, too.

Honakura sat, waiting, hiding a rising excitement.

Nnanji threw away the towel and quietly closed the aft shutters for privacy. Then he stooped to retrieve his harness and the seventh sword from the floor. "Have you, Lord Honakura, in all your years on the temple court, ever heard of a valid excuse for civilians killing swordsmen?"

Aha! So that was it?

"No, adept. I have been wondering the same. But, no. I have never heard of one."

Nnanji rubbed his chin thoughtfully. "One isn't enough—we need two, don't we? I think I've found them, but I'm not sure of the words. I need your help, my lord."

††† †††

Long before sunset the wind failed utterly, and *Sapphire* dropped anchor, still in mid-River. The evening meal was brought out early, and the fare was sparser than usual. There were jokes about starving to death if the calm continued—black humor. Black was the prevailing mood on board these days.

Brota had found one very, very tiny ray in the darkness—for the first time, she thought Shonsu seemed a little better. Reluctant to raise false hopes, she said nothing.

Tomiyano's stupidity in taking on a swordsman at fencing had cast a deeper pall than ever over *Sapphire*. He had tried to administer a beating and had thereby almost lost the first few passes. That had shaken his nerve, and then Nnanji had countered his every move and gone on to swamp him with innumerable complicated routines. She had recognized Shonsu's techniques, of course, and probably Tomiyano had, also, but never in time to block them. In a real fight her son would probably be still the better man, for in a real fight repetition did not matter. But Nnanji had coached Thana and Matarro, Tomiyano's pupils, and had also watched him fight against Shonsu. That experience had given him advantages Tomiyano had not foreseen. No matter how gifted, an amateur should not meddle with a professional.

But now the crew were more worried than ever, and there were dark whispers of caging Nnanji in a cabin. She had refused to listen, for she knew that the swordsman would fight if they tried it. For the first time since Tomminoliy had died, her leadership was being questioned, and the air smelled of mutiny.

Since the fencing, Nnanji had stayed out of sight in the deckhouse. Either he was being surprisingly tactful, or else the old priest had taken him in hand. He had appeared only once, when Tomiyano returned to collect his sanding blocks, coming out and offering to help with the work. That had been a peace offering, but the sailor had rejected it with obscenities. And the ship was too small to keep them apart for long.

So Brota abandoned her usual eating place. She sat herself on the aft end of the forward hatch cover, next to her still-resentful son. It was not a position she favored, for the flanking dinghies cut off her view of the River, but she had Tomiyano under control and could keep an eye on the deckhouse door. The rest of the family collected food and spread around the deck as usual, but there was little conversation and much angry brooding.

Jja appeared. She laid a few scraps on a plate, smiled faintly when spoken to, then hurried back to her master's sickbed. Katanji, ever sensitive to mood, had put himself in a far corner and was being invisible. The old priest arrived. He took a slice of bread and a lump of soft cheese over to the forward end of the other hatch cover, facing Brota and Tomiyano. That was an odd choice, and Holiyi had to move to make a space for him. Was the old man keeping an eye on Tomiyano, also?

So everyone was eating except Nnanji, and normally he was first pig at the trough. Then the sound of boots . . .

Brota lost interest in the plate beside her. The red-haired young swordsman was not going toward the food. There was a strained, tense look about him.

He stopped by the mast, facing her. But it was not she that he wanted.

"Captain Tomiyano?"

The sailor's hand slunk near to his dagger, and she prepared to grab his arm if he tried to draw it. "Well?"

Nnanji pulled in his chin and said gruffly, "I owe you an apology."

Surprise! No, astonishment! Formal apologies from swordsmen were rarer than feathers on fish.

Tomiyano's fingers moved up to touch the new scrape on his ribs. A half-healed scab had been knocked off; it was trivial. "I accept that this was an accident," he said gruffly.

"Not that, sailor." Whatever was coming, Nnanji was finding it difficult. He was taut. "I apologize for causing you worry. I made a mistake last week, when Novice Matarro asked me what would happen if Lord Shonsu were to die."

Goddess be praised!

"I said that I should have to avenge him. I was wrong."

Relief! The onlookers began to smile.

Nnanji took a very deep breath, all his ribs showing as they moved below his harness straps. "The oath we swore is very unusual, Captain. Of course he is not going to die, but even if he did, I misinterpreted that oath." Another pause, an even deeper breath, as if he had to force the words out. "Because, if Lord Shonsu were to die, you would not be at fault."

Tomiyano was suspicious, hunting for traps. "That's very nice. Why?"

"He empowered you as a posse. He told you to drop the sword, but he did not use the correct words. You were entitled . . . you were *required* . . . to continue obeying his previous order. When a civilian has been deputized, then the swordsman who warranted him is responsible for whatever happens."

"You're saying that Shonsu ki—wounded himself?"

Nnanji tensed even more, clenching his fists. "Legally, yes."

Tomiyano emitted a loud bellow of scornful laughter. "Well, that is very nice indeed! So I have nothing to fear? I can sleep sound, now? I don't need to worry about you creeping up on me with a sword?"

"Tom'o!" Brota wanted to strangle him.

"It means that I bear no onus of vengeance for what happened to Shonsu." Nnanji was glowering. "It does not mean that I may not take offense on my own account."

Before the sailor could reply, Brota said, "That is good news, adept. We are very relieved. Now, perhaps, you will join us in our evening meal? Tom'o, how about some wine to celebrate?"

Thana ran forward, took Nnanji's hand, and placed a quick kiss on his cheek. Color flooded into his paleness, but he did not look at her, or smile as he should have done. The old man was still watching carefully. There was more to come, then, although almost everyone else was grinning with relief and starting to chatter.

"It would be a strange case, Captain," Nnanji said loudly. The listeners fell silent. "It would mean that a civilian had slain a swordsman and escaped punishment. That never happens."

Thana backed away. Tomiyano went very still.

Nnanji looked at Brota and bit his lip. Then he said quickly, "Where is Yok, mistress?"

She took tight hold of Tomiyano's wrist. "Ten days up from Hool. Why?"

"You have never been back to Yok?"

"Since when?"

"Since your son was killed."

She looked at the old man. He had known this was coming. There must be more to it than an impetuous, arrogant young swordsman's suicidal blundering. "No. We never went back."

Again Nnanji seemed at a loss for words. Then he shouted, "Tell me!"

Tomiyano jerked his dagger hand free and threw his plate down. Sausage and carrots and pastry scattered at Nnanji's feet. "You don't want to know, sonny!"

"I must know! I can't denounce you, there is no one on board to judge."

"But there will be at Dri."

"Then you won't let me reach Dri. You know you won't."

Now the silence was unbearable, as sailor and swordsman stared at each other, Tomiyano dark with anger, Nnanji grim and pale. Again Brota looked to the old man, but he was being inscrutable.

"As you wish," Tomiyano said, baring his teeth. "Thana? Tell your nosy friend what you did at Yok."

Thana was pressing herself back against the starboard dinghy, shocked. "Mother!"

Brota shrugged. This was some sort of showdown, and she did not understand. It was too late to stop it, though. "Tell him."

"But, Mother—"

"Tell him!"

"I was still only a First," Thana whispered. "I went ashore with my sword on. Landlubbers don't like girls wearing swords."

Nnanji had turned to face her, grim and intent. Tomiyano's hand sneaked back to his dagger, and again Brota took hold of his wrist . . . *wait!*

"There were four of them," Thana said, speaking faster. "A Fourth, two Thirds, and a First. The adept challenged me . . ."

"And you made obeisance," said Nnanji, "of course."

She nodded. "Then he told me to strip. We were behind some bales on the dock."

Nnanji's lip curled. "And the others?"

"They were laughing . . . and making jokes. I dodged by them and ran back to the ship. They followed."

His face murderous, Nnanji swung back to the captain. "Did you drain them all?"

A long pause . . . long enough to die in.

"Eventually. But that didn't bring my brother back. Or Linkaro. And Brokaro died a week later."

Nnanji raised a hand, and Tomiyano tensed, but he was merely wiping his forehead with his wrist.

"Well, adept?" Brota spoke into silence. "Now you have it. We are swordsman killers. Assassins. There was no posse that time."

He frowned. "You could not have used a posse, mistress. A swordsman must not interfere in an affair of honor, and if the Fourth had properly challenged and Thana had made obeisance, then it was an affair of honor."

Tomiyano sneered. "Some honor!"

"Legally. Having made obeisance, Thana had lost a duel. She had to do whatever he demanded, until he sheathed his sword."

Oligarro and Maloli clambered to their feet at the side of the deck and moved closer to fire buckets. Holiyi copied them, reluctantly. Nnanji stood alone in the center, like a stag in a wolf pack, facing the captain's scorn.

"Even that, swordsman?"

Nnanji nodded. "A winner can demand anything, because the loser can still refuse, to preserve his honor."

"But then he may be killed?"

"Then he must be killed. Of course it was shameful! A Fourth should not challenge a First. Nor make villainous demands. Had I been there I would have warned him that I would challenge, afterward. But he was within his rights. No, legally you are assassins."

"And so you will denounce us when we get to Dri?"

Nnanji swallowed hard and shook his head.

The captain snorted in disbelief. "Why not?"

"Because you never went back to Yok. The Goddess could have moved you there. She could have prevented you from leaving."

There was a puzzled silence, a dawn of hope. Then the old man broke in, with his slurred, toothless voice. "Normally, of course, that is not a defense, mistress. As I explained to Adept Nnanji earlier, when we were discussing a parallel, but hypothetical, case, the gods can strike any sinner dead, so absence of divine intervention may not be construed as innocence."

If anyone still had doubts that he was a priest, then that speech would have drowned them.

"But in this case," Nnanji said, "She did move you. She brought you to Aus, to that quarry. You dragged your anchor; you were taken a very long way—an unusual display of Her Hand. The Goddess has judged the case Herself. Your penance is to help Lord Shonsu. No swordsman, or priest, may interfere when Her will has been made known. A similar thing happened to us at Hann. She has pronounced sentence Herself, and no human judge can overrule Her."

"You believe that, old man?" Brota demanded. He must have been behind all this. No swordsman could think that way, certainly not Nnanji.

He had guessed what she was thinking. "I agree with the adept's arguments, yes." He grinned toothlessly.

"I don't believe them!" Tomiyano jerked his hand free from

Brota's grip again and jumped to his feet. "And I surely don't trust them!"

Nnanji flushed. "I will swear an oath for you, sailor. But I shall need to draw my sword."

Tomiyano hesitated. He was well within range. "Let's hear it."

Deliberately, making no sudden move, Nnanji drew the glittering Chioxin sword and raised it to the oath position. It flamed blood in the rays of the setting sun. "I, Nnanji, swordsman of the fourth rank, oath brother to Shonsu of the seventh rank, do solemnly swear that all members of the crew of *Sapphire* have been cleared of wrongdoing in the deaths of four swordsmen in Yok; and this I swear upon my honor and in the name of the Goddess."

The seventh sword hissed back into its scabbard.

Astonished pause.

"And your boss?" the captain said. "If he recovers . . ."

Nnanji smiled wanly, looking more nervous than he had up until now. "He and I swore the swordsmen's fourth oath, Captain. My oaths are his, so I have committed Lord Shonsu, also. And no Seventh will ever overrule another. A priest might, but there would be no one to carry out his sentence. You are out of danger."

"You're a Fourth! You think you can bind all the Sevenths in the World?"

Nnanji's nervous smile grew wider, rather like his brother's juvenile, impudent smirk. "It is a grave responsibility! I warned Shonsu when he told me about that oath . . . Yes! All Sevenths. So all the swordsmen in the World, I suppose. Forever. Absolutely. Even if I am mistaken, we can only leave you to the Goddess."

"Old man?" Brota snapped.

He nodded his hairless head. "That is correct, mistress."

She was taking the word of a beggar?

Then Thana rushed forward and threw her arms around Nnanji. This time he laughed and embraced her, also, returning the kiss.

Tomiyano said, "Well, I'll be . . ." He looked at Brota as she rose. Everyone looked to Brota.

Too choked to speak, she nodded, smiling.

The long terror was over. Cheering rang over the deck. People were scrambling to their feet, wives embracing husbands, children screaming with excitement. Katanji was flat on his back with his arms around Diwa and Mei, as they both tried to kiss him at the same time. Thana was still clutched in Nnanji's arms, getting back much more kiss than she had planned to give . . .

"Nnanji! Nnanji!" Jja pushed her way through the throng.

A flushed Nnanji broke free of Thana so roughly that she almost fell.

"Nnanji!" Jja grabbed his arm. There were tears in her eyes. "He's awake . . . he says he feels hungry."

††† † †††

Shonsu was going to live, the trading was good, every day brought new lands to see. *Sapphire* sailed on in a glow of summery contentment. Swordsmen were not so bad, after all. Jonahs brought profits.

Sapphire came to Dri.

Dri was a city of haze and sunlight flickering over water, a city of misty glitter and iridescence, where gondolas and galleys plied busy canals. High-arched bridges linked wide piazzas; eggshell domes and alabaster towers faded back into the sky. The air was pungent with the scent of exotic spices and blossoms, vibrant with color and old sad songs being sung by undernourished gondoliers. Ornate ships made stately progress between edifices encrusted in marble trelliswork, beneath the steady gaze of severe ancestral statuary.

The officials were the worst Brota had ever met. They reached out in boats to meet *Sapphire*, as if impatient for their prey. They took her gold and directed her to a berth at one of the lesser trading islands.

Shonsu was still very weak. Even Tomiyano made no more than halfhearted suggestions that he be put ashore, and Nnanji had no intention of leaving the seventh sword unguarded, or of risking it on his own back near other swordsman. So the swordsmen stayed on board, and the sailors prepared to trade.

Brota sold the furniture easily, and the price was fair, even after a predatory customs had sucked its due.

"Rugs," Tomiyano said, and pointed to the nearest warehouse once again. Brota marched across at his side, and together they inspected and peered and fingered rugs, and haggled and pondered. The trader was difficult and insisted that he could only sell to a trader . . . meaning a fee for one of his relatives to act as agent. There would be another tax. Brota was more cautious than she had been with the brass. Trading should be based on experience and knowledge; at Ki or Hool she had known what to buy, what would sell, what things were worth. This strange Goddess-driven commerce was a gamble, a leap of faith that made her nervous, but at last she decided, and hands were shaken. Slaves began to carry the carpets and pile them by the ship, for yet another officer must inspect them before they were loaded.

She came out into the noisy, busy street with her son, and they stood in the sunlit throng and grumbled to each other, wondering if they had done right. A group of street musicians twanged and chirped on one side of them, a hawker was shouting the merits of his flowers on the other. Carts and pedestrians shoved and jostled and bustled.

Somehow, Brota thought, she was missing something. The rugs just did not feel right, although now she had shaken hands and could not renege.

"We shall still have space to spare," Tomiyano suggested, equally unsatisfied.

"Mistress?" said a voice at her elbow. She turned around to frown at the interruption, raising the frown to a glare when she discovered a slave, who should know better. He was very young, browner than most, skinny enough to show every rib. He wore only a scrap of black rag. He had dark curly hair and large, bright eyes.

She recoiled. "*Katanji!*" She gasped. "By all the gods, boy! You're out of your mind!"

He had drawn a black slave line down the center of his face.

It concealed his single swordmark, and the tiny crossbar could be seen only by a close inspection—and who ever inspected slaves closely?

Tomiyano grabbed his arm. "That's an abomination, my lad," he whispered. "If anyone notices, you'll be a slave forever and they'll put that mark on with a hot iron. Back to the ship, quickly!"

Katanji squirmed loose. "But wait! It was all right—I was round in the back, and it was dark in there."

Brota looked at Tomiyano, and Tomiyano at Brota; and then they both looked at Katanji.

"Doing what?" she demanded.

"Inspecting rugs." He pointed to his fathermark. "I know rugs! I saw you go in, so I did a little scouting for you. The slaves know all about the business and they don't care about their owners' profits, so they tell the truth—to another slave."

There could be truth in that. "And what did you learn?" Brota's curiosity was aroused.

"The silk ones are the best, aren't they? They're great!"

"Some of them. But you must buy ten wool for each silk. It's a city law. The other traders said the same."

The boy grinned. "That's only for traders! The locals buy them. A swordswoman could buy them!" He was becoming so excited that he seemed to be bouncing on the cobbles. "Did you see the one with the golden mermaids? Magnificent! And the only one they have from that shop, because city folk usually buy them all. I know where to go, and how much the locals pay."

Brota looked at Tomiyano, and Tomiyano looked at Brota. Smuggling?

"The wools are bulky," Brota said. "But even a gondola could hold quite a few silks."

Tomiyano nodded thoughtfully. "You'd have to buy the gondolier. He could lose his boat. Or his head."

"The regulars wouldn't dare—their ships could be impounded."

But no one will impound a ship with Shonsu on it.

"Let's do it!" Brota said. "Tom'o, you see to the loading. And you, novice? How do we get you back on the ship?"

He grinned again. "I'll see you on board, mistress." He stepped back and vanished like a soap bubble.

Tomiyano scowled and went running, dodging wagons and people. When Brota reached the gangplank, he was already in conversation with an official, but he paused to shake his head at her. "I thought he might have left a port open. But he didn't."

When the ship was docked, unlocked portholes were almost a capital offense—they could admit rats, four-legged or two-legged. She glanced around, but there was no sign of Katanji— which was hardly surprising on a dock so littered with piles of trade goods, with wagons and people. The official was being officious, clicking his abacus expensively . . . another bribe needed.

Her cabin, when she got there, was hot and airless. The seven-times-damned port official had cleaned out her supply of cash. She bolted the door, eased down to her knees, and slid open a panel. Of the many hidden compartments on the ship, this was the one she used most often. She eyed the hoard inside. How many rugs, even silk, could fit in a gondola? Not many, but perhaps almost as many as she had bought already, with *Sapphire*'s hold filling up with the wools. The boy had been quite right, it was the silks that would bring the profit. If you weren't sure of your market, stay with quality. The wools were not in that class. That lad was a born trader.

She selected a small leather bag. It held one hundred golds, and she was sure that a gondola would not take that much, maybe not half that much. Then she put on her sword and combed her hair and went back on deck.

As she approached the deckhouse, she heard a steady thudding. The ship was motionless, of course, and someone was taking the opportunity to practice knife throwing. She was stunned to discover that it was Nnanji, sitting on one of the chests because of the low head room, working his way through a collection of a dozen or so blades. From the look of the target board, he was doing very well.

He grinned at her surprise. "Quicker than swords!" he said.

He looked rather embarrassed, but obviously pleased with his native skill.

"I thought those were about the worst abomination in the canon, adept? Have I missed a new sutra?"

"My suggestion, mistress." That was Shonsu. He was sitting up now, leaning back against a heap of cushions, still very thin and wan, but certainly on the mend. Every day he was visibly stronger. "You know what the sutras say about sorcerers?"

If she confessed how many sutras she knew, Adept Nnanji's ginger hair would turn white instantly. "Can't say I've ever thought about it."

"Nothing! They're not swordsmen, so the ways of honor do not apply. They're armed civilians, an abomination in itself—so anything goes."

"But knives?" Even a water rat could feel uneasy at the thought of swordsmen hurling knives. Worse, Jja was sitting quietly in a corner, stitching at one of Shonsu's boots, and there was one of Nnanji's beside her. Concealed knives were worse yet.

Shonsu shrugged. He looked tired. Thana was kneeling attentively at his side. She had been playing nurse ever since Shonsu recovered consciousness and could appreciate her efforts. Brota did not think her daughter would succeed any more with Shonsu than Nnanji was succeeding with her, but a Seventh was worth the effort.

"When I met the sorcerers in Aus," Shonsu said, "they made me stand back from them. I wondered if they might need time to chant their spells, or whatever it is they do. And everything we've heard about them suggests that speed is the only effective attack. So—knives!" He sounded defensive about it, though.

"I'm not arguing, my lord! Thana, I need you to come ashore with me."

Thana turned solicitous eyes on Shonsu. "You can spare me for a little while, my lord?"

"I think I'll manage," he said politely.

Thana patted his hand, rose in a leisurely display of long, brown limbs, and sauntered catlike to the door. Her sashes were becoming quite indecent these days, hardly more than ribbons, and Brota caught a whiff of musk and violets that would have choked a goat. She would have to explain subtlety to Thana.

Nnanji threw. *Thud!* Bull's-eye. He smirked and reached for another knife.

Jja rose and went across to her owner, receiving a smile of welcome that spoke more than a dozen sutras. Then he looked to Brota again. "Mistress? I've been trying to make sense of what happened in Wal. You, Sailor Oligarro, Nnanji, and the captain, none of your stories are quite the same. The thunderbolt—you said the man vanished in the smoke, but you saw no flash. Oligarro says he fell off the gangplank, and there was a flash. Nnanji could not see . . ."

She had told him three times. Of course eyewitnesses would never agree. "What does Novice Katanji say, my lord?"

Shonsu and Nnanji exchanged surprised glances. "I was not aware that he was present."

Demons! She had just thrown away her guide to the source of illicit rugs. "Oh, yes! He was there, my lord."

Nnanji sprang off the chest and headed purposefully for the door. Brota followed him out on deck. Katanji was standing by the forward gangplank, wearing kilt and sword and boots. How had he managed . . .

She hurried after Nnanji, dodging rolls of carpet being carried aboard.

"I need a word with you, protégé!" he said ominously.

Katanji opened his eyes wide. "Of course, mentor." The only trace of his slave disguise was a faint oily smear on his nose. His face had been smeared that night in Wal, too. "Did you ask Mistress Brota about that sutra?"

Nnanji hesitated, then turned to Brota with a grin. "Can you explain one thousand and forty-four to me, mistress?"

Fortunately, a Fifth need only know up to nine eighty-one. "I'm not familiar with it, adept."

"Lord Shonsu threw it at me. He says he doesn't understand it, either, but I'm sure he's fooling." His eyes went blank and he quoted in a voice very like Shonsu's: "'On Lack of Footprints: It is better to give a blunt sword than a sutra to those beyond help.'"

Brota shrugged. Landlubber piffle! How was she going to

extract Katanji, or even get a quick word with him? "It doesn't seem to make much sense, does it? How can you give anything to someone who's beyond help?"

Nnanji nodded glumly. "I thought it might mean that it's better to give any help you can, even if it's not much, rather than just advice?"

"Where do the footprints come in, then?"

"Well . . . even if there's no fame or honor to be gained?"

"Could it have two meanings," Katanji said, "so you could take whichever one you wanted?"

"What's the other one?" his brother demanded cautiously.

Thana drifted out of the fo'c'sle door, wearing her best satin wrap and yellow sandals. She had her sword on her back. Nnanji's eyes wandered in that direction.

"Pirates leave no footprints," Katanji muttered, as though deep in thought. "Not like brigands on land. And 'blunt sword' could mean . . . a foil? And the frees can't help sailors . . ."

"That's it!" Nnanji shouted. "You've got it! It means you can teach fencing to sailors! Thanks, nipper!" Sorcerers forgotten, he spun around and ran for the deckhouse.

Katanji watched him go, shaking his head pityingly. Then he smirked at Brota. "Let's get the hell out of here!" he said.

Brota chose the largest gondola she could see, but it heaved mightily when she clambered in. She seated herself facing the gondolier to keep an eye on him. He was a skinny, sun-dried man with wide shoulders, about the right age to have many mouths to feed. Thana and the boy sat in front of him, facing her.

The gondolier pushed off, and the boat slid out toward the harbor. He sang a short welcome, tourist stuff, and then said, "Where to, mistress?"

"Into the city to make a few purchases and bring them back to the ship."

He guessed at once. "Rugs," he said, and his face went wooden. Thana helped in the negotiations, leaning back to smile up at him and let him peer down the top of her wrap while she wheedled. It was an article of faith in the family that Thana always got her own way. Wide-eyed and damp on the forehead, the gondolier settled for a lot less than the port officer had.

The boat glided forward again through sheets of light coming off the water. Misty towers glimmered in the distance. "Where to?" asked the gondolier again.

"Where to, novice?" Brota asked. The rugmaker would think he was furnishing a barracks when he saw three swordsmen arrive.

Katanji tore his eyes away from stately tall ships, the graceful galleys, the scurrying small craft. He smiled angelically. "What's my share?" he asked.

The boat flowed onward for a few minutes, and the only sounds were the music and port noises drifting over the harbor.

"What did you have in mind?" she demanded, deciding that five silver was tops.

He grinned. "I get first choice, and you transport mine free of charge to *Sapphire* and on *Sapphire* to wherever I want and unload for me." Then he paused, and his face grew serious. "And you promise not to tell Nanj. He says trade isn't honorable for swordsmen!"

Thana began to snicker. Brota didn't know whether to be furious at herself or amused at the lad.

"We don't allow private trading on *Sapphire*," she said grimly. "The crew all know that they have a share, and if anyone wants to leave he can take it then."

"With respect, mistress," Katanji said, not looking very respectful, "I'm not crew."

She surrendered with a wry smile, conscious that Thana was enjoying this and would love to tell the story to the rest of the family. "No, you're one of the Goddess' men, aren't you? All right, it's a deal. But don't you tell anyone, either. Or you, Thana!"

He leaned forward and held out both hands for the traders' shake, which amused her even more. Then he told the gondolier the Canal of Seven Temples and went back to eyeing the busy port.

Suddenly Brota remembered that this First had at least fifteen golds in his pouch. She'd been thinking that "first choice" meant one rug. He wouldn't dare . . . would he?

Before she could ask, Thana beat her to it. "How much are you planning to spend, trader?" she asked.

Katanji gave her a big, toothy smile. "Sixty-four golds," he said.

BOOK FOUR:

HOW THE SWORDSMAN EARNED AN ARMY

†

Casr, next city after Dri, lay also on the right bank, swordsman country. The Wind God continued to perform His duties apathetically, and when at last Casr came in sight, one hot and tranquil afternoon, Wallie was sufficiently recovered to be out of doors. Wearing nothing but his kilt, he sprawled on a hatch cover with his head on a pillow, soaking up sunshine like a millionaire on a private yacht. The boards were warm beneath him, and sails filled the sky.

By him lay his crutch, made for him by Sailor Holiyi. On his other side sat Jja, clad now in sailor breechclout and bra sash. They had to be black for a slave, of course, but they showed off her delectable figure in a way that Wallie found thunderously provocative. From time to time he would squeeze her hand, or she would squeeze his, and then they would smile to each other in silent contentment. Thana, praise to the Most High, had at last become discouraged in her wooing and was nowhere around.

The World crawled along at its leisurely preindustrial pace. It was a very peaceful way to go to war. Wallie was being given time to recover his health and apparently he was going to make a full recovery. The pious might class that as a miracle cure.

Sailors sauntered by upon their daily tasks, tending ship and children, clothes and food. The glances they sent his way were at best friendly, at worst respectfully polite . . . and that was another miracle. Their former hostility had vanished, being replaced by a grudging acceptance of the passengers. Brota had even found cabins for them, doubling up youngsters and clearing out storage.

Up on the poop, steel clashed on steel as Nnanji coached Mata. Since his mentor had uncovered that curiously ambiguous sutra, ship life had been transformed for him from a hell of boredom to a heaven of day-long fencing. No longer was he restricted to teaching Thana, Katanji, and Matarro. The sailors welcomed the instruction. On the River, it was wise insurance.

Wallie was still savoring that thought when a shadow warned him and he raised his eyes to see the humorless face of Tomiyano like a dark cloud in the sky. He sat up.

"Casr in sight . . . my lord." Tomiyano no longer thought murder when he looked at Shonsu, but neither did he experience ecstasies of brotherly love. "Just wondering if you felt able to recruit some swordsmen yet?" He was obviously resigned to a negative reply.

Wallie shook his head. He tried a smile, but it was absorbed and not reflected. Moving the crutch out of the way, he gestured to the hatch beside him.

"Not yet, Captain. But sit a moment and let's discuss it."

Tomiyano shrugged and perched on the edge as if not planning to stay long. His bruises were gone now, the scrapes healed. The burn on his face had developed white strands of scar tissue. A proud man—proud of his ship, now appropriated by the gods; proud of his physical self, eclipsed by the titanic presence of Shonsu; proud once of his independence . . .

"I'm not fit for duty yet," Wallie said. "But one day, Captain, you'll get your ship back. One day I'll have cleaned up the sorcerers. Then we'll both be free agents. And perhaps, when that day comes, you and I can meet in a bar somewhere and clean that up together? Or clean up each other, if you prefer. I'll spot you one friend or two chair legs, and I'll flatten the furniture with you. After that's over, we could tear up the whole dock front? Go wenching and start a legend? Build the sort of hangover that makes a man suicidal? Riot and pillage and . . ."

Tomiyano's face stayed wooden. He laid his hands on the hatch as if about to rise. "Anything else, my lord?"

Wallie sighed—wrong approach. "Yes. After Casr, I believe, comes Sen. But that's left bank. Next swordsman city is Tau . . . a week, maybe?"

"If we get some decent wind."

"Well, I should be mobile by then."

"You'll be disembarking in Tau?" The sailor's expression was cautious.

Wallie knew what was bothering him. "As soon as I'm fit and we reach a city with some reasonable swordsmen, then your obligations are ended, the contract fulfilled. We'll disembark. Fair enough?"

The sailor was also a trader. "Define 'reasonable swordsmen.'"

"A pair of Thirds? Able-bodied types, of course. Yes, I'd say that two Thirds would do to start with. They, at least, could cover my back."

The sailor nodded and again seemed about to depart.

"Stay awhile," Wallie said. "If you have a minute? I've a problem you may be able to help me with."

Tomiyano settled back, his face revealing nothing, but at that moment an outburst of laughter came wafting down from the fencers and their audience on the poop, with Nnanji's the loudest of all. The captain glanced that way, and his eyes narrowed.

"Now there's a miracle for you," Wallie said softly.

"Miracle?"

"Nnanji. Not many men can overcome their own prejudices as he did, Captain."

Tomiyano scowled. "Prejudices? Prejudices would be opinions not based upon experience, would they not?"

"Or on experiences not relevant." Wallie found it hard to be patient around Tomiyano. "Think what he started with—years of consorting with almost no one but swordsmen. Of course he regarded civilians with scorn—it was how he was trained to think. He was also taught that assassination was an absolutely unforgivable crime, the ultimate atrocity—"

"You disagree with that oath he swore?"

"Not in the slightest. What I mean is that he found that his training was inappropriate and he rose above it. Few people ever do that, Captain. The old man swears he played no part—

it was all Nnanji's idea. When we first came aboard, he believed that you and your family should be proud to serve him, just because he was a swordsman. Now he regards you as friends and allies. That's quite a feat of adjustment, is it not?"

"It's an improvement."

"And you? You believed that all swordsmen were murderers and rapists. How are your prejudices coming along, Sailor Tomiyano?"

The captain flushed. "My opinions were based on experience."

"But not relevant experience."

"I admit I was proved wrong, in your case. Only in your case."

Wallie shrugged, knowing that most swordsmen would have been ready to draw blood for that remark. But a ship's captain ought to appreciate leadership, and Nnanji had demonstrated a faculty for leadership that Wallie had never suspected behind that flippant juvenile grin. He had been guilty of prejudice himself, thinking of his young assistant as merely a useful ax-man and a handy walking reference library. So there was another niggling question: how large a part was Nnanji destined to play in Shonsu's quest?

Tomiyano went back to business. "What was the problem you wanted to discuss?"

"In a sense, my problem is knowing what my problem is, if you can follow that. A god told me I had a mission, but he didn't say what it involved, just that it would be revealed to me. Well, now I've met the sorcerers, so I know *what* I'm supposed to do, even if I still don't know *how*. But he also gave me a riddle."

The sailor's eyebrows pushed the three shipmarks up into his chestnut hair. Petulance succumbed to curiosity. "A riddle, my lord?"

"A riddle. And this is the part that concerns you:

When the mighty has been spurned,
An army earned, a circle turned,
So the lesson may be learned.

"We assume that a swordsman of my rank qualifies as being mighty, and spurning is a mild description of what I got in Aus."

Obviously intrigued, Tomiyano scratched his head. "How do you earn an army?" he asked warily.

He did not speak the natural continuation of the question: How did Lord Shonsu earn an army after what he had done in Aus? If that tale arrived before him, he would be refused at best and denounced at worst. If it became known after he had enlisted swordsmen, then it would detonate a mutiny. His contract with Brota had specified that he was to be given passage to the nearest city where he could recruit swordsmen, but could Shonsu ever recruit swordsmen now?

Which might be why Honakura had been suggesting that *Sapphire*'s crew might be the army in question. They had all been nimble with a sword even before Nnanji began his lessons, and his training was rapidly giving them a versatility and polish they had never had before. Nevertheless, Wallie could not believe that he was expected to fight several cities' worth of sorcerers with a dozen or so amateurs, half of them women, and he certainly was not going to mention the idea to Tomiyano. The swordsmen and their companions might be tolerated now as a necessary evil, but *Sapphire*'s crew were not soldiers. Warfare had no appeal for them, and fire demons were certainly not in the contract.

"I don't know how one *earns* an army," Wallie said. "I am sure that the lesson part concerns the sorcerers—somehow, there must be a way to fight them. But it's the circle part I wanted to ask you about."

"What circle?"

"The one we're turning!" He chuckled at the sailor's puzzled frown. "So far we know of four swordsmen cities to our left, on the right bank—Ki San, Dri, and Casr straight ahead there. Tau comes next, I'm told."

"So they say." Then the sailor pulled a face. "We're traders, Shonsu, not explorers. Traders trade back and forth—usually between two cities, sometimes a stretch of three or four. If the Goddess does not return us to Hool, then we'll trade here just as happily. Ki San and Dri will do fine. I admit I like the climate, though I'm told the winters are bad. We'll study what sells and what's needed. We weren't even planning to go on to Tau, but I suppose we still have to find you some swordsmen. If there are none in Tau, then we'll bring you back to Casr. Or Ki San. You'll be on your feet by then."

Wallie had been hoping that Tomiyano would have been more inquisitive. He ought to know more of the geography than Honakura and Katanji had been able to uncover; but obviously not. Brota had shown the same lack of interest.

"On the left bank, Captain, we know of Aus and Wal—sorcerer cities. Next comes Sen. But I know of another one ahead, further upstream."

"What's that?"

"Ov."

"But . . ." The sailor scowled. "That was where you'd come from, when we met you? That's weeks back, Shonsu!"

To a sailor there were only two directions in the World: up and down River. Distance was measured in days. Patiently Wallie began to explain, drawing invisible maps on the hatch cover with his fingers. The River made a loop—north from Ov, then west, around or through the mountains, and then south to Aus. The Black Lands upstream from Ov were the same Black Lands that lay downstream from Aus. There was the god's circle that must be turned.

He had worked it out during his convalescence, only to discover that his companions already knew. Honakura had seen it first, on the top of the pass, or so he claimed, when Wallie had pointed out the River ahead and had argued that it must flow south. Nnanji had probably learned it from Katanji.

Eventually logic overcame the sailor's prejudices. He nodded. *Sapphire* was sailing up the west side of a loop. Already the mountains of RegiVul lay to the east and south, and they had been northeast of Aus. At Ov, they had lain to the northwest.

"You expect us to take you all the way around to Ov, Shonsu?" he demanded angrily.

"I have to go back to Ov, Captain, and turn the circle. Whether that means the city itself or the manor house where we started, I don't know. Whether we travel there on *Sapphire* or not, I don't know. But it would help if you asked some sailors in Casr. How far is it? How many cities have the sorcerers seized? The old man says he knows, but he's just guessing."

Seven, of course, Honakura said—it would have to be seven. Wallie had not disputed the point, because he was developing a hard respect for the priest's superstitions.

Then boots thumped on the old polished planks, and there was Nnanji, hot and sweaty and grinning, fencing completed for the time being. Behind him, the city of Casr was drawing near. "You will be staying on board, my lord brother?" he inquired.

"I will," Wallie said. He noted once more the subtle signs of change in Nnanji—the tiny pause that came before he spoke and after others did, the calculation hidden below the habitual joviality, the secret pride in his own competence. Wallie's lectures on the theory of thinking and responsibility had been promptly followed by practice in white water, and no one of Nnanji's age could have come through that without a few scars. On the surface he was still the same impractical idealist, an irrepressible rapscallion, but something deeper had been awakened now. Blind hero worship had become considered respect. Being Nnanji, he would forget nothing.

"I'll stay, but I don't see why you can't do a little exploring," Wallie said. "You could visit the garrison in Casr and talk with the reeve."

Nnanji's smile vanished. Evidently he had already considered the possibility. "I think that might be inadvisable," he said softly. "They will ask if I have a mentor—who and what rank. And if the reeve hears that there is a Seventh in town, then he will certainly come to call."

Wallie was about to suggest that Nnanji could tell lies—but of course he wouldn't. Based on his experience with the venal Hardduju at Hann, and the Cowie incident in Ki San, Nnanji now had a strong distrust of reeves.

"You might learn something about sorcerers, though."

"I still think it would be inadvisable . . . brother." Nnanji was being respectful, but he was prepared to be stubborn. "You are not yet restored to health."

Wallie sighed. "As you wish. But, Nnanji . . . that oath we swore was the oath of brotherhood."

"Yes?"

"Not motherhood."

Nnanji grinned and pointed a lean arm at the fo'c'sle. "Go to your room, Shonsu!"

Evidently Tomiyano was still mulling the god's riddle. "Suppose we did sail all the way to Ov, my lord? Why Ov? What happens there?"

"Captain," Wallie said sadly, "I'm damned if I know. Maybe I missed something?"

††

After Casr the weather broke, as if to hint that summer was aging and might die soon. In rain and fog and gloom they came to Sen. Black Sen, the sailors called it, and the name fit—black basalt walls and black slate roofs, morbid buildings over noisome narrow alleys glittering icily in the wet. Cramped against the River between two cliffs, the town had bloated upward in tenements of five or six stories, turning cramped streets into tenebrous canyons. Even the docks were black, and the sorcerers' tower seemed no more depressing or ominous than the rest of the city. The pedestrians and the horses cowered along in the wet, hunched and dejected.

Katanji watched the arrival through the porthole in Diwa's cabin. So far he had not been summoned to the deckhouse, where Shonsu and Nnanji would skulk while *Sapphire* was in port. It was too late now to send Nanj to get him, for the ship was already close to the dock, but they might yet send Jja.

Diwa fretted nervously at his side. He had his slave loincloth ready, and his makeup. That was a mixture of lampblack and goose grease, Matarro had said. They used it to lubricate the capstan. Matarro did not know that Katanji had purloined some, or the other use he had found for it.

Shonsu had torn him apart when he had learned that Katanji

had gone ashore in Wal to talk to the slave gang under the wagon, although he had been pleased enough to get the eyewitness reports that Katanji had gathered. The port officer had fallen off the gangplank when the thunderbolt struck him. He had not been turned into smoke, as Brota had said. There had been two sorcerers waiting on the dock . . . the man had been dead or unconscious . . . they had taken his pouch and pushed him over into the River . . .

That news had pleased Shonsu, but he had still been molten, claiming that Katanji had disobeyed orders. That had not been true. As they left Aus, he had been told not to go ashore if *Sapphire* ever returned there. Nothing had been said about other sorcerer ports. Nanj had confirmed that, quoting the big man's exact words.

"Very well!" Shonsu had said, glaring black murder. "But in any other sorcerer port, you don't set foot on the gangplank! You don't even go on deck! Is that clear?"

Perfectly clear—Katanji went in and out portholes when he was being a slave, anyway. Tactfully, he had not mentioned that he had gone ashore again in Wal, the next day, and had roamed the town for hours.

And now Shonsu had asked Brota to visit Sen so he could gather wisdom. Sailors and one old priest—what could they learn? What could swordsmen discover by hiding in the deckhouse and peering out windows? Wisdom was Katanji's business; the god had said so.

Sly, sneaky old Honakura had found out what he was up to, and he had deflected Shonsu a couple of times when the conversation had veered onto dangerous territory. But even he now said that next time must be the last time. "Then you must tell them novice. And they'll have to stop you. But it's worth one more try."

The dock was coming up fast now, on this side. Had the ship turned, then he would have had to nip across to the cabin he shared with Matarro.

"Good!" Katanji said. He pulled off his breechclout and began tying on the black loincloth.

He had Diwa well trained now. She held up the mirror she

borrowed from her parents' cabin. He reached for his grease pot and spatula.

"Hold it still, wench!" he said. Her hands were trembling.

"Oh, Katanji! It's so dangerous!"

"I've told you! I'm a swordsman. Danger is my business. A swordsman's woman must be strong as well as beautiful . . . and you *are* beautiful."

That took her mind off danger. She blushed a rich, dark shade—very rewarding—and her hands steadied. He smiled and concentrated on his makeup again. "Only the fair deserve the brave, Nanj says."

She whimpered a little. She was a pretty thing, nicely rounded. A few more years and she'd be as disgustingly fat as her Aunt Brota, but right now she was just very cuddly.

"There!" He had done. It was nice to have a girl he could look down at. Mei was too tall for him. "I can't kiss you now, or I'll smudge it. But I'll make it up to you tonight."

She laid her cheek against his neck. "Be careful, my darling. "I'll feel terrible if anything happens to you."

The ship bumped gently into fenders. He put his arms around her and was surprised to discover how hard it was to take them away again.

"Nothing will. Now, keep a good lookout. And get down here fast when I signal!"

He opened the porthole a crack. The lines had been tied. There was a pile of bales just in front . . . perfect. He opened the flap wider and slithered out onto the cold, wet dock.

The crowds were thin because of the rain, but people were walking with their heads down, not looking around, and that suited Katanji very well. He kept his head down, also, walking with a slave's listless shuffle. It was good to get out of his boots; he shucked them whenever Nanj was not looking, but rarely got away with it for long. The wisp of loincloth was lots more comfortable than that kilt. He felt like a kid again, running around with the sun shining on his butt, not having to strut about with his head up, being a swordsman. He still could not think of himself as a swordsman, no matter how much Nanj shouted at him.

He headed up one of the narrow streets. It was gloomy enough that no one could possibly see anything wrong with his slave stripe. This would be the last time, and he must make it pay, gathering lots of wisdom.

He chuckled at the thought of Nanj. His ponytail would stand straight up, and he'd scream like Aunt Gruza. Shonsu would roar, but in secret he would approve. Yet he would not overrule Nanj in a thing like this. The big man liked to learn things—so did Katanji, and there were not many people like that around. Well, today he would find out plenty to add to what he had learned in Wal. Then the two of them would sit down together, and he'd give Shonsu all the wisdom, and Shonsu would shake his head admiringly and say, "Well done, novice," in that deep growl of his. Then even Nanj could not scream too much.

He caught a glimpse of the tower down another alley and turned that way.

Then he reached the square and ducked into a doorway to take a look. Just like Wal and Aus—the bag-heads had pulled down buildings to make their tower and leave an empty space around it. This was as close as he had gone at Aus, but in Wal he had walked right by the tower and picked up some of that swordsman intelligence that the sutras listed. He could do that now, but this tower looked exactly like the others. He could see a big raised door for unloading wagons, so there would be another, smaller door on the far side. No windows for at least three spans above the ground, then there were thirteen layers of windows in all. The stairs they would have to climb! But exactly alike. Sorcerers must have a sutra for building towers.

He walked across the square, counting his paces to the tower and alongside the tower and past the tower. Then he worked his way round the streets to come out another alley and did the same thing in the other direction. Square tower, twenty-two paces each side, as he had expected. The doors were the same —heavy wood with bronze scrollwork on them, bronze feather shapes. And again there was a pit in front of each door with a bronze grating over it.

Why? The pit was shallow, and the gratings did not look hinged, so they were not traps.

A lot of bronze: expensive! Birds, too. There had been birds round the other towers, strutting about on the ground and fluttering clumsily out of his way as he passed. Something to do with feather facemarks? He was standing on a corner, wondering what to do next, when the small door opened and a sorcerer of the Second came out with a basket and started throwing something on the ground. The birds all gathered around, so it must be food.

He wondered if the birds were sorcerers in disguise. What would happen if he grabbed one? If it changed back into a sorcerer would its feathers turn into a gown, or would he be naked? Or were the birds prisoners, changed by sorcery, hanging around the tower in the hope of being turned back into men? He shivered.

Then a boy came across the square pulling a cart with fish painted on its sides. He stopped at the small door and spoke to the Second, who opened the door for him, and he started carrying boxes into the tower. Katanji came out of his corner and crossed the square in the slow, lazy lope of a slave who had been told to run. He grabbed a look in the boxes as he went by. Octopus? *Yuck!*

That was enough for now, so he wandered off through the town for a while, enjoying the smells, the people, the smell of people, the old familiar feel of horsedung between his toes. Ship life got boring for a city man.

He headed back to the docks to check on *Sapphire*. Two traders were trudging up the plank to haggle with Brota. That was all right, then. He had hours yet.

He went exploring the alleyways, looking for a slave hole. As a kid he had gone slaving often with Kan'a and Ji'o . . . what would they be doing now? Kan'a had sworn to the fullers. Ji'o was probably a draper now, like his dad.

The three of them had learned more from listening to slaves than their parents had ever known. Sometimes they had even drawn slave lines on their faces, although that was so risky that it had made his gut quiver and usually they had not done that. He had assumed when he got pricked as a swordsman that his slaving days were over. Then he had seen that a slavestripe would cover up a single sword, and the temptation had been too much to resist. He had gone down to the dock in Wal in the thunderstorm and gathered a lot of wisdom sitting under that wagon. Two golds . . . it had been worth at least two hundred to Brota.

So the Goddess had approved, and the next day he had gone slaving around Wal.

Slaves were slaves. Slave holes were slave holes. He found a deep alcove between two buildings, where a wooden stair went up. There was just room to squeeze between the steps and one wall—slaves were never fat unless they'd been gelded. He squeezed through, and there, sprawled underneath in the dark and filth and stink, were three slaves, assiduously shirking.

They just grunted, so he joined them, finding a place next to one of them where there was no dung on the ground. He sat down and huddled up for warmth, listened to their talk for a while; listened to the rain drip and a billion baritone flies. Just like old times.

The talk was of women, of course—bragging about what their mistresses demanded when their masters were away. None of them believed the others, it was all wishful thinking, and they all knew that. It made him horny listening to them, though, and he started thinking about Diwa. Maloli would kill him if he found out what had happened to his dear little, innocent, virgin daughter, or how much his dear little daughter enjoyed it.

But who would tell? Matarro knew; he'd wakened up at least once as his roommate came home at dawn. Truth be told, Katanji had been a little clumsier than necessary that first time. Stepping on his fingers had been a bit excessive. Later Matarro had tried to frighten him, saying Brota had put Diwa up to it, wanting to trap Katanji because he would make a good water rat. He did not believe that. He did not *think* he believed that. You could not trap a swordsman on land that way, but the riverfolk had narrow ideas. Certainly it would create a hell of a fight—he had been told not to use the women. But Matarro was a good kid. Very naïve, being just a sailor, but he wouldn't split.

Very gently he edged into the conversation. New slave in

town: what's this sorcerer business? How many of them? What do they do? Could they cast a spell to make a slave a free man?

"They'd sell you a magic potion to do it," one of the men said, and one of the others laughed. They worked together, these two. What's so funny? asked the third—younger, not much older than Katanji.

"You know what they make those potions out of?" the first said. "Horse pee."

The third said manure they did.

"Fact. Our owner has a stable. Collects the horse pee and the sorcerers buy it off him."

Manure again.

"Manure you!" the first growled. "Fact. You go walk by that tower of theirs. You'll smell it. Stinks like a stable, but there's no horses there."

"I used to belong to a tanner," Katanji said. "Now there was stink!"

"None of those around here. Sorcerers ran them out of town."

Again! The same as Wal—what did sorcerers have against tanners? "How about dyers?"

"Them, too. Why?" The oldest slave was getting suspicious of so many questions.

But there had been no dyers in Aus or Wal, either. Shonsu would love this.

"I'd heard that," Katanji said. "Didn't believe it. What about thunderbolts? Fact?"

"Fact," the oldest said. "Big noise and fire and smoke. Seen one."

"No big noise," said the middle one. "Seen one, too. Big flash of light was all."

They got to arguing. The first man had been walking along a street when a madman came out of a house, a slave gone weird, waving a bloody ax. He had killed three people inside and got two more in the street. Then a sorceress of the Second—piddly little girl—had stepped in front of him. Big noise, smoke, dead slave.

So even a Second could cast that spell? Shonsu would not like hearing that.

That was *all* manure, the other said, pure, adulterated manure. He'd seen *swordsmen* killed by a thunderbolt. The others scoffed, so he went into details. Couple years ago—dark night, clouds over the Dream God ... coming home late from a woman, he'd been making a shortcut across the square and seen three swordsmen—ponytails, swords, the whole rig. They must have come off a ship. They'd been carrying bundles. He'd stopped in the shadows to watch, because there had not been swordsmen in Sen for years, and he'd made out the bundles. They'd been faggots. The swordsmen had run across the square to the small door of the tower, and he'd guessed that they were going to set a fire against the door. He thought they'd been drunked up pretty good.

They'd stopped at the grating, suspicious, and put down the bundles. He thought a window had opened high up, but he was not sure. Then the swordsmen had gone to look at the door and there'd been a big flash of lightning and screams. No big noise, just a sort of glass-breaking sound; loud for glass, but not thunder.

Two of the swordsmen had come back and gone by him, one helping the other. The third had stayed, dead.

"Cooked," he said. "They went right by me, and I could smell roast meat off the hurt one. He was making nasty noises and smelling like pork. You go look at that door on the tower! You can still see the scorch marks."

Two types of thunderbolt? Or a demon?

The nearest slave put his arm round Katanji. "You're a nice kid," he said.

"No!" Katanji tried to wriggle loose.

"It's all right if it's all you can get," the slave said, without much conviction. "Try it, come on!"

"No," Katanji protested, not daring to shout very loud.

"Oh, let him go," the youngest said. "I'll do it with you."

Katanji left then.

He checked on *Sapphire* again, and she was unloading cargo, so he still had time. He must try to find more wisdom. He went back to the square, and the rain was even heavier, the clouds lower and gloomier. A group of slaves was waiting by the big door, ten or twelve of them. He hung around, watching, beginning to feel frustrated.

Then a wagon came grumbling along the street behind him, heading for the square and the tower. It was big—four horses. Maybe from out of town? From Vul, even? Shonsu might know. It was loaded high with something, a leather cover over it. More slaves walked behind. Two slave gangs? He could join in, and then each would think he belonged to the other. When the wagon and its followers passed him, he tagged on and trailed after them across the square before he had time to get scared.

Halfway there his insides began to leap up and down. What in the names of all the gods was he doing? He must have been out of his mind, but it was too late to stop now. If he tried to bolt they'd start a runaway slave cry, and the whole town would give chase. *Goddess, preserve me!*

The big doors were opened. The teamster maneuvered the wagon onto the grating, against the loading door. Three sorcerers appeared, a Third and two big Firsts. They tried to keep the load dry, holding up the cover so that the slaves could pull out the sacks and hustle them inside. Katanji climbed up on the dock with the others, and no one looked at him twice.

He must tell Shonsu that the walls were an arm's-length thick. There would be no knocking holes in those.

A sack was dumped on his shoulder, and his legs almost crumpled. He staggered into the tower, following the man in front.

He was crazy! What had possessed him? They would hear his heart!

They would hear his knees—either his terror or the load he was carrying was making them knock like castanets.

The air did stink of horses. Phew!

It was dark in there, a big, high room reaching right up to the first windows, and probably half the width of the tower. He could look up and see great massive beams supporting the ceiling. The place was cluttered, but the sack hid everything to his right, and on his left was just a wall of bins, some of them open, holding herbs.

A swordsman spying inside a sorcerers' tower... what would they do to him if they caught him at it?

The slave in front stepped into a sort of big closet and

dumped his sack on a pile and came out. Katanji copied him with relief. Two sorcerers stood by the entrance, watching—a Fourth in orange, and a Second, whose yellow gown shone bright in the gloom.

Remembering to keep his head down, Katanji emerged from the closet, still following the same slave. He rubbed his back . . . mucking heavy, those sacks! Then, as he was going past the sorcerers, one of them reached out and tapped him on the shoulder.

†††

Sapphire was still gliding toward the dock in Sen, while Honakura sat on an oak chest like a ragged black owl and Nnanji slouched restlessly by the windows and Wallie thudded knives into the target board. Then Brota swooped into the deckhouse, swathed in an enormous madder-colored leather cloak, more huge even than usual, an angry cumulus cloud. Water was puddling all around her as it ran off that great expanse of stitched leather and dripped from her ponytail. It shone on her plump brown face and white eyebrows.

"I don't like the look of this place," she grumbled. "What do you think you're going to learn here, my lord?"

"I don't know, mistress."

"Traders expect shelter. They'll want to come in here!"

Wallie had not thought of that. There was nowhere else he would be able to see much at all. The portholes would be level with the dock, or lower. "Hang a drape? Yes—I've seen washing hung in here, haven't I?"

Brota rolled her eyes at the thought of swordsmen hiding behind laundry, but she swung around and went off to organize.

"Where's our mascot?" Wallie asked. "Perhaps we should keep him under our eye."

Nnanji nodded. He was turning for the door when Honakura said, "Lord Shonsu? What would you say was the most unusual thing the sorcerer did, the one who came aboard in Wal? And you, adept? What do you think?"

"Killing a man with a snap of his fingers," Wallie suggested.

"Not killing me with another!" Nnanji grinned as if that were funny.

The old priest shrugged his huddled shoulders. "We knew they could do something like that. And you were not trying to draw your sword, adept. Not like the late Swordsman Kandoru . . . No. That's not it." He looked puzzled.

"Tell us."

"That spell of good fortune he offered to put on the cargo!"

What bright thoughts were sparkling below that polished scalp? "He must have known of the fire," Wallie said.

"Exactly! It's like that bird that they magicked into the kettle for the captain, isn't it?"

"It is?"

Honakura scowled at the obtuseness of swordsmen. "When you capture a dangerous prisoner, Lord Shonsu, do you demonstrate your swordsmanship? Do you throw apples in the air and split them?"

"Showing off?"

"Like little boys! Why?"

It was a curious point, possibly significant. Honakura had a finely honed instinct for people.

"Katanji says he was lumpy. That interests me more," Wallie said.

"Lumpy? Boils?"

"No. Their gowns are made of very heavy, stiff material, but the wind was blowing hard that night, and Katanji says that either the man had packages strapped around him, or a great many pockets. He's a very quick little rascal, that one. Which reminds me. Nnanji—"

Honakura leered. "That's not all he's quick at."

"What do you mean? He was told—"

The old man put a warning finger to his lips as Brota came in with Mata, bearing bundles. Quickly they strung a line along the length of the room and draped wet sheets over it. Nnanji pushed the chests to one side, so the swordsmen could sit unseen, yet would be able to see and hear whatever was going on. They would be on the landward side, Brota assured them, and able to watch the dock, also. It was ingenious but not very plausible, for nothing would dry in Sen on this drippy day. Wallie wondered if sorcerers could see through cotton—but then they might be able to see through timbers as easily.

The deckhouse began to fill up with wet people, including children, giggling at the novelty of wearing capes. Their play would be a good distraction if anyone became suspicious, for nothing could seem more innocent than children's laughter.

As *Sapphire* nestled against the dock, Wallie remembered Katanji. Too late now to send Nnanji. Honakura, who had just wandered away so ingenuously, had deliberately diverted Wallie's attention from the boy, and not for the first time, either. Katanji must be up to something, and Honakura was covering for him. Still, the novice had been ordered not to go ashore in sorcerer ports, so he could not get into too much mischief. Wallie put Katanji out of his mind.

Tomiyano had announced that if sorcerers in Wal could stomach Nnanji on a ship, then a burn mark was not going to upset them, and he stayed in view, wearing the dagger. Jja entertained the toddlers, leaving sailors free to attend to business.

The port officer was an old woman, twisted and lame from arthritis, sad and respectful. She ignored the captain's scar, muttered quickly that no swordsmen should go ashore, accepted two golds, and limped away. Wallie concluded that she was probably genuine and probably frightened of her masters.

So the sorcerers were succeeding in their efforts to cure corruption among the officials. In the ports on the right bank the swordsmen either could not or did not try, and graft persisted in traditional fashion. The only crimes that swordsmen recognized were the violent varieties. Wallie could not imagine a Nnanji-type swordsman trying to unravel the intricacies of embezzlement or fraud. The sorcerers wanted to encourage trade. Again, the swordsmen would not care. Wallie, being a very atypical swordsman, rather approved of that. He found the notion amusing, remembering the words of the demigod: "You do not think like Shonsu, and that pleases me."

An awning had been jury-rigged over the top of one gangplank, where Brota had made herself comfortable in her chair, and the edge of the dock below was cluttered with her samples. Old Lina wandered down the other plank to inspect the hawkers' wares. Rain splattered and dripped.

Wallie began to grow bored and frustrated. These damn facemarks! How could he run a war with such a handicap? If the enemy could become invisible, or change their crafts at will, then they could penetrate the swordsmen cities easily. It was not fair! He grew short-tempered, wanting to shout at the children to be quiet.

Quite soon, though, Brota brought in two traders and argued them up from one hundred and fifty to two forty-five, while the eavesdroppers listened in amusement behind the draperies. Hands were shaken, and the traders went off to watch the unloading of the baskets and leather goods.

Then came Holiyi. He was the youngest of the adult sailors, skinnier even than Nnanji, and notoriously short of speech— amiable enough, but apparently able to go for days without saying a word.

"Ki San, Dri, Casr, Tau, Wo, Shan, and Gi," he told Wallie. "Aus, Wal, Sen, Cha, Gor, Amb . . . and Ov!" He smiled, turned, and stalked out. For him, that had been a notable oration—and a fine display of the trained memory expected among preliterates.

So Tomiyano must have ordered him to inquire about the geography, and he had done so. Honakura had been correct, then—seven cities on each bank. Seven free cities lying on the outer rim of the River's loop, and seven lining the inner curve seized by sorcerers? Assume so—based on superstition, which seemed to work as well as evidence in the World. For the millionth time, Wallie wished he could write. Of course he could sketch a map—with charcoal, say—but he would not be able to attach labels to it. He had tried, and it did not work. He asked Nnanji to repeat the lists for him while he pictured how the River must flow: north out of the Black Lands near Ov, charting a wide circle counter-clockwise—around Vul?—and back south into the Black Lands again at Aus. The only gap in this River-drawn circle would be the neck of land between Aus and Ov, which they had already crossed.

Wallie was still mulling over his mental map when a curious procession came marching up the plank. The slaves had only just begun removing the cargo, and here was new business already. With a little luck, *Sapphire* would soon be able to leave this dismal place.

The leader was a middle-aged Fourth, followed by two younger men who wore brown robes and were therefore likely priests, for other crafts kept to loincloths at their age. All three carried leather umbrellas. The last man was younger, a Third. He was husky and earnest-looking and soaking wet, his hair plastered over his face. After a word to Brota, they all trooped into the deckhouse, followed by Brota herself and Tomiyano.

Listening and watching behind the curtain, Wallie learned that the burly, bedraggled youngster was a stonemason. His father had sent him downriver from Cha to buy marble, and now he had a load to send home. If *Sapphire* was heading upriver, then would she transport his purchase?

Wallie found that an interesting problem in an illiterate world. There was no bills of lading, or banks, or letters of credit, or even any effective policing outside the cities. Straight buying and selling was simple, but obviously merchants must sometimes wish to ship goods on order. He could not think of any effective means. Obviously Brota could buy the marble and then resell it, but then she must trust the man's word that his father would be willing to take it, or else her own judgment that it would sell for a fair profit. But she would also be free to sell it to his competitors. If he merely entrusted his cargo to her, then she and her ship could vanish with it forever. If he sailed along with it, then the same thing might happen, with him feeding the piranhas. Any course seemed to call for impossible trust by somebody, even without the complications introduced by the fickleness of the Goddess and the variable geography of the World.

So Wallie sat behind the curtain, listened to the terms being discussed, and learned that there was a way. The wagon with the marble was standing by, and Brota purchased the stone for one hundred and sixty golds—grumbling that it could not be worth half that. The trader, a local worthy who would be collecting a commission, swore that he would buy it from her in ten days for two hundred if she brought it back. Tomiyano, as official captain, swore that he would take it to Cha, Brota that she would sell it to the stonemason for no more than two hundred.

Very ingenious, Wallie concluded; they spread the risk around. The young man would probably get his marble transported for forty, or even less if his father beat Brota down a little. She was sure of forty golds if she had to make the round trip, and the marble was overpriced so she would not be tempted to abscond with it. Wallie enjoyed that, and also the oath ceremonies. The priests were witnesses. The mason swore by his chisel, Brota by her sword, Tomiyano by his ship, and the trader by gold.

Wallie mused how much easier things would be if writing had been invented in the World. He wondered why it had not been. Was that an intervention by the gods?

The bulky baskets were soon removed, and *Sapphire* began to load the marble. Now Wallie discovered why a mere seven or eight days' sailing could command so high a fee. Marble was a dangerous cargo. It was the first time he had seen the boom in use, and everyone seemed to stop breathing as each great block was swung inboard. If one slipped, it would go straight through the keel, and a helpless, invalid swordsman would be stranded in a sorcerer city. When that realization came, he began muttering curses: damn Brota for making such a deal in this place!

But no rope broke, no block slipped. Eight times the boom lowered its load in safety, while *Sapphire* cowered lower in the water. Then the wagon and witnesses departed. Honakura, who had been snooping as usual, came dripping up the plank. Wandering crew members returned and prepared for departure.

The visit seemed to have been almost pointless from Wallie's point of view, although likely Honakura would have uncovered some information on when and how Sen had been invaded by sorcerers.

"I shan't be sorry to leave here," Wallie remarked. "It's a depressing town."

Nnanji nodded in agreement. "And lunch is overdue."

The first of the two gangplanks was hauled in with a clatter.

At the sorcerer's touch, Katanji jumped like a rabbit, and a small squeal of terror escaped before he could stop it. Every gland on his skin started spurting sweat. He turned around, still staring hard at the floor, expecting to see all his insides drop out of his loincloth at any moment.

He tried to say "Adept?" but all that came out was a croak. His very fear would betray him.

"That one hasn't got much meat on his bones," the Second remarked.

What were they going to do, cook him?

"Don't want meat," the Fourth replied in a deep, rumbling voice. "Endurance is what we need—stamina."

Torture? *Oh, Goddess!*

Neither sorcerer spoke to Katanji, so he just stood there, quivering. Other slaves paraded past with sacks and came out of the closet without them. Then the Fourth tapped another. "You!" He was not much older than Katanji, taller but just as stringy, and he reacted with an even louder, gibbering wail. Katanji could see his knees shake. So all slaves were frightened of sorcerers, and his own terror had not given him away. But when they looked at faces . . .

"And you!" the Fourth said, choosing another. "Come with me."

Leaving the Second to watch the unloading, the Fourth swung around and led the way, going between a big iron range, very hot, with two big caldrons boiling on it—more foul stink—and a stack of firewood, then a pile of sacks. One of them was open and there was charcoal falling out of it. Beyond the sacks was a long table, cluttered with big pots and little pots and giant bottles of dark green glass and three of the big copper pots with coils on top that Shonsu had seen in Aus, dented and black with long use. And beyond the range was a furnace, like a blacksmith's but bigger, and a near-naked youth working bellows furiously, gleaming sweat. He glanced up as Katanji passed, showing the single feather on his brow. Being a sorcerer First was less fun than being a swordsman First, obviously, and he looked at least as old as Nanj.

Then they came to a stairwell. A big wooden vat of water sat in the middle, and the stairs spiraled up around the walls. Metal steps; more bronze.

As Katanji reached the vat and was about to put his foot on the first step, with the sorcerer three or four steps up already, the vat suddenly spluttered and hissed and blew steam. Katanji jumped and squealed in alarm and very nearly lost control of his bladder.

The sorcerer laughed. He stretched out a hand and wailed a brief incantation in words Katanji did not recognize. "Now he won't hurt you," he said. "Come on!"

Trembling, Katanji started up the stairs, the other two slaves following him. Then the vat hissed again, and they wailed quietly, so they were just as scared as he was. And they did not have swordmarks on their foreheads.

The stairs went round twice before they reached the next level, and the vat hissed five times below them. More stairs . . . they climbed three floors and were all puffing. The sorcerer marched along a dim corridor, passed two closed doors, and then turned into a big room. Katanji looked nervously at a hole in the floor with ropes hanging in it, and a huge wooden thing like a long drum in a rack, tangled with ropes and wheels. One wall was stone and had a window—the sutras said that window size was important—and two walls were wooden, and the fourth was almost hidden by piles of sacks. There were four sorcerers waiting there, two Firsts and two Seconds. Katanji gazed in growing horror at the drum thing. Torture?

The Fourth pointed at it. "Hurry up! Get on!" he said.

Katanji did not understand, but the other two slaves pushed past him to grab hold of a bar across the top and climb up on the drum, which had paddles along it. He copied them, and the drum began to turn slowly with a loud squeaking and clattering of the ropes and wheels. Big slab things began to sink into the hole.

"Flames!" muttered the Fourth. He picked up a whip from

somewhere and cracked it loudly in the air. "Work, or I'll skin you!"

So the three slaves pushed up against the bar and pushed down with their feet. The drum began to move faster and make louder noises, creaking and rumbling. Katanji was in the middle, looking at his thin arms between two sets of thicker arms, and beyond those was the big hole in the floor, and the ropes were moving. Soon he was running, trying to keep up with the others, wondering if he was going to be run to death. When he saw that the ropes were coming up, he worked out that this was not sorcery—the drum was winding the ropes. He and the other two slaves must be lifting that whole closet thing with their feet. It was nitty hard work.

The whip cracked again, and he remembered that he had no scars on his back. Would the sorcerers wonder about that? Almost all real slaves did. Would they be tempted to put some there, just on principle?

Faster and faster—he was gasping for breath, and his face and armpits were dribbling sweat. He could smell sweat in the air. His heart hammered and his mouth was dry. The other two were gasping, also, and both were bigger youths than he. Then gradually the pile of sacks rose right out of the floor, and the Fourth threw a handle. The drum locked and the three slaves almost jumped right over the bar. The sorcerers all laughed, as if they had been waiting for that.

The other two slaves lifted their arms and wiped their faces. Just in time Katanji did not. It was brighter in this room than downstairs—would anyone look hard at his slavestripe? Grease and lampblack . . . was it spreading with all this sweat? He kept his head down with his hands out, resting on the rail, and he panted his heart out. The other two slaves were doing much the same. The junior sorcerers were unloading the sacks and stacking them carefully and neatly. There seemed to be some way of telling one type from another, for they went to various places along the wall, but all the sacks looked the same to the watching swordsman.

"Ready!" the Fourth shouted when the closet was empty; he threw the handle again and the drum shifted under Katanji's feet. The slaves started treading, but it was almost as much work to lower the thing back down again as it had been to bring it up—and that did not seem fair, somehow. Then he heard more sacks being thrown in it.

He thought with dismay of the size of that wagon, and its load.

He wondered about *Sapphire*. What would he do if she sailed without him?

The whip cracked again, and the torment began again . . .

It took at least twenty trips to empty the wagon. By then Katanji was shaking all over with exhaustion and did not really care if they saw he was a swordsman, if they would only let him lie down somewhere. His mouth tasted like mud, and he thought his heart would burst. Sometimes the room seemed to darken and fade; then he knew he was close to fainting. Slaves were always worked like that, but if he fell over, they would see his face.

The Fourth cracked his whip often, but did not use it, although the last couple of loads took a long time. One of his juniors said perhaps he should go and get some fresh livestock, but the Fourth said almost done, not to bother.

At last he led them into the corridor again. Katanji hung back, limping slowly—and it was not hard to do that. It was hard to walk at all. His legs were paste. The two doors were open now, throwing patches of light, and he slowed down as he went by each, trying to grab a picture in his mind. In the first room a sorceress was sitting at a table, a Second, with her cowl back. She was doing something with a plate, rubbing it round and round on something—casting a spell, he supposed, looking bored. Mostly he just noticed her face, saw nothing behind or around her. She was about twenty-five, quite pretty, but she had three facemarks, not two for her yellow gown. They were not feathers! He was not sure just what they were, but they did not have the curved shape of feathers.

There was no one visible in the second room, just a couple of tables and some chairs. One of the tables seemed to be a shrine, for it had tall feathers standing on it in silver holders—something to do with the facemarks, he supposed. The far wall was lined with shelves, laden with hundreds of brown boxes of various sizes, made of leather, he thought. Then he was at the stairs.

He clung hard to the rail as he went down, because his legs were quivering so much. The thing in the vat hissed and spluttered, and he did not care. He tried to see more things in the big room, but it was gloomy, and his eyes had not had time to adjust. It was a very big room, half the size of the tower, he guessed. There were two windows on one long wall and one on each of the shorter walls, so that would be right. Racks and shelves ran the whole length of the room, with bottles and bundles on them—how could anyone remember which was what? The bellows man was still pumping. Another First, in a gown, was grinding something in a mortar as big as a washtub.

He wanted more time, time to study it all, and he dare not stop. His brain would not work, he was too tired. Through a gray fog he noticed a copper snake at the far end—much, much bigger than any he had seen before—and a grindstone, and a smaller edition of the treadmill upstairs, underneath one thing that he could never overlook: a great big gold ball on a pillar near the door, big enough for a man to stand up in if it were hollow. That must be a very big sorcery, or perhaps it was a sun god idol? There were many pipes snaking around, too, and ropes hanging . . . a couple more tables of junk and two more piles of bags and sacks . . . and then he was at the loading dock, and the wagon had already gone. The two slave gangs were standing outside, waiting.

He was trapped! He stopped on the dock to try to think. His two sweaty companions from the treadmill dropped down limply, heading for different groups. Which one should he go to? The sorcerers were waiting to shut the doors. He rubbed an eye as if he had got something in it and got shouted at, so he scrambled down, legs still shaking madly.

He stood on the bronze grating and hesitated. But both slave gangs were complete, so both turned and walked away, each boss thinking that the last slave belonged to the other. With a sigh of relief Katanji followed after one of them, and the big doors clunked shut behind him. The rain was gloriously cold on his hot skin. He began to drop behind the slaves, farther and farther, and then edged in behind a portly matron of the Third, following her as if she owned him until they reached the buildings and he could go off on his own. He had started to shiver in the cold.

Sapphire would be gone, and they might not miss him for hours. He was a swordsman, trapped in a sorcerer town. He would have to go to the temple, he supposed . . .

"Katanji?"

He jumped. It was Lae, bony old Lae, her wrinkled, motherly face frowning at him.

"You all right?" she demanded.

He stopped his jaw rattling long enough to say, "Yes, I'm all right. I was just coming back." His eyes prickled, and he lowered his face as a slave should.

She frowned. "Shonsu and your brother are eating the shutters in the deckhouse. You were very nearly left behind! I guessed you'd be around the tower somewhere. Come on!"

He fell into step beside her, then remembered that he was a slave and fell back a pace. She twisted her head a few times to look at him. "You look as if you've had a hard day." Her voice was more gentle.

He managed to grin, beginning to feel better. "I've been inside the tower."

She stopped dead so that the other pedestrians had to dodge around them; it was a narrow street. "Gods, boy! You've got more guts and less brains than your brother! I did not think that was possible."

He had more brains, but he did not say so. And, yes, maybe he did have guts.

"Oh, it was not hard. Very interesting, really. I saw lots of things . . ." He was going to start babbling and he had a crazy desire to laugh, so he bit his lip and forced himself into silence.

"Getting in might be easy," Lae said, "but you got out again! You look beat. Come on, then."

They reached the dock road and walked along past the ships. Two patrolling sorcerers went by without a glance at him. Lae stopped again and asked some questions, studying him carefully.

"I'm going to take you on board," she said firmly, "and you're going to have a shower and then you'll sleep in my cabin. Shonsu and Nnanji can't leave the deckhouse until we're out of port, and I'll see they stay away."

"Thanks," he said. Brota liked to think she was ship mother, but anyone with a problem went to Lae. A sleep would be good, but could even Lae hold off an angry Seventh?

He saw both grins and glares as he went on board, but Lae kept the others away. She stood outside the door while he showered. His muscles began to knot up in lumps of agony as he worked the pump. He was trembling even more now, damn it! Then she handed in his kilt, and he stumbled along behind her, down to the cabins.

Hers was just like the others, a little box with a chest and a roll of bedding, but she had bright drapes beside the porthole, a little rug on the floor, and an embroidered bedcover. The air smelled of lavender, like his mother's closet. He unrolled the bedding and lay down stiffly and looked up at her.

"You need anything else, novice? Food?"

"A drink of water, Sailor Lae," he said, "and thank you."

She smiled, thin-lipped. "I'll see that you're not disturbed."

He thought he would go to sleep at once, but he lay there, and his shivering grew worse instead of better. He took off his kilt and pulled the covers over him and that did not help. He decided he had caught a chill.

He ought to say some prayers, he thought. Then the door opened and his drink came in, but it was Diwa who brought it. She shut the door and bolted it.

When he put the beaker aside, she sat down and started sliding into the bed beside him.

He gulped. "No! You'll be missed!"

She chuckled. "Don't worry—they know about us. Oooo! You're cold as a fish! Lae said this might help."

It did help. It helped worlds. She put her arms around him, tightly. He pushed down her bra sash with his chin and cuddled his head between her breasts. They were big and soft and warm and smelled of fresh bread; lovely things, they were. He shed tears over them, because they were so lovely, and hoped she would not notice.

Eventually he stopped shivering and began to feel warm. He thought he ought to do the manly thing for Diwa now, because this might be his last opportunity, but then it was too late, because he was asleep . . .

†† † ††

Of course it was Diwa who stopped *Sapphire* from sailing. Sniveling and shaking, she was thrust into the deckhouse ahead of an enraged Brota to repeat her confession to the swordsmen and explain that Katanji was ashore. Tomiyano was right behind, his face dark with fury. Others came crowding in, filling the dim, shuttered room with wet, furious people. The draperies of damp laundry were ripped down to make more space; voices were raised.

For the third time the ship had visited a sorcerer city. For a fourth time she had been put in jeopardy. The sailors were frightened and therefore angry. Wallie was horrified by the risk to Katanji. Nnanji was disgusted at the disgrace of a swordsman playing slave. Maloli—a stocky, heavyset man whose face was rubicund at the best of times—was ablaze at the shame of it all. Only the calming influence of his wife, Fala, was restraining him from words that would have forced Nnanji to take offense; and even the unexcitable Fala was thin-lipped and bitter. Katanji had been in their daughter's cabin; she had been compromised. Everyone was shouting and arguing at cross-purposes.

"Quiet!" Wallie bellowed, and there was quiet.

Then he spoke quietly. "Mistress, we can discuss blame later. I ask you now to send out search parties. If he's been caught, then we must be able to leave quickly. How many can you spare?"

"If he's been caught, then the demons may be here any minute!"

"That's true. But remember the sorcerers in the quarry—

they did nothing to stop us sailing away, so their powers do not extend very far over the River. If he has been captured, then I shall offer myself in exchange—"

"A Seventh for a First?" Nnanji shouted.

"It's my fault. Be quiet, brother, please. Mistress?"

Had it been any one of the passengers other than Katanji, Brota would have cast off and sailed. Wallie knew that. But Katanji had charm. They all liked Katanji. As tempers began to cool, the sailors remembered stories they had collected about sorcerers and torture. Reluctantly Brota agreed that they would stay and look for him, at least until there was evidence that the sorcerers had been alerted. If they had to leave swiftly, then anyone left behind would rendezvous at the temple at midnight and wait for a dinghy...

The sailors trailed out.

Wallie was feeling sick. If he had failed to control one novice, how could he ever run an army? "I told him not to go ashore!"

"You told him not to set foot on the plank!" Nnanji snapped. He bared his teeth. "Disguise! A slave!"

"I set the example there," Wallie admitted.

"At least you never tampered with facemarks." That was an inordinate sin among the People; their whole culture was based on facemarks.

But then they were interrupted as crew members took shelter from the rain, and they could say no more.

And time seemed to stop. A port officer came by and inquired why they had not sailed yet, if their trading was done. The berth was needed. Brota spun a yarn of stomach cramps and a hurried trip to the healers.

The rain grew worse.

Wallie's frustration grew almost unbearable.

How long until the sorcerers extracted the truth from the boy?

And what happened then? The ship was being jeopardized on a faint chance of saving one raw recruit. Cold mathematics suggested that *Sapphire* should sail while she could. A good general would make that calculation and act on it. Wallie could calculate, but he could not act.

Little Fia ran in, screaming with excitement—Lae and Katanji were coming along the road.

Wallie relaxed with a huge sigh of relief and said a silent prayer to the Goddess, and to Shorty.

"I'll skin him!" Nnanji muttered. But his eyes were shiny.

A few minutes later, a wan Katanji limped up the plank like a beaten dog and headed forward behind Lae. The sailors hurried to their posts, and at last the swordsmen were left alone— two swordsmen and one ragged old priest, sitting on a chest and smirking.

Now the blame could be distributed.

Wallie pointed an accusing finger at Honakura. "You knew what he was doing!"

The old man nodded smugly.

"You let that boy go into danger—"

"Danger?" Nnanji shouted. "That's his job! But to violate the laws—that's an abomination!"

"Indeed?" Honakura raised his eyebrows. "Laws are tricky, adept. Unlike sutras, they have no exact words. What is the precise law in Sen that your protégé has broken?"

"I . . . exact?"

"Oh? You don't know?" Honakura beamed up mockingly. Nnanji was turning bright red with fury.

"All laws forbid changing facemarks!"

"He hasn't changed his. It is still there. He painted a stripe over it, but that will wipe off."

"Then it is an abomination to change one's craft!"

"Slavery is not a craft."

Reluctantly Wallie began to appreciate the humor. The old priest was going to tie Nnanji in a marlinespike hitch. And he himself could see nothing wrong in a plainclothes swordsman; it was the answer he had been seeking. Katanji could gather wisdom for him, as the riddle had suggested, so this was part of the gods' plan. He felt more hopeful.

"It is always an abomination to change one's rank!" Nnanji persisted.

"I disagree. Any law I have ever heard forbids one to raise one's rank. Your brother lowered his."

Nnanji's reply was incomprehensible.

"Did Katanji understand that, old man?" Wallie asked.

"Perhaps not at first," Honakura admitted. "But I explained it to him."

"You corrupted my protégé, you—"

"Steady, Nnanji!" Wallie said. "He has a good argument. There would seem to be no breach of the laws. Who would make a law forbidding a swordsman to wear a slavestripe? It is still the danger that bothers me . . ."

"Honor!"

The door flew open to admit young Matarro, with eyes big as *Sapphire*'s scuppers. "He went in the tower, my lord!"

"He did *what?*"

The boy nodded wildly. "He's been in the sorcerers' tower! Lae says he saw all sorts of things!"

And Novice Matarro vanished again to attend to his duties. *Sapphire* was departing.

From another wisdom gain. Wallie turned to Nnanji—and even Nnanji was looking startled. "Adept, I congratulate you on the exemplary courage displayed by your protégé!" There was no higher compliment one swordsman could pay another, because the craft believed that courage and honor could be taught only by example.

Nnanji's mouth opened and closed a few times in silence. Then his principles and his anger prevailed. "Does courage alone justify dishonor, my lord brother?"

"I see no dishonor! He cannot yet serve the Goddess with his sword. He was trying to further Her purposes by the best means he has. I am amazed by his dedication. I applaud his heroism."

Nnanji took a few deep breaths, calming himself with a visible effort. He smiled uncertainly. "Well, he is a spunky little devil, I suppose . . ."

"He seeks to be worthy of his mentor."

Nnanji's face went red again. He mumbled something and

turned away. Wallie and Honakura grinned at each other.

But now it was also time to think about repairs. Relations with the crew had been damaged.

"Tell me, protégé!" Wallie said. "Did you not instruct him to stay away from the girls?"

Nnanji turned around again, looking surprised. "Well, yes! But of course . . ." He shrugged.

"Of course *what?*"

Nnanji smirked. "Of course he knew I did not mean it. No swordsman would take that order seriously, my lord brother!"

"I meant it! I took it seriously!"

Nnanji seemed puzzled. "Why? A swordsman? It's an honor . . ."

"Sailors may not think so!"

"Well, they should!"

Gods give me strength! Wallie thought. Somehow Nnanji managed to combine the ethics of a puritan with the morals of an alleycat.

"I've told you, we're not free swords. Even if we were . . ."

Again the door swung open, this time to admit Tomiyano. He marched across to Nnanji and held out a hand. Tomiyano *smiling?*

"You should be proud of that brother of yours, adept!" he said. "He's been in the tower!"

Nnanji shook hands, vacillated, and then registered modesty. "It was his duty, sailor."

"Maybe so, but it took more courage . . ."

Sapphire was heading out into the River. News of Katanji's exploit had flown through the ship like a flight of gulls. He being unavailable, men and women and children came flocking into the deckhouse to congratulate Nnanji instead. He began to swell like a pouter pigeon. Wallie and Honakura grinned at each other again.

Then Maloli arrived, and there was a sudden tension.

"Adept," he muttered, "I'm sorry if anything I said earlier . . . We can all take pride in your brother. We're glad that Diwa . . . was able to be of assistance. He is a courageous lad—and a man of honor!"

"Of course!" Nnanji shot a smug, I-told-you-so glance at Wallie.

"A good influence on Diwa, we're sure," said Fala. "Now we understand why he was in her cabin and we are glad that she could be of service to him."

Nnanji kept his face straight, but only just. "He knows how a true swordsman should honor a lady, naturally."

Uncertainly Fala said, "Naturally." And blushed.

Wallie gave up. They were not all talking the same sort of honor, but he suspected they all knew what they meant—and he was the stranger here. Who could grudge anything to Katanji now?

By nightfall the rain had stopped, and Katanji appeared on deck for the evening meal. He was still shaky, and so stiff that he could hardly walk, but he put on a superb performance as Imp of the Year. Wallie and Nnanji, having obtained permission from Tomiyano to draw their swords on board, gave him the Salute to a Hero. He grinned mightily and kept his arm firmly around Diwa.

Yet damage there had been. Brota stated emphatically that Tau was the limit. *Sapphire* would continue as far as Cha to unload her marble, but no farther. If Lord Shonsu could not enlist his swordsmen at Tau, then he was going to be taken back to Casr. Then the family would settle down to a routine trading existence once more, probably on the Dri–Casr run. Their obligations to the Goddess had been satisfied, they said. Whether the Goddess agreed, of course, was something that only time would show.

Fair weather returned, and the River flowed now from the east. The mountains of RegiVul lay to the south. For several days, Wallie and Honakura stripped information from Katanji, layer after layer, as if they were peeling an onion. Nnanji sat beside them as recording secretary and filed it all away in his memory.

Katanji cooperated as well as he could. His powers of observation could not be faulted, and even under the terrible stress of imminent danger, he had continued to look. Yet everything he had seen had to be filtered through his own experience before it could be told, and through Wallie's to be understood. Somewhere on that journey, facts became guesses.

Obviously the sorcerers had limitations. They could certainly be fooled, and that might be the most important lesson of all. But gold balls? Feathers in silver holders? Wallie began to feel that he was viewing a madhouse through a distorting glass. What was achieved by all that frenzied activity in the tower? What was being ground up with mortar and pestle—demon bait? What lived in the tub? How many sorts of thunderbolt were there, and why had fire demons been invoked only at Ov? How he wished that Katanji had been able to carry a camera on that perilous expedition into the tower!

What did sorcerers have against dyers and tanners? How much of their behavior was effective, and how much mere witch-doctoring? Some of it must be as meaningless and illogical as medieval alchemy, or Honakura's fixation upon the holy number seven, and the more Wallie learned, the less sense it all seemed to make.

Day by day his frustration continued, until at last *Sapphire* drew close to Tau.

Although he still limped, one morning Wallie took up foil and mask. He would not yet dare to take on a highrank, but he could handle Nnanji. When the score reached twenty-one to zero, even the sweating redhead admitted that Shonsu was now restored to health and no longer in need of mothering.

"And me, my lord brother?" he inquired eagerly.

"Yes," Wallie agreed. "You're coming along well."

"Fifth?"

"Very close. Certainly worth a try."

The sun god in all his splendor could not have shone more brightly then. In a small army Lord Shonsu would not need a Sixth, so if Adept Nnanji could become Master Nnanji, then he would be sure of being second in command.

††† †††

It was good to be ashore after so many weeks, even if his leg did hurt a little. It was fun to limp along the narrow, crowded streets with the seventh sword on his back, studying the traffic and the buildings while civilians warily made way for him. And Tau itself was a joyful surprise.

Each city on the River was different. Tau was barely a city at all, no more than a small market town. Watching it as *Sapphire* approached, Wallie had felt a strange recognition: thatched roofs, brown oak beams showing on the fronts of the buildings, earth-toned pargeting. At first he had identified the style as medieval European, but he decided that it was more like Tudor when he started along the lane that professed to be the main street, for there he saw older structures, whose beams had turned black and pargeting white.

So Tau was a stage set of Merrie England. Upper stories jutted out to shadow the cobbled filth underfoot, while the strip of blue sky above was fringed by bristling eaves. Shiny bottle glass in the diamond windows obscured the interiors and flickered many-hued reflections back at the viewer; hanging signs portrayed the wares available within. Despite a constant lack of headroom that made his progress hazardous, Wallie was fascinated. Of course the loincloths and gowns were inappropriate, but he felt as if he had been transported to Shakespeare's London, and he kept wondering whether there was a theater in town, and who composed its plays.

Brota had solemnly promised not to sail without him. He had come to seek swordsmen, but he felt as if he were a prisoner released, a child at a fair. At one point, when even his rank and prestige could not immediately clear a way for him, he turned around to grin at Nnanji and announce, "I like this town!"

Nnanji pinched his nose and said, "Yeech!"

Well, there was that . . .

The main thoroughfare was so narrow that two men's arms

could have spanned it easily, and here it had packed solid. Now Wallie saw the cause of the delay. A cart full of apples had locked wheels with one overloaded with glossy blue tiles, and the impact had spilled a shower of shiny red fruit into the mire. Peering over heads, he could see small boys squeezing in and out to retrieve this treasure, and its guardian engaged in a contest of oaths with the pusher of the tile cart. The invention was becoming more lurid, the genealogy more improbable, and the anatomical instructions more ruinous by the minute. A wheel on the tile cart had left its axle, and the entire load was in danger of collapsing. The resulting fistfight might easily grow into a riot. The crowd's good-natured mockery was already turning to abuse as those with urgent business attempted to squeeze by with their bundles.

In the midst of all this confusion, a sword hilt was bobbing around like a floating cork, but its owner was apparently being ignored, unable even to get close to the problem. Wallie decided that the time had come for him to do a little swordsmaning.

He began to push and he cleared a path with sheer size where his rank had failed. With Nnanji at his heels, he reached the center of the turmoil and laid a heavy hand on Tiles' shoulder. Tiles looked around angrily, then up apprehensively, then fell silent respectfully. Apples stopped a detailed pedigree of his antagonist at the fourth generation. Both waited with relief for instructions. Wallie ordered Apples and a beefy slave to lift one end of the tile cart, while he took a grip on the other and shifted his weight to his left leg. The cart was raised, and Tiles replaced the wheel on the axle. Nnanji had already begun to clear an exit for him. Soon the jam was thinning out in a few final ribald comments.

The ineffective local swordsman remained, now revealed as a very young and very small Second, staring white-faced and horrified at the visitor. He could not be much older than Katanji and he was no bigger—small wonder he had failed to impose his authority.

He reached a shaky hand for his sword hilt.

"Leave that!" Wallie commanded.

Gulping, the Second obeyed and made civilian salute, identifying himself as Apprentice Allajuiy. Wallie responded, but did not waste time presenting the youngster to Nnanji.

"I came to call on the reeve," he said. "Lead the way to the barracks."

His obvious nervousness increasing, Allajuiy pointed in silent dismay at the nearest doorway. Above it hung a bronze sword that Wallie ought to have noticed, side by side with an oversized boot.

"And where is the reeve, then?" Wallie asked.

"He . . . he is in there, my lord."

Wallie glanced at Nnanji and received the puzzled frown he had expected. The two of them moved toward the door, and Apprentice Allajuiy took to his heels without waiting for formal dismissal.

The swordsmen stepped down into the cordwainer's shop. It was small and cramped by tables of shoes and boots, the beams of the ceiling perilously low. Under the window, a Fifth and two Seconds were hammering away, their lasts on their laps. The floor around them was littered with scraps of leather, and its pungency perfumed the air. The door closed over the sounds of the street.

The Fifth rose hastily and turned to greet his visitors. At once his face took on the same apprehensive expression as the young swordsman's had. He was around forty, heavyset in his red gown, and almost bald. He had arms like a wrestler, an old scar across his forehead, and a remarkable cauliflower ear. Cobbling must be a rowdy profession in Tau.

Wallie returned his salute.

"I seek the reeve," he said.

The cordwainer's craggy face did not welcome the news. "My father has the honor to be reeve, my lord. He will, of course, be honored to greet you, if your lordship can wait a few minutes?" He turned and plodded out quickly through a door at the back. His two juniors scrambled to their feet and fled after him.

Wallie's quizzical smile earned a scowl from Nnanji.

"Something tells me that I shall not be doing much recruiting in Tau," Wallie said. "I can't consider a denunciation from you, oath brother—but they won't know that. This might be a good chance for you to try conducting an investigation!"

Nnanji nodded, without losing his frown.

It was some time before the cordwainer returned, and he came alone. He had changed into a cleaner robe, but it was an older man's garment. Nnanji's brows dropped even lower.

"My father will be here shortly, my lord. He . . . he is elderly, and sometimes a little slow in the mornings . . ."

"We are in no hurry," Wallie remarked cheerfully. "Meanwhile, allow me to present my protégé and oath brother, Adept Nnanji. I believe he may have a few questions to ask."

Worry became open terror. The burly man's hands shook as he returned Nnanji's salute, and Nnanji's questions began at once.

"Tell me the names and ranks of the garrison, master."

"My father, Kioniarru of the Fifth, adept, is reeve. His deputy is Kionijuiy of the Fourth . . ." Unhappy silence.

"And?"

"And two Seconds, adept."

Nnanji's eyes flashed a predatory gleam. "Nephews of yours, by any chance?"

The cordwainer shuddered and nodded. "Yes, adept."

"And where is . . ."

At that moment a young woman led in the reeve.

He was a Fifth, but at least eighty; bent, wrinkled, toothless, and senile, grinning inanely around him as he was brought forward. His ponytail was a faint white wisp, the sort of thing that grew on grass stalks in ditches. He beamed at the sight of the visitors and tried to draw to make his salute. With much help from his son, he eventually did so, but then the cordwainer took the sword away from him to sheath it safely. Wallie managed to contort himself enough to make the appropriate reply under the low ceiling.

"In what way may I be of service to your lordship?" the reeve quavered. "Kionijuiy handles most of the work now. Where is the boy?" he demanded of the cordwainer.

"He's out just now, father," the cordwainer shouted.

"Where's he gone, then?"

"He'll be back soon."

"No, he won't! I remember—he's gone to Casr, hasn't he?"

Master Kioniarru showed his gums triumphantly. "Went to the lodge!"

The cordwainer rolled his eyes up and said, "Yes, Father."

"Lodge?" Nnanji shouted. "There is a lodge at Casr?" He glanced momentarily at Wallie. "And who is castellan?"

"Eh?" The old man cupped his ear.

"Who is castellan of the lodge?" Nnanji bellowed.

"Castellan? Shonsu of the Seventh."

The solid cordwainer was now close to nervous weeping. "No, no, Father, this is Lord Shonsu."

He did not notice the way Lord Shonsu and his protégé were staring at each other. Wallie did not need to ask what a lodge was—that had been part of Shonsu's professional memories and had therefore been passed on to him. A lodge was a union hall, an independent barracks where free swords might seek rest, news, and fellowship. A lodge was a logical place to try to enlist swordsmen. A lodge was a logical headquarters for a war against the sorcerers.

And for Shonsu? The Shonsu who had failed disastrously?

The sorcerer in Aus had said, " . . . when you return to your nest."

"I'm sure it was Shonsu," the old man quavered. "I'll ask Kio'y. He'll know." He turned and tottered back to the rear exit, already shouting, "Kionijuiy?"

The woman, who had been watching in unhappy silence, followed him sadly out. The others observed a moment's silence, out of pity. The cordwainer, left to face the wrath of swordsmen, muttered something about one of his bad days.

Then Wallie folded his arms and leaned back against a table displaying boots. He did not need to tell Nnanji to go ahead—he could not have stopped him now. The questions came quick and angry.

"So your brother is the only effective swordsman in Tau?"

"Yes, adept."

"But he has gone to Casr?"

"Yes, adept."

"Why? For promotion?"

"He hoped . . . Yes, adept. He should be back—"

"Take off that robe!"

He was older, bigger, and of higher rank, but civilians did not dispute with swordsmen. In abject silence, the cordwainer untied his garment and pulled it down as far as his waist.

"Put it on again. How many more brothers have you got?"

"Five, adept."

"Crafts?"

"A butcher, a baker—"

"And do they also bear foil scars?"

The cordwainer nodded miserably.

A man with only two Seconds for practice would hardly be trying for promotion to Fifth. And a lodge would be a logical place to seek promotion—having missed that opportunity, Adept Nnanji was not likely to be sympathetic.

"So your brother—your *swordsman* brother—has gone off to advance his career, leaving the town unguarded?"

"The Seconds could call for a posse—"

"An apprentice does not have that authority!" Nnanji was seething with fury, but he took a few minutes to reflect before he decided, unconsciously rubbing his chin. Then he said icily, "I am ready to proceed, mentor."

The cordwainer looked ready to faint.

And Wallie had to decide what to do now. Possibly this was another of the gods' tests, or perhaps it was some sort of a clue. Certainly Nnanji had a watertight case. Tau was so small that most of the time one swordsman would be ample to keep it peaceful. Likely Kioniarru had been reeve for decades, and any time he had needed help, on festival days when the drunks prowled, he had called out his sons. The elders would have approved, because they had no extra wages to pay, so they were not guiltless. But the old man had taught his sons to use swords—a sensible precaution and a flagrant abomination. Butchers and bakers were not sailors.

Wallie could not hear a denunciation from Nnanji, and priests should not judge violations of swordsmen sutras. Brota could, of course.

He needed time to think. If he let this prosecution go ahead, he was going to strip Tau of any protection at all. Even a cordwainer would be better than nothing. Even a cordwainer who had ignored a near riot developing right outside his shop.

"What penalties would you demand?" Wallie inquired.

"Death—what else?" Nnanji snapped.

The cordwainer moaned.

"A little extreme, perhaps?"

Nnanji bristled. "I have no doubts, my lord brother!"

Wallie had asked the wrong question. "What penalties would you assess if you were judge, then?" Nnanji as prosecutor would always ask for the death penalty, to show he was not afraid of losing his case.

"Oh!" Nnanji pondered. "The old man wouldn't understand, would he? He's confused . . . cut off his ponytail and break his sword. The civilians . . . the right hand."

The cordwainer cringed.

"Then they will starve, and their children, also," Wallie said.

Nnanji frowned. "What sentence would you impose, mentor?"

Very grateful that the case was still hypothetical, Wallie said, "I think a flogging would suffice. Their father was the main culprit."

Nnanji thought about that, and then nodded. "Yes, that's true—a thorough flogging, in public." Nnanji had mellowed!

"And Adept Kionijuiy? Or Master Kionijuiy, if he has won his promotion?"

Nnanji's eyes lit up—challenge! That need not be hypothetical! "He might still be at Casr when we get back there? Or even here, when we return from Cha next week?"

"If he is, then you can have him."

"Thank you, brother!" Nnanji beamed.

Wallie suppressed a shiver and looked at the quaking cobbler. "Adept Nnanji and I have pressing business elsewhere. We cannot stay to administer justice at this time, but we shall be back. Warn your brothers, all of them. And I intend to send word to the lodge at Casr, stating that Tau has need of swordsmen."

Obviously astonished by this reprieve, the cordwainer wiped sweat from his brow.

It was amazing that the old man, and later his swordsman son, had managed to hide the nepotism so long. Perhaps only the very closeness of a lodge had made it possible—any free swords who had chanced by had been easily diverted to Casr.

Now, if they had any sense, the whole family would leave town.

The swordsmen emerged again into the smelly, bustling street. Wallie stood for a moment with his back against a wall, thinking. He could not easily talk to Nnanji when they were walking.

It was still not a very satisfactory solution. If Kionijuiy's brothers all fled, then Tau would be left unprotected, at least for a few days.

"We are going to the temple?" Nnanji asked.

"You are, as soon as you see me safely to the ship. Here." Wallie handed over a couple of golds. Priests were the only messengers who could be trusted not to pocket a fee and forget its purpose.

Nnanji raised his eyebrows.

"Send word to the lodge. But also ask if they know the castellan's name—I can't do that now, can I?"

Perhaps the old man had been mistaken; or perhaps not.

If Shonsu had been castellan of the lodge at Casr, then word of Wallie's disgrace at Aus. would certainly have been carried there by sailors. When *Sapphire* had docked at Casr, he had tried to persuade Nnanji to visit the garrison. That might have been a very narrow escape. And what was he expected to do now—go back to Casr, or continue the circle to Ov?

"It's a puzzle, isn't it?" Wallie looked around with enjoyment at the pseudo-Tudor buildings and the bustling people detouring nervously around him. "Maybe I'm supposed to stay and take over here! It's a cute little town, this."

"You're joking!"

"Not entirely," Wallie said. "When we've completed our mission, what are you going to do afterward? Marry Thana and be a water rat?"

"Thana's great, but . . . me—a water rat?" Nnanji shrugged. "Be a Seventh?"

"Certainly, in time. Doing what?"

"A free sword. Honorable and true to my oaths." Nnanji looked puzzled by this sudden philosophical discussion. "You?"

"I want to see more of the World. But eventually, I suppose, I'll settle down in some quiet little town like this and be a reeve." Wallie chuckled at the notion. "And raise seven sons, like old Kioniarru. And seven daughters, also, if Jja wants them!"

Nnanji stared at him incredulously. "Reeve? Why not king?"

"Too much bloodshed to get it, and too much work when you do. But I like Tau, I think."

"If you want it, my lord brother," Nnanji said respectfully, "then I am sure that the Goddess will give it to you." He wrinkled his snub nose in disgust. "I'll try to deserve something better."

Wallie had feared that the sailors might be fretting and eager to leave, but Brota had discovered that Tau was a source of fine leather. While *Sapphire* was heavy-laden with the marble, her holds were far from full. Brota dearly enjoyed trading . . . and sorcerer towns had no tanners. Thus the swordsmen returned to find the ship smelling like the cordwainer's shop, while the usual panting slaves raced up and down the planks, loading boots and shoes, bulky but not heavy.

Brota and Tomiyano scowled at the news that Lord Shonsu had been unable to enlist helpers in Tau, but they did not seem surprised. Nnanji headed off to the temple, and Wallie sought out Honakura for a consultation.

The evenings were growing shorter now, and the weather uncertain. By nightfall, a storm front had moved in, and *Sapphire* jerked peevishly at her anchor in mid-River, her center of gravity strangely lowered by the marble. Rain splattered everywhere and dribbled from the scuppers. Cold, damp darkness flooded into the deckhouse before the meal was finished.

Wallie was even more puzzled than before. The priests had promised Nnanji they would pass the message to the lodge. The castellan there had been a Lord Shonsu until recently—so they had said—but they thought there was a new one now, name unknown. Castellans came and went frequently. So what was Wallie supposed to do? Go back to Casr, or continue to Ov? Casr was logical, for there he must find swordsmen, but he would be in grave danger of a denunciation for cowardice. Ov seemed to be what the god's riddle demanded, but it made very little sense.

Sitting on the floor and cuddling Jja for warmth, he passed on the news that there was a lodge in Casr.

Holiyi broke a two-day silence to say, "Heard that. Didn't know it mattered."

"Casr it must be, then," Brota proclaimed firmly. "Three days to Cha, then back to Casr!" The next city was always going to appear in three days, but in practice always took longer.

A wordless murmur from the shadows indicated that the family agreed with her. The Jonahs were not resented as bitterly as they had been at first, but these riverfolk wanted no part of divine missions. They felt they had done their share now and should be allowed to go back to minding their own business.

"What would a priest say, if we had one present, old man?" Wallie asked.

"How should I know?" Honakura protested, and there were a few chuckles. "I agree that the signals are contradictory, my lord. You must pray for guidance."

Prayer might help, but Wallie decided to try a little morale boosting. "Nnanji? Sing us a song, the one about Chioxin."

"No, let's have a romantic one!" protested one of the women—Mata, he thought.

"Don't know any romantic ones," Nnanji said. "They weren't allowed in the barracks."

Then he started, and his soft tenor drifted anonymously out of the shadows:

> "I sing of arms and he who made
> The greatest swords that men have wrought,
> Of how the price of life was paid,
> The seven years Chioxin bought."

In a few minutes Oligarro's mandolin picked up the melody. It was a mediocre ballad, and whichever minstrel's voice Nnanji was copying was not especially tuneful, but it was new to the audience, and soon they must have seen why it had been chosen. Battles and heroes, monsters and villains, blood and honor floated through the gathering dark and out into the night: six swords, six heraldic beasts holding six jewels, many legendary warriors . . . then silence.

"Go on!" Matarro shouted eagerly.

"Forgotten the words?" Tomiyano asked sarcastically.

"I only know one more verse," Nnanji said, and quoted the lines he had sung once to his liege lord as he sat in a bathtub:

> "A griffon crouched upon the hilt
> In silver white and sapphire blue,
> With ruby eye and talons gilt
> And blade of steel of starlight hue,
> The seventh sword he wrought at last,
> And all the others it surpassed."

Silence again.

"That can't be all?" Diwa protested.

"No," said Nnanji. "There's a little more, but I never heard it. Chioxin died. The seventh sword, he gave to the Goddess. No one saw it for seven hundred years."

The deckhouse was black as a coal mine now, the Dream God obscured by the flying clouds, the shutters mostly closed against the wind.

"And She gave it to Shonsu?" Matarro asked breathlessly.

"She did. It's here, in this room. The saga isn't finished. The greatest part must be still to come. And you're in it!"

"Oo!" said a few juvenile voices, and there were adult murmurs there, also.

"I don't want to be in it!" That was Tomiyano. "And I don't want the damned sword on my ship!"

"Tom'o!" Brota's voice was reproving, but a few others muttered agreement.

"Nor swordsmen! Who needs them?"

The ensuing embarrassed silence was suddenly broken as the bar dropped across the door. Feet ran up the steps outside.

Engrossed in the song, Captain Tomiyano had forgotten to set guards at nightfall. *Sapphire* had been boarded.

The deckhouse was filled with shouting and panic. Wallie was sitting directly below a window. He rose and swung open the shutter. Leaning out backward, he looked up at the blackness of the bulwark against the almost-black sky. He could reach the rail if he stood on his toes. Then a darker darkness loomed above the rail, and a blade glinted. Behind him, the brightness of the River . . . hastily he grabbed the sides of the frame and threw himself back, hanging over the water as steel whistled where his head had been an instant before.

He slid back into the deckhouse. Think up plan two . . .

"Here," Nnanji said softly at his side.

The noise was subsiding.

"Men to the middle, everyone else back against the walls," Wallie said. Silence returned, except for one of the adolescents, who was snuffling.

All the shutters were open now and a very faint grayness filtered in. Even on deck there would be little light, with clouds covering the Dream God. The rain seemed to have stopped, but there were footsteps on the deck above.

"Tomiyano? Holiyi?" Wallie said quietly.

"Here."

"Here."

"I'm going to lift Nnanji up. You two hang on to my back straps, or we'll tip out. Okay? Then I'll follow him, but the rest of you stay here. Leave it to the professionals. Nnanji, I'll let go the right ankle when you're up there. Better have your knife handy for openers. This way." He led them over to the aft port window.

The panic had gone. They were a tough bunch, these sailors.

Nnanji turned his back to the window. His eyes seemed to shine by themselves, but it must have been the light from the other side of the room. Wallie crowded close to him, positioned Holiyi's foot behind his own on one side, Tomiyano's on the

271

other, felt them grip his backstraps. Then he squatted down, ignoring protests from his not-quite-healed wound. The sailors took his weight, stopping him from falling over backward. He gripped Nnanji's ankles.

"Ready?" he asked, his voice muffled in Nnanji's kilt.

He felt Nnanji chuckle. "Ready!" He leaned back.

Wallie lifted and then straightened his knees: Ummph!

Nnanji shot upward and out, swaying as Wallie rose and leaned forward. The two sailors grunted, catching the sudden stress on the straps and the backward slip of his feet, slamming bodily against the window frame. In one long movement Wallie had unfolded from a squat to his full height, raising his arms and propelling his protégé skyward—a remarkable feat of strength, but there was no time for admiration.

To the pirates waiting above, the swordsman must have materialized from nothing, suddenly suspended outside the rail, higher than they were. A flash of teeth and eyes, perhaps, and then Nnanji threw his knife into the nearest watcher and drew his sword. Another man sprang forward and his blade was parried. He recoiled against a mizzen backstay and was struck. He screamed, his sword missing Wallie by inches, then hitting the water with a loud splash. Nnanji swayed precariously as his ankle was released, parried again, put his right foot on the rail, grabbed the stay, blocked another lunge, pulled his left foot free, parried—then he was on the rail and down on the deck.

At that point the fight was as good as lost for the pirates. Nnanji could hold them off while Wallie pushed his supporters away and scrambled out through the window. Then he was over the rail also, and the sharks were in the swimming pool.

It was a monochrome nightmare, black on almost-black, lit only by faint gleams from silver shreds of clouds and shards of the Dream God and bright water. Slaughter and injury and death, no affair of honor, proclaimed by heralds, diluted by the convention of equal facing off against equal . . . Wallie used a battle cry to tell his companion where he was: "Seven! Seven!" like a tuba in the mounting noise. He heard Nnanji's laugh, then: "Four! Four!"

Wallie parried and thrust, and someone screamed. Another dark shape loomed at him, eyes and blade shining, and he slashed and felt his sword cut into meat and strike bone, heard another curse of pain. A body hit the deck. "Seven!" "Four!" He could barely see his opponents, but they were worse off. His supreme skill, his knowledge of the deck, his certainty that they were all enemies and not friends, even his size and strength, together made him unbeatable. Shonsu was the World's best, and on this deck Nnanji was almost a Sixth. It was no contest, just hot-blooded murder. The swordsmen were outnumbered, but the pirates were outclassed.

"Four!"

"Seven!"

A voice shouted, "Three!" and tailed off in a gurgle and another tenor laugh from Nnanji. Then the pirates fell back, and for a moment there was a pause, a circle of armed men facing two over a clutter of four or five bodies, one of them screaming in a high voice like a boy or a woman might use. It was better not to see the carnage, to fight by sounds and the feel of things, not to know what one was doing to living men—or women.

"Come on, then!" Nnanji jeered, and they came, at least six of them together, and it must have seemed a reasonable idea. It was folly, for they tripped over the bodies and jostled each other, while the swordsmen had their backs to the rail. Cut. Slash. Oath. Scream.

"Seven!"

"Four!"

Then they broke and fled, the swordsmen close behind, lions after Christians. A hand grabbed Wallie's ankle. He stumbled, slashed, and was freed. He fought his way down the steps, and the brightening ringlight showed people scrambling over the rail forward.

"Hold it!" he panted. "Let them go."

The wind was cold as death on his sweaty skin.

Nnanji stopped to watch also, wiping his face with an arm. "That was fun," he said. "The trouble with our craft, brother, is too much rehearsal and not enough acting."

Then the fo'c'sle door slammed shut. The pirates had vacated the deck, but there were others below. Wallie stalked forward, warily checking for ambushes behind the dinghies. He looked over the rail and saw a group of boats.

"Wait for your wounded!" he called, and received a chorus of obscenities.

"I am a swordsman of the Seventh. I swear by my sword that there will be no tricks. We'll return your wounded. How many went below?"

The replies were too jumbled to be audible. He went over to the door and kicked it. "Can you hear me?" No reply. He grabbed the door and heaved, jumped back and sideways. He was facing utter blackness and he didn't need Shonsu to tell him that he would be visible against the sky and could be knifed.

He repeated his oath—no tricks, and they could leave in safety if they came out. Silence, the only sounds a muffled clamor from the deckhouse, a distant weeping from the wounded, and the slap of water against the hull.

"We'll starve you out," he shouted.

No reply.

"I've told you that you can leave. But only if you come now."

More silence.

"I'm a swordsman!" Wallie shouted, and he could hear his despair in his voice—and hoped the pirates could. "The sailors will be here in a minute. Hurry!"

"With our swords?" asked a voice from just inside.

"Yes. I swear."

Nnanji growled angrily.

Wallie snarled at him. "Keep watch on the boats!"

"I'm coming!" said a woman's voice. A shape materialized in the doorway and ran toward the boats.

Nnanji grabbed her arm with his free hand. "How many more in there?"

"Four more," she said.

Then there was confusion as the crew came streaming across the deck. Someone had climbed out a window and unbarred the door. Wallie swung around, and now he had to threaten his friends to defend their enemies. Tomiyano would have attacked them with his dagger if Nnanji had not blocked him. He was raving with fury, screaming over and over that they were pirates and ought to die.

Finally Wallie grabbed him with his left hand, angry that he must take his attention off the fo'c'sle and the captives, who might yet be dangerous.

"They're sailors," Wallie roared. "Half of them are women. There are children out there in the boats! Where did your grandfather get this ship?"

It was only a guess, but it silenced Tomiyano. The last of the pirates slipped over the rail to their boats. A splash from the stern warned Wallie that the crew were starting to clean up. He turned and ran, hoping that that body had been dead, and he almost had to use his sword again to defend the three surviving wounded from his friends. Next to fire, they loathed pirates most.

The wounded were bandaged and helped into a final boat. Wallie leaned wearily on the rail, feeling the blood drying on his arm and chest, feeling the sullen throb of protest from his leg, hating this barbaric World, watching the sad little cavalcade drift away. It was an endless, savage game, with its own rules. Had the attack succeeded, then by morning *Sapphire* would still have been a trading ship, but under new ownership. Brota and her family would have been fed to the fish, unless they had been granted mercy, in which case they would have been in the boats—with swords or without—homeless refugees and potentially pirates themselves.

He shivered at the wind on his heated face. The light was growing brighter as the clouds were ripped from the Dream God.

"I think I did four and wounded one," Nnanji said. "So that would be three dead, two wounded for you, right?"

"I didn't count."

Then Thana came hurtling out of the darkness and threw her arms around Nnanji. Wallie was suddenly enveloped in a sobbing Brota. His back was being slapped, his hand pumped with laughter and cheering. He was astonished at one point to be hugged by Tomiyano, now recovered from his fury and gruffly apologizing for everything he could think of. The swordsmen were heroes.

He slipped away by himself up the fo'c'sle steps and leaned on the capstan and shivered. It was there that Jja found him.

She put an arm around him. "What's wrong? Are you hurt?" The shivering was getting worse.

"No." That had been a mere river skirmish, and he had seven cities to take back from the sorcerers. How much blood? How many dead?

"You did your duty, love," she whispered, sensing his horror at the slaughter. "What the gods wanted."

"I don't have to like it, do I?" In the battle on the holy island he had let the Shonsu bloodlust drive him. Perhaps he could have called it up for this one, but he had not felt it and had not raised it. This had been Wallie running things; and hating it.

"No, you don't have to like it," she said. "But it had to be done. They are your friends—Wallie's friends." She very rarely called him that, except when they were making love. He hugged her tightly and buried his face in her hair.

Yes, they would be friends now—there was a party developing down on the main deck. Someone had just tipped wine over Nnanji's head.

Rain began to fall on his back, increasing his shivering. Voices were calling him to come down and drink.

The pirates had died to fulfill the god's riddle. He had earned his army.

Murderer!

BOOK FIVE:

HOW THE SWORD SAVED THE SWORDSMAN

†

Next morning, while Nnanji was teaching fencing to Matarro, Tomiyano came to Wallie with a rueful smile and two foils. It was a declaration of surrender, but it merely confirmed what Wallie had already guessed—from now on *Sapphire* was his to command. The family had had close calls from pirates before, but never that close, and they had suffered no losses. They understood. They would cooperate. Moreover, they were genuinely grateful to the swordsmen. There would be no more talk of putting the passengers ashore, and now even the surly captain began to thaw into friendship.

Two days later, carefully primed by Wallie with a few fiendishly complex and obscure routines, plus a brief lecture on Nnanji's shortcomings, Tomiyano beat that young man soundly, to his great indignation. From then on their daily match became the ship's national sport. Wallie could hardly find a peaceful moment without one or other demanding another lesson. The standard of fencing on board rose to giddy heights.

At Cha, Novice Katanji was astonished to discover that slaving was not merely permissible now, but encouraged. Entering towers, talking to sorcerers, or any other such foolhardiness was still forbidden, but he seemed unusually sincere when he promised to be careful.

At Cha, also, Brota disposed of the marble and footwear and bought wine, great fragrant hogsheads of wine. Without discussion, *Sapphire* continued her voyage upstream, and the mountains edged around from south to southwest.

That first night out of Cha, the meal became raucous as a feast of gulls—Tomiyano was passing round samples of wine.

"Ensorceled wine!" he proclaimed. "You wouldn't believe what the vintners charge for it, but there's a good market for it on the right bank. I've been checking."

Wallie could guess before he tasted it, and not only from the choking and gasping that accompanied its progress around the circle. "At least six times the price of ordinary wine?" he asked.

The captain nodded suspiciously. "About eight times. Why?"

Wallie sipped cautiously. It was almost straight alcohol, flavored with wine—a crude and powerful brandy.

"If you have some ordinary wine, Captain," he said, "then tomorrow I shall ensorcel it for you. But you'll only get about a fifth as much of the ensorceled wine as you have of the ordinary." He laughed at the captain's skeptical glare.

The copper still from Ki San had remained in a corner of the deckhouse, unclaimed by either Tomiyano or Nnanji. Next morning Wallie took it down to the galley and carefully distilled some wine for the dumfounded sailors.

"There you are," he said. "If you want to settle down ashore, then you can be wine ensorcelers; but I suspect that the sorcerers would resent the competition. You might die of a nasty accident fairly soon, so I don't advise it." They stared at him with superstitious awe and disclaimed any such ambition.

It was obvious that the sorcerers, having stills for whatever purpose, would sooner or later have discovered alcohol. What was more interesting to Wallie was the revelation that they were making money from it. He added to his list of things he wanted to know: What else did the sorcerers sell, apart from magic potions and spells and ensorceled wine?

Cha on the left bank . . . the next city was Wo on the right bank. They alternated like footsteps. As *Sapphire* docked, a band led a parade along the road. The port official reeled up the gangplank, and Tomiyano reeled, also, catching his breath from his salute.

"Welcome to Wo and carnival!" the official declaimed, and staggered slightly.

Brota rubbed her plump hands at the thought of carnival time and a load of ensorceled wine to sell.

A dark suspicion settled in Wallie's mind. He turned to Nnanji. "I'll bet you tomorrow's latrine duty that we don't get to speak to the reeve."

Nnanji would not take that bet—he trusted his mentor's hunches too much. They settled on a wager of an hour's fencing as a sure win for both.

"Go ahead and sell your wine, mistress," Wallie told Brota. "I know what the rest of us are going to do. Right, brother?"

"Right," said Nnanji. "Carnival!"

Wallie turned to Jja. "Dancing!" he said. "Wine and song and beautiful ladies in gossamer dresses."

Jja dropped her eyes. "I can't dance, my love."

"And masks," Wallie said quietly.

He had been right about the reeve: the only swordsmen they could locate were two juniors so totally drunk that they could not have found their sword hilts. Nnanji was enraged and wanted to chop off their ponytails, but Wallie dragged him away before he could start. There was no chance now that Brota would put him ashore if he found enlistable swordsmen, but evidently he was still not permitted to meet any. He was on a voyage of discovery and must find out for himself. By Ov, hopefully, the lesson would be learned.

He had been wrong about the beautiful dresses. The standard of living was not high enough to allow such luxury. Participants in carnival wore the minimum of clothes and a complete coat of body paint, which acted as costume and mask in one. A supply of paint was quickly obtained, and the younger folk divided into couples to decorate each other. Nnanji offered his services to Thana, but had to settle for Katanji.

Wallie and Jja retired to their cabin and discovered that body painting was even more fun than the dress designing they had enjoyed long ago in the temple barracks. They smudged several attempts before being able to concentrate on art.

That night they danced in the streets by the light of bonfires while the music played and the wine flowed. The air was cool on skins wearing only paint, but they were warmed by giant bonfires, by frenzied tarantellas and torrid fandangoes, by hot wine mulled with cinnamon and sweet cloves.

Jja was a born dancer, the best of them all, and soon was teaching her owner. They all danced until dawn had turned to morning.

Nnanji wore four shades of green, like a red-haired leprechaun, and Thana was a golden sprite from some legendary Arcadian forest. Leaping with little skill but unbounded enthusiasm, those two won the endurance dance.

Jja shone in midnight blue with silver stars, Wallie was Harlequin. They were awarded the grand prize for the handsomest couple in the carnival. Of course.

From Wo to Gor . . .

At Gor, two sorcerers stopped Tomiyano in the street and questioned him about his scar, his ship, his business, and his personal habits. He returned to *Sapphire* cursing, red-faced, and obviously intimidated; vowing to stay out of sight in future.

Slowly Wallie was gathering wisdom about sorcery, but not the one wisdom he needed—how could swordsmen fight sorcerers? There were more stories of thunderbolts, various tales of mysterious powers—some of which he was sure were legend —and a harrowing eyewitness account of the destruction of the swordsmen of Gor, who had charged the line of sorcerers across an open pasture under a cloudless sky, only to die simultaneously in one great thunderbolt. Or had that been another manifestation of fire demons? The bodies had apparently been badly chewed, as at Ov.

The towers were places of dread for the townsfolk, who stayed away at night, fearing the strange noises and lights. All the towers were identical, Katanji insisted, and they all had birds around them. At least one other tower purchased horse urine, and a second time Katanji saw octopus being delivered. The sorcerers seemed to do well out of their wine ensorceling. They purchased all the finest leather. They sold love potions and would foretell the future for a fee. Their garrisons seemed always to be slightly smaller than the swordsmen garrisons they displaced, but who knew who was a sorcerer? There might be many around in disguise.

Wallie could find no limit to their power, no chink in their armor. If the World contained a sorcerer kryptonite, he did not hear of it. The colors of fall began to tint the hills and the days flew away like swallows. The mountains slid round to the west. Crew and passengers became almost indistinguishable, and even Nnanji at times donned a breechclout and ran aloft with the others.

Thana continued to vamp Lord Shonsu and ignore Nnanji's passionate yearnings. At first Wallie had dismissed those as mere lechery. Then he had concluded that they were only a juvenile infatuation—Thana was probably the first woman who had ever genuinely refused Nnanji and she was also the only target in sight. Now his unflagging persistence was beginning to seem quite out of character, another of those complexities that Wallie had not previously suspected in him. Unfortunately, his social skills remained primitive, and his courtship was still much like his table manners—long on enthusiasm and short on finesse. He did not know how to woo a lady. Until he sought advice, his mentor was not going to offer any, and evidently Nnanji was too proud to ask.

Gor on the left bank, then Shan on the right, a pleasant little town of potteries and dairies, where *Sapphire* loaded great yellow cartwheels of cheese, and the crew joked that the Goddess was rewarding even the ship's rats.

Rather nervously, Wallie went hunting for the reeve, wondering what disaster this action might call down on the unsuspecting victim. The reeve and his deputy had gone duck hunting. Wallie was not surprised. For the first time he did meet some competent swordsmen—a half-dozen middleranks, awed to find themselves entertaining a Seventh—but all of them were happily married and beyond the age of seeking adventure. He made no attempt to enlist any, and none of them knew or cared very much about sorcerers.

Then Amb, on the left bank. There Brota purchased long rolls of sailcloth and bundles of tools; saws and axes and shovels and kegs of nails. As the last of these were being carried aboard, *Sapphire* had a visitor, a wizened, graying priest of the Fifth, mincing up the plank behind the diminutive figure of Honakura.

Wallie, Nnanji, and Tomiyano—the three who must not be seen in sorcerer country, the three wise monkeys, Wallie called them—were watching from the deckhouse. They could not hear what was said, but they saw gold being passed and then the priest depart. Honakura came wandering in to explain, looking pleased with himself.

He settled wearily on one of the chests. "An interesting development, my lord," he said. "We are on a mission of mercy!" Then he would say no more until he had sipped a glass of wine and eaten some of Lina's fresh gingerbread.

Wallie knew that he was being teased and would have to wait. The old man was a wonder to him. He gave the impression that he was enjoying every minute of this wandering, dangerous life, so unlike his pampered past. At every city he scouted with the sailors and he provided more useful information than anyone except Katanji, for he had both judgment and skill.

He also had an invaluable source of gossip in the priests. While they were unhappy with the rule of sorcerers because they demanded that altars to the Fire God be maintained within the temples and prayers offered to Him, their unhappiness did not seem to extend to contemplating revolution. The sorcerers were being very skillful at keeping the population content. In Wallie's view, their public relations were much better than the swordsmen's.

"Ah!" said Honakura, refreshed at last. The ship was preparing to leave. "You know that Mistress Brota purchased tools? I was just returning when I saw the holy Master Momingu arrive at the trader's, so I made myself known to him."

"And what is so interesting about Master Momingu?" Wallie

asked patiently. Nnanji and Tomiyano were almost ready to start strangling procedures.

"He had come to purchase a shipload of tools and charter a vessel to carry them. The temple wants to send succor to the city of Gi, next port up on the right bank. I explained that we were heading that way, and Mistress Brota agreed to sell her cargo and accept the charter."

"The devil she did?" Tomiyano muttered.

Honakura twinkled. "I think she made a small profit, Captain. Of course, the reverend Momingu had expected to accompany the load and supervise distribution, but I was able to persuade him that such was not required in this case."

"And why should the priests of Amb wish to buy tools and send them to the city of Gi?" Wallie asked, as expected.

"Because," the priest replied triumphantly, "the sorcerers have informed them that a great fire is burning there! Much of the city has already been destroyed, and many people are homeless. The temple is also chartering ships of food and lumber."

"*Is* burning?"

"Is. It started this morning, they say."

His listeners looked at each other. "Three days to Gi," Tomiyano said.

"Exactly!" Honakura rubbed his hands and beamed at Wallie. "A test of the sorcerers, my lord!"

Wallie nodded. The sorcerers had known of the downed bridge in the mountains, but Gi was a long way off and was also in swordsman country. Nor had the sorcerers offered to transport the tools and lumber by magic. "Very interesting, old man. Very interesting, indeed!"

Hard-nosed traders though they were, Brota and Tomiyano were not without compassion or faith in the Goddess. They sailed late and weighed anchor early, and now the winds were favorable. Two days brought *Sapphire* to Gi.

There were cities of wood and there were cities of stone. Gi had been of wood, spread across a delta plain between two gentle hills. For hours before *Sapphire* arrived the air was tainted by an acrid stench of burning. As she drew close the whole company assembled on deck to stare in shock and dismay at the devastation.

The plain was gray, a giant's thistlefield, a petrified forest of chimneys, its deadly sameness broken only by a few roofless skeletons of temples. Lonely wisps of smoke showed where remnants still smoldered, but tiny shanties of charred fragments were already clustered around some of the stark chimneystacks. The wind lifted clouds of ash and stirred them around contemptuously. From the stone facing on the dock all the way back to the hillsides, hardly a whole building stood. Even as the watchers absorbed their first horror, people began to rise out of the wasteland like ants. They drifted toward the harbor, thousands of them, homeless, hungry ghosts, the same deathly gray as their city.

Wallie was the first ashore, Nnanji at his heels, and they had to push their way into the crowd and force it back to allow the ship to be properly moored. The mob was filthy and shocked—white eyes staring out of ash-covered faces. People shouted and struggled, and there was danger of a stampede that would hurl hundreds off the dock and into the deadly waters.

Drawing his sword and waving it high, bellowing to enforce order, Wallie called for swordsmen, and eventually three or four came struggling through to the front. They were as black and as confused as the civilians. He could not tell their ranks and he had no time for formal salutes. He barked orders and was obeyed. Discipline appeared like a sudden rain in the desert, and the danger of panic subsided. He jumped up on a bollard and shouted the news: Food ships were coming, help was coming, pass the word, and make room.

So that day *Sapphire* went into the relief business. The sailcloth was ripped into tent lengths, and some of those torn small to hold nails. One tool or one poke of nails to a customer—let them cooperate as best they could. The crew worked as dock slaves, carrying the cargo to shore. Other ships began to arrive, sent by the priests of Amb and Ov, or by chance, or by the Hand of the Goddess. They brought food and lumber, and one was a cattle boat whose crew set up an abattoir on the dock. Wallie conscripted every water rat from every ship and built himself an army, which he used to organize and pacify. Eventually he found the reeve, but he was elderly and shattered by bereavement. Wallie declared him deposed and replaced by his deputy; no one questioned a Seventh's right to do anything he wanted. By evening tents and shacks were beginning to spread across the plain, while *Sapphire* had turned gray herself and stank of dead fire like the devastated city. But civilization had taken root again.

Incredibly, Brota had found trade. Several of the warehouses had held bronze ingots, great flat slabs with a lug at each corner, the shape that the Greeks had used and called oxhides. Many had survived the fire and lay in heaps amid the rubble. She bought a load of them, and Wallie had no doubt that the price was good. Nor was there need to hire a slave gang; hundreds of sooty men were willing to work for a copper until they were sweat-streaked like zebras. By the end of the day there was one woman smiling in Gi.

At last they had done all they could. They spread the grubby sails and stood out into open water and untainted air, weary and filthy, and sad. Fire was even worse than pirates.

Slumped beside a sooty and equally exhausted Nnanji at the rail, Wallie reflected that for once he had truly enjoyed being a swordsman of the Seventh. Power itself held no appeal for him, but sometimes it could be used for good purposes.

Then Jja came by, clean and delectable in her black bikini, much amused that she had won first place in the lottery for the shower, taking precedence over her mighty owner. She made a great performance of leaning forward and pursing her lips to get a kiss without being soiled by him. Chuckling, she went off to help with the children.

Wallie sighed and made a remark that was to have a curious sequel.

"If only a slave could wear jewels!" he said. "If she could use them, I would buy beautiful things and give them to Jja. There are few easier ways to honor one's lady."

Getting no answer, he turned to glance at his companion and intercepted an amused look. He turned away quickly. Nnanji had seen right through that little deception and knew that he was not talking only of Jja.

"Thank you, brother," Nnanji said quietly. "I should have thought of that, of course."

Wallie turned back to him, knowing that his face was burning under its film of ash. "Forgive me," he said. "I keep treating you as the Second I found on the beach. I forget that you have come a long way since then."

"If I have, then the credit is yours," Nnanji said graciously. He went back to looking at the ruins of Gi. Incredibly, a tear trickled down his cheek, clearing a path through the dust.

††

The rain god had been about his business in the night, washing the rigging, but the sails were striped with his leavings and the deck blotched with mud. The crew set to work to clean up, singing river chanteys in the morning sunshine.

Wallie swung a mop in the line of workers, perhaps the first swordsman of the Seventh ever to undertake such a task in the history of the World. He would have been quite happy at it, had he not been working alongside a certain nubile, slender lass. He was being kept extremely conscious of her shapely form in its saffron bikini, of her calendar beauty, of her classic profile crowned with shiny black curls and adorned with the sexiest eyelashes in the World, for Thana had mysteriously become left-handed, which put her off center, and every few minutes her flank or arm would gently nudge against his. "Beg pardon, my lord," she would whisper. "My pleasure," he would reply. It was very annoying, because he knew that she was doing it deliberately, that he was reacting, that she knew he was reacting, that she knew he knew, and so on. Had Shonsu been in better control of his glands? Probably not, but likely Shonsu would not have cared.

Then Nnanji threw open the fo'c'sle door and came striding along the deck with a bag in his hand. Behind him, almost having to trot to keep up, came Katanji, wearing sword and kilt and boots. For once, he looked concerned, and there was obviously trouble in the air—so much trouble that Nnanji did not even notice Thana.

"I should be grateful if you would accompany us, my lord brother. I need speak with Mistress Brota."

Wallie was wearing his sword, but his feet were bare. "If you hold on a moment, I can get my boots," he said, but Nnanji was already bounding up the steps to the poop. Wallie glanced at Katanji, who brashly rolled his eyes in an attempt to appear less worried than he obviously was. They both followed.

Brota was sitting like a giant red puffball at the tiller and her moon face was totally expressionless as the deputation arrived. Wallie was not surprised to find that Thana and Honakura had come along also—they both liked to be in on any excitement that was brewing. Thus there were five people who formed up in a semicircle in front of the helmsperson.

"You're blocking my view!" Brota barked. Nnanji growled, but all five sat down. First point to Brota, Wallie thought; now she was higher than they were, and being angry was harder when sitting than standing. She had no real need to see, anyway. *Sapphire* was heading up an empty River, with very few sails in sight—blue sky, blue water, golden fall hills against the smoke-colored ranges far to the northwest.

A moment later Tomiyano slid into view and stayed leaning against the rail, watching with cynical suspicion. Seven was the magic number, Wallie remembered. Could this be some divinely decreed event? They had as near a complete set of ranks as could be assembled on the ship, too—little, desiccated Honakura in his black, then the lithesome Thana in skimpy yellow... Next to her, Katanji was as dark-skinned as she, and looked darker because he was wearing a white kilt, unusually clean for him. Nnanji was a tangle of lanky and paler limbs protruding from an orange kilt, his anger making him seem more awkward even than he normally did. Brota loomed above them all in her wind-rippled crimson, Tomiyano was a silent audience on the fringes in a brown breechclout, and Wallie himself, huge in blue. Only a Sixth's green was missing.

Nnanji looked at Wallie. "The day you were wounded, brother, I took your money to look after. I gave mine to Novice Katanji, so they would not get mixed up. I gave him forty-three golds and some change. When I sold Cowie, I gave him another ten. He had five of his own. I asked for three back in Wo, but I haven't needed any more. Today I asked him for the rest of it."

Planning to buy a present for Thana, of course.

"Fifty-three of yours and five of his makes fifty-eight," Wallie said, knowing that mathematics was not his protégé's strong point. "Less three makes fifty he owes you?"

Nnanji nodded grimly. "He hasn't got it. All he has is this."

He tipped the bag he had been holding, spilling a glittering heap of rubies and emeralds and pearls. The circle of onlookers muttered in astonishment. Nnanji stirred the heap with a finger.

"Three golds and some silver," he said, picking out a few coins.

"Obviously the gems are worth more than fifty golds," Wallie said. "He can certainly repay you as soon as he gets to a free city."

Nnanji's eyes were icy. "But I want to know where he got them, brother. He denies stealing, but says he promised Mistress Brota that he would not tell. That's what concerns me!"

"I've never seen those before," Brota said hurriedly. She started scanning the horizon as if looking for landmarks. No one wanted to speak next. Wallie decided that this was a matter between Nnanji and his brother, but he was curious to see how Nnanji would handle it.

Getting no help from him, Nnanji took a deep breath and said, "Mistress, would you please explain how a protégé can keep anything secret from his mentor? Do you consider it seemly for another swordsman, like yourself, to suggest that he should?"

Point to Nnanji.

Brota grunted without looking down. "No! But I don't recall telling him to do that. As I remember, it was the other way. I promised him that I would not tell you."

Nnanji swung a triumphant gaze on Katanji, who was attempting to look like a very small boy confused by the affairs of adults. He was less convincing than he would have been once; the weeks on the River had lengthened him and filled him out. He would never be big, but he was visibly closer to manhood than he had been when Wallie first met him. He looked healthier, too, and he even had a stump of a ponytail now, although it curled up in a knot. "I bought some rugs, mentor," he said. "Brota helped me."

Thana was instantly overcome by a life-threatening attack of giggles. Brota glared at her in angry silence, but that merely made Thana's fit worse.

"Let me tell!" she said when she had recovered.

Out came a story of silk rugs and of negotiations in a gondola. Wallie was soon digging his nails into his palms to stop himself laughing aloud. He risked a glance at the old priest, who raised one eyebrow—Brota outwitted by a scratcher? Certainly a miracle!

Katanji had bought all the best rugs in the shop in Dri for sixty-two gold pieces, filling the gondola. Brota had gained nothing by her bargain. Indeed she had been out the costs of the ride and bribing the gondolier, out even the risk of smuggling, for the authorities might have seized her ship. Wallie knew that she would have felt bound by her handshake, but that did not explain how she had managed to resist drowning the brat.

"And how did you sell them?" he asked.

Katanji had recovered his confidence, but he was still somehow projecting an appearance of great youth and innocence as he took up the story. Now it was even better.

At the next port, Casr, he asked that his rugs be unloaded and placed on the docks next to Brota's. There was a fierce but whispered argument. He retorted that she had agreed to unload them where he wanted and if they were too close to hers, then she could have them moved, but he could not do that himself, and the crew would wonder why. He promised that the sailors would not discover his private trading as long as she kept them away, especially Diwa and Matarro. Wallie guessed that by this time Brota was too fascinated by his display of precocity to do more than cooperate and watch. So Katanji arranged his rugs in a heap and sat on top of it to play a solitaire game that involved moving pegs around a board.

When the traders came, Brota tried to sell her rugs, but the finest in sight were under Katanji. She could only refer the traders to the boy. He politely showed the goods, but explained that he was guarding the rugs for his father, who had gone into town. So they were not for sale? Well, his dad had said he could sell the whole pile for a hundred and twenty golds. When would his father be back? Katanji merely shrugged and returned to his solitaire game. He wore a rugmaker's fathermark, so the story seemed believable.

He had nothing else to do with the day; the ship could not sail without Brota; Brota could not leave without selling her goods—for the traders were interested—and Brota was not going to sell much with that pile of superlative rugs sitting there next to hers. The traders, baffled by having no one to haggle with, hung around, waiting for the imaginary father to return. After a couple of hours, when the waiting seemed likely to last until sunset, one of the traders confirmed with Brota that the boy had authority to sell and handed over the full amount. As Katanji went back on board, he placed the solitaire game on Brota's table . . .

That last piece of studied insolence was too much for Wallie. He leaned back on his arms and bellowed with laughter. Nnanji scowled and looked at Thana, who was equally helpless. Tears were pouring down Honakura's cheeks. Brota was smiling thinly—obviously it hurt too much to laugh. Then a raucous noise from the rail showed that Tomiyano, also, was overcome by the story. Outraged, Nnanji glared around at him, then turned back to his brother, who was very wide-eyed and hopeful . . . but this time he had gone too far. Nnanji was not going to see the joke. This was a matter of honor.

"Right," he said coldly, when calm had been restored. "So you spent sixty-two out of . . . how did you get to sixty-two?"

He looked in puzzlement at Wallie, who agreed that they had not accounted for sixty-two, even with Katanji's own five.

"You had nineteen silvers, mentor," Katanji said reluctantly. "And I had two . . ."

"That makes one more gold."

Katanji sighed. "When you tried to buy the pot from the captain? He didn't take the money. He kicked it away."

"And you picked it up afterward, of course!" Nnanji glared. "That is Lord Shonsu's money. No, it is the captain's."

"But he didn't want it!"

Even Wallie was having trouble keeping track by this time,

but they eventually established that Katanji, after he had sold his rugs, should have had one hundred and twenty-two left, of which five were either Wallie's or Tomiyano's. Then they learned of two more that he had weaseled out of Brota in Wal . . . one hundred and twenty-four.

"How much is all this worth?" Nnanji asked suddenly, peering at the heap of jewels. Thana bent forward and spread them out.

"At least five hundred golds," she said. Brota nodded in agreement.

Nnanji fixed his gaze on the sinner. "How much?"

Katanji pouted. "Between seven and eight hundred . . . nearer to eight."

The congregation exchanged glances.

"I bought some jewels in Casr. Look, see this ruby? I bought that and another for sixty, then I sold the other in Tau for fifty, but it was bigger. And I bought two amethysts and four topazes in Wo and sold them in Shan."

"How do you know about jewels?" Wallie demanded. There seemed to be no bottom to Katanji's hidden depths.

Nnanji turned pink. "Our grandfather was a silversmith. Katanji used to hang around his workshop, my lord brother, till he died. About four years ago," he added in a small voice, and Wallie then knew where the money had come from to bribe Nnanji's way into the temple guard.

"He was going to let me apprentice to him, my lord," Katanji said, eager to change the subject.

"How did you get from one hundred and twenty-odd to seven or eight hundred, though?" his brother demanded.

Katanji looked appealingly at Brota. "He did some work for me," she admitted, then grudgingly explained. Katanji's unique ability to extract information from slaves had not been used only in sorcerer cities. At Casr, Tau, Wo, and Shan, he had undertaken industrial espionage for Brota. His price had risen every time, until now he was charging ten golds. Brota had paid, because haggling was much easier when she knew her opponent's unit cost.

Nnanji looked disgusted. Even Wallie had lost track of the

mathematics. "What did you have when you got to Gi?" he demanded.

"One ruby, two emeralds, and one hundred and eleven golds, my lord."

Three coins left . . . "You bought the rest of this with one hundred and eight golds?" Wallie asked and Katanji nodded guiltily.

Supply and demand—in a world without banks the ultimate store of value was land, but for movable property was gold or gems. The survivors of Gi would have saved their jewelry if nothing else, but they would have been in need of hard cash. Jewels had suddenly become cheap and money dear. Katanji had seen the opportunity of a lifetime. Wallie looked at Brota, and she was scowling ferociously. She had been wasting her time on bronze ingots, while Katanji had been working his way up into the senior class.

"That's horrible!" Nnanji said when it was explained to him in simple terms. "They were starving! Homeless! Don't you have any pity at all?"

He looked at Wallie in disgust. Wallie wondered if Nnanji would have felt such compassion when he was Katanji's age. Perhaps not, but he had changed and learned. Katanji never would.

"He probably regrets only that he didn't hold back enough cash to repay you," said Wallie. "Then you wouldn't have known. He got greedy."

"I was going to, my lord," Katanji said sadly, "until I saw the pearls." He reached into the heap and lifted out a glittering string of light. "I couldn't resist them. I got these for twenty— and they're worth at least two hundred."

No, he had no regrets.

"From now on," Nnanji said, "you will not go slaving without my permission! Is that clear?" His brother nodded glumly, and Brota pouted at the skyline. "Slaving may be honorable when it is done to aid the gods, but not for money! Now, how much could you get for . . . this?" He pulled out a brooch of gold and emeralds.

"Seventy or so," Katanji suggested cautiously.

Nnanji handed it to him. "Then take it, sell it, and pay back what you started with. Keep anything extra."

Katanji's eyes gleamed.

Then Nnanji looked doubtfully at the rest of the treasure, silently sought help from Wallie and then Honakura, and saw that they were leaving it up to him. "Who owns this?"

"It's mine!" But Katanji's voice lacked conviction.

"No it isn't!" Even sitting on the deck, Nnanji could look down on him like a wading heron eyeing a fish. "As a First you can own nothing. And even if you were a Second, this wouldn't be yours. If I told you to look after my cow, and she calved, then the calf would still be mine. That's the law." He glanced at the priest and got an amused nod.

He scowled in thought for a while, the others waited for his decision, and the ship glided through the morning sunlight.

"I think it's tainted," Nnanji said. "It ought to go to the Goddess at the next temple we reach."

Katanji and Brota exchanged looks of disgust.

"Just a minute," said Brota from her throne, a crimson Buddha about to impart enlightenment. "Shonsu, you've seen Katanji fence. What sort of a swordsman is he going to make?"

"A dead one."

She nodded. "Nnanji, you know this, too. The kid has no future in your business, but he's a natural trader, like my oldest, Tomiyarro, was, maybe even better. He will do very well on the River, even if he never does get more marks."

"He's not quite as bad as he makes out," Wallie said. "He fakes it."

Nnanji looked suspiciously at Katanji, whose face now wore a studied absence of expression.

"But," Wallie added, "he's never going to be a Third if he lives to a thousand. Nnanji," he said gently, "the lady has a good point."

"Let him swear to me," Brota suggested, "and be a water rat. It's his natural calling. One day he can marry a trader, and they can own their own ship. That's better than being dead, isn't it?" She gave Katanji a motherly smile and probably meant it.

Nnanji colored. "A swordsman engaging in trade?"

"Kindly explain what is wrong with that?" Thana asked in a voice dripping poisoned honey. "Mother and I need to know."

A silence grew, while Nnanji studied the jewels intently, and the sides of his neck turned as red as his cheeks. He had just dug his grave with his tongue, Wallie decided, and waited with interest to see if he could extricate himself.

"Is that what you want, protégé? To be a water rat? A *trader*?"

Katanji hesitated. "I think I would be a better trader than a swordsman, Nanj," he said quietly. "But I want to stay with you—for a few years, anyway."

"Well, if you do become a water rat, then I suppose you could use this," Nnanji said reluctantly.

"But my honor, mentor?" Katanji's eyes were very big and very innocent.

Nnanji glared. Then, choosing his words with great care, he said, "It is wrong for a garrison swordsman or a free sword to engage in trade, because it distracts him from his duty. But a water rat has obligations to his ship, so trade is permissible for him. Is that clear?"

Katanji sighed. "It's clever!" Then he looked up again at his brother. "But what would Aunt Gruza say?"

More silence . . . a sound like escaping steam . . . then Nnanji exploded into laughter at last, and Katanji joined him, and they howled in unison at some family in-joke that the others could not share. The onlookers watched in amused and puzzled silence.

Nnanji could not speak. He beat his fists on the deck. He wiped tears away a couple of times and tried . . . then he would catch his brother's eye again, and again the two of them would collapse into hysterical giggles. Whoever Aunt Gruza was, her name was a word of power.

To Wallie it was a touching reminder that these two had shared childhood together—and not very long ago, either. He was trying to fight a war with very young assistants. And, in spite of their extreme differences, these brothers were actually very fond of each other.

At long last, the fit passed, and Nnanji regained control.

"All right, nipper," he said. "You can keep it . . . except for these." He reached into the hoard and lifted out the string of pearls, which writhed in his fingers like a captured sunbeam. "Mistress Brota, will you seal the rest of this in a bag and put it in a safe place for us? If anything happens to me, then it belongs to Katanji."

"Of course, adept," Brota said.

Nnanji studied the pearls for a moment. "And these . . . these are the most beautiful, and they are honest—they brought out the story. So I shall keep them in view, to remind us to be honest. But I shall hide their beauty by putting them against a greater beauty."

He rose, hung the pearls around Thana's neck, and walked quickly away.

Thana gasped and raised her hand to them: *two hundred golds?* She looked at her mother, then at Wallie. Then she jumped up and ran after Nnanji.

Katanji quietly muttered, "Oh, puke!" in unbounded disgust.

"Perhaps you would witness the sealing, old man?" Wallie asked. Honakura took the hint and led Katanji and his fortune away. Tomiyano followed, leaving only Wallie sitting on the deck, looking up at Brota.

"That should do the trick," Wallie said.

And Brota studied him in silence for a while. "You are a man of great honor, my lord. Very few men, of any rank, would have refused what has been offered."

"I think there were conditions attached," Wallie said. "But what of Nnanji? You know, sometimes I think of him as an egg, a great big egg that I found on a beach. Every now and again another piece of shell falls off, and I get another glimpse of what is going to hatch. Whatever it is, it will be remarkable. Who would have thought that he was capable of that gracious little speech just now?"

"What are you implying, my lord?"

"That Thana has been missing a very good bet."

Brota nodded thoughtfully. "A mother should not say this, Lord Shonsu . . . but I doubt that she is worthy of him."

"Someone's coming now!" Nnanji said, and slapped at a mosquito, bringing his score up to a hundred or so.

The undulant profile of mountains along the western skyline was sharp and black like obsidian, below a colorless, limpid sky. The sun had gone, but true darkness was slow in coming, here in the deep shadow of RegiVul. The cliffs and the River were gloomy, drab, and sad. A cool wind ruffled the water, but failed to discourage legions of the nastiest biting insects Wallie had ever met.

At noon, *Sapphire* had slipped by the sorcerer city of Ov, feeling her way cautiously southward amid shallows and sandbanks. Now she lay in mid-River off the Garathondi estate.

Her dinghy was tied at the end of the jetty. It had been there for what seemed like a dozen hours, and must be at least two. A couple of ramshackle fishing boats were tethered nearby. The River was much higher than it had been when Wallie had first come to this place—and how long ago that felt!

Peering along the surface of the ancient, scruffy planks, he heard what Nnanji's ears had discerned over the slap of the ripples: hooves, and a creaking axle, and wheels on gravel. The dinghy rocked gently.

"About time!" said Tomiyano.

There were five of them—three swordsmen, counting Thana, plus one sailor and one slave—or six if you also counted the sleeping Vixini. Holiyi had been sent inland to find Quili.

Holiyi had been gone too long, so something had not gone as expected. With Holiyi the delay was certainly not due to idle gossiping, and Tomiyano had begun muttering dark threats of vengeance if anything had happened to his cousin.

The circle had been turned. This was where the mission had begun, here at the end of this jetty, waiting for Nnanji to scout and return. By coming back, Wallie had followed his orders. He had met the problem here, crossed the mountains, sailed around—turned the circle. Now the lesson might be learned. Maybe. He wished he had more confidence in his own ability to learn it. He was depressed by a nagging conviction that he had overlooked something, somewhere.

Damn horseflies! He slapped at the back of his neck.

A wagon came into sight at the bottom of the canyon, drawn by two horses. Two people dismounted and began walking. A third remained and commenced a long, painful effort to turn the vehicle. Horses would not step into the waters of the River, and there was little room with the River so high.

One of the pedestrians was Holiyi. The other was a woman, but not Quili.

"The rest of you stay here!" Wallie stepped up on the deck and strode forward to meet the visitors, his boots making hollow thudding sounds in the evening stillness.

Holiyi, when he came near enough to be clearly seen, was sporting his usual sardonic grin, which was reassuring. His companion was middle-aged, almost elderly. She wore the orange gown of a Fourth, and Wallie registered vaguely that it was of much too fine a velvet to be sweeping its lace-trimmed hem over this dirty, scabby jetty. Her hair was silver and well tended, her fingers jeweled. She was a priestess, and obviously a prosperous one.

"Adept Valia, Lord Shonsu," Holiyi muttered.

Salute and response.

"You had trouble?" Wallie demanded.

Holiyi shook his head with a relaxed and noncommittal shrug.

"Priestess Quili is well, my lord," Valia said, "but unable to come and see you at the moment. She is entertaining sorcerers." She smiled, being graciously amused at his reaction. Valia's manner was friendly enough, but she obviously fancied herself as a grand lady.

"That's not trouble?"

"Not as long as they do not know you are here, my lord! And I am sure that they will not find out."

Wallie turned and waved for his companions to join him. He

could ask Holiyi for details, but it might take an hour to drag them out of him.

"Explain, please, adept?"

But boots were drumming, and bare feet. The others came running, and then Valia had to be presented to Nnanji, and the others to her.

"What a beautiful baby!" she exclaimed.

Vixini, grumpy from being awakened, did not feel like a beautiful baby. He buried his face in his mother and declined conversation.

Wallie said a silent prayer for patience. "We cannot offer you a comfortable chair, adept, and the air swarms with vampire bats, so perhaps we should get the story quickly?"

Valia inclined her head in regal assent. "I have the honor to minister here now, my lord. Priestess Quili is my protégé. She is also my secular superior, but that is no problem. We work well together."

"I don't think I quite understand," Wallie said. "I am delighted to hear that Quili has achieved promotion to Third. What of Lady Thondi?"

"She is with the Goddess."

"I would be hypocritical if I expressed regrets."

He received a slight frown of priestly reproof, then the smiling condescension due a Seventh. "Perhaps understandable. I believe that you yourself consigned her to the justice of the gods. Your prayer was heard, my lord, and her passing was not easy."

"Explain!"

Adept Valia glanced around the group, relishing an attentive audience for a good story. "She came down to this jetty to embark on the family boat, meaning to travel to Ov on business —not long after your departure, Lord Shonsu. A rotted plank failed beneath her, and she fell through."

"Goddess!" Wallie muttered. His skin crawled. Why did he feel guilty?

"Undoubtedly! Several large men had preceded her, and she was not a weighty person, as I understand."

"So the piranha got her?"

He had been expected to ask. "No. They rejected her. That

does happen, of course. The current swept her out of reach, underneath. She was trapped, and she drowned. No one was able to reach her in time." The priestess was savoring her audience's reaction.

Jja slipped a comforting arm around her master. Nnanji and Tomiyano were looking impressed.

"I can show you the exact spot, if you wish," Valia offered.

"Thank you, no! And her son?"

"The Honorable Garathondi is in poor health, my lord. A few days after his mother's death, he suffered a seizure. He has been paralyzed and speechless ever since. The healers hold out no hope of recovery and do not expect him to live much longer."

"That's horrible!"

The priestess looked surprised. "You question the justice of the gods, my lord, when you yourself invoked it?"

"I didn't mean . . . Tell me about Quili, then. I trust her news is better?"

"Excellent. I have never seen a happier couple."

Wallie restrained a strong temptation to stun a holy personage. "She married Garadooi?"

"Of course! And they are so well suited! True lovebirds."

Feeling Jja's arm squeeze him, Wallie looked down at her smile. Some things did not need to be said.

"Please give them our congratulations."

"I certainly shall. And you, my lord? You have recovered from your injury?"

"How the . . . how do you know of that?"

Valia again displayed ladylike amusement. She was much less exposed to the wind and the bugs than the others were. "Some weeks ago, the sorcerers informed the builder that you had died. You had been seen in Aus, and then in Ki San, but very ill, from the effects of a sword cut. The healers had despaired of your life. Naturally, Quili was overjoyed when she heard that you were here this evening, and that the stories were all lies."

Not all; Wallie did not look at Nnanji. His mind was swirling with the implications. The sorcerers' powers were terrifying. They had agents in Ki San, then, at the very least, even if the healer himself had not been a sorcerer. But the healer had been wrong. That might by why *Sapphire* had not been more closely examined in Wal, when the sorcerer came aboard. The sorcerers had given him up for dead. Again that sense of power wasted by human fallibility...

"Not all their tales were false," he admitted. "But what is their business here tonight?"

The priestess chuckled. "Work on the sorcerers' tower is proceeding very slowly since Builder Garadooi shortened his slaves' work hours. He has also banned all physical punishment without his personal approval, my lord."

"That could be deleterious, I suppose."

"But output from the estate itself is markedly improved recently, I am told."

It sounded like Garadooi. He would be giving his slaves meat next. Maybe he already had. Beds, even.

"And the sorcerers?"

"Honorable Rathazaxo came to call today," Valia said, with a cynical smile. "He wanted Builder Garadooi to return with him to the city and take over supervision in person, as his father did. There was some loud discussion. Even through closed doors, it was loud."

"The tower is not being completed?"

"The tower itself is almost finished, I understand, but there is still work needed on the adjacent plaza. I think the contract will be fulfilled, my lord, eventually. Of course his honor and his companions were invited to stay to dinner. That was when Sailor Holiyi arrived at the tenancy. Word came to the manor. There was some problem in passing a message—I was at the dinner, also."

Holiyi had been told to find Quili, but the presence of two priestesses might have caused some confusion. Hence the delay, passing information under the ears of sorcerers.

"Quili and I managed to slip out for a quick word together," Valia explained, "at the end. She dares not leave yet. If you wish to come back with me, then we should wait awhile, to be sure. If not... she sends her love to you and Adept Nnanji, my lord."

Nnanji grinned. "Give her mine."

"And certainly mine," Wallie added. "How many companions did this sorcerer of the Sixth bring with him?"

"Two. Both Thirds."

Wallie's pulse began to beat a little faster. "But Builder Garadooi will be returning to Ov with them?"

Nnanji stiffened slightly.

Valia indulged a genteel laugh. "If they cast a spell on him. But it will take a strong one! He did promise that in a couple of days..." Then she guessed, and her lips clamped together in angry silence.

Tomiyano had arrived there also. "The road runs by the River?"

Nnanji nodded. "There is a ferry," he said softly.

"They were being very insistent that he go with them, my lord," Valia protested. She was frightened now, furious at her own stupidity. "And he was still trying to persuade them to spend the night. The family boat will be arriving in the morning—"

"But you invited us to the manor. You thought they were leaving."

She would not admit that. "They may have."

Wallie ignored her then. He had often watched Honakura twist the truth without actually lying, and the old man was much more skilled at it than this pompous priestess was.

In the gathering gloom, the light from the River was reflecting in Nnanji's eyes, making them shine. But the bloodlust that should have been there was missing. He was watching Wallie intently, very still, not seething with excitement as he should be at the prospect of action. Nnanji knew the answer and was waiting to see if Wallie did.

"Then here's your chance, Shonsu!" Tomiyano rubbed his hands gloatingly. "Five of us and three of them. Not bad odds, wouldn't you say, when we have surprise on our side?"

Wallie said, "No."

"What! Why not? Kill two, take one alive! It's your chance to find out what they have in their pockets, man! A heaven-sent opportunity! We'll tie him up and gag him—"

"No."

"Why not?" the captain shouted. "What's wrong with it?"

"Lord Shonsu is not Swordsman Kandoru," Nnanji said, more quietly than ever.

"What's he got to do with it?" Tomiyano was looking from one swordsman to the other, baffled.

"He drew against a guest."

Thana was as puzzled as her brother. "She said we couldn't go up to the house yet—we've been refused hospitality. We're not guests!"

"But they are." Nnanji was smiling faintly, approving.

"We shall not move against the sorcerers, adept," Wallie told Valia. It was crazy. Tomiyano was quite right—this was a heaven-sent opportunity, a chance to capture a sorcerer of the Sixth. But Valia had unwittingly betrayed her guests to their enemies, and to take advantage of that error would not be honorable. Good manners did not permit a war to be fought that way . . . crazy! Insane! But Nnanji was pleased—Lord Shonsu was a man of honor. Why should Wallie care what Nnanji thought? Why did that wry smile feel good? Penance for what he had done in Aus? Crazy!

Tomiyano snorted in disgust. Thana shook her head over such landlubber nonsense.

"I thank you, my lord," Valia said humbly. "The blame would have been laid to Quili . . ." There was less great lady now. "Will you not come up to the manor?"

"I think the hour is late," Wallie said. "We should return to our vessel before true darkness."

"As you please, my lord." Valia hesitated. "I was not going to mention . . . this was told in confidence, but there was no oath. I think my duty is to pass it on. You would find out soon anyway."

Wallie felt a sudden tingle of premonition. "Yes?"

"It seems to be the cause of the sorcerers' impatience." She was incapable of coming straight to a point. "Honorable Rathazaxo reported that a tryst has been called."

"*A TRYST?*" shouted Nnanji. "*Where?*"

Valia recoiled. "At Casr, adept."

"When?"

"Yesterday."

"And has She blessed it?"

Valia backed away before his vehemence. "Apparently, adept."

"Her swordsmen are coming?"

"So his honor said . . ."

Nnanji stepped across the circle and grabbed Wallie by the shoulders. If he tried to shake him, nothing happened. "That's it, brother! You were wondering how to fight sorcerers, and there's the answer! Why didn't we think of it?"

"What the demons is a tryst?" Tomiyano growled.

"It's a holy war! It needs two Sevenths, a swordsman, and a priest—" He swung back to Valia, growing shrill with excitement. "And bullocks? They had the bullocks?"

She nodded.

"Why bullocks?" Tomiyano asked. "A barbecue?"

"No, no, no!" Nnanji was almost dancing. "There hasn't been a tryst for—oh! centuries. It takes a priest and a swordsman to call one, and they wade into the River. The bullocks go first."

Tomiyano's eyes popped wide. "It would take more than bullocks to get me—"

Nnanji spun back to Wallie. "But if the stories are true and the swordsmen are coming, then the Goddess has blessed it! So it's a real tryst! The saga of Arganari . . . Za? Guiliko?"

"Who leads this tryst?" Thana asked with a glance at Wallie. "The Seventh who called it?"

Nnanji paused and frowned. "No, I don't think . . . not necessarily." His lips moved as he pondered. "Leadership is decided by combat, I think. The best swordsman." He swung round to face Wallie again and shouted. *"The best swordsman in the World!* Of course! And remember the ballad of Chioxin, brother? The emerald led a tryst, and so did the ruby! The fourth did, too! That's what your sword is for!"

And the leader's aide-de-camp and oath brother could be certain of an honorable mention in the epics to follow. Nnanji was as thrilled as a medieval squire given tickets to the next crusade. Thana and Tomiyano also had caught the excitement. Even Jja and Holiyi were beaming. Of course—a tryst against the sorcerers, led by Lord Shonsu and Her own sword.

So here was something else to think about. Lots of things.

Perhaps Wallie had been interpreting the riddle wrongly. The army might not be *Sapphire*'s crew after all. A tryst was a real army, the greatest the World ever knew. He had done nothing to earn that.

Nnanji lapsed into silence, his lips moving again as he recited epics to himself, researching trysts.

"I cannot persuade you to come up to the manor, my lord?" Valia asked. "Quili is anxious to see you, and the builder will be, also, if he did not accompany the sorcerers."

But Wallie had too much on his mind—riddles and trysts, circles and armies, Casr and Aus. And he did not want to face his former helpers and have to confess that what they had been told about him was true.

"I think not, holy one. Give them our love and, again, our thanks. Tell them we shall continue the fight against the evil ones, and that it progresses. I think we must return to our ship before true darkness."

Or would *Sapphire* have vanished, and the dinghy find itself delivering the seventh sword to Casr? Under that bitter thought he tasted relief that Jja and Vixini were with him.

"And on to Casr, my lord brother?" Nnanji said eagerly.

Wallie sighed. "Yes. She has summoned Her swordsmen, so yes, we must go to Casr."

Then Thana's eyes went wide, and a brightness seemed to glow in her face. Before she could speak, the others wheeled around, staring to the north. Huge, but very distant, a giant rose of flame was unfolding graceful petals into the somber dusk— higher, higher, and ever brighter, belittling the range on which it grew, lighting the dark landscape below, setting the very sky ablaze. Then the darkening crest reached into the heavens themselves and was touched by the rays of the invisible sun, blooming pink and gold.

A volcanic eruption . . . the blast would arrive later, but the wind would carry the ash westward, toward Casr . . . Wallie was still analyzing, when he realized how this would appear to his companions.

"The Fire God rages!" Valia exclaimed, making the sign of the Goddess. "He fears the tryst called against his sorcerers!"

"He didn't fear it until he heard who was going to lead it!"

said Nnanji. He grinned proudly at Wallie. A little hero worship was creeping back. Lord Shonsu was a man of honor.

†† ††

The first thing the sun god discovered when he returned to the World was the monstrous mushroom standing high above Regi-Vul, dwarfing the mountains themselves. Playfully he painted it red, then gold, and finally a very pale blue, but the Fire God still tinted the underside with angry rosy flickers. A little later the sun observed *Sapphire* as she headed into Ov.

Wallie had slept little and badly. He had been counting on the god's riddle to solve his problem for him. Turn the circle, he had thought, and some divine revelation would show him how to fight sorcerers. Instead his problem now looked worse. The sorcerers had known of his sickness at Ki San. They had demonstrated again an inexplicable ability to pass information. A tryst had been called. As a swordsman, he now had a sacred duty to head for Casr. Certainly the tryst explained why he had been given the legendary sword, but for Shonsu to return to Casr would be virtual suicide. Now he must beware not only denunciation but also challenge, for other Sevenths would flock to a tryst.

In the bitterest hours of the night, he had reproached himself for another blunder. He should have ambushed that so... Sixth as he headed home to Ov, instead of pandering... stupid scruples.

But had he turned the circle? During... run halfway to dawn, Honakura had... had not yet done... *Sapphir...* ship cal... was ver... bly ale... cal ex... bronze...

a discussion that had
suggested that perhaps he
had fallen to the sorcerers;
back ran by Ov, so let the
of a better plan, but no one
he sorcerers would be dou-
over, *Sapphire* had no logi-
was a tin-pting center; the
chased at a knock-down price

... to Nnanji's
... ter

Gi had themselves come from Ov. To offer them for sale there would make no sense and might rouse suspicion.

A short visit, then, Wallie suggested, and offered to pay the dock fees. Brota accepted that suggestion without argument.

Ov was huge, bigger even than Dri or Ki San, the sailors said. It sprawled in patches and weals on the higher reaches of a low gray landscape, whose hollows were fetid swamp. The buildings themselves were a drab gray, also, monotonous and ugly—a city built of fossilized business suits, Wallie concluded peevishly. Amid such tedious dullness, the sorcerers' tower was a welcome relief, black and vertical, evil instead of merely funereal. It stood, as usual, about a block back from the River. Its exterior seemed to be complete, and sunlight streaked from glass in at least one of the high windows.

The River was shallow, and the dock unlike any other Wallie had seen, a long pier extending far out from shore, branching at the end to form a T. Each captain tried to moor as close to the city as he dared approach, so the vertical part of the T was crowded, the crossbar almost empty.

Wallie, Nnanji, and Tomiyano, the three wise monkeys, gathered in the deckhouse as Brota brought *Sapphire* in. She found a berth about halfway along the vertical, on the downstream side.

"Good position," Tomiyano said. "Cut the cables and the current will sweep us away. Good for a fast escape." He glanced at Wallie.

"Good fighting terrain," Wallie agreed. "No warehouses ...king us—they could only bring up reinforcements from ...Then he caught the captain's eye, and each admitted ...was uneasy. Seven times they had risked ...of the Seventh to a sorcerer city in viola-... was the end of the line. Superstition ...oing to happen, it should happen ...the World.

...lso. Half the night, Nnanji ...s—the Tryst of Rof and ...deri's Tryst—honor ...d succumbed to

overlo...
one side." ...
in silence that he
bringing a swordsman ...
tion of the local laws. Th...
said that if something ...
now. Superstition work...
Nnanji had caught ...
had been in spate o...
the Tryst of Za, Gi...
and glory and blo...
the prevailing dre...

His brother strolled into the deckhouse in his slave costume.

"You don't have to," Nnanji said, "if you don't want to."

Even Katanji seemed more subdued than usual. He hesitated and then said, "My duty, mentor?"

Nnanji bit his lip and nodded.

"Keep it short, though," Wallie said. "Just a quick look at the tower and then right back, okay?"

Sapphire bumped gently against the fenders.

The Fire God was angry . . . Honakura wandered in. "Too far to town for my old legs," he muttered, and hauled himself up to sit on a chest.

They all felt it, but no one would say it: Something was going to go wrong.

A wagon went by and made a drumming, roaring sound on the roadway that was built of timber over stone piers. It was also narrow and cluttered by ships' loads on both sides.

"Phew!" Nnanji pulled a face. "Now we know why this spot was empty!" The vessel on the opposite side of the pier was a cattle boat, as evidenced by mournful bellowings and an unmistakable stench.

"Must have swordsmen aboard?" Tomiyano suggested, and dodged the ensuing punch. For a moment the two of them indulged in a wrestling match. Wallie was amused, remembering the beginning of the voyage. *Sapphire* was a much happier ship now.

Nnanji broke free of the unequal struggle and slapped at his shoulder, muttering. If mosquitoes in the World carried malaria, Wallie thought, then Ov could not be a healthy place. Already the deckhouse swarmed with them.

"The circle turned," mused the priest in his corner. He looked tired and even older than usual. "Have you decided what to do next, Lord Shonsu?"

"Yes," Wallie said. "Nothing."

Nnanji gasped. "Nothing, brother?"

"Tell me how to fight sorcerers," Wallie replied.

"Pah!" said the old man. "They're fakes!" His audience swung around to stare at him indignantly.

"Fakes?" Wallie sneered. "If you count up the garrisons and the other stories—how many now, Nnanji?"

"Two hundred and eighty-one," Nnanji said.

"Two hundred and eighty-one swordsmen have been killed. A man died out there on that deck. Fakes?"

"True," Honakura admitted. "But they're still faking. I'm sure of it. Why did the sorcerer offer to put a spell of good fortune on the cargo when he already knew it would fetch an unusually high price? Why was the captain given a demonstration of birds coming out of pots? It all stinks of showing off, like little boys do. They're not as powerful as they want you to think!"

He had argued this before, and certainly the sorcerers did have an aura of showmanship about them. But they also had deadly powers that Wallie could not explain in an iron-age culture.

"So what are you going to do about them?" Honakura demanded again from his perch across the deckhouse.

"The answer is still 'nothing,'" Wallie said. "In every city it's the same story: the sorcerers appear, and the swordsmen march out and—*zap*! It started fifteen years ago, in Wal, and every couple of years they do another. I expect they'll cross the River soon. Does it matter? The swordsmen have learned nothing in fifteen years—nothing! I don't know what to teach them, and they wouldn't learn anyway. They'll try to take the cities back with the same techniques that lost them. I want nothing to do with it."

The old priest made the sign of the Goddess. "But the edict of the gods!"

"So She doesn't like Fire altars in Her temples? What does it matter? Even the priests don't care much! For thousands of years Her swordsmen have been swatting sorcerers like bugs. Now the foot is in the other shoe, and She starts sending miracles."

Honakura spluttered. "Blasphemy!"

Wallie was beginning to convince himself and was also losing his temper as his sense of failure and frustration boiled over. "All right—*blasphemy*! So throw me in the River as you did the last time! Denounce me to Brota. I don't know what happened fifteen years ago. Did the sorcerers find a better thunderbolt, do you suppose? Or did they just get tired of being stamped on by swordsmen? The people don't mind. They're just as miserable under sorcerers as they were under swordsmen; no more, no less. And they certainly won't want battles being fought in their streets, civilians killed, swordsmen killed, houses burned. You saw in Gi what a fire can do.

"No. I shall do nothing." Wallie went back to staring out the window.

Nnanji was incredulous and upset. "But the tryst, my lord brother?"

"I think the sorcerers could zap a tryst as easily as they can zap a garrison. It will be a disaster."

Shonsu had failed disastrously, but that was another mystery. In all their inquiries, the *Sapphire* detectives had heard no further word of Shonsu. He had been castellan of the lodge at Casr, but that was all they knew. They had uncovered no news of any slaughter later than the conquest of Ov. There was no explanation of Shonsu's departure from Casr and his pilgrimage to Hann, driven by the sorcerers' demons.

"Remember the riddle?" Wallie said. *"Finally return that sword?* I shall return it all right—to the Goddess. I'll give it to Her temple in Casr. Then the tryst can fight over it. I shall buy a blue breechclout and be a water rat. Want a strong back on your ship, Captain?"

"You are lying, Shonsu," Tomiyano said cheerfully. "Swear an oath on that?"

"Tell me how to fight sorcerers," Wallie growled and turned back to peer out the shutter. Then he added: "Port officer!"

Honakura and Katanji came to the windows as the plank clunked down to the dock.

She was elderly, white-haired, plump—a something of the Third, in a brown wool gown, with pink cheeks and a friendly smile. The big, embossed leather pouch of office hung at her waist. She came puffing up the plank to the deck.

Wallie thought she seemed a motherly, neighborly sort, and at once wondered if that was what he was meant to think. Then he hissed, for there were two sorcerers behind her, a Third and a Second. They glided up the plank with less effort and onto the deck without asking permission; they stood there like hooded statues, faces invisible, hands in sleeves.

"Uh-oh!" Nnanji whispered.

"If they search the ship . . ." Wallie drew the knife from his boot.

"I'll take the woman," said Tomiyano, who knew that swordsmen had sutra problems fighting women. "Shonsu the brown, Nnanji the yellow."

Oligarro was being captain, and Brota was close beside him. Half the crew hung around the deck, wary and frowning at the sinister intruders.

The port officer made the salute. "I welcome you to Ov, Captain," she said, "on behalf of the king and the wizard. What swordsmen do you have on board?"

Brota stepped forward and made the acknowledgment of an inferior, then accepted the resulting salute.

"Me, my daughter of the Second, and a First."

"That is all?" one of the sorcerers growled, and the watchers could not tell which one spoke, although it was probably the brown Third. "No frees? You will swear that on your ship, Captain?"

"Certainly," Oligarro said. The crew all knew now that their passengers did not classify themselves as free swords.

"Mistress, you also swear that there are no free swords aboard?"

"Certainly," Brota said. The sorcerers pivoted and floated away down the plank.

"That's new, isn't it?" Brota demanded.

The grandmotherly type nodded. "Started today. Something's chewing the baggies' bottoms." She shrugged. "Don't know what."

Wallie knew what. He was relieved to see that Brota looked as suspicious of this sweet old dear as he was. No port officer had ever talked like that before.

"Well, let's do business," Brota said. "How much?"

"Five," the port officer answered sweetly.

Oligarro frowned. "I thought two was the fee?"

"Perhaps it is, perhaps it isn't," she said. "But you are going to pay five, and who's to know?" She shook her leather pouch, making it jingle, and she smiled again.

Brota scowled and Oligarro argued, but he paid in the end.

The dear old lady took the money, made a polite farewell, and limped away. Brota made a vulgar gesture at her back. Then she headed for the deckhouse to collect from Lord Shonsu.

As a slave Katanji could be so inconspicuous as to be almost invisible. Wallie caught a glimpse of him slouching down the plank, and then he had gone. Brota headed out back to supervise, but the crew was already doing everything required. Wallie turned to regard the dock, in time to see two more sorcerers gliding by. "Why do they never show their hands?" he asked, and got no reply.

Holiyi and Linihyo staggered down to the dock with an ingot, then took another and leaned the two together like a tent for elves. Hawkers came by, and Lina haggled with them for groceries and fresh fruit, while other crew members drifted off along the pier in search of information, most going left to the city, a couple heading right toward the River. Brota parked herself in her chair at the top of the plank and waited for business.

People and wagons swarmed along the roadway, with masts and rigging forming a double avenue of winter trees above them and the wheels rumbling thunderously on the hollow planks. The drivers cursed and roared at the sailors and slaves; the sailors replied as loudly and continued to pile goods in heaps along both sides, steadily encroaching on the right-of-way. Pedestrians dodged and jostled. Birds that looked like gulls perched on the yards and made lightning dives into the traffic in search of garbage.

A party of horsemen arrived, and the cattle were unloaded, turning confusion into chaos for a while. Eventually the bawling died away as the herd was driven into the city; the cattle boat cast off and sailed away, leaving no regrets on *Sapphire*.

Nnanji started to do exercises. Honakura sat on the chest and seemed to be thinking hard. Wallie and Tomiyano took a window each and stared despondently at the crowd. All of them slapped petulantly at mosquitoes.

As usual, sorcerers patrolled the docks in pairs, gliding along unperturbed by the crush, ignoring the impatience of those who wanted to get by them but dared not get too close. They had no set beat, and Wallie could not decide how many there were in total; all he had to go on was the color of their gowns, and they seemed to change partners frequently.

Then Tomiyano suddenly snapped, "Shonsu! That Fourth! Recognize him?"

"Our soft-handed friend from Ov!"

"Ixiphino?" Nnanji came over to look.

It was the port officer from Aus, slim and handsome in orange breechclout and shiny leather sandals; still looking to Wallie like a beachwear model. Beside him walked a sorcerer of the Fifth, red robed, cowled, tall, and stooped. Behind them, and apparently in their service, a slave pulled a cart loaded with cubical baskets. They were heading away from the town.

"That settles any doubts in my mind," Wallie said. "He's a sorcerer! And look there!"

Not far behind was Katanji. He must have met that little procession somewhere and now was tagging along behind, to see where it was going. Sharp kid!

They watched the quarry out of sight behind the next ship, one anonymous slave boy following. Tomiyano went out and ran up the rigging like a squirrel.

Thana came in to ask if they had seen the sailor.

Jja arrived. Wallie kissed her and told her the news.

Two more spies returned. Fala had discovered little of interest, but Lae had seen the fake sailor and his sorcerer companion in the town and had trailed them, also. She had waited a while on the dock to make sure she was not being followed. Lae was competent at anything, even spying.

"They came from the tower, I think," she said, and her sure manner suggested that a theory from Lae was as good as a fact from anyone else.

Tomiyano slid down a rope and hurried in. "They turned right at the junction," he said, and hurried over to one of the stern windows. "That ship there, the white one."

The crossbar of the T was less crowded with shipping, and the ship he indicated was near the end, clearly visible and isolated. It was small and single-masted. If the cart was there, it was hidden by the hull.

"Tell a landlubber about boats," Wallie said. "Surely a small one like that could come much closer in? Why would they berth out there?"

"Doesn't follow," the captain said impatiently. "That babe's built for speed. She probably draws more water than *Sapphire* —big keel. Too big to use a center board."

Wallie turned back to Lae. "Did you happen to see what they had in the baskets?"

Lae glanced at Tomiyano and her wrinkles deepened in a hint of a smile. "Birds, my lord."

Tomiyano growled obscenities about sorcerers and their birds.

Time continued to pass imperceptibly...

Then a small candle flickered in the darkness at the back of Wallie's mind. Katanji had always seen birds around the towers, birds that walked on the ground. The sorcerers fed the birds. True, they had feather facemarks, but... he tried to recall the bird that he had seen magicked from the pot. Square baskets? "What sort of birds, could you tell?" he asked and held his breath for Lae's reply.

"They sounded like pigeons."

"Great gods!" Wallie said. "Octopus and feathers!" The candle flame blazed up like a bonfire. The others looked at him in surprise, but he was lost in thought and did not notice their stares or the half-amused, half-worried glances they exchanged. His mind raced as he tried to absorb the implications of pigeons in baskets and a fast boat.

"My lord brother?" said Nnanji at last, concerned.

Wallie snapped back to the deckhouse and thumped him on the back so vigorously that he almost fell over. Jubilation! "Got it!" he said. "It's not much, but I've solved one of the sorcerers' secrets." He turned his smile on Tomiyano. "You get black stuff out of an octopus?"

"Ink, you mean?" the captain asked, looking annoyed at this puzzle game.

"Ink?" A new word for Wallie. The former Shonsu would have known nothing of octopus, except possibly as food. Sepia —squid ink! And the feather marks meant quills. Quills! Ink! Honakura had said that the sorcerers had once been associated with the priests—scribes, by the gods! And homing pigeons were no use without messages, and messages meant writing. That was how the sorcerers had known of the downed bridge, of the fire in Gi, how word had come so soon about the tryst.

Pigeons, moreover, would only fly one way—homeward. So a messenger service based on pigeons needed a distribution network, and the fastest way of getting around would be a swift boat . . . and of course the overland shortcut from Aus. That was one reason why the road had been repaired. The sailor they had recognized had brought pigeons from Aus and probably Wal, for use in Ov and Amb. Check!

The implications were immense: find a trader or merchant who kept pigeons in a free city and you had a sorcerer spy. Hawking was a common sport—hawks could cut the lines of communication. Wallie still could not fight sorcery, but he had a start for fighting sorcerers.

"I can't explain now," Wallie said. Perhaps he never could, for writing was beyond their experience. It was also social dynamite, and even to reveal the principle might break the sorcerers' monopoly and rock the whole framework of their culture. The gods might not allow that. No! The *sorcerers* did not allow it! Now he remembered his half-joke about ensorceling wine. That was why writing was not invented—it had been invented once and it was a sorcerer monopoly. He had discovered the sorcerers' business. That was why they prowled the World in disguise—to stamp out any reinvention of writing. That was how they built identical towers, with blueprints.

Wallie was starting to twitch with excitement. "Nnanji! When Katanji was leaving the tower he saw shelves with boxes on them. How did he describe them?"

"'Leather boxes,'" Nnanji said with a frown. "The second time he said 'brown leather boxes' and the next time, 'flat boxes.' Lots of them, he said."

Books! Sorcerers bought all the finest leather—vellum! Would it even be possible to steal books and learn to read again? To learn magic? This changed everything! *Sorcerers were literate!* Meanwhile . . . "What the devil do you suppose is keeping Katanji?"

Then birds hurtled skyward, horses reared in their traces, and heads turned. Out by the fast boat where the cart had gone, where the sorcerers had gone, where Katanji had gone, a cloud of smoke rose slowly into the air.

The hard, sharp crack of a thunderbolt rolled over the harbor.

Wallie Smith knew that noise.

That was no thunderbolt—that was a shot.

The coming of wisdom.

†† † ††

So the lesson may be learned.

Idiot!

Tomiyano and Nnanji collided in the doorway and the swordsman lost. The captain went aloft at high speed, and every rope in the moorings was bouncing as other sailors did the same. Nnanji recovered his balance and made a second try at the door; then discipline asserted itself, and he rushed back to his mentor.

"Katanji!" he said. "I want to go and see!"

Wallie stared blankly, right through him. The rest of the crew came hurrying in with frightened looks. Out on the roadway the patrolling sorcerers started to move quickly, heading riverward and almost running. Braver souls in the crowd followed them, while the more timorous headed toward home.

"My lord brother! Lord Shonsu!"

"Horse pee," Wallie replied in a whisper. His mind was in turmoil. He had barely recovered from the staggering discovery of writing, had not had time to work out all the implications of it. Yet perhaps without that shock to disturb his thinking he might not have made this other incredible leap. The mental bonfire blazed like a sun. Ideas were racing through his head so fast that he could not keep track of them. The World had turned upside down for him.

He had been a blind, witless, stubborn fool! It had all been there for him to see. He screamed and thumped his fists against the deckhouse wall in a fury. Horse urine and fire blazing in dark forests. Thunderbolts and mining near volcanoes. Fire demons and boiling tubs. Magic fifes and mosquitoes. Birds in pots and long sleeves. Maniac! Why had he not realized?

My lord brother!

Wallie roared: "Tomiyano?" He looked around and To-miyano was missing. He grabbed Brota by the shoulders. "Aus!" he shouted. "The ship where I met Tom'o. What was it loading? Did he tell you?" Then he realized that he was shaking her and stopped.

She gaped at him in terror. "He said sulfur, my lord!"

"Sulfur?" Another new word to Shonsu. "What is it used for?"

"I use it to fumigate the cabins sometimes, my lord." Brota was quaking before the madman.

MY LORD BROTHER!

Sulfur it was, then. A whole shipload of sulfur? He should have guessed right there. The sorcerers exported sulfur from Aus to the other towers. And Katanji had seen charcoal in the tower. Gunpowder! Primitive black powder: fifteen parts potassium nitrate, three parts sulfur, two parts charcoal . . . The Goddess had chosen the soul of a chemical engineer, and he had been too damn dumb to see why. They would know potassium nitrate as saltpeter, perhaps, a meat preservative . . . never mind now. That tub in the stairwell of the tower that had frightened Katanji so much when it spluttered . . . that was why the sorcerers built towers, or one reason—they were shot towers. Drip molten lead down a tower into a vat of water—of course it hissed and steamed! But that meant that they likely did not have rifling yet, only smooth bore.

Fire demons were cannons full of grapeshot, or possibly shrapnel bombs—no wonder the bodies had been ripped and shattered!

"Katanji!" he wailed. "You told me! You offered me wisdom, and I didn't take it!" The others looked at one another in dismay.

So the sorcerers had skulked for millennia in their mountain retreats, hemmed in by the swordsmen, but they had known of writing. With writing knowledge became cumulative. They had piled up knowledge, age after age, until they discovered gunpowder. The Chinese had known of gunpowder for centuries before they made weapons from it. The sorcerers had invented firearms, primitive certainly, but enough to kill swordsmen.

But not likely very accurate. Slow to reload! That was why the sorcerer in Wal had not shot Nnanji—he had not had time to reload after killing the port officer.

The coming of wisdom—the coming of sorcery. Wallie had wondered why the sorcerers had never seized cities until fifteen years ago. That fact alone should have told him. Only a leap in technology ever changed the course of history like that.

Then the fog began to clear, and the first thing that came into view was Nnanji's face, distraught and bewildered—Nnanji, bereaved of the last of his family and now betrayed by a mentor behaving like a raving madman. All around him clustered the shocked and worried faces of the crew, a deckhouse full of frightened people looking to him for leadership. Nnanji first.

"I want to go and see, my lord brother!" Perhaps Nnanji had said that before, several times.

"No! You could not help." What to say? Wallie plunged ahead. "Nnanji, the tryst has begun. If Katanji has died, then he is only the start. The minstrels will sing his name forever, first in the list of the glorious!"

That was the right note. Nnanji's bony shoulders straightened, and he nodded solemnly.

Wallie said, "But suppose he isn't dead? Put yourself in the sorcerers' place. You have uncovered a spy; what do you do?" Five minutes before he would not even have considered the possibility of a thunderbolt spell missing its target.

"Take him in to the tower for questioning, of course," Nnanji said. "No!" His lips moved as he began to run through the sutras, the Manual of Swordsmanship. "It's likely he came from a ship, and they'd have to pass by too many ships. Take him on board their own boat to be safe. Alert the tower against an attack. Post guards at the end of the dock to protect the tower? Start a ship-by-ship search."

"Good!" Wallie nodded. "I was thinking the same. But we're swordsmen, and they're not! They might just be stupid enough to bring him past here."

Nnanji's eyes gleamed, then his face fell again. "That's only if he's alive, my lord brother."

Then he yelped and Wallie realized that he had taken hold of Nnanji's shoulder and was squeezing it like putty. He let go. "Let's assume he is until we know otherwise. We'll ambush them!" There were mutterings of disbelief around him: fight thunderbolts? Had Tomiyano been there he would have made one of his sarcastic comments about swordsmen.

Then Tomiyano's feet thumped against the deck and he came bounding in. "He's alive!" he shouted. "It looks like he's hurt, but they've got him on his feet."

Tumult and cheering.

"Quiet!" Wallie roared. He swung around to look at the crowd in the deckhouse. That was bad. The sorcerers would want to know where this disguised swordsman had come from, and if the tower was watching for unusual activity, then an entire crew pouring through one door would wave flags galore for them. Casting a spell by rubbing a plate? "If they bring him past here, then Nnanji and I are going to rescue him. Do you want to help?"

"Yes," said the crew, almost as one.

"It'll be dangerous," he warned. "We may lose more lives in the attempt."

Uproar! They were with him; damn the torpedoes! Ever since the pirates, Shonsu had had an army ready to hand.

Nnanji was grinning wildly now. His hero was heroing again, and there was going to be action.

Wallie closed his eyes for a moment, rattling plans around in his head like dice in a box. Then, "Okay!" he said. "We have very little time. Do exactly as I say, with no arguments at all. First thing—when I shout 'Charge!' you all throw yourselves flat on the ground! Got that? It's a code. 'Charge!' means lie down. Fast! 'Up!' means up. Think of these thunderbolts as throwing knives—they probably have about the same accuracy, but I think that each sorcerer can only throw one, and then there will be a space of a few minutes until he can throw another. Have you got that?" He repeated it.

If he was wrong on that guess, he was going to lose a lot of friends very shortly. Why did he think that, anyway? Part of his brain was throwing up answers to questions he had not had time to ask it yet. Because the sorcerers had only been acting this way for fifteen years, since they first seized a city, and a technology that succeeds does not advance very far in fifteen years —that was why. The fire-demon cannons might be new, but there were none of those here. With a sensation of launching himself into space he started throwing out orders, hardly knowing himself what words were going to come out of his mouth.

"Linihyo, Oligarro, Holiyi, Maloli, you bring those ingots up from the dock and—"

"They don't matter," Brota began.

"Quiet!" the swordsman roared again. "I said no arguments!" No one had spoken to Brota like that in years. She crumpled into shocked silence. He turned back to the sailors. "Get as many more as you can manage up from the hold. No time to rig the boom. You'll have to manhandle them. Stand them on edge against the bulwark on the dock side. Okay? Move!"

The ingots were incredible good fortune—if the gods were withholding miracles, they were still allowing good luck. A bronze ingot would stop a lead musket ball.

"Nnanji, take off your sword for now. I want six good swordsmen down on the dock, scattered around and out of sight. Women—they'll be less conspicuous. Place them and then come back for weapons. Move!" Nnanji's sword and harness fell by the doorway, and he was gone, shouting names as he went.

"Sinboro, take Fia and Oligata, go aloft. You stay, send them down when there's any news.

"Diwa, all the children and noncombatants belowdecks and keep them there unless the ship goes on fire. Lina and the old man, as well. And not in the cabins, right down in the hold.

"Lae, an ax beside each cable. You may have to cut and run if this doesn't work.

"Cap'n? How many sorcerers?"

Tomiyano hesitated. "Demons! Didn't count. I think just two or three out where Katanji is. The patrols . . . maybe another eight. They'll be out there, too, by now. That's cowls only."

Wallie nodded, satisfied. "It's only cowls I'm worried about. Get the swords up." He ran his sketchy plan through in his head, and it was not good enough—he would get himself killed. "Brota, I need something that looks like a head."

Her fat face quavered all over. She did not know whether to laugh or scream. "A head?"

"With a foil on it." That took time to explain. By the time she stumped off, the first messenger boy was back from the lookout—Oligata.

"They're bringing him in," he said, panting and wide-eyed with excitement. "Seven sorcerers and Katanji."

"Great! Tell Sinboro to keep an eye on the town. There may be reinforcements coming. Back to your post, herald!"

Sword in hand, Wallie led the rest out on deck and told Nnanji that his brother was coming, the ambush was going ahead. The sailors had strung ten of the ingots along the side against the bulwark, invisible from the dock. But would they be strong enough? He moved two single-handedly, putting one beside each of the cables.

Brota reappeared with a foil and a head-sized basket wrapped in black cloth. The end of the cloth even looked like a ponytail. He stuck the foil through the knot and studied it with a grin. "Puppet show," he said.

"You're madder than usual today, Shonsu," she remarked nervously.

"On the contrary. I'm sane for the first time since Aus." He glanced around the deck, wondering how many dozen things he had overlooked. "You and Jja lie down by the hawsers, behind those ingots, because I think they'll stop the thunderbolts. But first I need cloths to cover the swords."

"It will take a large ingot to hide me!" Brota rolled her eyes and waddled off obediently.

Wallie turned to watch the crowd, which had not thinned out much. There might be a lot of innocent people hurt soon. He was suddenly tempted to call the whole thing off, to pull in his troops, and run. The only thing that stopped him was the thought of torture. Oh, Katanji!

He had five men and one boy on deck, standing expectantly around him. Nnanji with six women and girls on the roadway —he could see Fala by a heap of bales, talking to a woman from another ship, and Mata on the other side chatting with two sailors. The space by *Sapphire* was comparatively clear, as they had unloaded no cargo, but the rest of the dockway was cluttered with heaps, and there were wagons waiting, people pushing or standing, more wagons coming. This was going to be chaos on top of chaos.

He turned to the shiny-eyed Nnanji. "Take swords down to the others. Keep them wrapped until they're needed." He motioned the men in to listen. "Remind them to lie down fast whenever I shout 'Charge!' Nnanji, the one thing I'm most worried about is torture. We musn't leave any wounded, and that includes your brother!"

Nnanji just nodded, but his grin showed that he was not contemplating failure.

Wallie explained. "We're going to show ourselves on deck and challenge, then duck. I hope that that will draw their . . . their thunderbolts. It will be noisy! Then we attack before they have a chance to cast any more spells."

Tiny Fia dropped to the deck, wrapping her hands under her arms to cool them. "Shonsu, they've turned the corner."

"Okay. Go back up. Tell Sinboro that you're all to stay up there now. Expect lots of noise!

"Off you go, Nnanji. Stay out of sight until we come over the rail. Oh, Nnanji? Tell everyone to aim for arms, not head or body."

The ginger eyebrows shot up, and a question was stopped on the brink of being asked. Nnanji dashed off with his bundle of wrapped swords in one hand, his own sword and harness in the other.

"Why arms, my lord?" Holiyi asked.

"Because they have things in their gowns," Wallie said cryptically, and they all accepted that. There was another reason that he could not tell them, a promise. *The first sorcerer I meet, I shall spare for your sake.* Of course there was also the possibility of reprisals against the sailors or townsfolk, although he did not really expect that; but he might leave some of his force behind alive, in spite of his gruesome warning to Nnanji. They might fare better if no sorcerers had died. And he just wanted to avoid deaths if he could.

"Shonsu!" Sinboro was shouting from the masthead. "More coming!" He pointed toward the town. Wallie waved an acknowledgment. Then he took his small army over to the rail and ran through the drill twice.

Then another shout from the masthead warned him that the sorcerers were almost there.

††† †††

He crouched by the top of the gangplank, sword in hand. Opposite *Sapphire* a ship had unloaded a pile of shabby brown bales and sailcloth in long, buff rolls to make an excellent road-block. All the traffic detoured toward him to get around it; it also made good cover. Fala was sitting on a bale with a sword beside her, but her companion of a few minutes before had gone. Perhaps she had recognized the sword in its wrapping.

To his right, in the direction from which the enemy would come, the way was squeezed between a heap of grain sacks on the nearer side and a wagon loading crates on the other. Nnanji was squatting behind the sacks, sword in hand. That seemed an odd choice—why would he not have put himself at the city end of the ambush in case the sorcerers tried to run for it? Fala and Mata were beside the wagon.

To his left he could see none of his warriors, but his view was as much obstructed as the sorcerers' would be by two more wagons, one piled high with yellow baskets and the other with warm red bricks. Another wagon bearing lumber was scraping through between them with loud exchange of insults. Leaning on his cart of glistening fish, an elderly hawker plodded past *Sapphire*. Two more wagons were coming from the right, and the sorcerers were behind those, a glimpse of yellow cowls above the crowd.

There were fewer people nearby as the swords were noticed and the wise departed. This was a loyalty test for the riverfolk and the citizens of Ov: Would anyone run to warn the sorcerers? Of course that was why Nnanji had gone to that side. If they were alerted, they would turn around and retreat with their prisoner. The thought gave Wallie goose bumps, for his plan to draw their fire would have been thwarted, and Nnanji would certainly pursue.

He made a last check of the deck and of his army, all crouching by the ingots, swords in hands, watching him nervously. He gave them the local equivalent of a thumbs-up sign, and then saw Honakura standing by the mast and smiling complacently.

"Go below!" Wallie yelled.

The old man pouted and shook his head. "I collect great deeds, as well as miracles!" He smirked.

"You'll collect a thunderbolt, you flaming idiot! Go up on the fo'c'sle, then, and stay behind the capstan."

The priest scowled, but sauntered forward.

Now the lumber wagon had made it through the gap and pulled up by *Sapphire* until the way ahead was clear. Fortunately for the ambush, the teamster was selfish enough to hog the middle of the road. The oncoming traffic would have to pass him on Wallie's side. A spurt of pedestrians flowed through the gap and hurried by.

The first of the two wagons rumbled past the crates and then by the ship, its cargo of barrels sending out a strong smell of beer. The second followed, carrying a precariously high load of what looked like lobster pots.

Then came the sorcerers—yellows, a red, and browns. They walked in two lines of three, warily eyeing the ships and the crowd, every man with his arms in front of him and hands in sleeves. In the center was Katanji, tiny and barely visible. Wallie saw that his right arm was bandaged and in a sling. There was a rope around his neck and behind him, holding the rope, walked a very tall Fifth, keeping his eyes firmly on the prisoner.

Wallie's pulse was pounding, and his mouth was dry. The lobster pots passed below him, and he got his first clear glimpse of the captive. Katanji looked shaken and pale and very small. He was keeping his eyes down to avoid looking at *Sapphire*, but his face was bruised and bleeding. The sorcerers had obviously done some preliminary questioning.

Bastards!

"Up!" Wallie roared. "Sorcerers! I am sent of the Goddess!"

He stepped forward to the top of the plank so that they could have a clear view of his blue kilt. He raised his sword.

The sorcerers' eyes swung toward the shout. They saw a Seventh and a group of men with swords and they reacted instinctively, pulling their weapons from their sleeves. Seeing battle impending, bystanders and pedestrians screamed and started to run.

Wallie yelled, "Charge!" and hurled himself flat on his face.

Roar!—a very loud and jagged explosion. He felt the ingots beside him shudder. Splinters of wood flew across the deck. He grabbed the foil with the basket and thrust it up over the rail to draw any more thunderbolts, but nothing happened to it. He scrambled to his feet and he did not die.

Chaos he had predicted, but not this. The amount of smoke from the primitive black powder was astonishing; the air was thick with it and full of terrified screams from people and horses. Especially horses, plunging horses, churning the crowd. The lobster pots were a lightweight load and that wagon had bolted straight left, into the beer wagon, and barrels were cascading down. The basket wagon came charging to the right, into the sorcerers, scattered them, plowed over the sailcloth, and toppled onto its side. Baskets bounded into the roadway among the barrels and milling civilians.

He was halfway down the gangplank when he saw Nnanji impale his first sorcerer. But where was Katanji? Then he caught a glimpse of red through the smoke, as the big Fifth disappeared around the beer wagon and headed toward the town. Wallie left the battle to his army and gave chase.

Now the barrels and baskets were a hindrance instead of a helpful distraction. He dodged and sidestepped and cursed until he was past the worst of it and had a clearer view. The Fifth, with his prisoner over one shoulder, was in the middle of a panic-stricken crowd streaming toward the town through a maze of goods and wagons and skittish horses. Wallie threw people out of the way as he ran, but the big man was a powerful runner, also, even with his burden, and it took long minutes to catch him . . . almost to the end of the dock. Then Wallie came up behind him and thrust his sword between the man's legs.

The sorcerer fell headlong on top of Katanji, rolled over, and started to pull something from a pocket. Wallie was briefly conscious of a hate-filled face glaring up at him. He kicked. The first sorcerer Wallie had met was out of the battle then. Maimed perhaps, but probably not dead, so the swordsman had kept the promise he had made in Aus.

Katanji sat up shakily, looking dazed, saw Wallie, exclaimed, "Oh, Lord Shonsu!" and burst into tears.

Wallie glanced at the crowd ahead and saw cowls fighting their way toward him. He was almost into the reinforcements coming from the tower. He sheathed his sword, threw Katanji over his shoulder, and began to run.

The dock had emptied of people, and now he needed them for cover. He pounded down the roadway as hard as he could go, with his scalp prickling, waiting for more thunderbolts. He started to veer from side to side, even when there was clear space ahead, and he heard Katanji groan at the shaking he was getting. He saw *Sapphire*'s blue hull still a long way ahead along that cluttered avenue between the wagons and the heaps, an avenue walled by the sides of ships, arched over by the webbing of masts and rope and yards. It seemed to stretch forever.

There was shouting close behind him, very close. Then something kicked him in the back with the strength of elephants and proclamations of thunder. He was hurled forward and for the second time the unfortunate Katanji acted as landing pad for a large man.

All the breath went out of Wallie, and the impact rattled his bones from his feet to his teeth. Half stunned, he could only lie and gasp like a landed fish.

Then his arms were grabbed and pulled behind him and something cold went round his wrists with a click.

"A Seventh!" said a jubilant voice. A foot crashed into Wallie's ribs. "Up, swordsman!"

He gasped and was kicked again. He was dragged to his feet, reeling and dazed. Every rasping breath was an agony. There were sorcerers of various colors all around, even a green.

"A swordsman of the Seventh!" the Sixth exclaimed, and then laughed. He smiled up at Wallie. "You are a welcome guest, my lord! We shall have much entertainment from you."

Damned handcuffs! Manacles! He swayed and looked to see Katanji being hauled to his feet, also, although he seemed barely conscious and his sling was soaked with blood. "Let the boy go!" Wallie said.

"Hors d'oeuvre," the Sixth said, a smallish, wrinkled face peering out of a green cowl. "You can watch him go first. Shonsu, of course? You are hard to kill, swordsman! But this time we shall make sure. There will be no haste."

Then he frowned and turned to stare toward the River, and Wallie became vaguely conscious of a rumbling noise.

He struggled to focus sense out of a many-colored, whirling mist. A wagon was moving. Two men were standing up in front, one flogging the horses, and the other waving a sword. It carried a whole company of sword-waving figures. More men were jumping on it as it reached them. Swordsmen! They were pouring off the ships as it passed and being hauled aboard.

From a million miles away, from a million years ago, someone was shouting inside his head, very faintly. It sounded like Wallie Smith. The chief sorcerer started yelling orders in a shrill voice. Then Wallie made out that thin, far-off internal screaming: "Delay them! Distract them!"

His tongue was a dead fish in his mouth. "Honorable . . . Rathazaxo!"

The sorcerer paused and stared in surprise. "Well done! How . . . No matter. You will tell, later. Everything, you will tell."

He turned back to consider the onrushing wagon.

Wallie flogged his mind and voice. "The tryst is come, sorcerer."

This time he got a glare. "You could not know!"

"The gods told me. Did you think your pigeons could do better than the gods?" Everything was going round faster and faster. "Ink and feathers, little bits of leather?"

He had scored. Not only the green—half a dozen sorcerers were staring at him openmouthed. Their age-old secret?

"How do you know of that, Shonsu?"

"Sulfur . . . charcoal . . . horse urine . . ."

Anger and fear showed within the cowls.

The rumbling grew louder. Then the Sixth awoke again to danger. He shouted orders. Wallie was shoved back to the side of the road. He stumbled and fell heavily on a pile of bales, and a flame of agony in his back dragged a scream from him. The rigging swayed before a darkening sky. He thought he would vomit . . .

Yet he hung on. He twisted his head to see. The hollow rumbling was growing louder, the wagon picking up speed, the shouting becoming clearer. Now the two men were distinguishable, even to Wallie's muddled vision—the heavyset bulkiness of Oligarro driving the horses, yelling and whipping, Nnanji's matchstick lankiness, whirling his sword as he yelled for swordsmen, his ponytail a banner of blood in the wind. The water rats were responding, leaping off the boats and coming to help against sorcerers. And armed sailors, also . . . even a few free swords in ponytails and kilts . . . Oligarro had not been the only liar in port.

Louder and louder came the juggernaut, gathering speed even as it gathered passengers. Then Wallie saw what the sorcerers were trying to do. He twisted and scrambled frantically until he got to his feet, his head a whirlpool of pain. Katanji was staggering about behind them, in the path of the coming destruction, too dazed to understand. Wallie backed up to him, grabbed his good arm with manacled hands and towed him to the side of the road, knocked him down yet again, and turned his muddled attention to the eight sorcerers lined up across the road. They were all standing with legs apart. They were all holding pistols.

"Ready!" the Sixth shouted, and the sorcerers raised their arms outstretched before them. The wagon was plunging forward, and in the midst of the dust and the noise and confusion Wallie registered the terrified eyes of the horses.

"Aim!" the Sixth shouted.

Then he opened his mouth again, and Wallie hurled himself bodily into the nearest man. He teetered and fell against his neighbor. Had Wallie had his wits and normal strength he might have felled the whole line, like dominoes, one into another. As it was, he ricocheted limply off and fell once more, thumping his head on the timbers as a hail of knives flashed over him and the pistols roared, squirting great clouds of smoke. Half the sorcerers fell, and the wagon plowed into and over the rest.

There were swordsmen everywhere, screams and swords and yells and knives and cheers and smoke and blood.

The smoke cleared, the noise stopped.

He was lifted more gently—but not much more gently—to his feet. Eight dead sorcerers . . . a crowd of swordsmen—free swords in kilts, water rats in breechclouts, sailors . . . Tomiyano and Holiyi and Maloli, even a few women. They were cheering and laughing. Then Nnanji threw an arm around him, grinning and exultant.

"We did it, brother! Wiped out the lot of them!"

"Well done," Wallie whispered. "Oh, bravely done!" But he did not think he was audible.

Nnanji was. *"On To The Tower!"*

Cheers! "On to the tower!"

"No!" Wallie yelled. He lunged at Nnanji as he started to move away and then gasped again with the pain. The tower was booby-trapped. There would be cannons and grapeshot and shrapnel bombs . . . "You can't take the tower! Back to your ships!" Gods! It hurts to speak!

Anger and disappointment rumbled around him. Wallie leaned weakly against Nnanji. "Back to your ships!" he repeated faintly.

"Brother!" Nnanji pleaded. "We have a victory. We must follow it up. The sutras . . ."

That bang on the head—he couldn't think, and his tongue was all over his mouth. "I ama theventh," Wallie mumbled.

"Brother!"

"A Seventh!" Wallie repeated faintly. His knees were paper. The howling of the wind . . .

He was a Seventh. Muttering, they turned and headed back.

"Katanji?" Wallie said. The dock road was swaying nauseatingly, the storm drowning out everything.

"He's on his way back." Nnanji was beginning to look worried.

"Casualties?"

"Only Oligarro, brother. Not serious."

Earthquakes, now; the dock was going up and down in great fuzzy waves.

"He's got a little round hole through his shoulder," Nnanji said from a far distance. "I think he'll be all right, if there's no curse on it."

There was something very important that Wallie had to say, if he could only remember...He slid to his knees, and the World faded behind the gray roaring.

He thought of it again as they carried him on board *Sapphire*, when he saw the other pile of dead sorcerers. His orders to wound, not kill, had not worked very well. He tried to speak, to tell Nnanji to collect weapons. If he made the words they were not heard.

They laid him on a hatch cover and sailed away.

††† † †††

He had been studying a fire bucket for some time—perhaps only a few minutes, perhaps longer. He had not been conscious of being unconscious... He remembered them cutting off his manacles, unbuckling his harness, and laying him gently on the cover. He was lying there now, on his side with his head in Jja's lap. Delayed shock? Not the sort of thing that a hero was supposed to get. He tried to turn over, winced, and made do with twisting his head to look up at her. This was an interesting viewpoint, and he studied contentedly for a while, then looked beyond, to where her face hung against the sky, the most beautiful and certainly the most welcome face in the World, a miracle of golden brown against blue.

"That's the sort of smile that drives men mad," he said. The smile grew broader, but she did not speak. "What's so funny, then?"

The smile became broader still. "Not funny, my love—happy."

Again he tried to move and grunted with pain. "I don't think you should smile like that when I'm dying. See that hole in my back? Those broken white things are ribs. The puffy pink things are bits of lungs."

"There's no hole in your back." Soft as snowflakes, her fingers stroked from his shoulder blade down to the base of his ribs. "You have bruises, that's all. A bump on the head. No bones broken, Brota says."

Wallie said, "Brota can only look at the outside. Inside feels like a junkyard." He decided that the smile was fifty percent relief and fifty percent the sort of smile she gave Vixini sometimes and fifty percent some sort of admiration. All the rest of it must be love. Hell, it was a good smile to be given. Yet . . . "What is so funny, wench?"

Jja snickered. "You have a mothermark. I know it wasn't there this morning."

Another battle won—after the last battle, his right eyelid had suddenly gained a swordsman fathermark, but his left had stayed blank, uniquely blank in the World.

"Tell me," he said, wondering what the little god had made of a crime reporter.

Jja's smile broadened. "It's a feather, my love!"

A scribe, of course. Or was the god playing his jokes again? The sorcerers were a lot more than scribes; they were also chemists, and the new Lord Shonsu was a blend of the old Shonsu the swordsman and Wallie Smith the chemist. *Very funny, Shorty! I thought you promised no miracles? What are the swordsmen of the tryst going to think when they see that?*

Sorcery as technology? That was going to need some re-thinking.

He had been thinking of spy stories, and whodunnits. But it had not been a whodunnit, rather a *howdunnit*. His eyes had told him, Katanji had told him, and he had paid no heed.

Gunpowder certainly—the smell alone confirmed that. What else did they have? Probably not much; Honakura had been right, they were mostly charlatans. Whatever had caused that ancient quarrel between the priests and the scribes, the swordsmen had sided with the priests. The scribes had been driven out and herded up into the mountains. In self-defense they had claimed magical powers and probably devised all sorts of clever little tricks, like the sleight of hand that could steal a sailor's knife. That explained the sleeves and the hidden hands.

And sleight of hand explained the magical bird. Tomiyano had not opened the pot, because he had been holding it. The sorcerer had lifted the lid, and the bird had come out of his sleeve. Put a bird in a dark pocket, and it would freeze. That had not been all meaningless mumbo-jumbo, though. A pigeon could carry a message, but it could also be a signal. No message meant *send help*. The purpose of the exercise had been to release the pigeon, and the other sorcerers had shown up very soon afterward.

Burning rags? Lights in the forest? Phosphorus! Quite possible—middle sixteen hundreds on Earth, but not all technologies would make discoveries in the same order, so phosphorus was possible. Urine, both human and animal, would be the source of phosphorus, as well as of nitrates for the gunpowder. That was why the tanners and dyers were evicted; those crafts used urine, also, and the sorcerers wanted to corner the supply. Why had he not seen that? The scar on Tomiyano's face was an acid burn, of course. What else? He would have to rethink everything he had learned and reinterpret it. Surely all of it would have a rational explanation now—sorcery or science, but never both.

It had all been there for him to see that day in Aus: distillation coils, sulfur, pigeons. Even earlier—what would be mined in volcanic terrain except sulfur? Dumb swordsman!

He had come so close when he had Kandoru's murder reenacted. Had he followed his own logic through to its proper conclusions, he would have seen that the tune had been a stage prop, the fife a weapon. Then he would not have locked his mind into a belief in sorcery; things would have turned out differently then.

He twisted around and saw Nnanji and Thana standing by the rail watching him, so he made an effort, and Jja helped him to sit up. He had indeed been unconscious, and for some time, it seemed. *Sapphire* was already in among the islands north of the city, winding her way along a channel in a line of ships, all fleeing from Ov and the sorcerers' wrath. The sun shone on blue water and the hot fall tints of dogwood and willows on those islands. White herons stalked the beaches. The massive white cloud over RegiVul was almost invisible in its remoteness, its shadows the same soft blue as the dome of heaven itself. Brota was humped by the tiller, probably finding her helmsman solitude relaxing after the excitement. She saw him move and raised a fat arm in salute.

Nnanji and Thana came hurrying over, hand in hand.

"Where's Katanji?" Wallie asked.

"He's below, resting." Nnanji shook his head sadly. "It will take a real miracle to make a swordsman out of him now, brother! His arm is smashed. Brota says we can't even put a cast on until the swelling goes down."

"The Goddess rewards those who help us," Wallie said awkwardly. "If Cowie went to live in a palace, then I think Novice Katanji will be looked after."

Nnanji nodded, and Wallie asked what had gone wrong, what had happened. Very simple, was the answer—mosquitoes. Katanji had been slapping, like the rest of them, and had smudged his slavestripe. The fake sailor had noticed as Katanji edged close to see what was in the baskets. But Oligarro was fine, Nnanji said, a clean wound, no bones or arteries.

His grin would not stay away long: "And no one else but you got as much as a broken fingernail! We should have had minstrels with us, brother!" He hugged Thana tightly. "The first victory of your tryst, Lord Shonsu!"

"It's not my tryst! Ouch!" He had moved again. "What's that?"

Gingerly Nnanji held up a thin silver tube. "I found it on the dock. Is it safe, my lord brother? I can throw it overboard . . ."

"Oh, it's safe if there's nothing in it! You didn't pick up anything else, did you?"

"No, brother."

Pity! Wallie took the fife and looked at it. There were only three finger holes, so it would not be capable of much music, but drilling finger holes without spoiling the bore must be tricky. He tried blowing, achieving a wince from himself and nervous cries from the others.

"Kandoru didn't draw his sword, Nnanji, and he could have done, easily. He reached up and then he turned around, but he hadn't drawn. He hadn't been trying to draw!"

Nnanji looked blank.

Wallie sighed. "He thought he'd been bitten by a mosquito. But his fingers found a little dart sticking in him, and he turned round to see where it had come from."

Of course, it had come from a blowpipe, a convenient short-range weapon. Good indoors, or when there was no wind—that was why he had seen one in Aus. The air had been still that afternoon, when the sorcerers had cornered Shonsu. It would have been as reliable as a pistol at close quarters, and more dramatic to the onlookers. The sorcerers were showmen, murderous tricksters!

Quietly the crew was gathering around, and Wallie explained the blowpipe, and poison darts.

"Give me my sword."

They passed him his harness. In the middle of the decorated leather of the scabbard was a round hole, the edges burned. Wincing again, he drew the sword out, and there was a dark burn mark on the blade, very close to the image of a maiden stroking a griffon.

"Is that where the thunderbolt struck?" Nnanji asked solemnly. "I suppose a sorcerer's spell couldn't prevail against the Goddess' sword?"

"Nor against Brota's ingots. Did you look behind them?" Wallie asked. Nnanji shook his head and went to do so.

Wallie squinted along the blade, but there was no kink in it—a fine tribute to the metallurgical skill of Chioxin, for a lesser sword must surely have broken when hit by a musket ball. He would have to test it to make sure that the steel had not been fatally weakened. A fraction to the left or right and the ball would have missed the blade. Indeed if he had not been carrying Katanji, the scabbard would not have been pushed over to the left so far . . . hastily he dropped that line of thought.

He eased himself around and looked at the rail. There were two holes through it and big chunks had been blown out. Then Tomiyano saw him looking.

"We'll have to charge for repairs," he said solemnly. "Passengers aren't supposed to damage the ship." Then he laughed, which was almost unheard of.

"Don't!" Wallie said quickly. "They're honorable battle scars."

Nnanji had managed to drag one of the ingots aside. He came back holding two shapeless lumps.

"I found these," he said wonderingly. "They look like silver."

"They're lead," Wallie told him.

"Why would you not let us go on to the tower, my lord brother?" Nnanji asked regretfully. "Fighting sorcerers wasn't so difficult after all! Fifteen dead!" Then he paused and smiled suspiciously. "Or was it only fourteen?"

"Fourteen," Wallie agreed. "I don't think I killed the Fifth." Nnanji shook his head in affectionate disapproval of this swordsman who didn't like killing.

"We were lucky, Nnanji, very lucky! They aren't much good at fighting are they? Did you count their mistakes?"

"Dozens!" Nnanji snorted. "Lining up across the path of a charging wagon? They should have let us go by them, then commandeered a ship. They should have dropped you in the River before we arrived, brother! Amateurs!"

That was worth knowing, though. The swordsmen were trained fighters, the sorcerers merely armed civilians. They had lost their heads. Yet Nnanji could not suspect a fraction of it. The tower doors were certainly booby-trapped. Defenders could drop antipersonnel grenades. A skirmish on a jetty was one thing; an assault on a tower would be another matter altogether. Then another piece of the puzzle fell into place—Katanji had reported bronze gratings at the tower doors and had seen a big gold ball on a column—an electrostatic generator, of course. Burglars were electrocuted.

"You saved my life again, brother," Wallie said. "I thank you."

Nnanji grinned. "I was rather good, wasn't I?"

"Not good—magnificent!"

Once Nnanji would have blushed scarlet at that. Now he just chuckled and said, "Thinking?"

"Very fast thinking!"

"Judgment?"

"Great judgment!"

"Tactics?"

"Superb tactics!" Wallie laughed with him, and then wished he hadn't. "Sum it up in one word, brother: leadership! You're not just a Fifth in fencing, Master Nnanji, you're a leader. You'll be a Fifth and a good one!"

Where now was the gangling, awkward kid whom Wallie had found on the temple beach? Few swordsmen of any rank could have reacted fast enough and efficiently enough to have organized that rescue. Wallie had not thought of calling on the water rats as reinforcements, but Nnanji had, and thought of taking a wagon, too.

Thana was standing beside him; they had their arms around each other again. Now she spoke for the first time. "Sixth?"

Wallie tried to shrug and regretted that, also. "Soon," he said. "Very soon."

Nnanji's eyes glinted. "We are going on to Casr, then, brother?"

Yes, Lord Shonsu would have to return to Casr. He might have to face a denunciation for what he had done in Aus—but now he had a victory to set against it. He wondered what other time bombs might be ticking there, what buried mines his predecessor had left. "We are, if She wills it. You will get your promotion. You've earned it, and it will be our first business there."

The rest of the crew was standing or sitting around—smiling in approval, waiting for him to recover, patient to hear what fate he had in store for them. He was admiral, he had been granted wisdom, he was the Goddess' champion, he would decide their fate.

"And the tryst, brother?"

Wallie sagged his shoulders to seek a more comfortable position. Tryst? Now he knew how to fight sorcerers, but that did not mean he would succeed.

Nor was the god's riddle much help now. *First your brother* ... fine, he had done that. *From another wisdom gain*—that was his new insight into the sorcerers. He had been spurned in Aus, turned the circle back to Ov, earned his army for the battle on the jetty...

Finally return that sword, And to its destiny accord. But

what did that mean? When was "finally"? Destiny? The destiny of the sword might be to lead the tryst, but the sword had never truly been in Casr, so returning it to Casr was not the answer. Was he truly supposed to return it to the Goddess at Her temple there, so that some other leader could have it? He gazed lovingly at that superb hilt, the silver griffon, and the sapphire. *Over my dead body!*

Lead a tryst? Other Chioxin swords had done so. Somehow he felt that the destiny of the seventh should be more than that.

"The tryst?" Nnanji asked again.

"I don't know." Wallie sighed. "Maybe we'll join the tryst —and if we do, then I don't intend to be assistant quartermaster. I'll be leader, and you'll be my deputy!"

Nnanji's teeth gleamed as he smiled at Thana—fame and glory!

"Or maybe we'll have to stop the tryst, to prevent a massacre."

"Stop the tryst!" echoed Nnanji in horror.

It was Cortez versus Montezuma again, a few firearms against a primitive civilization. The smart money went on Cortez. The swordsmen were at about the level of the Greek phalanx, the sorcerers were Early Renaissance—and that was a different league.

One thing was certain: if the tryst of the Goddess' swordsmen went heads-down against the Fire God's sorcerers using their traditional tactics, they were going to be devastated. Wallie's duty—to his craft, to the Goddess, to his own conscience —was clear. He must prevent disaster.

How?

He would have to do some hard thinking before he got to Casr. Four or five weeks' sailing to Casr . . . unless the Goddess wanted him there by lunchtime. The crew's smiles were fading, and he could see that his doubts had alarmed them.

He put his arm around Jja and grinned to reassure them all. "Or perhaps the tryst is just a blind to distract the sorcerers, Adept Nnanji, while you and I do something else?"

"Do what, brother?" Nnanji asked, eager to hear and willing to follow his oath brother into hell if he was asked.

"Ah!" Wallie had no idea. "That's the big question, isn't it?"

He mused for a while, but his mind was a blank. "Answer that one, friend, and you win an all-expense-paid trip for two."

Nnanji looked puzzled. "To where?"

"To Vul, I suppose," Wallie said, and then he laughed. "No, that's just an expression. Don't take me seriously."

Wisdom seldom gave answers; it only redefined the questions. He had not known how to lead an army of swordsmen against sorcery. Against technology, though . . . well, that was another story altogether.

That other story is
THE DESTINY OF THE SWORD
which concludes the saga of
The Seventh Sword

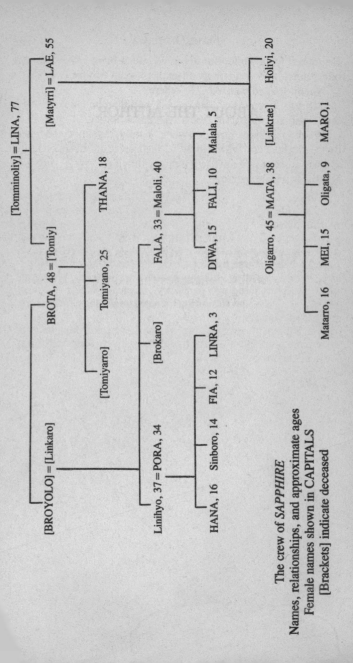

The crew of *SAPPHIRE*
Names, relationships, and approximate ages
Female names shown in CAPITALS
[Brackets] indicate deceased

ABOUT THE AUTHOR

Dave Duncan was born in Scotland in 1933 and educated at Dundee High School and the University of St. Andrews. He moved to Canada in 1955 and has lived in Calgary ever since. He is married and has three grown-up children.

Unlike most writers, he did not experiment beforehand with a wide variety of careers. Apart from a brief entrepreneurial digression into founding—and then quickly selling—a computerized data-sorting business, he spent thirty years as a petroleum geologist. His recreational interests, however, have included at one time or another astronomy, acting, statistics, history, painting, hiking, model ship building, photography, parakeet breeding, carpentry, tropical plants, classical music, computer programming, chess, genealogy, and stock market speculation.

An attempt to add writing to this list backfired—he met with enough encouragement that he took up writing full-time. Now his hobby is geology.

DAVE DUNCAN

Fantasy Novels:

The Seventh Sword